BOOK THREE

A KING IN WAITING

MICHAEL CRONK

To the BookTube and Indie Publishing Communities
Especially Elliot Brooks and Michael R Miller
With my eternal gratitude

Contents

Chapter 1   1
Chapter 2   11
Chapter 3   21
Chapter 4   33
Chapter 5   41
Chapter 6   52
Chapter 7   67
Chapter 8   77
Chapter 9   92
Chapter 10   104
Chapter 11   117
Chapter 12   137
Chapter 13   153
Chapter 14   164
Chapter 15   174
Chapter 16   192
Chapter 17   204
Chapter 18   216
Chapter 19   239
Chapter 20   256
Chapter 21   274
Chapter 22   290
Chapter 23   299
Chapter 24   311

Chapter 25   319

Chapter 26   336

Chapter 27   348

Chapter 28   356

Chapter 29   369

Chapter 30   378

Chapter 31   389

Chapter 32   399

Chapter 33   415

Chapter 34   428

Chapter 35   445

Chapter 36   454

Chapter 37   463

Epilogue   468

Acknowledgments   474

About the Author   476

Chapter 1

A loud bang startled Jason awake.

His eyes snapped open. His body was jolted out of a deep sleep and immediately became tense and alert. The room was pitch black. Jason threw back the covers and leapt to his feet. He shivered as the freezing night air clawed at his skin. "Silvana?" he whispered into the darkness. "Did you hear that?"

He could see her outline moving from the bed to wrap a dressing gown around her lithe form.

"The front door," Silvana replied.

"Don't suppose you're expecting visitors and just forgot to tell me?"

"Not at two in the morning. My visitors come at midnight."

"Of course. I forgot."

Jason held his breath and listened. The house was silent. The suburbs of Plymouth were always peaceful at this time of night. So why was there someone making a commotion at their front door? He waited. Nothing else happened.

"I think…"

The door banged again, making Jason jump.

"Hello?" a voice cried in a hoarse stage-whisper from outside the house. It was too breathy to tell anything about the speaker.

Jason pulled his handgun out of the bedside drawer. He was only wearing boxer shorts and didn't pause to put anything else on. He wanted clear aim. He moved to the bedroom door, but Silvana cut him off.

"Stay behind me," she instructed.

"Yes ma'am."

Silvana stepped out of the bedroom first. Jason followed with his gun aimed at the ground in a two-handed grip. In the hallway they found their roommate Freddie, shirtless and holding a hammer at shoulder height. He shrugged at them in question and Jason waved downwards to signal absolute quiet. The three of them turned towards the front door. Jason steadied his breathing as Silvana walked up to the handle.

"Who is it?" she barked in a loud voice.

"Oh, thank the stars!" a voice cried out. "I thought no one was home. Is that Silvana Clarke, of House Romanov?"

A chill ran down Jason's spine. Whoever this person was, they knew Silvana's true identity. It could only mean one thing. This was an Immortal.

"What do you want?" Silvana snapped.

"I need you to save my life," the person cried, their voice thick with desperation.

"What?" Jason called. "Save your life?"

"Someone's trying to kill me. I need your protection."

'Protection?' Silvana mouthed. She looked at Jason, pointed at the doorknob, and shrugged. He nodded once and so she threw open the main door.

The person outside was enveloped in a black robe, their face cloaked by the darkness. The only thing Jason could say for certain was they were below average height.

"Who are you?" Jason asked.

"My name is Leslie Toussaint."

Of course it's a genderless name. They pronounced the last name Too-san, with the slightest inflection. Jason couldn't learn anything from the voice. The name sounded French, but they had clearly lost any French accent they had in the past and now sounded distinctly British. The voice was neither deep nor high-pitched, instead hovering right in the middle.

"Hey," Freddie called, still clutching his hammer tightly. "I think the better question is *what* are you? You a shapeshifter? A wizard?"

"A witch," Leslie replied.

"Oh, a witch?" Freddie quipped. "Do you ride on broomsticks? Do you have a black cat?"

Leslie's face was hidden, but Jason got the distinct sense they were rolling their eyes. "I have no need for broomsticks, since I can teleport. And no, I don't have a familiar. Now will you extend me your hospitality? I'm very exposed out here. I swear by the stars I will not do you any harm and I'll answer all your questions."

Jason could feel everyone's heavy gazes settle on him for a decision. He grimaced. He didn't have enough information to make a call.

"One question first," he said. "Why'd you pick us for protection? We're just two mortals and a vampire. Surely there are others more powerful? A wizard or something?"

"Undoubtedly," Leslie admitted. "But you're also a detective, Jason Turner. You're the one who uncovered the Yamato plot six months ago, and slew the wizard Erickson before that. I need a detective, because I don't know *who* is trying to kill me."

Jason growled under his breath. "Ah, fuck." Then said a little louder, "Let them in."

Silvana stepped aside. Leslie stopped to politely take their shoes off before ducking into the house. They paused as soon as they saw Jason's gun aimed at the ground. "Please," Leslie said, hands raised. "There's no need for weapons. I assure you, I'm not using any magic.

Why would I threaten you when I need your help?"

Jason lowered the gun even further, but did not put it down. "Please, come and sit down," he said, using Immortal formality. "Do you require food or drink?"

"No, but I thank you for your hospitality."

That sealed it. Leslie now had guest rights in this home, which was as good as a signed peace treaty. Jason continued to eye their guest as they moved towards the dining room table. The house felt cramped. It was filled with cheap Ikea furniture with no cohesive style or theme. Dust lined the floors and cobwebs filled the roof corners. *Probably a step down from what this Immortal is used to.* Freddie turned on a single light and started making coffee.

"Anyone else?" he offered.

"Not for me, thanks," Jason said. "I have to be up in four hours."

"Well, I need one. I still haven't gone to sleep," Freddie said.

"Come on, man."

Leslie sat at the head of the table and finally pulled back their hood. Noticeable wrinkles covered their pronounced, asymmetrical cheekbones as their blue eyes gleamed with wisdom. Jason guessed they were about seventy, which in Immortal years meant they could be as old as eight hundred. Silvana sat immediately next to them.

"So, is it Mister Toussaint, or Miss?" she asked.

"If you please, just Toussaint will do fine," Leslie said. "I've never been one for labels."

Jason nodded. "All right, Toussaint. What makes you so sure someone's trying to kill you?"

Leslie scoffed. "Because I found a dinosaur in my home."

Freddie choked on his coffee. "Whoa, an actual dinosaur? What type?"

"Freddie!"

"Tyrannosaur."

"Oh my god, an actual T-rex! That is so cool!" Freddie glanced around the table. "Oh, come on! How am I the weird one here? You should all be *way* more amazed by this."

Jason sighed. "Just go on with your story, Leslie. A T-rex was in your home? Was it magic?"

"No. It was a flesh and blood Metamorph." Leslie seemed excited, and hurried to explain. "They make the best assassins. All the royal houses have a few Metamorphs in their employ. Think of them as hitmen."

"A shapeshifter?" Freddie asked.

"Yes, but it's impolite to call them that," Silvana whispered.

"Begging your pardon, young man," Leslie said, "but what House do you come from?"

Freddie stammered, "Uh… this one?" He sipped his coffee.

Leslie looked to Silvana. "He's a regular mortal? Forgive me for asking, but why is he initiated into our culture?"

"I thought you wanted our help?" Silvana said, raising an eyebrow.

"Right. My apologies." Leslie grimaced. "Look, I came home a few hours ago to find my library had been ransacked. Thousands of priceless books, shredded to pieces." Leslie clutched a hand to their chest in horror. "When I entered the room, a great man-eating cat leapt at me, obviously trying to take me unawares. I managed to fight it off with several hexes, but it cornered me and transformed into a Tyrannosaur in the middle of my house."

"So cool," Freddie whispered to no-one in particular.

"Luckily, I had already set up a reversing hex on my property for just this reason."

Jason frowned. "Wait, a reversing hex?"

"It takes a spell and flips it so the opposite happens. Even Metamorphs are using a form of magic when they change form, so my spell reversed theirs."

"So, instead of turning into a t-rex...what? A triceratops?"

"Well that's hardly the opposite. A big reptile would normally turn into a little amphibian. But the hex didn't quite work. For some reason, it only latched onto part of the spell. Specifically, the size altering part. So the assassin still turned into a T-rex. It was just two centimetres tall."

"No way!" Silvana whispered. "So..."

"I think there's part of him still stuck to my shoe."

"Fucking hell," Jason muttered.

"And now you've carried that into my house," Freddie said with mocking disapproval. "You know I'm the one who does all the vacuuming. How can I explain mini T-rex goo to my landlord?"

"I took my shoes off when entering."

"Oh. Well never mind then." Freddie chuckled. "Honestly, I wouldn't even be mad. Imagine, a freaking T-rex corpse in my carpet."

Jason groaned. "Alright, so someone tore up your library and tried to kill you too. What's so important about you, Leslie, that someone would want to kill you?"

"Because of my job."

"Your job as a witch?"

"What? No. Mr Turner, do you think my job is to *be* a witch?"

Jason gave a helpless shrug. "Um...yes?"

Silvana rolled her eyes.

Leslie raised their head high. "I'm a keeper of Imperium records. You might call me a historian."

The room went silent. Jason could feel the darkness of the outside world lingering just beyond the solitary dining room light. A lonesome vehicle accelerated in the distance before the night became silent once more. It would be all too easy for an Immortal to be out there somewhere, listening in, planning to strike once again at a moment's notice. Jason shivered, wishing he'd grabbed a jumper.

"I've heard of your title," Silvana said. "You know all the histories of Houses. All the family trees, names, and marriages."

"That's true."

"It's also said that you know all the secrets of the High Kings. All the histories they've tried to erase. All the great mysteries of the time before Zapherahleous's ascent and the coming of Immortal kind."

Jason blinked. Did she really just say 'all' the mysteries? This could mean a wealth of knew knowledge for his ongoing investigation into Immortal secrets. He raised an eyebrow at Leslie.

"That is just a conspiracy theory," Leslie said. "It's somewhat exaggerated."

"Only somewhat?" Jason quipped. Leslie said nothing. "So you are one of the few people in the world who know the secret histories of the Imperium? And someone just tried to kill you." He looked between Silvana and Freddie. "I think someone wants to make sure a secret is never revealed."

"Exactly," Leslie said. "But I know many secrets. I don't know which one is the reason for this attack."

"Well, there's only one thing for it," Freddie said. "You have to tell us all your secrets, just to cover all our bases."

"Out of the question," Leslie snapped with an edge in their voice that made Jason reach for his gun on impulse. Leslie cleared their throat. "My apologies. But I have sworn a magical vow to keep these secrets." Leslie held up their hand and drew up their sleeve, revealing a blue tattoo etched into the forearm. It was several runes that seemed to form a word.

ᛖᛁᛚᛗᚾᛏ

"This signet is the vow of the historians," Leslie said. "It's a powerful spell I've held on my person for hundreds of years. I am literally incapable of sharing my knowledge of Imperium secrets. Even if I found a way around it to tell you something, the signet would reveal this to my superiors. I would almost certainly face execution."

"That's still kinda cool," Freddie said. "What are those runes exactly?"

"They look Norse. Do they translate?" Silvana asked.

Leslie blushed and pulled their sleeve down to cover the signet again. Silvana and Freddie looked noticeably disappointed.

"Well, that complicates things," Jason grumbled.

"Fear not," Leslie said. "I've lived with this for a long time, and I'm familiar with the legal ways around it. I can give you clues in order to investigate. I even have a few suspicions regarding what this might be about. But before we go any further, you must swear to take on this case."

Jason let out a laugh and threw his hands in the air. "What case? I'm sorry, but you're giving me almost nothing to work with. I need suspects to investigate, and that comes from understanding your business so I can find *motive*. Without a motive, the list of suspects is too long. Besides, I don't even have any authority within the Immortal community. I'd be working in an unofficial capacity. I can't just demand entry into someone's home to investigate them."

"Perhaps you'd like to discuss your fee instead."

"This isn't about my fee! And I'm not haggling. I'm trying to explain that I don't have the resources."

"How does one hundred sound?"

"Whoa whoa whoa!" Freddie cried out and held up a hand. "A hundred, you were saying? A hundred what exactly?"

Leslie shrugged. "Pounds."

Freddie's face seemed to scrunch up in confusion. "What!?"

"Isn't that a lot?" Leslie said.

Jason explained, "Some PI's make about a hundred pounds per hour."

"Oh! Sorry, I don't pay much attention to recent history," Leslie said.

Freddie balked, "A hundred dollars hasn't been a lot of money for a while, old timer."

"Fine. How's a million pounds?"

Jason's jaw dropped. He looked at Freddie, who was nodding eagerly. But Silvana had a strange glint in her eye. "Silvy?" he asked. "What do you think?"

Silvana appeared deep in thought. Jason saw movement in his side vision, but it was just a house spider spinning its web in the corner of the roof. *Damn, maybe we could use the money to hire a cleaner.* "Silvy?"

Silvana finally spoke. "A million pounds, plus the information I require."

Leslie held up their hands. "I told you, I'm sworn to secrecy on certain…"

"It's about a royal house. I want to track the linage of someone I know. A vampire called Dorin." She looked across the table at Jason. "We met at the gala six months ago in Dubai. I'd like to know what family he came from."

Jason remembered seeing Dorin. They had only met briefly when he said he knew Silvana from before she was adopted. He claimed to know where she really came from. But an explosion at the party had separated them before he could say more. In six months of searching, Jason had barely found any news on him. All they knew was that Dorin was a member of the Royalists, a dangerous movement within the Immortal community who wanted to reinstate the monarchies. The Royalist organisation were like the terrorists of the Immortal world. And they were very skilled at covering their tracks.

Leslie nodded. "The name is familiar. It'll be hard to find which house they're from, if that's all the information you have. But I can do it. My only stipulation is that we look into this *after* our current crisis." They held out their hand. "Do we have a deal?"

Silvana looked at Jason with a look of desperation in her blue eyes. She wanted this. She *needed* this. Jason sighed as he took Leslie's hand.

"Deal."

Jason spotted something shift in his peripheral vision again. A frown creased his brow and a strange sense of unease spread through him.

"Huh, that's weird," Silvana said.

"What?" Freddie asked.

"Just a spider. It fell out of its web—"

Jason understood at last. "The shapeshifter!"

Everyone leapt from their chairs, just before the table shattered in an explosion of wooden shards, and the hulking form of a grizzly bear emerged in the middle of the dining room.

Chapter 2

Silvana was swatted backwards by a massive paw to the face. She tucked her legs and backflipped to land on her feet in a crouch. The other three people in the room had been knocked down by the bear's sudden arrival. Now the shapeshifter assassin was standing on its hind legs and raising a thick paw to swipe at Leslie. Silvana only had a second to decide how to react.

She launched herself at the bear.

Her blood supply was high, so she fused it all into her core and arms as she crashed into the grizzly bear with tremendous force. Her momentum knocked it off balance and it fell against the wall, smashing the plaster and wooden beams. As the Metamorph thrashed on the floor, Silvana landed against its chest, lost amongst its sheer bulky mass. The creature roared and tried to swipe at her with its claws, but Silvana was inside its defences. She landed an uppercut on its snout and heard the small bones in its jaw snap.

The creature morphed, but only the arms changed shape – shrinking down into the limbs of a smaller animal – while the rest of its body remained as a bear. Its shorter arms sliced at Silvana with sharp claws, sending a searing pain burning down her ribcage.

"Silvana!" Jason roared and drew his handgun.

The creature morphed again. This time just its legs changed into the long thrashing tail of a python. It flicked out its tailpiece and swatted Jason's gun aside before it curled around his chest in a crushing grip. Jason let out a strangled groan as the tail-end of the giant serpent wrapped around him twice.

"Jason!" she cried.

She couldn't even see Freddie. Was he underneath the creature somehow? The two mortal men had little chance against this foe.

"Stand back!" Leslie roared. The witch stood before Silvana like a shield. Their hand lit up with an emerald glow as they shouted, *"Shrorantha Hars!"*

Light burst from Leslie's hands and expanded to fill the room. The bear's face seemed to slacken as its mouth opened wide. It was a strangely human expression. It almost looked like a grin.

The assassin's smiling. Why...

The light suddenly jerked and rebounded back onto Leslie. It struck them hard in the chest with a sharp crack of lightning, deafening in the confined space. Leslie shrieked in pain and collapsed, unconscious.

"Oh god," Silvana gasped.

The bear let out a surprisingly human laugh. It shifted onto its paws and changed shape again. The python's tail curled tighter around Jason while the creature's head morphed into a lion and the chest changed into something like a horse.

It's a chimera. A true chimera. The greatest of all Metamorph abilities. The ultimate assassin.

Silvana still couldn't find Freddie. Meanwhile, Jason was clawing at the snake's body as it encircled his stomach for a third time. He looked up at Silvana. There were tears of pain in his eyes.

Silvana roared at the top of her lungs as she stepped forward and crouched low in a fighters pose. The assassin turned to her. She paused for only a second, then kicked at its face with vampire speed.

But the chimera's jaws were quicker. A curved canine tooth dug into her calf and tore a long gash into her muscle. Silvana shrieked and grappled with its face to release its bite, but a huge lion paw swiped at her shoulder, streaks of blood dampening her dressing gown. Silvana had no choice but to retreat out of its reach.

"Silvy!" Jason wheezed through a strained breath.

His face had turned purple, his cheek muscles twitching. The python tail continued to squeeze his chest, and even though Jason's hands were free to pound at the scaly mass, Silvana knew he couldn't claw himself out of that grip. She wanted to help him, but blood dripped from her multiple wounds. Her vampire healing abilities would not be quick enough to mend her wounds in time. The chimera growled as it came closer. She couldn't beat the chimera in a battle of strength. But for Jason's sake, she had to try. She climbed to her feet once more.

"Hey, Aslan!"

The lion raised its head just as a glass vial broke in its face. Green liquid spilled over its muzzle and the flesh sizzled wherever it touched, melting skin and exposing bone. The chimera gave a monstrous roar of agony that sounded like a dozen creatures at once. A bitter haze filled the room with a scent powerful enough to make everyone's eyes water.

Freddie appeared from the back of the house with a large hunting knife and started slashing at the python tail still holding Jason. With every cut, thick gouts of blood splattered the room. Freddie snarled with each clumsy hack, but it was enough to break the serpent's grip. Jason gasped with relief as he wiggled free.

The chimera clawed at its rapidly changing face. It morphed through a dozen bestial heads, all of them shrieking in animalistic distress. Silvana waited for it to take a weaker form. If it changed into something small for just a second, she could break its neck with one quick snap.

But the chance didn't come. The chimera's hind legs morphed into a giant bestial form and kicked downed the dining room's back door. Its whole form shifted into a tiny bird before it zipped outside and out into the night's darkness.

"Damn," Silvana muttered, even as relief flooded through her.

They were safe for now. But it would be back.

"Jase, you ok?" Freddie called.

Jason continued to cough and gasp for breath. Silvana tried to move to his side, but a sharp pain shot through her leg. The gash in her calf was much deeper than she'd realised. Now she was able to get a good look at it, she became more aware of the pain. The scratches on her shoulder were burning with every movement.

"How'd you do that, Freddie?" Silvana asked.

"Acid elixir," he said.

Jason coughed again and cleared his throat. "You just carry acid with you now?"

"I bought it off Edward. You know, in case something weird attacked us. Call me crazy, but that scenario just seemed likely."

"Yeah, that's fair enough."

Silvana grinned at him. "I think you just saved our lives."

Freddie beamed at her, before his eyes grew wide at the blood dripping from her body.

"Shit. I'll get some bandages or something." He grabbed a couple of towels from the kitchen drawers.

"You ok, sweetheart?" Jason asked, coming to her side. "That looks bad."

"It hurts, but it's not dangerous."

"Do you need more blood?"

"I'll let you know."

Jason looked across the room, to where the witch Leslie was

sprawled on the ground, unconscious. "What the hell happened to them?"

Silvana shrugged. "Leslie tried to use magic. It looked like it reflected back on them."

"I thought Metamorphs couldn't use magic?" Jason asked.

"They can't."

"Then what does that mean?" Freddie asked as he started wrapping rags around Silvana's wounds.

"I have no idea." Silvana steeled herself to speak through the pain. "Listen. That Metamorph was a proper chimera. Only the greatest and most powerful Metamorphs reach that level of transformation. That's why it could take multiple forms at the same time. They are the greatest assassins in the Imperium, outrageously expensive to hire, and bound to a code of honour." She pointed to the kicked-in door. "It'll be back. And soon. It won't stop until we're all dead."

"Shit," Freddie said. He jumped over to Leslie's side and slapped them on the face. "Hey, witchy person. Wake the hell up and tell us what to do!"

"We have to get out of here, now," Jason growled, moving to the hallway cupboard to grab a backpack. "We're not equipped for this, not at this house. Jesus Christ, the fucking back door is gone!" The entire living quarters were exposed to the cold British winds common for this late in the year. Silvana noticed Jason shiver as he crossed paths with the damaged door, grumbling, "What about Edward's place?"

"He's three hours away," Freddie said as he ducked into his bedroom and started packing a bag. "What about your family, Silvana?"

She caught Jason looking at her, waiting for her to speak for herself, but failing to hide the disgust on his face.

"They wouldn't be any help," Silvana said, and she watched Jason sag in relief. "My aunts and uncles have the same skillsets as Jason and I. The chimera would likely just tear through them too." She knelt by Leslie's side, checking they were still breathing. "What about the police, Jason? They've got guns."

Jason had disappeared into their shared bedroom. She could hear the sound of his drawers opening and shutting, interrupting his shouted words. "Cops wouldn't work for this. Could you imagine a chimera moving between a group of armed gunmen? There'd be more friendly fire than anything else."

"Really?" Freddie shouted back across the house. "It's not like police to shoot innocent people."

"Damn it, Freddie!"

"Well it's fucking true, innit?"

"Not the time to have this discussion…" Jason started.

Silvana shouted, "What about Khadija?"

Both men appeared in their respective doorways, staring at her with wide eyes. "Silvana," Jason whispered. "That's a pretty big risk. I know Khadija's technically an ally, but I'm not sure we can trust her."

"She's dangerous," Freddie said and shivered, "or unhinged is more like it."

"I think I'd rather call the Vigiles," Jason said. "At least with Desdemona you know what she's capable of. Khadija is unpredictable."

Silvana shook her head. "The Vigiles already know about the chimera assassins and do nothing. They'd be more likely to bury this case than actually investigate. Worse, what if the assassin is working for a High King? The Vigiles would probably report everything back to their bosses and paint a target for the assassin. No. Unless either of you have a better idea, we need to call Khadija."

Jason grumbled. "What if we start driving to Eddies now?"

"That chimera would catch us along the way. Birds can fly a lot faster than cars can drive."

"We could drive really, really fast?" Jason asked hopefully. Silvana glared at him. "Fine! We'll call Khadija." He threw his hands in the air and went back into the bedroom.

"And I'll get a bucket of water for Khadija," Freddie said. Silvana glared at him too. "I'm joking! I know it wouldn't really melt her." He raised an eyebrow in question.

"It won't."

"Damn it. Fine. I'll just… fucking pray, I guess." He returned to his room and Silvana heard him open his cupboards with more force than necessary.

Silvana whipped out her phone and texted the one person able to help them.

Khadija, emergency. Life or death. Please help ASAP. Current location safe for travel, but not for long.

She hit send.

"You're not going to call her?" Jason asked, appearing fully dressed now in his combat trousers, shirt and jacket. He had his Romanov sword and gun holster strapped to his hip and a backpack slung over his shoulders.

"She's a VIP. She might be in the middle of something. Besides, I told her it's safe to teleport here."

"Wait," Freddie called as he appeared with a packed back too, though still in his boxers. "Did you tell her my address? Does this crazy lunatic know where I live now?" Freddie jolted. "Oh crap. Is she right behind me?" He slowly glanced over his shoulder at his empty bedroom, and sighed with relief.

At that moment the room began to spin and fold in on itself. The roof bent at an impossible angle. The floors began to twist in a circle, and Silvana caught a glimpse of some sort of laboratory with work surfaces covered in beakers and flasks. Then a woman was standing in the middle of the room. Dressed in a long black robe and aviator sunglasses, and her thick wavy hair framed her lean olive-skinned face.

It all happened in the time it took Freddie to turn back around. Khadija was now standing a foot in front of him.

"Jesus!" He shouted and shoved her away without thinking.

Khadija staggered before whirling on him with a snarl and a hand wreathed in blue flame. Her sunglasses reflected the light of the fire so that she appeared almost wraith-like with pits of flame instead of eyes.

"Khadija wait!" Silvana cried as she snatched up the wizard's wrist. Khadija growled, and Silvana felt an invisible presence trying to shove her backwards. She clung on. "You're with friends. Freddie didn't mean to hit you. He was just surprised."

"All right, I got it!" Khadija cried and shrugged herself free from Silvana's grip. "You said it was an emergency. Forgive me for being a little jumpy." She squinted at Freddie. "Besides, I think this mortal could benefit from a reminder to mind his manners."

"Consider them minded," Freddie replied meekly before he slunk away.

"Thank you for coming, Princess Al Khalifa," Jason said. "The House of Romanov thanks you for your timely aid."

"Save it. What happened here?" She gestured at the broken wall and the unconscious Leslie who still lay slumped on the dining room floor.

"We had a random visitor," Silvana explained. "This witch arrived asking for Jason's help. Then, not five minutes later, an assassin appears in the room and nearly kills us all."

"They shapeshifted into a bear and a lion," Freddie chimed in.

"And a big damn snake," Jason added.

"So?" Khadija replied with a quick shrug. "One Metamorph shouldn't have been too much for you."

"Um… they were all those creatures at the same time," Silvana said.

Khadija's eyes widened. "By Allah…" Then she launched herself at Silvana, snatching her up by the lapels of her dressing gown. "A chimera? You fought a fucking chimera? And you didn't tell me *before* I came here?!" Her voice had risen to a high-pitched shriek.

"Hey, calm down," Jason growled as he took a step towards Silvana.

"*Think!* You ignorant fool," Khadija snapped as she released Silvana and pointed a finger at Jason. "The chimera has to erase all witnesses! Everyone in this room is now officially on the chimera's kill list. And your wife has brought me under the same doom without properly warning me what I was getting into!"

"But… the chimera didn't see you!" Silvana insisted. "If you get us out of here soon, they'll never know you were here. You're in the clear."

"Oh, right. They'll just assume two knights and a vampire used wizard magic to teleport themselves elsewhere." Khadija threw her hands up in the air. "Chimera's are top-tier assassins, Silvana. Even the High Kings fear them, as well they should. Every mosquito, every fly, could suddenly shift into a creature big enough to rip your guts out. They could hide under your bed as a viper and kill you with one venomous bite. They can track you as a bird before they drop out of the sky as an elephant and crush you."

"Like drop bears." Everyone turned to Freddie. "Like in Australia. Bears that drop out of trees and kill tourists exclusively."

"My god, Freddie," Jason moaned.

"I'll shut up now." Freddie put a hand over his mouth.

Khadija huffed in annoyance. "My point is that this assassin could be anywhere. We are all its targets now. One way or another, it will keep coming until we're all dead. Anyone we speak with will become a target too."

"All right," Jason snapped. "So we find out who hired the assassin and work it like a case. Leslie is the real target and we're all just collateral. We have to track down whoever put a hit on Leslie. That's the only way out of this, right?"

Khadija grumbled, "First we have to go somewhere safer than here." She gestured at the small house, screwing her nose up as she took in the mess.

"We were thinking Edward's place. The alchemist," Silvana said.

"You know he'll come under the same doom," Khadija warned.

"Do you have another location?" Silvana drawled.

Khadija rolled her eyes. "Fine. But out of politeness, I insist you warn him properly before I take you there."

Freddie nodded. "I'll call him."

Chapter 3

Silvana found herself sitting in an armchair and sipping a steaming cup of tea.

It was a bizarre feeling. After being happily asleep just thirty minutes ago, she'd since fought a master assassin, allied with an angry wizard, packed a bag of clothes and been teleported to an alchemist's mansion.

To be fair, it's a rather nice mansion.

Their host, Edward, kept his lounge room tidy and immaculate. He didn't seem to believe in decoration. The walls were covered in an old green leaf wallpaper, and nothing else. The room desperately needed an artwork to hang on the wall or a splash of colour. Edward himself was an Immortal alchemist who appeared to be in his late twenties, with blue-grey eyes and a long fringe of hair. He stood before them in brown robes with long sleeves, and a bright pink nightcap. He walked around the circle of old leather couches and poured steaming hot tea from a pewter jug into porcelain cups.

"Drink it," he muttered. "It will cure the shock and nerves you're feeling."

"Thanks, Eddie. You're the best, man," Freddie said, then raised his cup to click it against the jug. "Cheers!"

Edward grimaced, and Silvana couldn't help smiling at the missed social cue. It had taken her a while to understand Edward's autism. Yet the more she worked on overcoming her prejudice, the more endearing Edward became.

Jason moved about the room, scanning the corners of the roof. "Eddie, do you use some sort of magical bug repellent on this place?"

"Sure do. I haven't seen a cockroach in decades. It's a tricky potion to make, and you have to smear it in a perfect boundary around the property." Edward produced a satisfied smirk as he explained the process.

"Excellent," Jason said and tapped the gun holster on his hip. "So, if I can see a bug, I can shoot it on sight? That'll surprise the bastard."

"I've also turned my house invisible again," Edward said, ignoring Jason's comment. "And I've got several nasty surprises waiting for any intruder who tries to break in." He tapped his vest in a meaningful way, and Silvana heard the quiet chink of glass vials knocking together.

Silvana remembered the first time they visited the alchemist and how, at first, his whole mansion had been invisible. She hadn't realised until now it was something he could adjust at will. Maybe this place would be more secure than she thought.

"Would you relax, Jason?" Khadija drawled. "The assassin will take time to find us here."

"They found Leslie at our place pretty damn quick," Jason replied, checking the kitchen windows and back door, his sword swinging at his belt from the rapid movements.

"I'm here this time," Khadija said. "The assassin will have a harder fight with a wizard."

Silvana shook her head. "There was a magical barrier on them. You should be prepared for your spells to fail."

"Then I'll throw stuff at him with magic," Khadija drawled. "Come on, Jason, we have things to discuss."

Jason reluctantly sat on the three seater couch, with Silvana in the middle and Freddie on her other side. Both men were leaning forward, their backs rigid like they might need to leap into action at a moment's notice. She wondered if they copied each other on purpose, or if they both simply wanted to protect her.

"What about our guest?" Jason asked, pointing to the witch – Leslie – who was slumped on a couch, drool running down one side of their face. "Do you have something for them?"

"No idea," Edward muttered.

Jason smirked. "Um… would you mind explaining?"

"Well, I'm not a witch. I don't know what the problem is. I can't just start giving them random elixirs. You should ask the wizard."

"Don't look at me," Khadija said, her legs sprawled to the side and her back slouched. She still wore her aviator sunglasses and almost looked like a badass biker. "The witch had their own spell backfire on them. I don't understand witch's spells."

"We can't just sit here and hope for the best," Jason growled.

"That's exactly what we're going to do, sir knight," Khadija said. "Until Leslie wakes up and tells us what spell they cast, we won't know what magical problem we're facing. Besides, there's a more pressing matter, don't you think?"

Freddie barked a laugh and raised his cup, which happened to have pink lilies on the outside. "Are you sure? We're being hunted by a super assassin. That's just a Tuesday for us." He grinned, and found everyone staring at him. "What?"

"Focus up, mortal," Khadija growled.

"Well, excuse me, princess!" Freddie cried. "This is a load-bearing sense of humour. My entire psyche will crumble without it."

She pinched the bridge of her nose. "Men."

Silvana stepped in before the tension got any worse. "So Khadija, it's been a few months since we last saw you. How have you been?"

The Khalifa princess gave her a smile back. "I'm ok. Things with my family are good. It's just…"

"Samantha?" Silvana asked.

"Yeah." She took a long sip of her tea, clearly steadying herself. "I haven't seen her in six months. It's been really hard." Her flat tone couldn't hide the pain in her words.

"I'm so sorry. Is there any progress on getting her released?"

"None. The bastards are stalling me. I think the Imperium are freaking out that she technically came back from the dead. I fear they're studying her more than trying to help her recover." Khadija sighed. "Still, there's nothing we can do for her now. We best deal with the situation at hand." Silvana understood this meant she was done talking about this topic. Still, Khadija gave her a slight nod of thanks.

"So," Silvana began, "a world class assassin is coming for Leslie, and by extension, all of us. Therefore, we cannot call anyone else for help. That means no police…" She looked to Jason. "No allies…" She pointed at Khadija. "…and no other vampire family members." She raised her own hand in acknowledgement. *Not that I've spoken to any of them in weeks. They probably wouldn't help anyway.* She pushed aside her resentment before it boiled over. "So, we have to work together. The only people we can trust are the six people in this room."

"Well," Khadija said, "that's a sobering thought." She pointedly looked at Freddie, and he just raised an eyebrow as if to show how little he cared.

"We need to view this as a case," Silvana said, looking to Jason. "Do we have any leads?"

He stared at her, a questioning look in his eyes.

"What?" she asked.

"Nothing," he said. "It's just… you're taking charge. I like it."

Khadija sneered, "All right, enough googly eyes, kids. Can you be adorable later?" Silvana couldn't help the blush that warmed her cheeks.

Jason slipped into his professional detective demeanour. "We have no leads. The assassin could be hired by anyone. Although, that assassin had some form of magical protection which blocked Leslie's spell. But I guess that could just mean the assassin organisation has a wizard in their employ. Doesn't mean a wizard hired them and shielded them. There's not enough information until Leslie wakes up."

"I actually… disagree," Silvana said. Her tone was gentle, but she felt an instant stab of panic. She still hated any kind of confrontation with family. Her hands were fidgeting, until Jason placed a reassuring hand on her own. *God he knows me so well.* "Leslie is a historian for the Imperium. They keep secrets. So clearly, someone is trying to keep something hidden."

"It's still too vague," Jason said. "The Imperium is thousands of years old. That's a lot of history. Lots of room for a lot of secrets."

"Then it's not about history," Khadija said. "Something is happening *now.*"

Silvana clapped her hands and pointed at the wizard. "Exactly! Someone could be planning to repeat history, and they want to remove the people who might see the signs and stop it."

Khadija smiled warmly. "Brilliant. Finally, someone capable on this team."

"Oh, come on," Freddie growled.

Silvana ignored him and smiled back at Khadija.

"Then we investigate the Immortal Houses," Silvana said. "Someone must be up to something."

Jason sighed. "Someone's always up to something. I'm sorry, Silvana, but I still don't think we have enough information. Not until Leslie wakes up…"

"Where's Eddie?" Freddie asked, looking around.

Silvana scanned the lounge room. Now that Freddie had pointed it out, she noticed the alchemist was gone. Jason was on his feet, his gun held in both hands and aimed at the ground. "Where did he…?"

Edward appeared in the doorway, and immediately splashed a vial of liquid onto Leslie's sleeping face.

Everyone cried out at the same time in overlapping voices.

"Whoa!"

"Dude what the hell? Don't do that!"

"Not again! Didn't you learn from last time?"

"You just said we had no idea what would happen…"

Leslie gasped. The witch sat up, clutching their chest and breathing rapidly. They looked around as recognition lightened their eyes at the people sitting around them. After a moment's hesitation, they sat back against the couch with a sigh of relief. All the lines on their face slackened.

"Thank the stars," Leslie whispered.

"Well," Freddie said, "Nice job Eddie. I take back all my criticism."

"I don't," said Khadija.

Jason holstered his gun and knelt before the witch. "Leslie? You ok?"

Leslie groaned and sat up. "What just happened? And where am I now?" They blinked. "And who are these other people?"

"Relax. They are friends of ours. You were hit by your own spell. It bounced off that chimera."

Leslie scoffed. "That's impossible, I…" Their eyes focused on Khadija and grew cold. "Wizard."

"Witch." Khadija's voice was like ice.

"I would not have thought you capable of such a generous rescue," Leslie said.

"Funny. I would indeed have thought you capable of knocking yourself out with your own spell."

Leslie scowled. "I know you. You're that princess, Al Khalifa. What's wrong? Are you hiding out here because daddy picked another ugly man for you to marry?"

Khadija's jaw clenched, and Silvana's enhanced eyes noticed the room grow the tiniest shade darker. "There's always a cost to ruling the world. Not that you'd know."

"Must be nice to rule the world," Leslie said in a pleasant voice. "Committing genocide. Covering up genocide. Honestly, where *do* you find the time for the little things?"

"There's always time for a little ass kicking," Khadija growled, and the walls behind her filled with shadows.

"All right!" Jason said in a loud, calm tone. He stood up in the centre of the room. "Can someone tell me what your problem is with each other?" Both wizard and witch went silent, and the shadows seeped away.

Edward cleared his throat from the corner of the room. "Wizards run the Imperium. Witches live in a mostly subservient role. Has been this way since the Imperium came into existence two thousand years ago."

Jason sighed. "Just what we need. A new prejudice." He rubbed his hand over his eyes. "Look, it's very early in the morning, and we've all just woken up and narrowly escaped death. Can we please hate each other later?"

Wizard and witch eyed each other. Silvana was ready to leap at Khadija and hold her down if a fight broke out, but it seemed both witch and wizard were keeping their cool. At least for now.

"Are you a man or a woman?" Edward asked bluntly. He was looking at Leslie, a small frown creasing his brow. "I can't tell."

Leslie gave a gentle smile. "Does it really matter, my friend?"

"Oh. Of course." Edward nodded as if that made perfect sense and finally sat down at last in a relaxed pose.

Silvana wished he'd asked a few more questions. The whole gender thing still confused her and she didn't know how to ask about it politely.

"My friends," Leslie said. "I am grateful for your rescue, and I am ashamed I was no help in the battle. Now I must ask, how did we survive?"

"Freddie here used a potion," Jason said.

Edward clapped his hands together. "Oh, which one? The Ignis Elixir?"

Freddie grinned. "Nah man, the acid one! Melted the dudes face off!"

"Oh, the one that burns green! Is that why your eyes were all red when you arrived? I should have guessed. How did you recover from—"

"Boys," Silvana said and waved the pair into silence. She leaned forward in her chair. "So…" she struggled at what honorific she should call Leslie. *Damn, all titles are gendered. That doesn't seem fair.* At last she said, "Leslie. While you were unconscious, we were discussing possible avenues to investigate your attacker. We were hoping you could give us some sort of new information that would help."

"First," Jason said, "how long until the assassin finds us? What are we dealing with here?"

Leslie gestured to Khadija. "If the wizard teleported us, then they won't be able to track my magic like they did last time. We could have several days, or only one. I don't know precisely. But I know we must use this precious time to find out why they've been sent after me."

"We figured," Jason said, "that it's likely to do with your research as a historian. You probably know something that someone else is trying to keep hidden."

Leslie held up a hand. "Let me stop you right there. If you're about to ask me to spill the Imperium's darkest secrets, you know I can't. I already showed you my signet."

"Wait! I didn't get to see it," Edward said eagerly. Leslie patiently rolled up their sleeve again for Edward's interest. "Norse runes. It means 'silent.'"

"Very good," Leslie said, genuinely impressed. "So you know I cannot reveal Imperium secrets."

"Ah, but this is to save your life, mate." Freddie raised an eyebrow at Leslie.

"If I told you the Imperium's secrets, my life would be forfeit anyway. No use escaping one attacker just to anger the High Kings themselves."

"Ah. True," Freddie grumbled.

"All right then," Jason said. "Keep your secrets." He gave a sly wink at Freddie, who nodded approvingly. "But can you give us a hint? Tell us which Houses we should be looking into."

"I can't do that either." Leslie was already waving away their objections. "Not because of the signet, but because I don't know. If I knew where to start, I would have done it myself. But I have no *clue.* Someone's trying to kill me and I don't have the faintest suspicion of why. This is the reason I came to you, sir knight. You've solved two Immortal crimes and stopped their ultimate plans from coming to fruition. I'm hoping you can do that a third time."

Jason shook his head and scoffed, looking at the roof in dismay. "Leslie..." he groaned. "I'm not a miracle worker. I solved those crimes because I had *information.* I was able to piece together the facts. Right now, there are *no* facts. I don't have contacts, or super powers, or even any qualifications. I'm not even a real detective yet.

I'm a beat cop!"

"Which only makes your accomplishments even more impressive."

Annoyance flashed over Jason's face. "That's not…" he growled, but stopped himself with visible effort. "Then, can you at least be sure this isn't about you personally? Do you have any enemies who might want to hurt you? An ex-partner you broke up with? A colleague whose promotion you stole?"

Leslie shook their head. "Mr Turner, I'm certain. I conduct myself with the highest integrity. There's nothing in my personal life that could cause this, and nothing in my professional life either."

"How can you be certain?"

"Do you know how old I am?" The room went quiet. Leslie grinned to themselves, like that solved the matter.

"No," Freddie said. "Maybe…fifty?"

Leslie blinked. "I'm in my eighth century of life."

"Oh."

"I was born in France in 1263." Leslie's voice rose in fervency and command. "I lived through the Hundred Year War, the Crusades, and the Mongol Invasion. I met Joan of Arc, Johannes Guttenberg, Da Vinci, Columbus. I fought against the hordes of Genghis Khan. I defended France from British invasion time and time again. I witnessed the charge of the Light brigade with my own eyes. I slaughtered fascists in the Second World War."

They flicked their hand, and the room seemed to explode in colour. A kaleidoscope of swirling lights and flickering stars filled the little space, all spinning like revolving galaxies. Silvana stared right at it but could not understand what she was seeing, whether it was a glimpse into deep space, or every nucleus on a subatomic level. "I am a witch at the height of their powers. I can do things you couldn't even imagine. And I am very, very smart. So yes, Jason. I am *certain*."

The room went back to normal. Silvana had to rapidly blink to clear the flashing dark spots from her eyes. *What was that?* Silvana had seen a lot in her ninety-three years of life, but today she was reminded of how young she still was within the Immortal world. *Leslie must be the witch's equivalent of a High King. Someone at their maximum power level.*

Jason had slouched back into a nearby chair during the display. He spoke in a whisper, "Then why do you need me? What can I possibly do that you can't do yourself?"

Leslie smiled widely at him, before letting out a warm laugh. "Because I believe in the power of little things." Leslie's face was alive with joy as they spoke. "I have seen empires that were supposed to last forever fall into dust. I've seen the mighty and the powerful show stupidity like you wouldn't believe. I've seen cities disappear off the face of the earth. Yet time and time again, I've seen little people succeed where they had no right to hope for victory."

They looked around the room at Freddie. "I've seen bravery succeed against power." At Edward, "I've seen ingenuity change the world." They looked at Silvana. "I've seen simple kindness shatter the might of kingdoms."

Leslie faced Jason again. "So when I found myself attacked by the ultimate assassin, with the might of the Imperium backing them, who should I turn to? Another High King? A president? No. I turn to one individual, unique out of all the people I've known in my eight hundred years of life, and I trust that their mind is exactly what we need."

Khadija sneered. "So you trust in God to save you? Through his *messiah*, Jason Turner?"

Leslie sneered right back, mimicking her tone. "I have never trusted God. I trust in the capability of humanity. The uniqueness of the individual. You might even say, I trust in the beauty of life itself."

"Then you're a fool," Khadija said. "Surely you've seen power triumph a thousand times over good people."

"Well, a wizard would know about that." Leslie laughed again. "You're absolutely right, of course. Power wins most of the time. But if you can't beat power with power, then courage and cleverness are the only options left." Leslie looked to Jason. "Though, they are still pretty good options. I guess you might say, I'd stake my life on that."

All eyes turned to Jason. Silvana couldn't imagine what he felt like in that moment. She wanted to reach out to him. But she trusted him and waited in silence.

"I understand," he whispered. "You don't really care for qualifications. Or power. You just want people who are willing to try."

"Indeed. Now, sir knight, what are you willing to try?"

Jason nodded to himself. "Eddie? Do you have a whiteboard of some kind?"

"I have several chalk boards."

Jason grinned. "Of course you do. Can you bring them in here? We need to start brainstorming."

Chapter 4

The first rays of morning light peeked through the gaps in the curtains. Jason took another sip of coffee and paced the living room.

"Read it back to me again," he asked.

"Jason," Khadija groaned. "You can just look at the board. It's literally within arm's reach."

"Just let him work," Freddie said. "He's got a process."

The team of six were still gathered in Edward's lounge room now with the signs of a plan slowly coming together. A plate of biscuits, cheese, dips and strawberries was set on the coffee table. Silvana was lying sideways on a stack of pillows, Freddie was slouching with one leg over the arm rest, and Khadija had her couch in full recliner mode. Only Leslie sat up straight and alert. Meanwhile, Edward and Jason were standing in front of a chalk board covered in writing.

Edward cleared his throat. "Resources are limited," he read. "Anyone we speak to can become a target of the assassin. That rules out help from mortal means, or the Romanov family. Technically, Al Khalifa family connections are still an option, as Khadija's involvement is not open knowledge just yet."

"For now," Khadija said, her aviator sunglasses making her appear asleep.

"Next," Jason prompted.

"Primary goal is information gathering," Edward went on, twirling his piece of chalk between his fingers before pointing at the board. "We have three main options. Option one; Investigate the assassin organisation."

"Definitely our weakest option," Leslie muttered, but Jason politely shushed them.

"Infiltrate the Metamorphs and find all active contracts. Find out who ordered the hit. The pros are that it's definitely the simplest option. The cons are that it will be almost impossible to execute. The order of assassins are unapproachable except by those already in the know. Virtually nothing is known about their organisation. Likely that contracts are highly secure and assassins will die before revealing anything."

"Option two?" Jason called out, still pacing.

Freddie helped himself to a pile of cheese.

"Investigate the Immortal Houses. Tug on every string and find news on current activity that may be relevant. Pros, probably the safest option. It can be done within means of normal operation. Cons, it's likely to find a plethora of irrelevant information, existing plots, and possible distractions. Also, very time consuming. Metamorph assassin likely to find us within that time."

"God," Jason groaned. "Next?"

"Final option three," Edward read. "Investigate the histories of the Imperium. Look for anything that might be relevant to current events and could be cause for attempted murder of a historian. Pros, it will be fun and interesting."

"Take that off!" Khadija said, tilting her head up and glaring at Freddie. "Why'd you tell him to write that?"

"Cause it's the secret history of the world! I want to know."

"Now is not the time."

"If not now, then when?"

Khadija growled in frustration, sinking her head back into the couch. "Why are you even here, mortal? What do you bring to the table other than pointless comic relief?"

Freddie cried out in mock horror. "That's really offensive! Comic relief is essential to any situation."

"Guys," Jason shouted. "Please, continue."

Edward tapped the board. "Other pros, this option is the most likely one to work, due to the least risk. Cons, we're also likely to find a plethora of irrelevant information and possible distractions."

"Unless Leslie gives us direct answers?" Jason asked with a raised brow in the witch's direction.

"Sorry," Leslie shrugged. "Even if I could just tell you all about the secret histories, I don't know what we're looking for."

Jason nodded. "Anything else?"

"That's all we have, Jason," Edward said mournfully.

"God damn it," Jason growled. He stopped pacing and collapsed on the couch next to Silvana. "That's still too little."

Khadija sighed as she moved her couch back into an upright position. "All right, we've been at this for over an hour. Maybe it's about time we just pick something. There's nothing else we can do now except take action. The sooner we start—"

Jason waved a hand at her dismissively, cutting her off mid-sentence. "Not yet. We could waste too much time on the wrong option. We have to pick the right one now."

"Face it, Jason," Khadija said, her tone not unkind. "There's no way to know which option is right. Like you said, we don't have all the information. You've got to guess."

"What if we split up?" Freddie asked. "There's six of us here. Two could pursue each option. Or three could choose two options. Or—"

"Or," Khadija cut in, "five of us could do whatever we want while

Freddie hunts down the assassins himself." She held up her hand. "That's my vote. Everyone else cool with that?"

Freddie sat up straight. "What is your fucking problem?"

"We don't need you to do long division."

Freddie mumbled, "Still rude."

"All right," Jason yelled yet again. "Final call. Does anyone else have any ideas?" Silence greeted him. "Anyone at all? Suggestions? Wild theories? Seriously, nothing's too weird at this point."

Freddie shrugged. "We could give up. Run and hide somewhere in Mexico."

Leslie shook their head. "We'd be looking over our shoulder all our lives, and we wouldn't even last that long. These chimeras are too good at hunting people."

"We have to make a choice, Jason," Khadija said. "I'm not trying to be cruel, but there's no other option."

"Maybe there is."

All eyes turned to Silvana. She had been silent the longest and still appeared deep in thought as she lay on the couch, but Jason could see the way her hands were pressed at her chin. Her mouth wavered. She was nervous.

"Silvy? I'd love to hear your ideas," he said.

She nodded and sat upright. "What if we searched for Dorin?"

"Ah yes," Leslie said. "I recall your stipulation. However, I thought we were going to do that *after* this calms down."

"Well, what if we did it now?"

Jason frowned. "I don't understand."

Silvana pointed at the board. "It comes under options two *and* three. Investigate the Immortal Houses *and* secret histories. Think about it. Dorin knows me, and claims to know about my past. All we know about him at this point is he's working for the Royalists."

"Royalists?" Edward asked.

Jason explained, "Immortals who want to bring back the monarchies and rule the mortal world openly. They're all extremists." Jason gave him a strained smile. "And we've managed to piss off several of them so far."

"That's my point exactly," Silvana continued. "The Royalist group could relate to an Immortal House, or a secret history. How about we pursue that? We don't exactly have a better option. For all we know, this could be the exact thing behind Leslie's assassin."

"Seems a bit convenient," Khadija said. "Sorry, sweetheart, but I have to question your motives here. Sounds like personal feelings are getting in the way."

Did she just call Silvana 'sweetheart?' Jason frowned. He was happy that Khadija was at least being respectful to someone in the group, but 'sweetheart' seemed too flirty for his taste.

"I know, I know," Silvana droned. "That's why I didn't say anything before now. But no one has a better option. Who knows, this could be something." She shrugged at Jason. "You're the detective. What do you think?"

Part of him thought he had to say no. It was such a random idea and it reeked of self-interest. Yet, she was right. He had no better option. At least with Silvana's idea, they could explore two of the options he'd put forward. He forced himself to relax and consider things from her perspective. It made more sense than he cared to admit.

"Alright," he said. "We can track down Dorin."

"Really?" half the room said at once, including Silvana.

"Really. After all, the Yamatos tried to destroy us in revenge for taking out their ally, Erikson. If Dorin is a Royalist too, this might be part of a similar revenge plot for defeating the Yamatos."

"Oh, come on," Khadija cried, then with great effort she stopped and took a breath to calm herself. She went on in a gentler voice.

"I'm sorry, Silvana, I don't mean to be rude, but I have to ask. You were adopted, right?" Silvana nodded. "And now you're not speaking to your adopted family? Well, maybe you're trying to find your real family just to get back at them? This could just be a very emotional decision."

"I agree with you," Silvana said. "That's why I asked Jason's opinion."

"Oh right, cause your husband's bound to be much more objective." Khadija sighed again. "Sorry. I'm trying to be polite."

Leslie was supressing a smile as they said, "How very wizard of you."

"Don't even fucking start with me, witch."

Jason shook his head. "Khadija makes a fair point. This could be a biased decision for both Silvana and me. That's why I don't want to commit everyone to this plan. I suggest some of us research Dorin and find out what he knows, and the rest of us pursue other options." He looked around the room and saw no complaints. "Excellent. So what other options do we have?"

Freddie spoke up as he leant forward to grab more cheese. "All right, I didn't want to say this earlier because it sounded biased, but since that's cool now," he winked at Silvana to show he was joking. "I still think we should look into the secrets of the Imperium."

Khadija rolled her eyes with a groan.

Freddie held up his hands. "I know, this is obviously an area of interest for me, I admit it. But don't you think it's just as likely to bring up more leads as looking for this Dorin guy? And yeah, we can learn some cool shit at the same time."

"I already told you," Leslie sighed. "I'm not telling you anything."

"Well, maybe you don't have to," Freddie countered. "You're a historian, right? You know a lot of information. Surely you don't keep it all in your head. You must have some sort of Wikipedia." Leslie blinked at him. "An internet page. Somewhere you store all that information."

"You mean like a library?"

"My god, you're old," Freddie muttered. "Yes, like a library. How about you just give us a key to your office and let us research for ourselves. That way you're not technically breaking any vow."

Leslie paused with their mouth half open. "That's… actually an effective idea. It would be a perfect loophole to get around my signet. You could learn about the secret histories and find your connection to Dorin, all by yourselves." They smiled, causing the lines on their face to deepen. "Freddie, you'd make a good witch."

"Sign me up!" Freddie laughed.

"But there's a much larger problem here," Leslie went on. They pointed at Silvana. "I didn't have the heart to tell you before, but now it's unavoidable."

"Oh dear," Silvana muttered.

"If you want to find Dorin, you will need my books on genealogy and family lineage. They're at my workplace too."

"That's perfect!" Jason grinned. "We just have to get into your library and find the information we need." Only after he spoke did he see the grim look on Leslie's face. "Ok let me guess. There's something's terribly dangerous about that."

"Precisely. This library I work in is one of the most impregnable facilities in the world. There is both magical and technological security guarding it. Because if the information this library holds was ever to be released, the consequences could be irreversible."

"So it's Mordor," Freddie said. "One does not simply walk in. We get it."

"Oh no, my friend. Mordor has nothing on this place."

Jason eyed the witch. "Then… what is it?"

"The Library of Alexandria."

The room went silent. Jason sagged down into the couch and stared blankly at the wall. Too many thoughts were exploding in his head for him to focus on any given one. He had a few moments of sheer overwhelm. *It seems like I'm always aiming over my head these days.* Could this really be happening? Just a few hours ago, he had been asleep in his bed minding his own business. Now, he was the lead detective in yet another Immortal investigation. He looked up, and realised everyone was watching him. His dark mood was affecting everyone. He had to appear strong for the rest of the group.

"All right," he said. "So it looks to me like we need to break into the Library of Alexandria to find the secret that this assassin is trying to hide. If we find the secret, we'll find who hired the assassin and be able to stop them. Does that sound right to everyone else?"

No one spoke. But he could see the resolve on their faces as they nodded one by one.

"Ok then," Jason said in a loud voice. "Let's plan a heist."

Chapter 5

Freddie gave a loud 'whoop!' of excitement. It was just what Jason needed to lift him out of his funk. He smiled and stood from where he sat beside Silvana.

"Ok Leslie," Jason said. "Tell us about the Library of Alexandria. We need to know what we're up against, how to beat it, and what we're looking for once we're inside."

Edward immediately flipped his chalk board over to the blank side and poised himself to start writing. Jason gave him a nod of thanks, then checked on Silvana and Khadija. Both the women had looks of silent ascent.

"You're actually ok with this?" Jason asked.

"Makes sense," Khadija said. "It's the only way to get the information we need. Besides, I'm always up for a chance to undermine the absolute authority of the High Kings. Breaking into their top security fortress sounds like the perfect 'fuck you.'"

Silvana simply nodded. "I need to know," was all she said.

"All right. Leslie, what have you got for us? How much can you tell us?"

Leslie was chuckling softly to themselves. "You five are serious, aren't you? I've barely begun to explain how difficult this will be, and you're already willing to try."

"Well, this is a pretty good team," Jason said. "A wizard, witch, alchemist, vampire, and two knights. We're basically the Avengers in the first movie."

"Nice!" Silvana cheered.

Jason had recently watched all the Marvel movies to impress her, and referenced them every chance he got. It was definitely working.

"Oh, I like it," Freddie said. "Jase and me are the regular assassins. Leslie and Khadija can be Thor and Hulk. Nice."

"I'm Captain America, my favourite," Silvana said.

"Yeah, and Eddie is Iron Man! The super genius," Freddie said, and Edward had a very pleased smile on his face at that. "Good reference, Jase."

"Children…" Khadija groaned, running her hands down her face.

"My friends," Leslie said while trying to hide their smile. "This is harder than you think. You are not the first to attempt to infiltrate the Library. There have been teams with far greater power who have died in the attempt."

Silvana scoffed. "I thought you said you didn't trust in power. You trusted in the 'capability of humanity'?"

Leslie grinned at her. "Indeed I do. I'm just surprised you do too."

"We all have our reasons," Khadija said with a hard glare. "Though they may not be the same as yours. Now let's begin already."

"Yeah, I'm a bit concerned about the 'people dying in the attempt' part," Freddie said. "So what are we up against?"

Leslie stood up with a groan – their injuries clearly still causing them some pain – and moved to stand next to the blackboard. "You're in luck. I can tell you about the Library without compromising my signet. First of all, you need to understand that the Library is ancient. It was set up by Alexander the Great even before the Imperium existed."

"Hang on," Freddie cut in, and Khadija groaned. "Damn, I have like five questions already. For one, what's this about 'before' the Imperium? I thought it was ancient."

Leslie held up a hand to stop Khadija's complaint. "Listen, my mortal friend, before the Imperium existed, all of Europe used to be divided by warlords. Most of which were vampires. Have you heard of the empowered vampire?"

"Ah yes. That thing vampires do if they get too much blood. They go all superpowered and move stuff with their mind."

"Exactly. Now, unlike wizards and witches who require time and dedication to unlock their full power, a vampire can quickly gain power if they are…" Leslie trailed off for a moment, their eyes distant before continuing, "ruthless enough."

"Oh shit."

Jason glanced at Silvana, but she seemed ok with this conversation. He let Leslie continue.

"Just imagine it. Every young, violent, undisciplined vampire could go mad with power and bloodlust. A powerful vampire could gain a large portion of territory in a short amount of time, if they slaughtered their way through each place they wished to claim. It's the reason why humanity stayed underdeveloped for so long. Vampires ruled large portions of the world through sheer terror. Warlords destroyed whole people groups, entire civilisations, in their conquests. The mentally enhanced Immortals had little hope to stand against them."

"It's why there's still distrust of vampires to this day," Silvana said. "Why we have strict laws against vampires drinking too much blood. Even though that was thousands of years in the past."

Leslie nodded in agreement. "One of the most successful warlords was the aforementioned Alexander the Great."

"Wait," Jason said. "Alexander was a vampire?"

"It makes sense, doesn't it? One of the most successful conquests in history happened in a very short timeframe. Alexander was always on the front line. Even mortal records say he was one of the first over the walls at the siege of Tyre. The man was empowered."

"Huh," Jason muttered.

"Thing is, Alexander wasn't just power-hungry, though he was that. He also understood the fruitlessness of the endless vampire wars. He wanted to create a central government to unite the world and advance civilisation. Many historians agree that his ideas were the precursor to the Imperium. His problem was he wanted to unite the world behind *him.* That's why his empire fell apart the moment a witch's spell took his health."

"Whoa, whoa," Freddie said. "A witch killed Alexander the Great?"

Leslie gave him a dark grin. "If someone in history died of 'illness', about fifty percent of the time it was actually a witch."

"Well, that's kinda horrifying," Freddie said, and Jason nodded in agreement.

Perhaps Leslie was even more deadly than they realised.

"However," Leslie went on, "before Alexander's death, he did begin to build the foundation of a more civilised world. The Library was his crowning achievement. Some wizards tried to destroy it on a few occasions, including the famous fire. But the majority of the works were protected. Later, when the Imperium was formed, wizards took over its management."

"Hang on," Freddie said. "How was the Imperium formed?"

"Freddie," Khadija groaned.

"Hey," Jason objected. He turned to Leslie with a shrug. "It could be relevant."

Leslie smiled and kindly indulged him. "The Imperium started with Rome. What you know as the myth of Romulus and Remus, the twin brothers raised by wolves, is actually two wizards who were saved by a Metamorph to spare them from a vampire's wrath.

That one act of mercy changed the world. The female metamorph raised the brothers and protected them long enough for them to come into their power. They had enough strength to build Rome as a haven for wizards and other Immortals fleeing the vampire wars. In time, it became an established front of power in Europe. Remus eventually warred with his brother and Romulus destroyed him. However, Romulus stayed in power for over eight hundred years, nearly the full length of the Roman Empire. He destroyed many vampire warlords. Eventually, his kingdom expanded until it covered most of Europe. That's when he founded the Imperium by allying with other wizard kings."

Freddie held up a hand. "What year was this? Do you have a date?"

Leslie grinned. "Year One."

"What?"

"You've probably heard that BC stands for Before Christ, AD is Anno Domini, the year of our lord. In the Immortal world, we refer to them as Before Conquest, and After Dominion. Year One marks the date when the Imperium was formed and control of Europe was successfully wrestled away from the vampire warlords. It's the date that the vampire laws were established, so that vampires must only take blood from their spouse to limit their power."

Jason couldn't help looking at Silvana. He'd spent a year disagreeing with the rule of vampire marriage, yet suddenly it made a lot of sense. He couldn't imagine a world where any vampire could become superpowered if they murdered enough people. One simple rule protected everyone. And yet… were the wizards any better rulers? He wasn't sure. Considering how cruel wizards could be towards the physically enhanced, they had probably forgotten they owed it all to one shapeshifter's act of mercy.

Khadija held up a hand. "Ok, that's a fascinating history lesson but let's bring it back to today. How is this going to help us with the

Library of Alexandria?"

"It's all relevant, princess," Leslie said. "You need to understand that the Library is older than the Imperium. It was built during the reign of the vampire lords. Therefore, it has magical protections that were created by a type of magic that no longer exists."

"Do you mean…" Silvana whispered, "…vampire magic?"

"Exactly. Something that almost no vampire has used in two thousand years. Even the High Kings don't fully understand it. Those who work at the Library have ways around it, but I'm not sure if we can duplicate those ways. Not unless we had our own empowered vampire." Leslie chuckled in derision.

Jason glanced over to Silvana and saw her nod.

"Uh, Leslie?" he said. "We might have one of those."

Leslie stared at Silvana. "Truly? You have done it before?"

"Just once." Silvana shrugged. "I've never been able to do it since."

Jason had to hide his wince. Silvana may have actually achieved an empowered state twice. The second time, however, she had changed. They had been fighting the Yamato's in their castle when a different personality took over Silvana. She became another person entirely and acted wild and violent. She didn't remember the episode, and despite six months passing, Jason still had not found the heart to tell her of what happened. He knew he should. The guilt ate away at him. Maybe he should tell her today?

"Well then," Leslie smiled, cutting off Jason's line of thought. "If this is true, then it changes everything. I think we might actually have a chance of success."

Leslie took a piece of chalk and started to draw a diagram. "The Library of Alexandria is still located in Alexandria, Egypt, believe it or not. There's been talk of moving it for thousands of years but we never have. To avoid attention, the full structure is underground." Leslie stood back to show a surprisingly skilled drawing. "I think we—"

Edward cleared his throat, cutting them off mid-sentence. "I'm the one writing on the chalk board."

Leslie paused. "I see. Sorry, I should have asked. Can I just do the drawing, and you do the writing?"

"That's a good plan," Edward replied flatly.

"Ok then." Leslie gave him a smile, which made Jason give a silent sigh of relief. "So the structure is underground. There is a single entry shaft reaching the surface, so there's literally just one way in and one way out."

The diagram showed a hexagon-shaped foyer in the entrance located above ground. It sat over a massive elevator shaft that lead down to a second foyer. This in turn led into a massive amphitheatre. The heart of the Library itself. "There are three checkpoints we'll need to get past. The first of which is the entry foyer. You'll need papers and identification to get you through."

"Oh," Jason remarked as Edward jotted down the words. "That doesn't sound so hard."

"The only one with clearance is me," Leslie said. "I'm not sure how to get anyone else the required authorisation."

"Oh. That's actually pretty complicated."

"Next," Leslie pointed at the foyer underneath the entry shaft. "Once we go down the lifts, we reach the second checkpoint where things get much trickier. The Imperium added this when they took over, so it's more modern magic. There are three very specific spells over this area. One is a spell of no violence."

"That's no problem," Jason said. "We couldn't use violence to get in anyway. It would expose us."

Leslie nodded. "Quite right. The second spell breaks any existing enchantment on a person."

"Crap," Khadija groaned. She was busy placing some cheese on a biscuit. "So if we use magic to get past the first checkpoint, then we'll be exposed at the second."

"Indeed. The third enchantment is perhaps the trickiest. You can only pass through this barrier if you've been given magical permission by someone who already has authority to cross the checkpoint."

Everyone went quiet, and Jason watched as they tried to make sense of Leslie's instructions. Freddie frowned at the chalkboard as if his stare alone could pull the answers from Edward's chalk script. Khadija had forgotten about her appetite and was now pacing the floor.

Silvana seemed to understand Leslie's words first.

"So the people who created that spell thousands of years ago had to give permission for the next people to enter, and so on and so forth, all the way up to today."

"Ah," Freddie said, "so it's like the Fidelius charm from Harry Potter."

"No!" Khadija growled. "It's nothing like that. Fuck you for saying so."

Freddie held up his hands in mock surrender.

"That's an easy solve," Jason said. "You can give us permission, Leslie. You have access."

Leslie shook their head. "It's a wizard's spell. I can't duplicate it."

"Then can you teach Khadija?"

"Our powers are different," Khadija replied flatly.

"Completely incompatible," Leslie said.

"Wait, what?" Jason groaned. "So, wizards and witches use different magic?" He shook his head. "Ok, never mind that. So this makes..." he counted off the board, "three spells to get past at checkpoint two. What's involved in the final checkpoint? Please tell me it's easier."

Leslie pointed to the diagram of the amphitheatre. There was an archway that joined the foyer to the Library. "That will depend on Ms Romanov here. The final checkpoint is at the entry to the Library itself. Only a vampire with their full powers unlocked would be granted access here. Of course, the historians worked a way around it."

The witch reached into their cloak and pulled out a golden ring with a strange blood-red gemstone set in the crest.

"This is a death diamond," Leslie said.

They held it up for everyone to see as the overhead light hit the jagged edges of the stone, reflecting the beams with a dark glint. It seemed to swallow all brightness.

"I've heard of those," Khadija whispered. "They're made from the dead. The corpse is crushed into a diamond."

"Hey, mortals have that too," Freddie said. "You can have a diamond made out of a loved one after they're cremated. Think they're called ash diamonds."

Leslie's expression was grim. "These are… a little different. They're made from the body of an empowered vampire." They glanced at Silvana in discomfort, but her face was a blank mask. "The wizards killed the original vampires who used the Library and turned their bodies into these stones. It gives access into the Library. The vampire magic of the Library accepts this and grants entry."

"Let me guess," Jason said. "I assume we can't just use that one?"

"Only I can," Leslie said. "It's bonded to me by my blood. I'd have to die for someone else to use it. So, either you find a way to get me past the other two checkpoints, or whoever gets to this stage will need to use their own vampire magic."

"Or," Khadija said with a grin. "We kill you and steal the stone."

"Khadija!" Jason cried. "The whole mission is to save Leslie."

"No, that's your mission. My mission right now is to survive this assassin."

Leslie glared at her. "What a *wizard* perspective."

"We're not killing Leslie," Silvana drawled. She looked at Jason. "I will find a way to use my vampire magic again. Trust me."

Edward finished writing down on the chalk board, *Third checkpoint = Silvana*, before facing the group.

"Anything else?" he added.

"Yeah, I have a question," Khadija said. "Once we find the books we need in the Library, how do we get back out again with said books in hand?"

"First of all," Leslie said. "You cannot take books out of the Library of Alexandria."

"What!" Jason cried. "You mean we have to study them on the spot?"

"We can't possibly remember all that information!" Silvana replied, throwing her hands up in despair. "How are we…"

"Wait, wait," Freddie cried. "This might not be so bad. How about we just film the books and look at them later? Leslie, can we take our phones in there?"

"No way. They'd get spotted at the first checkpoint."

"What if they were really small?"

Leslie paused. "I don't know. How small are mortal cameras these days?"

Freddie grinned. "Pretty damn small. All right, leave this one with me, everybody. I'll get some small cameras to smuggle in. We can record books and then reconvene back here to study them."

"Awesome! Good work, Freddie," Jason said, and Freddie beamed back at him.

Khadija was strangely silent. "What about getting us out?" she repeated.

Leslie waved away her concerns. "Much easier. At the second

checkpoint, there'll be a quick search to check we're not carrying anything out of the Library. If we aren't, they let you back up without any fuss. It'll be the exact same procedure as entering, just in reverse."

Jason nodded, though he noticed Khadija looking sceptical. "All right. Any other questions?" He gestured to the room. It remained silent. "Ok. Let's start working on ways to get past the three checkpoints and into the Library. We need ideas for the identity check at checkpoint one, and the magic spells at checkpoint two. Silvana will get us past checkpoint three."

"I have a question," Freddie said, raising his hand. "What do we do about the assassin in the meantime?"

All eyes turned to Leslie. The witch's old face seemed to bear the weariness of centuries. "It's like I said," they answered. "The assassin could be several days away. Or, they could be one."

"Then we assume it's one," Jason said. "We have to play it safe. Meanwhile, everyone needs to be armed at all times and try to avoid walking around alone. We have twenty-four hours to plan this heist." Jason sighed. "Let's get to work."

Chapter 6

"Igi-guri."

The words sent a flow of power through Portia's mind and into the universe. Her Will gave it shape, and the spell reordered reality itself to form a window in the air. She could see through the opening into another location halfway around the world.

She watched a government cabinet meeting from a magic hole in the ceiling. No one looked up, and even if they did, they'd only notice a slight haze on the roof.

The session had just begun, yet people were already in disarray shouting over the top of each other. Old men in fancy suits yelled at one another in an almost deafening volume. The one in the front was pounding his fist against the table crying for order, but it made no impact. It only seemed to spur on their anger. Portia ignored them all. *Posturing fools*, she thought as she scanned the back rows of civilian spectators.

"Hast thou found him?" Desdemona asked.

"Not yet, mistress."

The meeting had nearly two hundred people watching in the public section. Most had not bothered to dress up, instead wearing plain off-the-rack clothes of commoners. Portia scanned the faces slowly. She did not sense power from any of them, but that only meant there were no mentally enhanced Immortals in the crowd. There could still be…

There. A solitary man dressed in a white baggy top, with a red-brown vest covered in squiggly golden lines. The man's handsome face remained emotionless as his baby blue eyes watched the yelling men below.

"He's here," Portia said.

"Good work," Desdemona replied as she rested a tender hand on her shoulder.

Portia still struggled not to flinch from the physical contact. It had been six months since the incident with the High King, yet any form of touch still brought those memories rushing to the surface. She forced them down once more.

Her mistress watched through the window, with her face only centimetres away from Portia. "What art thou hiding, vampire?" she whispered.

"He is exposed. Vulnerable. The mortals would have scanned him to detect weapons before entering this place, so he must have none on him."

"A vampire hath no need of weapons." Desdemona cupped Portia's hand. "Nevertheless, we shouldst go there. He stands in a crowd of people. One touch from us can lay a tracing spell."

"Yes, Mistress."

Portia stared at Desdemona as she looked through the magic window. She had skin as black as obsidian and always wore her hair in long braids which cascaded down to her waist. She looked the perfect blend of beauty and ferocity, until her Mistress waved a hand and uttered a spell to change both of their appearances. Magic washed over the Vigiles. Desdemona's braided hair unfurled into long, luscious waves. The tuxedo she always donned, turned into a colourful skirt and a white blouse. She had never looked so… feminine.

"A bit traditional, don't you think?" Portia asked coyly.

Desdemona ignored her and waved a hand in the air. A red cloth wrapped around Portia's head, tucking her long, red curls back. "Thy hair is too noticeable," she said. "But forgive me. I could not bear to change its colour." She stroked a finger down the side of Portia's temple.

"Always so sentimental." Portia gave the most perfect smile. But there was no light in Desdemona's eyes. *She knows I'm pretending.* So Portia tried harder, and instead cupped Desdemona's hand and pressed it to her own cheek, before planting a kiss on her lips. "Thank you," she said with as much emotion as she could muster.

This time, her mistress's eyes glowed with genuine joy. *There. I convinced her that time.*

They held hands as Desdemona sent out another wave of magic. The portal disappeared as the room began to rotate around them at impossible angles. A hundred parts of the room moved in a hundred different directions at once, folding over the top of each other and overlapping seamlessly, until the pieces changed colour and shape. All the moving parts slowed down and coalesced into a single shape, and new location appeared.

The Vigiles stood in a dark stairwell. Portia could hear the muffled shouts of the government cabinet filtering through from outside, continuing their endless argument.

"We'll split up," Desdemona said. "Thou hast no need to rush. Ease through the crowd to avoid suspicion."

"Yes, Mistress."

The elder Vigile lead the way to the stairwell exit. The door swung open to emit a sheer wall of blinding light. Portia's eyes adjusted to see a hallway lined with velvet carpet and adorned with large paintings. They separated and moved several paces apart from each other towards the sounds of shouting.

They entered a massive amphitheatre. It looked completely different from the ground level, but it was definitely the same location Portia had spied upon moments earlier. She recognised the voices of the speakers.

"The president has once again shown his true allegiance to the Union and their Romanian Nationalism, and not to his own party!"

"The prime minister," a second voice replied, "is always quick to label anyone who disagrees with him as a Nationalist. He clearly thinks anyone who's not as far left as him must be alt-right."

Portia ignored them all as she moved through the crowd. There was a vampire somewhere on this viewing deck, and there was no spell in her repertoire that could reveal his location. She had to rely on her vision alone. And her intuition.

Where are you, traitor?

Someone shoved against her and she lost her footing. She could smell a foul wave of body odour wash over her. People were pushing back as she tried to move, some even blocking her way intentionally, thinking she was trying to steal their spot in the crowd. She shoved them back, even casting a muttered spell to make them stumble, allowing her to pass.

"This government has been crippled by inaction," a man shouted into a microphone. "And we all know why. Corruption and self-interest. The president and all his ilk would be better suited in a bank. That way when they spend their days lining their own pockets with cash, at least no one will be surprised."

"And where is all this money I supposedly have hidden?" another shouted back. "I wish I could agree with you, or I would have driven here in a limousine and flown home in a private jet. Has the prime minister found one iota of evidence to support his claim?"

Portia watched every face she passed. She looked for that handsome, blue-eyed face in traditional white and embroidered clothing. But it was all too common here. Every second person looked like her target.

Is this where he's from? It would explain his preoccupation with this government.

Portia had covered half the room by now. She could see Desdemona making her way towards her, still a ways off. Had the vampire slipped past her somehow? It seemed impossible. Surely, she would have seen him.

A cold hand gripped her at the wrist.

"Hello, Vigile," a warm voice purred in her ear.

Portia pulled at her wrist on impulse. She couldn't make it budge. The vampire had her in his grip, pinning her hand down discreetly and out of sight.

"I could burn you with a word, Dorin," Portia whispered.

Dorin's eye glittered with amusement. "And expose the Immortal world? We both know you wouldn't do that."

"It would be subtle. I could cook your brain from the inside. It would look like you suffered a stroke. Suffered being the optimal word."

Dorin only grinned. "I like your style, Vigile. Relax though, I'm no threat to you unless you strike first."

Portia's retort was cut off by a furious shout from the centre of the room.

"Our workers are slaving themselves to *death!* And what do they have to show for it? A president who's filthy rich. I'm sure that's a great comfort to their children when there's no food on the table again."

The crowd was in an uproar now. Hundreds of spectators stood against the railing and shook their fists, but Dorin only had eyes for Portia. She had to keep his attention locked on her for their plan to work.

Where is Desdemona?

"This is the world you've created, Vigile," he whispered, his grip keeping her at his side. "The world you uphold. Can't you see the misery these people live in?"

"Mere mortals," she replied.

"With the same capacity for pain and love as you. The Imperium has ignored their pleas for too long. But I am not deaf to their needs."

The president had to shout over the roar of the crowd. "My loyalty has always been to my people! To my country!"

The crowd drowned out his words. Portia could sense something building in the people, like it was one cry away from turning violent. She could feel her time running out. But she needed more information. She yanked her hand back, but the vampire didn't release his grip.

"Who do you work for?" she hissed. "Which High King do you serve?"

Dorin smiled. "You are mistaken, Vigile. The High King serves me."

"Release her!"

Desdemona was suddenly there, reaching for Dorin's face with an outstretched hand, and every fingertip held a focal point of darkness that sucked in all light.

The vampire smirked back, and the world exploded.

The ground dropped out from beneath Portia's feet as a loud crack rang out through the whole theatre. She fell, and she was aware of dozens of people falling with her.

Portia reached out with her mind. She shaped reality itself with her spell and folded the world around her, absorbing her momentum, and dropping her safely on the floor several metres away. She spun on her heel and threw off her disguise with a simple flick of her wrist, facing the vampire in her black Vigile suit and hair unveiled, ready for battle.

Instead, she saw devastation and rubble.

It took her a moment to recognise what she was seeing. The balcony had collapsed. An unknown number of mortals had been dumped onto the ground, three stories below. Some had landed on chairs and railings, their bodies limp and bent at odd angles. Others cried out from their positions on top of the rubble. Portia couldn't spare a thought for any of them.

How?! Was it a mortal weapon? A bomb? How did he time it so well?

"Art thou hurt?" Desdemona asked, appearing at Protia's side. She shook her head. "Dost thou see him?"

"He can't have gone far."

The Vigiles began running in unison. Desdemona sent out a brilliant wave of mental power, using skill that was two hundred years beyond Portia's ability. She folded space with such surgical precision that they arrived back at what was left of the balcony between one step and the next. The vampire was long gone. The remaining balcony was empty, now that the survivors had fled in terror. No one was left nearby.

"Didst thou place the tracer on him?"

"Yes, Mistress."

Portia reached out for the piece of her Will that she had bound to the vampire through their touch. She felt only the faintest tremor. Something was wrong. There should have been a beacon guiding her to him, as easy to spot as the sun. Instead, it felt like searching for a candle at a hundred paces.

"Well?" Desdemona snapped.

"There's interference. He's fighting me, somehow."

"He must be warded."

Portia turned to her mistress, half expecting to see a smile to show she was joking. Instead, Desdemona's face was hard as stone.

"That's not possible. How could a vampire be warded?" Portia cried.

"He has a powerful ally indeed," her mistress replied as she placed a hand on Portia's shoulder. "Summon thy full strength. Thou canst still find him easily. I am certain."

It was an old wizard trick. To speak with certainty in order to make the mind stronger. Yet even knowing it was just a trick, Desdemona's confidence still gave Portia the power she needed.

"He's on foot. I think he's heading for the street."

"Good girl."

Desdemona grabbed her hand and warped them both again. A heartbeat later they stood outside in the bright midday sun. The city street was almost calm compared to the scene of mass death and panic they'd just come from. A small crowd of spectators were looking towards the government building as if wondering what that loud bang had been. The first survivors were only just now coming out the front door. Portia searched the people this time with her magic, reaching out for that piece of her own mind…

There!

She shoved her mistress aside just as the vampire appeared before them with fangs bared and eyes glowing red.

He flew past them, his bite barely missing the side of Desdemona's face. His momentum carried him past the Vigiles and he landed on their other side. Both women spun to face him.

"Clever," he hissed as his eyes turned a bright blue. He appeared fully human once more. "But now you stand exposed in broad daylight. You wouldn't dare challenge me here."

"You're a real hero," Portia sung, putting on her cutest tone of voice. "You said you weren't deaf to the mortals needs. Yet you slaughtered how many to make your escape?" She gave a sweet laugh. "Some hero you are."

"You judge easily for one with so much blood on your hands," he growled back. "How many innocents have you slaughtered for your precious Imperium? Tell me, who are the real blood-sucking vampires?"

"Enough," Desdemona barked. "Thy meaningless moral dribble bores me. I will tear the truth from thy mind."

Portia sensed the power building up around the vampire's head, preparing to rip into his brain to tear the information free and shatter his psyche in the same blow. The vampire made no move. The wizard struck.

Desdemona's power seemed to hit a wall.

Portia couldn't even tell what was happening magically, but her Mistress's power hit a certain point then could go no further. She let out a gasp. In nearly two hundred years, Portia had never seen anyone overpower Desdemona. She was a prodigy. An enigma. A power that could stand next to High Kings one day. Yet, something blocked her now. And it could only mean one thing.

"Who dares!" Desdemona hissed, her eyes wide and feral with rage. "Which High King protects thee? Tell me, rat!"

Dorin only smirked. "Why don't you make me?"

This only enraged Desdemona further.

The vampire took a single step forward. In that instant, Portia felt true fear. The vampire was guarded by someone beyond her strength. Her magic was useless. And as a vampire, he was physically far superior. He well and truly had the upper hand.

"Your time is at an end," he whispered. "The Imperium will fall. Wizards will be quashed. And mortals will finally live free."

Desdemona took a step towards him. "Feeling confident, art thou?" she sneered.

Portia nearly cried out in terror. Even her mistress could not take on a High King. She looked tiny next to this man.

The vampire reached for her with slow, casual indifference. "Your arrogance makes you—"

Desdemona clutched his wrist. Dorin froze in place.

There was a sheer wall of Willpower emanating from Desdemona. Portia had never sensed anything like it except in the presence of High King Reynold the First. Somehow, Desdemona had broken through whatever protection lay on Dorin. Portia studied the magic being used. There were two spells in action. One was freezing Dorin's vocal cords. The second was causing every nerve in his body to flare up in pain.

He hasn't frozen. His body is just convulsing. My God, the agony he must be in! Yet any mortal on the street would see nothing out of the ordinary. Just two people holding hands as they spoke.

"I was merely playing," Desdemona said, before she leaned in close and whispered with a chilling smile, "Where is thy High King now?"

Portia put on her sweet voice once again. "My mistress is merciful, vampire," she pipped. "Answer her question in truth, and the pain will end. Simple, isn't it?"

Dorin started to move. It must have taken a tremendous effort to push through that much pain, but he was slowly gaining momentum. His body started to tremble. He moved both hands towards Desdemona, but Portia could feel the power emanating from her. There was no way he was ever getting past her.

"This is your final chance," Portia said. "Tell us—"

There was a flash of light. A loud bang. Something hit Portia with blinding force and everything went black.

Silence. There was danger, somewhere. There was a distant pain. Something was very wrong. If she could only remember what had happened. Remember her name or…

A loud ringing in her ears wouldn't stop. Someone clutched at her, jostled her, and pain ripped through her with the movement. She could feel air rushing through her throat and the resonating sensation that came with speech. But she heard nothing. Was she screaming?

I'm a wizard. A Vigile. I was hunting... someone. There was someone else I had to protect...

Magic filled her from her core. But it wasn't hers. There was pressure at her mouth. She felt her mind coming back into focus.

Desdemona!

At last, her eyes half blinked open, yet everything remained blurry. Her stomach felt like it was on fire. Her mistress kneeled over her and shoved an elixir down her throat.

An elixir! That's what's happening to me. But why do I need healing? What hit me?

Desdemona's mouth moved without making a sound. She held Portia to her chest and shifted their location with an effort of magic. But all that was secondary to Portia, who felt her body somehow both burning and freezing with the power running through her, and the searing agony in her gut all too slowly starting to ease.

"Rest, my love," Desdemona said audibly. "Thou art safe here." Another wave of magic washed over Portia and her eyes closed.

Portia stirred awake.

She lay on a four-poster bed in her own bedroom, staring up at a comforting pattern of red curtains. Her thoughts were sluggish as they formed into cohesion. Then she remembered, and felt a brief rush of panic, before her mind asserted control.

"That was close," she said out loud.

"Indeed it was," Desdemona replied, appearing at the side of her bed and once again dressed in the Vigile uniform. "The vampire had a mortal explosive taped to his chest. He was counting on his physical strength to save him. He must have had a kill switch somewhere on his person."

As she spoke, she magically summoned a table covered in food into the room. A wave of nausea made Portia clutch her stomach. A healing elixir always left it's user with a ravenous hunger, and Portia's healing must have been extensive to feel this much of it. Desdemona helped her into a seated position and stacked pillows behind her before rolling the table to rest in front of her. An entire roast chicken sat in the centre with an assortment of roasted vegetables set in dishes next to it. Portia dug in.

"I was already exerting magic at him," Desdemona continued. "It required a single thought to shape it into a shield instead. Alas, I had no time to offer thou protection as well."

"You got me the elixir in time," Portia said through a mouthful of food. "And brought me home. I am grateful. If you're thinking about apologising, you can forget it."

It was a private joke between them. Desdemona never apologised.

"Thou caused me great fear. I wish not to lose you."

She stroked her fingers down Portia's chin, tender yet careful not to interrupt her eating. *Always so thoughtful, even if she never says anything too direct.*

"You won't lose me," Portia said. "Though I must insist we murder the fuck out of that vampire."

"Agreed. Art thou ready to discuss?"

Portia wiped a dribble of chicken grease from her chin and nodded. In truth, she could use a whole day of rest before she was ready. But she was mad as hell. She figured her anger would give her the motivation she needed.

"Dorin is definitely a Royalist," Desdemona said. "Whatever he says his motivations may be. He still wants to threaten the High Kings, so that's all we need to know about that. The real question is which High King is backing him?"

"And if Dorin starts to succeed," Portia said. "Will his High King begin to participate more directly?"

"It's as we feared. This could mean an Imperium Civil War."

Portia sighed as she stuffed her mouth with carrots. Her stomach was starting to fill, but her body still yearned for more food. It was a bizarre feeling. She suddenly realised her mistress was quiet. She looked up, and found Desdemona staring at her. There was something in her eyes. *Concern? No. Pity.*

"My love," Desdemona said. "We need to speak to High King Reynold."

Portia froze with the food halfway in her mouth. A sharp chill ran down her neck, into her gut, and between her legs. She felt the need to squeeze her thighs together as if for protection. The mere mention of his name made her hands tremble. "And tell him what?" Portia was desperate to keep her voice flat and unconcerned. "We have yet to discover any hard facts. We still only have speculation."

"The risks are too great. If another High King is moving against Reynold, he needs to know. What if it's Louis? Or Alfonso? They have power enough to challenge him. That could disrupt his alliance, and that's all the excuse Jin Yu Qing needs to challenge the entire western world."

"Jin doesn't need to."

"My love, when have the High Kings ever acted upon true need? Thou knows as well as I the whims that dictate all their deeds." She stood near the edge of the bed next to Portia, as if the extra closeness would be any comfort. Portia avoided her eyes. "It is likely that he will have no interest in thee. He is fickle. Almost like a child. He may find thee unamusing this time."

"And that is all I can hope for, isn't it?" Portia said coldly.

"Disinterest. Because if he wants me again, no one will stop him. Isn't that right?" She looked at her mistress, but this time Desdemona avoided her eyes. "You fought a High King today. The one who warded the vampire. You resisted him—"

"Because he wasn't *there*," Desdemona cut in. "I was, which meant I had more power in that place. It was a simple mental trick, and one I wouldn't be able to duplicate in Reynold's very presence."

"He's old. Nine hundred and eighty. Surely you could—"

"I will do no such thing! Not without bringing down the wrath of the other six Kings and the entire Vigile armies. How could I claim to protect thou while incurring enmity with the entire Imperium?"

Portia wiped her hands on the towels and pushed the tray away. "Well excuse me for trying to find a solution. I would do anything if it meant keeping that creepy old man's hands off me."

"Thou speaks like a foolish child. Reynold is not some weak old man, and to see him as such is the greatest of follies. He is the closest thing we have to a god in this world. We do what we must to curry favour and ensure our own protection."

"Easy for you to say!" Portia felt her voice growing louder out of her control. "It's not your body he's interested in!"

Sudden pain flared in her stomach. She had moved too quickly in her anger and pulled something tender, causing a gasp to escape her lips.

Desdemona was instantly sitting at her side, as if they hadn't been fighting a second ago. Her hands were gentle as she held Portia's hand in comfort.

"Not today," Desdemona whispered back. "And not him. But yes. I know." Her voice softened to a whisper. "Believe me, my love."

Portia felt the rage draining from her. She knew precious little of Desdemona's life before she'd taken Portia as an apprentice and colleague one hundred and fifty years ago. Her mistress rarely spoke about it. But from the little she knew, she could believe Desdemona's claim.

"Then would you do it again?" Portia asked in a softer voice. "Would you willingly enter a situation like that by choice? Would you force the woman you love to do it?"

Desdemona stared at the wall. She was silent, her face as hard as stone. It almost seemed like she was summoning up immense magic for a powerful spell, even though her magic was unused at that moment. Just the sight of her in deep thought made Portia expect something to explode.

"As you wish," she said. "We will work this case a few days more. Find more evidence of this High King's involvement." She took Portia's hand. "But you must prepare yourself. We will need to see Reynold again very soon. It is inevitable." Desdemona stood and smoothed her tuxedo creases down. "Eat. Rest. And meditate to strengthen your Will. I am always nearby if you need anything."

Portia put on a mask. She forced down the growing tension in her stomach and the revulsion in her mouth, and used her obedient voice.

"Thank you, Mistress."

Her tone was perfect. Desdemona nodded in approval and swept out of the room, completely missing the insincerity of Portia's answer. Portia smiled in relief.

But, she couldn't help feeling disappointed at the same time.

<h1 style="text-align:center">Chapter 7</h1>

Jason groaned. "This was a horrible idea."

"Don't vomit!" Edward shouted. "That elixir took me an hour to prepare. I need to see if it works!"

Jason clutched his stomach as another wave of nausea threatened to send his breakfast all over Edward's neatly organised laboratory workbench. An icy chill spread down Jason's spine, tingling like pins and needles. His muscles cramped as a spasm rocked his body.

"You don't have to do this, Jase," Freddie cried.

But Jason held up a hand in protest.

"How… long…" he groaned again.

"Should only take a minute. Really, you're almost there," Edward said. "Just be patient."

"Patient?" Jason shouted, then clamped his mouth shut and winced as another shiver rippled through him.

Then the strangest thing happened. He felt his body start to move on its own, in a way he'd never experienced before. His body was changing shape. His facial muscles shifted. His toned muscles lost part of their strength, but his spine increased its length. His eyesight began to blur, and he felt a deep ache in his bones.

"Oh my god!" Freddie cried. "It worked!"

Jason glanced at himself in the mirror, and saw a completely different face staring back at him. No, Leslie's *face*. And Leslie's body.

"Holy crap," he said, and saw Leslie's mouth move and heard Leslie's voice correspond with his speech. "Ok, that is just weird."

He touched the face and felt a bizarrely different sensation. There was less facial hair, more pockmarks, and more lines. He was in so much shock, he only just realised that the horrible nausea had ended.

"Perfect!" Edward cried. "This change should last 24 hours, or until an antidote is administered. This should get us through the first checkpoint."

"You're a genius, Eddie," Freddie cheered. "Never doubted you for a second."

"Well, I doubted you," Jason grunted. "Clearly, I was wrong. I should have trusted yoooo—" the word was drowned out by an explosion of vomit.

Jason's original voice returned with a groan. The vomit stopped for a second and all seemed calm, before it suddenly burst out again. Jason bent his head between his knees, then hurled with such force that it pushed him backwards.

"Jesus Chriiiiiarrrrgh—"

Freddie was patting his back. "You're ok, man. Just let it pass. There can't be much more to—" he was cut off as Jason hurled so loudly it made his words inaudible. "Eddie?"

"He'll be ok. He's not going to die."

"Oh, well as long as he won't *die!*" Freddie cried sarcastically. "When will it stop?"

"When his stomach's empty. Even then, he'll probably gag for a while."

"Fuck you Eddie!' Jason growled, before hurling again.

"He doesn't mean that," Freddie said.

"The fuck I don't!"

Jason felt his stomach convulse again, but nothing came out except spit. Still, his body tried to vomit further. It felt like a super hiccup.

"All right," he said and sat down against a silver cabinet. The steel was cold against the warmth of his back, so he turned and pressed his face against it. "Sorry I snapped at you, Edward. Freddie was right, I didn't mean it."

"It's my fault," Edward said. "I used Ipecac."

Freddie mouthed it slowly. "Ipecac… isn't that used to induce vomiting in case of poison?"

"It had the magical properties I needed." Edward blushed. "I forgot to consider the… user experience. The potion won't work if you throw it back up."

"Yeah. Safe to say we tested that," Jason muttered weakly.

"I'll… uh… find a different binding agent."

"And I'll find a mop and bucket," Freddie said. "Jase, you just take five mate."

"Yep."

Jason slouched onto the ground and rested his head in his hands. *That sucked.* He focused on breathing deeply as his body still experienced waves of chills. It was hard to relax, with the smell of vomit everywhere. A loud crash came from within the lab as Edward moved glass vials and steel drums, banging them recklessly together. The noise made Jason's head ache.

"Hey Eddie?" he said in a calm voice. "You mind keeping it down?"

But Edward shouted back with sudden volume, *"I have to find a binding agent!"*

The sudden anger in the alchemist's voice made Jason's heartbeat start racing as Edward continued banging materials around in a flurry.

Jason took a breath and spoke softly. "Eddie? Are you ok, buddy?" Edward ignored him. "If something's wrong, you can tell me. I don't mind."

"I'm trying to fix the damn potion, what do you think?" Edward snapped. "I made a mistake, and I need to fix it."

"I understand, buddy. But everyone makes mistakes. It's ok that you didn't get it right the first time. No one's mad at you."

"You said you are."

Jason paused. "All right, that's fair, I did say that. But I didn't mean it. I was just in a bit of pain before and lashed out in the heat of the moment. I was wrong to do that. I'm sorry."

"You're still mad at me. I have to fix the potion."

Jason smiled as he finally understood. "Eddie, it's ok. Really! You don't have to fix the potion to make me happy. I'm fine! I'm really not mad, I promise you that."

"Well, I still want to be friends."

"Me too!" Jason cried, but it didn't seem to calm Edward down. There was something about his tone that seemed tense. He was pouring ingredients with a frantic energy. Jason eyed him for a moment. "Eddie," he asked gently. "Do you think I'm only friends with you because you're an alchemist?"

"It's what I'm best at."

Jason nearly let out an 'aww' sound, but thought it might seem patronizing. "Eddie, listen to me. I like you. You're my friend because you're a great guy. I don't just like you so I can get free potions. I like you because you're…" he struggled with the words. *How do guys say nice things to each other?* "Ok, you're really interesting. You're a genius. And you have a unique way of looking at things. I really enjoy that. So that's why I'm friends with you."

Edward stopped what he was doing. He looked at Jason directly in the eye, though it seemed like it required some effort for him to do so.

"So if I mess up an elixir, we won't stop being friends?"

"Eddie, we'll still be friends if you never make another potion."

"But I will always make potions."

Jason laughed. "I know, buddy. I'm just saying, hypothetically, if you didn't make potions, we'd still be friends."

Edward was motionless. "Why? Do you like my house?"

"No! I mean, yes. But I…I like *you*, Eddie. You're my friend because you're *you*. Does that make sense?"

"Not really." He shrugged. "But I know you're being nice, so thank you for that. I'm still going to try to fix this potion."

"Great. As long as you know we're still friends even if you don't get it right."

"But, I will get it right." Jason laughed again, and this time Edward seemed to understand. "Oh. You're saying we're still friends no matter what."

"Absolutely, mate."

Edward nodded to himself and went back to work, but with a slower, quieter rhythm this time. Jason couldn't help smiling at him. *God, he's like one hundred and forty years old, and we're probably his first friends. I can't even imagine what he's been through.* Come to think of it, Jason didn't really know much about Edward's past. The alchemist had never volunteered to talk about it, and Jason had assumed that was his preference. But maybe he was just waiting for someone to ask.

"Hey Eddie. How did you become an alchemist?"

"My father taught me," he answered immediately. "He was from Deutschland. You know, Germany. That's where I grew up. He started teaching me as early as I can remember. Mother thought he should wait until I was ten, but father saw my potential early."

Freddie came back into the lab with a mop. He handed Jason a towel and a bottle of water before patting him on the shoulder and cleaning up the floor. Freddie listened silently and started mopping up the mess while Edward began his story.

"Alchemy always made sense to me. The mixing of ingredients seemed obvious. The magic side of it was intuitive. I was creating elixirs as early as I can remember. Father thought I was a prodigy. The other alchemists thought it must have been a trick, that father was passing off his work as my own. But I never understood why people were confused. Father said the magic would work, and I believed him. It was as simple as that."

Jason nodded to himself. *Interesting. I wonder if his autism helped with his magic. He would have a strong belief the world should work a certain way, so it just did.*

"My father was a brilliant alchemist. He was among the first to experiment on the most advanced life-prolonging elixirs. They're still used among the elderly today. I think his version of the elixir was the best I've ever found. Problem was, he experimented too much. He often tried to make every elixir a little differently to test the effects. It used to frustrate mother, and especially his clients. People didn't want to buy from him because his spells would behave unpredictably. He always insisted that experimentation led to discovery. That's how people found new elixirs in the first place."

"When did you move to England?" Jason asked.

"After my parents died."

He stopped talking. Freddie had paused with the mop halfway out of the bucket. Jason and Freddie stared at each other while shifting their eyes meaningfully towards Edward. They argued silently back and forth with twitching mouths and head nods. Finally Freddie rolled his eyes, accepting defeat. "Do you want to talk about it?" he asked.

"About what?"

Freddie grimaced. "About how your parents died?"

Edward was quiet for a long moment as he poured water into a beaker.

Abruptly he answered, "Father attempted an elixir that was far beyond his skills. Mother knew it was risky. She was a mortal, but she had been raised by a witch. Sometimes she had strong intuitions, feelings that could pierce the future in small ways. She hid money away in fake accounts and purchased another home as a potential escape, in case father's elixir made enemies."

"How would it make enemies?" Jason asked.

"What kind of elixir was it?" Freddie added as he wrung the mop out one last time.

"Resurrection," Edward said simply. "The power to raise the dead."

Jason shivered as a chill ran up his neck. "Yeah. That would do it," he muttered.

"My father sold it to a wizard. He was so confident in its power that he never mentioned that it was still experimental. So when it failed, the wizard was furious." Edward took a thin needle and plopped a single green droplet into his cauldron. A burst of red cloud filled the room with a metallic scent. "I woke up that night and found the house on fire. The wizard had blown it apart with a spell. I was buried under a pile of rubble. My parents were screaming. I was pinned down. I couldn't move. I listened as the wizard brutalised them and tore them apart. He made my father watch first. He never even knew I was there. I don't even know who the wizard was."

Edward looked up at them. His face was calm, flat, as if unaware of the horror he had just spoken of. "The fire burnt through the rubble, weakening it until I could get free. I was burnt too."

He rolled up his sleeves and showed them a long patch of ruined skin covering his entire right arm, stopping just at the wrist.

"That's why you always wear long sleeves," Jason whispered.

"It's all over my back too. Thankfully it didn't touch my face or my hands, so it hasn't affected my mobility. But it always itches."

He rolled down his sleeves again. "I managed not to pass out from smoke inhalation by covering my face. I stayed in hiding and slowly made my way across the country. I foraged for materials to make elixirs and gave myself bursts of strength whenever I got hungry. I was a stowaway on a boat that brought me to Swansea. I found the home my mother prepared for me."

Freddie gestured around him. "Here?"

Edward nodded.

"How old were you?" Jason whispered.

"Nine."

Jason couldn't find anything to say. Even Freddie was speechless. Edward didn't seem to mind as he spoke an incantation and another wave of black smoke puffed out of his cauldron and dissipated into the air above. He looked up.

"It's almost ready. I just need another sample of Leslie's urine, and we'll be able to shapeshift into their form again."

Jason blinked. "What? You put Leslie's *piss* in it?"

Edward smiled back.

"Oh my god, you're joking!" Freddie cried. "You just made a joke!"

Jason sighed in relief, before roaring with laughter. Freddie joined him and in doing so they let out all the tension that had filled the room. Edward just kept smiling.

"Thanks for sharing your story," Jason said, though the words seemed insufficient.

"Yeah, thank you," Freddie echoed. "I never knew. So you still have no idea who that wizard was?" Edward shook his head. "Do you want to find them some day? Are you planning… revenge?"

"I do want revenge," Edward said. "But not by killing him. I want to finish my father's work."

Jason understood. "The resurrection elixir. The one you used on Samantha Kennedy. That was your father's work?"

Edward smiled again, looking immensely proud. "My father only created the formula. I've been working on it for over a hundred years." He reached into his robes and pulled out a small vial. "My elixir can resurrect someone within minutes of their death. Though, yes, as we saw with Kennedy, there are side effects on the mind of the user. It's a far cry from my father's plan to resurrect someone who's been dead for years, but it's a promising step towards that goal." Edward pocketed the elixir again. "One day, I will finish my father's work. That will be my revenge."

Jason could only shake his head. "Jesus Christ," he muttered. "Eddie… you are seriously badass."

"*So* badass," Freddie confirmed.

It seemed like a weak compliment, but Edward beamed at the praise.

"For what it's worth," Jason shrugged, still uncomfortable at saying it out loud, "I kinda know what you went through. My mum died because my dad was so horrible to her. I haven't seen him in thirteen years."

Edward frowned. "But I liked my dad. He was nice to mum"

"Oh! No, I mean my dad is like that wizard."

Edward simply nodded. "I'm sorry about your mother, Jason. Mortal lives are already so short. It seems especially cruel that fate would rob you of even that little time. She should have been able to meet Silvana. Meet all of us. Hold your first child. I'm sure it would have been perfect."

"Oh," Jason let out a short gasp and had to turn his face away from the alchemist.

The words seemed to hit his tear trigger, and now his eyes stung. *Oh mum… you would have loved Silvana. Why didn't you hang on just a little longer? We could have escaped him together. Oh mum!* He swallowed down the lump in his throat and kept his voice steady.

"Thank you, Eddie. That's very kind of you."

"Well," Freddie said in a louder tone to break the tension, "I get to talk to my mum all the time. She's awesome. But my dad's a dick. Does that count for anything?"

"I mean, sure," Jason said. "We were all hurt by our dads, just in different ways. Some intentional, some unintentional."

Edward gave a heartfelt nod. "But we all decided to become better men, didn't we? We didn't let them stop us."

Jason eyed him in surprise. "Yeah, Eddie. That was really deep."

"I don't know about me, though," Freddie said. "I'm still working through my dad's crap. I'm far from over it."

"But you did become a better man."

"Jase, I joined a cult."

"Well yeah. But you left."

Freddie rolled his eyes. "That's a low bar, but fine. Cheers to us for being awesome. Good job lads." He chuckled, and Jason just shook his head.

"I do actually need some DNA from Leslie," Edward said, standing awkwardly.

Oh, he's been waiting to leave. "Sure, mate. I'll come with you. I want to check on Leslie and Khadija, and make sure they're not killing each other."

"You fellas go," Freddie said and pulled out his laptop bag from where he'd stored it under a table. "I gotta do some shopping. Find those mini cam recorders I was talking about."

"Ok just watch yourself online. We don't want the assassin tracing anything back to us."

"Jase, I'm an Asian nerd. I know more than you."

"All right. But you're also mortal, and these are super beings."

"I know, buddy, trust me, I know." He set up his laptop, while Jason followed Edward out of the lab.

Chapter 8

The mansion was eerily quiet, and even in the light of day with the sun coming through the windows, Jason still felt like he was walking through the hotel in The Shining. *It's the long hallway with wallpaper that does it.*

Jason heard voices shouting from deep within the mansion, making his heartrate increase sharply. A memory stirred in the back of his mind, and Jason recalled being much younger and hearing another set of angry voices from down a different hallway. *Stupid trauma.* It sounded like it was just Leslie and Khadija arguing, but he still couldn't stop his mind comparing them to his parents. He hurried down the hall and checked cautiously around the corner.

Leslie was sitting at a table with a pile of papers before them. The old librarian was now dressed in thick grey trousers with sandals and a long black coat with gilded buttons that reached nearly to their knees. Meanwhile, Khadija looked like a pampered rich kid in jeans and a hoodie. She stood over the witch, pointing a finger and growling, "…pointless endeavour. You've clearly never communicated to another human being before."

"I've told you five times now, wizard, that I cannot be any clearer—" They cut off as soon as they saw Jason in the hallway. "Mr Turner, how can we help?"

Khadija gave a huff of annoyance and turned away.

"Eddie needs some more DNA," Jason said, standing at the table's edge. "Though, I'm just checking in. How's the work coming along?"

"We've made no progress at all!" Khadija snapped.

Leslie took a beaker from Edward and discreetly spat into it. "Magic works very differently for wizards and witches. What we're trying to do is almost impossible. Yet, Miss Al Khalifa seems to think I'm personally responsible for the fundamental laws of the universe."

"You said, and I quote, 'It feels tingly'. How the hell is that supposed to help?"

"When your enemy casts a spell on you, does the spell itself become sentient and teach you how to duplicate it? Cause I've never heard of a spell that teaches itself."

"You walked through that barrier every day for years. Surely you can describe it better than 'tingly'."

"It's someone else's spell!"

Khadija threw up her hands and turned around with more huffing.

"You know a real witch would have a familiar. You could just send a raven into the Library for us."

Leslie sighed as they handed the beaker back to Edward. "There's some good news," they said, ignoring Khadija's comment. "The papers are coming along nicely. I should have enough identification for three people who look like me. How's the elixir?"

"It's brilliant!" Jason said. He noticed Edward's worried expression, so he avoided mentioning the vomit. "It works perfectly. My face looked exactly like yours."

Leslie nodded to Edward. "Fantastic work, my alchemist friend. We're lucky to have you." Edward beamed. "The real question is how to make it last for just enough time to get through the checkpoint, then have it turn off before we get to the magic dampening barrier."

"Oh," Edward said. "I'd forgotten that part. Um… I could make it a minor dosage so it lasts anywhere between five and thirty minutes."

Leslie shook their head. "That's too wide a window. It has to be precisely between checkpoint one and checkpoint two."

Edward blinked rapidly and looked to Jason.

Jason wracked his brain for a solution. They needed an 'off' switch for the elixir. But there was no way to interrupt it once was it was already inside the user.

"Oh no," Jason groaned. "I just had a thought and it might be stupid, but what if we vomited up the elixir? You could use that… epic stuff?"

"Ipecac!" Edward grinned. "But I can't put it in the elixir… Oh!" he cried. "You can carry it as a second elixir. Administer it on the way. That's perfect."

Khadija laughed. "Oh yes, throwing up in the middle of the walkways. Sounds very subtle."

Leslie shook their hands. "There are bathrooms between checkpoints. We can step in there, throw up, come back looking like ourselves. If anyone asks, we can say we were out drinking the night before. That excuse will hold up. You have no idea how much librarians like to drink." They grinned widely.

Jason chose not to comment on that, instead asking, "But won't people notice if we go in looking like one person, and come out looking like another?"

"Good point," Leslie said. "I suppose we should wear something with hoods. Help to cover our face. No one will look too closely once we've gone through checkpoint one anyway." They nodded eagerly. "That's an excellent plan. Now if only we could get past the wizard's spell."

"If only you could tell me what it is!" Khadija growled again. "Honestly, I need better answers."

"Then ask better questions!"

Jason looked between the two magicians. He knew they were the only ones in their team capable of figuring out a solution and there was little he could do to help. But if they wouldn't work together, they were bound to fail.

"You know," Jason said, as he slowly sat down on the chair opposite Leslie and cupped his hands together. "Maybe I can help. I know nothing about magic, but it looks like you two could use a…" he laughed, "well, a moderator."

Khadija swore under her breath, still loud enough for everyone to hear. Leslie gave a nod. "Perhaps that would be helpful."

Edward cleared his throat suggestively. "Should I wait for you?" he asked Jason.

"I might be a while. Do you mind testing the next one on Freddie?"

"This one won't make you throw up."

Jason needed a moment to understand that Edward thought he was just trying to avoid testing the elixir again. "I believe you, Eddie. I just need to stay and help these two. I'm not afraid to try your elixir again. I trust that you've fixed it."

"Good. Cause I have."

"I'm sure! Tell you what, I'll try it after Freddie, just to be extra sure."

"Ok!" Edward held out a fist towards him. Jason paused again, before slowly extending his own fist and bumping them together. Edward grinned widely and left the room.

"What a beautiful soul," Leslie said fondly. "I never met an alchemist with his genius and skill. Yet when he talks to people, he's like a child needing reassurance."

"He would be famous in the Imperium, if anyone paid him attention," Khadija agreed. "Perhaps we're lucky he's an outcast."

Leslie pointed to Jason. "You want to know a fact from old history, my mortal friend?"

"Uh… sure? I guess."

"Over four hundred years ago, the French used to have two words for people like your friend Edward. Even before your time, wizard. The words were cretin and imbecile."

Jason's face turned cold. "Those are awful names. They're derogatory."

"Ah!" Leslie interrupted, holding up their hands in appeasement. "Peace, my friend. Those names weren't always so. 'Cretin' was a play on words. It's similar to the French word for Christian. We called them cretin to show that the intellectually disabled were still Christian. Meaning that they were still *human*. It was a term we used to bestow respect and kindness."

"Huh."

"Similarly, imbecile was an old word from the Latin language. The meaning was complex, as is often true for words. But one interpretation meant 'to weep for'. You would weep for the one who had suffered. We used the word imbecile for the physically disabled or the wounded, whereas cretin was for the intellectually disabled." Leslie wore a sad smile. "Many of us were trying to change the language we used to be more inclusive. We wanted to give the disabled more respect in society. Unfortunately, these words were quick to be used as insults. Eventually, that's all they became."

"That's awful," Jason said.

Leslie nodded sadly. "Such is the nature of mankind. We adopt words of kindness and turn them into piercing arrows. We show fear and prejudice towards everything not precisely like ourselves."

"Well there it is," Khadija groaned. "I was wondering who your story could be about. But you made it oh so clear in the end."

"I was making a general statement, princess," Leslie said. "If you felt called out, that's on you."

"All right," Jason said a little louder than necessary. He tapped the table softly with both hands. "I'll be mediating this conversation going forward. There will be no insults, no passive aggressive comments, and…what's the other one? Ah, no going into each other's lane."

"Lane?" Leslie asked.

"Oh. It's a mortal expression. It means don't put words in the other persons mouth."

"You mean with magic?"

Khadija growled. "How would it be a mortal expression if it used magic, imbecile?"

"Whoa!" Jason and Leslie cried.

"Ah, sorry! That's on me. The word was just on my mind." Khadija looked genuinely regretful.

"Ok but still, no insults," Jason insisted. "Khadija, please come and sit down with us." Khadija rolled her eyes but took a seat, dragging the chair along the floor. Jason ignored her attitude. "Now that the ground rules are established, where are you two up to in your work?"

The witch and wizard exchanged a look. Leslie gestured for her to speak, and Khadija pulled a face at them.

"I've been asking them questions about the wizard's barrier, trying to get any sort of useful information about it. But all they can describe is what it feels like to pass through it."

"Of course that's all I can describe. I'm a witch, and I didn't create the barrier."

Khadija opened her mouth, then closed it again. "Damn these rules make it difficult to say anything."

Leslie chuckled. "Well they wouldn't if you would…" Jason held up a hand. "Oh. I guess I see your point, wizard."

Jason sighed. "Let's look at it from another angle. What would be required to create this barrier in the first place? What spell?"

"It's not as simple as speaking a word," Khadija explained. "Wizards only use the word itself as the starting point for their spells. It's their thoughts that shape it into something specific. So I'm trying to find out what the wizard was thinking when they made that particular spell."

"All right. Let's work backwards for a second. Khadija, let's pretend you want to recreate that spell on this mansion. You want to put up an impassable barrier, but only you can give someone access to pass through. What would you need?"

Khadija looked like she was chewing on her own tongue. Eventually, she sighed and spoke with forced softness. "Well for one, I'd need about four times the magical power that I have now. So if you're willing to wait about five hundred years, we should be good."

Jason said, "That was passive aggressive."

Khadija clenched her hands into fists, and thin wisps of red flame briefly appeared around her knuckles. Then she breathed out slowly and relaxed. "Thank you for telling me, Jason," she said in a strained, sweet voice. "But for our purposes, I'm not trying to recreate the entire barrier spell. I'm just trying to recreate the part that allows *access*. I believe that should be within my power."

"Thank you, Khadija."

"The problem is, I don't know *what* I'm creating. I just know what it does. Imagine if… oh, I don't know what the mortal equivalent is… what if you had to build an airplane? You know what a plane is supposed to do, but that doesn't mean you could create one yourself."

"Yep. That's fair."

"Now I'm trying to reverse engineer a plane, but using only the descriptions of a witch who once looked at a plane engine, but doesn't fully know what they're describing. Do you see my problem?"

"We hear you, princess," Leslie said.

Khadija scowled. "I don't appreciate you calling me princess. It feels condescending."

Jason gave a nod of agreement.

"Ah. Yes, I can appreciate that." Leslie took a moment to compose themselves. "Khadija, no one is saying you have it easy. I'm just trying to say there's no choice. You are the only chance we have of getting past that barrier."

Khadija smirked. "Maybe there is another way past. We could find another staff member in the entrance and just fucking *make* them let us in."

"The anti-violence spell would catch us out. We'd be knocked unconscious."

Khadija groaned, and the table fell into silence. Jason started racking his brain trying to think of something. All he could think was, *why am I here? Khadija is one hundred and eighty, Leslie is like eight hundred. I'm twenty-five. I'm like an infant to them.* Yet, he remembered Leslie's speech from the night before. About how every mind was unique. If there was ever going to be truth to that, now was the ideal time to test it.

"This might be a dumb question," Jason asked, "but why does it have to be Khadija who gets us through the barrier? Why not you, Leslie?"

It seemed like exactly the wrong question when Khadija groaned, clawed at her face, and slumped into her chair until her face was level with the table. "We're all gonna die," she drawled.

Leslie held it together better than the wizard. "By the stars, Jason," they said his name as if speaking with a child. "If a wizard created the spell, then only a wizard can manipulate it. You basically just asked if a man can get pregnant."

"Well you know, that does happen in certain circumstances," Jason smirked, though the others didn't appreciate the humour. "Look, I'm asking because Leslie here threw a spell at the chimera assassin, and it bounced back and hit them. Leslie, you said a wizard put a protective spell on the assassin. So clearly, your different magics can still interact to some degree. Right?"

"Ah. Well, I guess I can see how it would look that way to you." Leslie pinched the bridge of their nose. "I was afraid of this. I'm not meant to share the secrets of a witch's power. But I'm not sure if we can plan this heist without it. Surely, you just trust me?"

"No chance, witch," Khadija said. Jason opened his mouth to object, but Khadija interjected. "Sorry, I meant no chance, *Leslie*. I've already shared with this mortal the secrets to a wizard's power. And you clearly knew those already. Time for you to address this imbalance."

Leslie groaned in discomfort.

Jason asked, "Is this something your signet will stop you from sharing?"

"No. It's just taboo. A big taboo."

"*Min 'ajl Allah*," Khadija grumbled.

Leslie sighed and began to explain. Jason listened closely for information to go into his report.

"You know how wizards use their power? They speak a spell and send out an effort of their Willpower. Well, witches don't work that way. We don't use our *own* Willpower. We use the Will of our targets."

"Your targets? How do you use someone else's Will?"

Leslie smirked. "Jason, if I were to throw magic at you, it would do exactly what you *think* it's going to do. It's your Will that shapes the magic."

Jason frowned. "That doesn't make any sense. I'm not thinking anything—"

Leslie screamed.

It was loud and sudden as they leapt across the table at Jason with wild hatred in their eyes. Jason flinched back with his hands up. At the last second, Leslie froze still. They spoke in a gentle, reassuring voice, "What did you think I was going to do to you just now?"

"You..." Jason felt his heart racing and forced it to calm down. "I thought you were attacking me."

"Yes, but *how?* What attack did you think I was going to use?"

"I…" he startled. "I thought you were going to punch me in the face."

"Excellent! That's it, Jason. That's what a witch's spell does. It makes your own fears come to life. I'm sorry for that, by the way."

"Oh. No it's cool." Jason shuddered. "That sounds like a dark power."

"Indeed. That's why there was such a hysteria over witches for hundreds of years. Because every time someone got afraid of a witch, their fear would make it real. That's how people got sick, struck down, or caused strange occurrences to happen. Not to mention there was good old misogyny mixed in. They feared witches because they feared a woman outside their control. It's why you still think witches are all women."

"My hero," Khadija said, pretending to swoon. "What an advocate!"

Leslie rolled their eyes and continued. "But it works in good ways too. Witches are the best healers in the Immortal world. Can you think why?"

Jason nodded. "Because if the patient wants to get better, the witch's magic makes them better."

"Exactly. That's also why it's taboo for witches to tell people how their magic works. If you know how it works, you can overthink the process and it'll stop working."

Jason thought about this. "Ok, so wizards use their own Willpower, and witches use other peoples'. That doesn't sound like it's that different. Shouldn't there be some overlap?"

"Ah, you are sharp for someone so young." Leslie smiled. "I started you off on the simplest difference. But the second is more complicated. In short, wizards and witches use entirely different sources of magic."

Jason stared back, eventually shrugging. "Ok?"

Khadija stepped in. "So wizards speak a spell and use their Willpower. But it's not the spell or Will that creates the power. That's just how they access it. The power is already there, in the world, all around us, waiting to be used."

"Well said, prin…Khadija," Leslie said. "Think of it like your mortal radio waves. The waves are always there, but you use a radio to tune into them. That's how magic works. Except witches and wizards draw from two different sources."

Jason nearly started explaining that radio waves were outdated and everyone used wifi now, but decided not to try. "That's actually not that complex. So you both have magic and you two pull from different sources. That's simple enough."

"But don't you see?" Leslie grew excited and sat forward with a grin. "We have no idea where these magics come from, or what they are. Or how they came to be. Or why there are two of them, no more, no less. Or why one of them can be shaped with your own Will, and why the other must be shaped by someone else's."

"Immortals have been debating where magic comes from for millennia," Khadija said. "I've been wondering about this all my life, and I only recently found out there are two sources of magic. This is a vast and deep philosophical topic."

Jason rolled his eyes. "I'm sure it is. But right now, all we're discussing is how to get past a wizard's barrier." Both witch and wizard looked disappointed. Jason couldn't help smirking at them. "So, where were we? I was asking about how Leslie's spell bounced off the assassin."

"Ah yes," Leslie said. "I cast a witch's spell, but the assassin was blocked by wizard magic. That means my spell couldn't latch on to his Willpower and rebounded. Though it should have bounced around the room and latched onto someone else. In many ways, we're lucky it hit me. It just knocked me unconscious. Might have killed yourself or Freddie."

"Well. How nice." Jason suppressed that thought before it could take hold. "So the barrier in the Library is made exclusively from wizards magic."

"And only a wizard can affect it," Khadija said. "I have to shape a counter spell with my own Willpower in order to have a chance. Witches power won't help."

"Ok, ok. But Leslie, if you must use someone else's Willpower for your magic, why not use Khadija's? It is possible your spell can… amplify Khadija's power? Give a boost?" They both groaned at him. "What?" he exclaimed.

"What you're describing is very risky," Khadija said. "Wizards have been experimenting with power-enhancement for a long time. More often than not, it kills the user."

"What kind of experiments?"

"Elixirs, for one," Leslie said. "There's a massive branch of alchemy devoted to finding boosts for wizards, either short term or permanent. But it takes extensive practice to actually wield that much power before you're ready for it. Wizards tend to kill themselves from lack of control."

"I did it once," Khadija said. "I had an elixir that was basically a bottle of whiskey without side effects. You know how alcohol lowers your inhibitors? It can make a wizard's mind more relaxed and their Will easier to access. But the lack of focus can also make you powerless." She shuddered. "I felt like a High King. The power was beyond what I'd ever dreamed. The problem was that my thoughts were so scattered that every single thought would trigger a spell. Imagine being in that state and thinking, 'Oh no, I hope I don't set my family on fire', and that's what happens."

"Oh shit."

"Exactly. That's not really an option I'd want to try in the middle of a sneaky mission. It's impossible."

"Actually," Leslie said, "it just might work."

"Huh?" Jason and Khadija cried out at the same time.

"I do know one spell of focus. I designed it centuries ago as a researcher to help my colleagues focus on a single task. It could block out all other thoughts except one. It was a way to help them speed up their brain power and process information quicker. But it could work for this." Leslie grew animated and pointed down the hall. "If Edward can recreate that drunk elixir you used, Khadija, and I put the focus spell on you to keep you thinking straight, you might just have enough power to break through the barrier. We wouldn't need to know the exact password. We could brute force our way in."

"Wait, but wouldn't the anti-violence spell stop us?" Jason asked.

"Ah, but would you consider opening a door an act of violence? I'm certain it will work."

Khadija winced. "But the other wizards will notice if I'm holding that much power."

"Then we make it quick. Do it in one stroke."

"Fuck no!" Khadija shouted. "I'm not giving you full control over my mind like that. I'd just be a puppet for you. How can I trust that you would relinquish control when I'm done?"

Leslie shrugged. "Well, in that state, I'd actually need to stay in control until your elixir wore off again, so you didn't cause havoc by accident."

"No! Absolutely not!"

"Khadija," Jason started.

"This was your plan, wasn't it?" Khadija rounded on Leslie. "This looked like a group idea, but it's what you wanted all along, isn't it? Your crawling fingers inside my mind, in the middle of an Imperium fortress. Why? What are you planning?"

"Nothing! I've told you the truth from the beginning. I've never lied once. I'm trying to escape the assassin, same as you."

"And the fact that you want to mind-control me is just a happy accident?"

"It's not like I'd be able to read your mind. I won't discover any of your secrets, if that's what you're worried about."

"Well I am now!"

"I have no need for your secrets. I'm a historian. I care about history, not the present."

"A likely story."

"Uh, guys?" Jason asked.

"I already know about your father," Leslie said. "King Al Khalifa, trying to ally himself with High King Siddig to present himself as a suitable heir. Anyone paying attention has known this for years."

"Aha! You reveal yourself. This is all about stopping my family's rise."

Leslie buried their face in their hands. "But I just said I don't care about your family."

"Well, you're clearly working for someone. You're Imperium staff, so which High King do you report to? Louis? Singh? Or Reynold?"

"Don't you dare!" Leslie growled, their face snapping up. "I would never work for Reynold."

"Shut it!" Jason shouted. "Both of you. I'm the mortal here, and yet you're both acting more childish than I am. Can you just fucking work together? Can we just assume I did some big speech about teamwork and the power of friendship and you just fucking got along? Because I don't want to die because of one of your *temper tantrums!*"

In hindsight, temper tantrums was a poor choice of words to scream hysterically.

He could tell that both witch and wizard were thinking it too by the way they pressed their lips together to keep from smiling. But neither said anything. Leslie calmly turned towards Khadija.

"If you like, we can practice the focus spell now until you're comfortable. You'll find I'm not really controlling you, just helping you focus. We can stop any time you're uncomfortable."

Khadija smirked. "Fine. Our safe word can be, 'temper tantrums'."

Leslie choked and squeezed their lips shut.

"Oh, real nice," Jason grumbled, and they both held back their laughter. "Let me know when you're ready." He stood up and left the kitchen, while the sounds of rising giggles followed him out. *Freaking jerks.* But he started chuckling too when he was out of earshot.

He began to head back towards the lab to check on Freddie and Eddie, but he was confident they were making progress by now. All areas of the plan seemed to be coming along nicely with checkpoints one and two seemingly covered. The only place he hadn't checked yet was Silvana, and her goal to reach the empowered vampire state to get past the final checkpoint.

Maybe he'd been avoiding her. When next he talked to her, he had resigned himself to tell her everything. He had to explain that alter ego he'd seen of hers, the feral vampire within. He had no idea how to bring that up. Still, it was cowardly of him to avoid it, and she needed help. He couldn't leave it all up to her. With a sigh, he headed upstairs to try to find her.

Chapter 9

"Silvy?"

She could hear Jason calling out from somewhere downstairs, but for a second, she considered staying silent and avoiding him. She knew this conversation was coming. She'd been hoping she could avoid it for longer, even though Jason had already left her alone for a strangely long amount of time. Maybe he was avoiding her too.

"Silvy?" he called again.

She sighed. Any longer and he'd start getting worried.

"I'm here, babe," she called, then remembered he didn't have vampire hearing. After all this time, she was still used to living with her aunts. She got up, opened the bedroom door and called into the hallway. "I'm here." Then she settled back down in her armchair.

Jason appeared in the doorway a moment later, still dressed and ready for combat with his sword and gun at his hip. He scanned the corners of the room for assassins, then closed the door behind him. He really did look the part of a knight. Noble, proud and strong. Yet she could already see the nervousness on his face. He probably thought he was hiding it well. *Or maybe I'm scowling and it was making him tense.* She forced her face to relax.

"What is it, darling?"

"What is it?" he chuckled. "I think we both know why I'm here."

"For this hot piece of ass?" she purred and rolled her hips onto the side. She meant it as a joke, but already she could see his eyes aflame with desire as they traced the curves of her butt and thighs. *God, he really is insatiable.*

"Uh…" he stammered. "I… I mean, if you think it would help." He coughed. "I was going to offer to help with your task. You know, the empowered vampire… thing."

"Ah. That minor thing."

"Yeah. Where our lives are at stake. No biggy." They each barked out a strained laugh, before they trailed off into silence.

Silvana let her eyes wander around the room. She had settled in one of the mansion's spare bedrooms, though it had none of Edward's usual fastidiousness. Where every other room was cleaned to perfection, this one was clearly nothing more than a convenient storage space. Dozens of old leather couches and aged oak cabinets were slowly gathering dust. A corner desk had a stack of faded old newspapers slowly biodegrading. A pile of clothes had been brushed to the side, clearly having been abandoned instead of put away. The room smelt of old musk and cotton balls. Even the bed was covered entirely with a jumble of household items. But she liked it. Strangely, it felt like home. Silvana had claimed the only chair without stuff on it. Jason looked around for a place to sit, before pushing a pile of clothes onto the ground and settling on the corner of the bed.

"So, any ideas?" he asked.

"None. You?"

"None." He sighed. "We spent a year thinking about this, since Peter's attack. I still think Desdemona's theory was the most likely. She said Peter's magic drained you of blood, and when you consumed blood again, his magic gave you a temporary power up."

"Desdemona could have been lying. That doesn't sound like how magic is supposed to work. Unless we asked Khadija to recreate the setting. She could drain me again…"

Jason winced. "Please, no."

"That's what I thought. Then unless I go into Swansea town and murder all the inhabitants to get empowered the old fashion way, we've got nothing."

"Guess we've got nothing then."

"Aw come on!" Silvana whined, smiling at Jason playfully. "It's just one little old English town. And Swansea at that."

Jason grinned back, but without sincerity. "Maybe it has to do with my blood. Remember, I had one of Edward's healing elixirs in me at the time. We could try that? I have an elixir then you drink my blood."

"I don't know." Silvana sighed. "Jason, the thing is… I feel a little empowered now."

"You do?"

"Yes, but not in the same way. It's hard to explain." She frowned in thought for a moment.

She had to explain something she herself didn't understand, and to a person who was even less likely to get it. There was so much she didn't know about vampire magic. If only there were some way to learn. She noticed the weapons at Jason's belt and an idea materialised in the back of her mind.

"Let me put it this way," she said. "When I was empowered in my fight against Peter, it's like I had a gun in my hands. It was so easy to use. All I had to do was think, and I could pull the trigger. Except now… something's missing, and I'm not sure what. It's like the gun is still there," she pointed to her mind, "but I just can't find the trigger. Or maybe I can find the trigger, but the gun has no ammo."

"Or the extractor's jammed," Jason offered.

She had no idea what that meant, but she shrugged. "Sure. Either way, something's wrong. But I can still feel part of that power in my mind. It's like it's just out of reach."

She saw him thinking it over. He looked as if he believed her. Maybe it was time to try her theory on him.

"Jason, this might sound a bit crazy," she said. "But the empowered vampire thing. I'm… well, I'm not sure if I need blood. Does that make sense?"

His face twisted into a confused frown. "So wait, you think you could become empowered without any blood at all? Just on your own."

"I don't know. Maybe? It's just a feeling. More like an instinct."

There was an instant flicker of disbelief on Jason's face. *Oh no. He doesn't believe me.*

"Look, Silvy," he started.

"No, forget it," she said. "It was a stupid idea. I shouldn't have said anything."

"Wait, what?" he cried. "Silvy, I didn't say it was a bad idea. I was going to say you were right."

"Really?"

"I'm serious! I just… Silvy, I'm worried that what I'm going to say is offensive."

"Ok." She gestured for him to continue.

He paused, taking a few moments to choose his words. "Ok. You remember when we were fighting the Yamatos? You had a moment where you lost control."

"I remember."

But in fact, Silvana barely remembered anything about that fight. It had just been raw animalistic rage that fuelled her. Jason had been stabbed by a sword through his stomach, and her mind had nearly shattered from the shock and fury. She didn't know he had already consumed a healing elixir, and that he had staged the wound in order to trick a more skilled opponent. All she knew was she'd attacked and attacked until her enemies were defeated and she realised Jason was beside her alive and well.

Jason continued. "Silvana, is it possible there's some link between… the state you were in then, and the power you felt while attacking Peter?"

Silvana shook her head. "I don't think so. The two are completely different. I wasn't moving things with my mind last time, was I?" Jason shook his head. "Besides, I've never experienced that state before. It was a one-off, emotional thing."

Jason looked sceptical. "How certain are you? I mean, you've had partners die in the past. Were you less upset then?"

"Of course I was upset."

"I'm just saying. What if you had a memory lapse in the past, but you didn't remember it?"

Silvana felt a strange sense of familiarity about the situation. Like déjà vu. *Something I didn't remember? What is he talking about?* "Jason," she asked, "have you seen me in that state before?"

"Well, no."

"Are you saying I've had blackouts and don't remember things? Cause if you are, now's the time to tell me."

"I…" Jason hesitated, then he gave a soft laugh. "All right fine, I'm sorry. I'm not trying to make you doubt yourself. You just seemed so sure you knew the difference between an empowered vampire and a memory lapse. I only meant to double check. But you would know best."

Silvana smiled at him. But something felt strange, as if he was holding something back. *Relax, girl. You're just being insecure. You know Jason loves you, now stop it.* She rolled her shoulders to ease the tension from her body. "I would like to do an experiment. May I please have just a drop of your blood? I want to see if I can feel the power in it."

"Sure."

"Ok, but it's more than that. I feel like if I can press my lips right to the source, that might help."

"You mean, drink directly from my veins?"

"Not drink. Just rest my lips there. Just enough to taste blood."

"Ok."

He didn't ask why.

Jason shifted to the edge of the bed. He had a slight scab around his wrist from when he donated blood. It only took a few scratches with his fingernail before he was satisfied.

"Gets easier every time," he said.

Silvana realised she had been sitting with her shoulders hunched and he was probably trying to reassure her. He offered her his wrist.

Silvana knelt before him, cupped his hand with a gentle touch and guided his wrist to her lips. He'd understood her perfectly. There was just the faintest outline of blood against his skin, not even a drop on the surface. She pressed her mouth down, letting her tongue run the length of the opening on his skin.

The normal sense was there. As a vampire, every tasting of blood filled her with more than nourishment. It was like an energy that filled every part of her body. Her mind grew just a little sharper. And deeper inside her was the part she wouldn't acknowledge out loud. The desire. The thirst. The urgent yearning for so much more. She forced it down and allowed herself to taste him. Not just his blood but the core of his being. Maybe it was just the comfort of being so close and intimate with a loved one, but there was a hint of something more tangible. Something more powerful. If she could just decipher what exactly—

"Feel anything?"

Jason's voice jolted her out of her reverie. She looked up at him with her mouth still pressed to his wrist, and she knew at that moment she wanted to claim him. The taste of blood always made her feel alive like a drug-induced high without any brain functions shutting down. There was always a sudden spike in her mental awareness, an energy spreading across her skin, through her muscles and sparking warmth within her body. And Jason, well, he was simply gorgeous. She just wanted to eat his face.

Careful. He's mortal. He does not find anything sexy about giving blood. And he's very stressed out about the assassin and the heist. I have to ease him into a sexual frame of mind. If I come on too strong, he'll withdraw.

"You know," she said as she removed her lips from his skin and cleaned herself with a quick swipe of her tongue. "I think I felt something. If I could just relax and focus, it might help. I don't suppose you could give me a head massage?"

"Sure," he said instantly. "If it'll help you, then absolutely."

Oh you sweet gullible fool.

She turned around, sitting on the ground with her shoulders between his legs and resting her head back against his stomach. She was careful to make sure at least part of her was pressing down near his crotch. His thighs pressed against her shoulders, and a moment later, his hands began to cup her head, and his thick fingertips pressed into her temples in circular motions.

She let out a soft gasp, knowing exactly how it sounded.

"That's good," she said, with a whispered purr.

Too much, and he'd catch on. She had to play this right.

His fingers kept moving without any encouragement. She waited patiently. Then, just as he pressed a little firmer than before, and she let out a small moan.

"Oh," she cried, breathy and low.

She shifted her posture as if relaxing into him, though she was actually aiming for the base of his thighs. *There.* She felt the first hint of his hardness.

"Hey," she said in a breathy voice, careful not to overdo it. "Can you do my neck while you're at it?"

"Uh, I can't quite reach from…"

"That's ok. I'll lie down on the bed."

"Oh…kay."

Silvana shifted onto her feet with ease. She walked around Jason and let her hand trail along his thigh, up his arm and over his shoulder. He gave a slight shiver, and she pretended not to notice. She lay flat across the bed, nestling her head in her folded arms and shutting her eyes. Everything was still. She could practically feel Jason's eyes on her. Finally, he moved to kneel over her, straddling her waist with his knees and resting his thighs against her ass.

This time when his hands touched her back, she let out a louder moan.

"Thank you, darling. This is just what I need," she said in a sweet, seductive voice.

"Is this helping you feel the power?" he asked, his tone flat.

"I think so. The massage is helping the blood flow. Can you keep going? It feels so good."

"All right."

He sounded sceptical. She waited and let him work through her knotted shoulders. It truly did feel good, but it wasn't what she wanted. It was killing her to lay in wait for so long. She held still until his thumbs began working down her spine. Then, just as he shifted over her bra strap, she moved at lightning speed.

"I'll get that out of the way," she said.

In one fluid movement, she pulled her shirt and bra up to her shoulders, leaving the garments sitting along her neck as if she intended to keep them on. Cool air caressed her exposed back making her skin prickle. Again, Jason was motionless.

"Keep going," she demanded without looking up, and a second later his hands returned to her spine, warming her flesh. He worked his way back up to her shoulders. As he leaned forward to reach her neck, she tilted her hips upwards, and felt the bulge in his pants digging in to her butt cheeks. *Yes! He's ready.*

"Can you do the lower back too?" she purred.

"Silvana," he whispered, his voice strained.

"Please, Jason," she begged. Her voice was now rich with subtlety and pleasure. "I really need this."

"Well…" he stammered. She made up his mind for him. She grabbed the edge of her jeans, and with a few quick wiggles, shifted them off her ass and down to her thighs. She even jerked up slightly to make it jiggle. "Fuck," he gasped.

"Please grab it Jason. Please squeeze it for me."

His fingers dug in hard, and she couldn't help letting out a squeal of delight. He pulled at the thickest part of her ass and ran his thumbs along the centre. It was driving her wild. Abruptly, she thrust her hips as high as they could go and arched her back, pressing her chest onto the bed. From this angle, she knew what he was looking at.

"Can you rub something else for me, darling?" she panted.

"Silvana," he moaned, the tension in his voice at breaking point. "I don't think this is helping. We should really focus."

She pulled her shirt off the rest of the way, then twisted her back around far enough to look at him. Now, he would be able to clearly see her breasts at the same time as everything else. She stared up at him, batting her lashes.

"What if I said this might genuinely help me find my power?" she asked innocently.

He stared at her, his face ridged, and his chest rising and falling rapidly. "I'd say you were full of shit," he growled, before all self-control broke and he was on her with a frenzied abandon.

His hands grabbed at her breasts, her ass cheeks, and for once he was squeezing as hard as she wanted. *I'm a vampire, you're not going to hurt me.* She must have told him this a thousand times. Now, he lay over her to plant a kiss on her lips, and she sat up to press her lips against his. She rolled fully onto her back and kicked her pants off her ankles.

"Hurry up," she whispered and reached for his pants.

He was out of them a second later. His cock fully extended and ready.

And yet, he still took the time to press his face down between her thighs.

"Good boy," she purred, her fingers coiling in his dark hair.

His tongue ran up and down the length of her entrance, then honed in just above, sending her nerve endings into a frenzy. His lips closed around the head of her clit, and his tongue began to slowly swirl and flick back and forth.

"You like that?" he said, his voice deeper and more gravelly than normal.

"Mmhmm."

He kept working her, and she let him. But it was burning her up to lay patiently. If she were being honest, he was still being too gentle. He was always too gentle. That had been great a year ago when they first got together and she was learning to trust him. But now… Why was he still holding back?

Could she just ask him for more? Maybe she should just tell him what she wanted.

"Hey, give me a turn," she gasped as she tucked her legs behind his hips, pulling him forward with her heels. Jason shifted his hips towards hers. "No, up here," she demanded.

Jason straddled her chest, pinning her to the bed with the weight of his body, and she took his cock into her mouth.

He immediately began to moan as her lips ran back and forth. His legs trembled and twitched with pleasure. He tasted like sweat and skin, with just a hint of that salty flavour still to come. She began flicking her tongue over the tip of his cock. Each motion leading to a corresponding tremor in Jason. Suddenly he thrust forward, and she took all of it at once. She made a choking sound, and Jason tried to pull back. But she clutched his butt cheeks and held him close to her, forcing it just an extra inch deeper.

"Silvy," he moaned.

She finally let him withdraw, letting the spit run down over her lips. "You're not going to hurt me," she said. "Now fuck me."

"Fuck yeah," he cried.

A second later, he was deep inside her.

There! Her mind nearly screamed in relief. *I told him what I needed, and he listened to me. God, why didn't I just tell him all along?*

Jason began pounding away in a stupor. Silvana worked to angle her hips at just the right position. He spent the energy, but she controlled the point of contact. This was best for both of them. Already, she could feel the build starting to grow between her legs. She did her best to hold it off for a few minutes. She wanted to go together.

Her mind was sharpening. Maybe it was the blood she'd just tasted, or how alive she felt, but something in her brain was working at full capacity. The power of Jason's blood was resonating within her, as if it could feel its donor just centimetres away. Her hunger for him was growing. She wanted more of his blood. More of *him. He* was all she wanted.

"Silvana, I'm..." Jason groaned, his sweat dripping over her skin.

She could still taste him in her mouth. She wanted him to explode. So she let her moans grow louder, her thrusting harder, and her grip tighter.

It worked. He shivered and twitched as he thrust as far forward as he could go. She felt the wetness inside her, and it was just what she needed. Her body responded and her back started to arch. Her legs straightened out as a huge wave of release ran up her core. She threw back her head and let out a cry of pleasure.

Something connected in her mind. She felt the power click into place. And when she cried out, a wave of force blasted outwards from her.

The bedroom wall exploded apart.

Silvana went still. She could feel Jason motionless on top of her. The bedroom wall next to her had completely collapsed. Plaster and wooden frames had shattered, exposing the room next to them.

And that's where Khadija was sitting. In a lounge chair in the room next to theirs, with one leg stretched over the armrest. Her thighs were wide apart, and her hand was down the front of her pants, and reaching between her legs.

"Oh," Khadija said in a calm voice. She slowly removed her hand and closed her legs. "Uh… ok yes, I was listening. But in my defence, I could have heard you two from any room in the house."

Jason pulled a blanket over the two of them. "And why exactly did you rip the wall down?" he asked, his voice cold. "Forgot yourself for a moment, did you?"

"That wasn't me," Khadija cried, holding up her hands.

Jason frowned, then looked down at Silvana. She flashed him a cheeky grin.

"I told you it might help."

Chapter 10

Portia sat cross-legged on a thick foam yoga mat. She wore long stretchy, skin-tight black pants and a sports top that showed her midriff, and her hair was in a messy pony tail. The floor underneath her was padded with foam, soft enough to avoid strain on her knees. She was in her second century after all. Knees were important.

She concentrated all her thoughts on the sensation of her breathing. In and out. She noted how her body responded to the motion of breath, her chest expanding and shrinking down repeatedly, her heartbeats slowing, limbs giving the faintest muscle twitch. Her mind was focused to the exclusion of all else.

"Tab Izī."

The word was a whisper, yet the true power of her Will shaped reality. Her mind was unfettered as every thought was focused on this one act of spell casting. Distantly, she heard the roar of an open flame coming from all around her, but it never entered her conscious mind. That part of her mind was focused on her Will.

"Tab Izī."

Her mind pushed out more power. Because of course there was more power. She was a wizard. A Vigile of the Imperium, an institution that had ruled the world for thousands of years. She focused on her name to give her strength. She was Portia. Portia was Immortal. Portia would live for another eight hundred years. Portia was barely a step below a god. The roar of flames became a thunderous song, harmonious in its consistent pitch. At this point, no one on earth could touch her. She was Portia. She was untouchable.

Except him. He could touch you.

Her control wavered. She pushed again with her Will to steady the overwhelming power she held. But the thought spoke again. *He can touch you as much as he likes and there's nothing you can do to stop him.* The spell trembled, and in doing so, the flames multiplied in heat and ferocity. It started to touch the walls. She was losing control of the heat. It was escaping her Will.

She quickly withdrew her power. The spell wavered on a knife's edge, ready to explode throughout her entire home. Yet her Will was sufficient. The flames whooshed like rushing air as they dissipated into nothingness and the room became a temple in the worship of silence.

Fury began building inside her. She knew what her mistress would say if she saw such a lack of control. *Damn it, that filthy old piece of shit is still in my head. I can't get him out.* She forced herself to keep focusing on her breathing. At least she had performed the spell to her full ability. And nothing had actually caught fire around her. Desdemona didn't need to know how close she'd come to burning their home to ash.

She ended her meditation early. With a wave of her hand and outburst of Willpower, she changed from her exercise clothes into her Vigile suit and gave her hair a flick to loosen it from its clasp. Portia left the gym to find her mistress.

Desdemona was at a computer, in her work gear, her face in its natural scowl. Portia stood before her and bowed. "Mistress. I am ready to return to active duty."

"Wilt thou burn the house if I refuse?"

Portia winced. So she had noticed the moment she'd almost lost control. Her senses were truly unmatched.

"My power is ready," she boasted. "My control is sufficient to the task."

Desdemona eyed her. "Let us hope so." She moved back to the computer.

It was the closest she got to offering real encouragement. Portia was used to her brisk manner, but sometimes, she couldn't help but wish for more.

"I'm searching through the financial records of the Royalists," Desdemona said. "But I fear I am not well suited to this task."

"Mistress?" Portia asked.

It sounded like an admission of weakness.

"It is beneath me." *Ah, there it is.* "I wish to seek an Imperium economist as a consultant."

Portia nearly sighed with relief. They should have done this from the start, as soon as they realised the Royalists were moving money around. Vigiles were not experts in all fields, as much as many of them seemed to think they were. Desdemona was always reluctant to hire experts like historians, doctors, lawyers, anyone who might know more than she did. Still, sometimes she gave in.

"Who did you have in mind?" Portia asked.

"Jacqueline Rothschild."

Portia couldn't help rolling her eyes. The Rothschilds were one of the wealthiest families in the world. Their economist, Jacqueline, was largely responsible for that wealth. She was a mega celebrity within the Immortal world and frequently gave talks on money management. It seemed typical that Desdemona would only bother speaking to a specialist on money if it was literally the world's greatest expert.

"It might take time to arrange a meeting," Portia said.

"I don't make appointments," Desdemona said. "Come." She held out a hand. Portia didn't bother arguing.

They teleported immediately.

Portia's heeled shoes touched down on gravel. She was facing a heavily manicured garden that spanned almost one hundred meters in length. It looked like a family crest of red and green crosses. Multiple groundsmen were working among the garden to maintain its quality. The sun was high overhead – the hottest part of the day – still they worked. Portia spun around to look in the same direction as her mistress and saw a massive manor looming over them.

The building was four stories high and stretched for one hundred metres both left and right. Several spires and turrets were mounted along the roof, and the brick walls were in pristine condition. Guards stood by the mansions entrance with automatic rifles held at the ready. Desdemona walked forward, and Portia followed.

"I recognise this place," Portia said. "What's it called again?"

"Waddesdon. Buckinghamshire."

The guards eyed the pair with nervous shifting eyes and clutched their weapons tighter. They wore red coats with blue trousers and a vest covered in adornments. *All those gold trims are about as useless as their rifles*, Portia chuckled to herself. Desdemona barged through the front door and announced herself to the staff.

"I am here to see Jacqueline."

Her voice echoed through the lobby, up the alabaster stairs and into the upper floors. Half a dozen staff members dressed in black pants and plain white vests exchanged worried glances with each other.

"Ms Rothschild is not on the premises, Vigiles" an older woman answered in a crisp cockney accent. She stepped forward and nodded. "This is a manor for entertainment and events, not a workspace."

"Then take me to her."

The woman gave Desdemona an exasperated smile. "She's not here, and I cannot tell you where she is."

Portia barked a high pitch laugh. "Oh dear! Sounds to me like you're opposing Imperium mandate. We're under orders from the High King himself." She didn't bother to specify. Or explain those orders had nothing to do with this. "Doesn't this mean we can tear them limb from limb?"

"It leaves such a mess," Desdemona said with disappointment. "I prefer fire. I like to think of it as a self-cleaning execution."

"Oh, clever."

The staff began to shift on their feet like they were considering running for it. One guard seemed to think about raising his weapon, then reconsidered.

"Madam, if you please," the woman begged. "I'm not trying to be difficult. This place is just a ceremonial estate. It's not where Ms Rothschild does her actual work. You're looking for her offices in London city. You're in the wrong place."

Desdemona did not look impressed. "Then thou will bring her here," she said simply.

"I…" the woman stammered. "Ms Rothschild is an extremely busy person."

"So am I. Now hurry." Desdemona turned around and walked to a desk that held a porcelain vase and a golden jewellery box.

With a flick of her wrist, all the objects flew aside and smashed violently against the walls. A woman on staff let out a high pitch squeal. Desdemona partially sat on the desk and faced the others with her hands clasped in her lap. She smiled.

"I'll get on the phone right away, Ms Vigile."

The staff stampeded out of the lobby and began whispering to one another before they were out of earshot in the next room.

Portia stepped towards her mistress, her heels echoing through the now empty room. "You know," she said. "You could always get things done without making the help fear for their lives."

"It would take twice as long."

"You're Immortal. You have the time."

Desdemona sneered. "The older I get, the more impatient I become. It's like my patience ran out years ago and everyone around me lives on borrowed time."

"I've always wondered why we don't have more visitors."

They waited only two minutes before the older woman rushed back into the entryway.

"Ms Vigile, ma'am, Ms Rothschild says she will see you momentarily. Would you like refreshments?"

"We'll be fine here," Desdemona said and did not move from her makeshift seat.

It was in fact an hour later when Jacqueline Rothschild appeared at the top of the stairs. Portia suspected they were kept waiting out of spite and pettiness – that's exactly what she would have done.

There was a faint trace of power around Jacqueline. Not as strong as wizard power, but something Immortal nonetheless.

Jacqueline's face was a kaleidoscope of plastic surgery. Everything looked like it had been worked on extensively. Her skin was tanned too orange to be natural, and her blonde hair was cut in a short bob and a long fringe like she was about to ask to see the manager. She wore a sapphire blue pantsuit, diamond earrings, and a golden Rolex at her wrist. She took one look at the Vigiles, and her lip curled like she'd bitten something sour.

"Come on, I don't have all day," she snapped and stepped away from the railing, moving out of sight.

Portia nearly groaned. Jacqueline was forcing them to walk upstairs as a power move, and it served no purpose other than to console her wounded pride. But there was no point arguing. They climbed the stairs, and Desdemona somehow made it look like that that was exactly what she wanted to do all along.

"Come on," Jacqueline snapped again and beckoned them into a boardroom.

A long mahogany table filled the conference room with a dozen plush, black, high-backed office chairs around the outside. Large TV screens hung from immaculate white walls. The room smelt of leather, stained wood, and the faint odour of cleaning products.

Jacqueline sat in a thickly cushioned chair at the head of the boardroom table. "You have five minutes. Make them count," she said. She pointedly looked at her Rolex to mark the time.

Portia raised an eyebrow towards her mistress. Desdemona remained standing in the doorway, her hands clutching at her waist and her face impassive. So Portia followed her lead and remained silent.

"I care little for your intimidation tactics," Jacqueline said. "If you wish to waste your time, that is your choice. Vigiles do not outrank me here." Her voice began to rise. "I handle the financials of the High Kings themselves. Who do you think they'd support here? The one who single-handedly gives them their trillions of wealth, or two faceless, replaceable lapdogs? You'll be hard pressed to overpower me."

Desdemona said nothing, which infuriated Jacqueline even further. So Portia let out a short, high pitched giggle for no other reason than to piss her off more.

"That's it! I don't have time to waste on this." Jacqueline stood and tried to storm past them, but Desdemona was clearly blocking the door. "Get out of my way." Desdemona made no move. "I said get out!" She pushed Desdemona.

Magic lashed out and seized Jacqueline, hurling her off the ground and across the length of the table, before slamming her into the TV on the far side. Glass shattered and the screen twisted on its hinges. Jacqueline hit the ground with a pained groan.

"Thou hast struck a Vigile of the Imperium," Desdemona said. "I would be within my rights to put thee in jail. Or execute thee on the spot."

Jacqueline shrieked, "You fucking bitch! You intended to goad me the whole time! Do you have any idea who I am?"

"Thy name means nothing to me. Thou wouldst do well to remember that."

"Ha!" Jacqueline snapped as she climbed to her feet. "I know you now. Desdemona, Vigile of the Imperium and so-called wizard prodigy." She brushed glass off her jacket and pants, though ended up smearing blood from her hands across her pantsuit instead. "If you're trying to goad me into fighting you, you can forget it. I don't have magic on your level. But you have no idea of the weapons I possess."

Desdemona simply resumed her silence.

"I can remove all your wealth and power in this world. I can leave you a shrivelled up sack of meat rotting on some street corner, filthy and ragged, desperate for your next meal and shying away from people in fear of them striking you. I can do that to you and everyone you've ever loved."

Portia couldn't help the laugh that escaped her lips. "I'm sorry, are you threatening my mistress with… homelessness?"

"That's exactly what I'm doing!"

"All right," Portia mumbled. "As long as we're clear, I guess."

"No one can remove my magic," Desdemona said. Yet there was something. A tremor in her voice. Was her mistress… shaken? "And I have no loved ones. Thou hast nothing with which to threaten me."

"Oh really?" Jacqueline smiled, revealing a mouth that had been artificially widened at the edges to make her smile broader. Her teeth were impossibly white.

Desdemona made a gasping sound. She stared at the floor with vacant eyes. Slowly, her eyes grew moist and reflected the overhead light.

"Mistress?" Portia whispered and clutched Desdemona's arm. It seemed to startle her. Her eyes settled on Portia, and with an effort of will, she seemed to settle herself.

"Thou art a telepath," Desdemona said with a sigh. "I should have seen it earlier."

A sudden crack rang out across the room and Jacqueline gave a loud cry. It sounded like a hard slap to the face. Desdemona had done so with a mere thought.

"Use thy power on me again," Desdemona said. "And I will spend a decade tearing thy body to shreds, one piece at a time."

"Fuck you!" Jacqueline roared. She straightened her hair and rubbed the red welt growing on her cheek, before straightening her suit jacket and regaining her composure. "Fine. What do you want?"

Desdemona let out a satisfied hum.

"Finally. Thou art most stubborn. I should think next time, thou wouldst be more cooperative with me. I don't do well with petulance." At last Desdemona moved to sit down at the table.

Portia mimicked her. They waited. When Jacqueline didn't move, Desdemona gestured casually towards the chair and waited as she slowly moved to sit, glaring the whole time.

"Thou art going to work for us," Desdemona said. "We have a case we want thee to handle."

Jacqueline scoffed, "Oh please. I don't do consultant work for law enforcement."

"Indeed, thou dost." That cut off Jacqueline's protests. "Portia?"

Portia took over. "You can read my mind. Surely you know what I'm going to say?"

Jacqueline gave an exaggerated sigh. "Your thoughts are too complicated. Just say it, please."

Portia shrugged. "We have been investigating the group known as the Royalists. Members include houses Yamato, Glucksburg, and several minor houses of little consequence. All of them have been moving money, but we cannot see what their purpose is."

"I imagine it's to make money," Jacqueline sneered.

"Cute. We want you to investigate all their books and find a pattern. Report back to us when you've found something."

Jacqueline gave a derisive laugh. "You can't be serious? First of all, do you have any idea how many projects I have in the works right now?"

"This takes precedence."

"I'm working for Reynold himself."

"So are we."

"I meant directly!"

"So did I."

Jacqueline growled, but forced herself to keep calm after a nervous glance at Desdemona. "You don't understand the impossibility of the task. Sometimes you just cannot tell *why* someone is moving money until after the fact."

Portia frowned. "What do you mean, after?"

"We move money when we expect the market to rise or fall. But sometimes you can't see the full picture until after the event. I moved money out of Lehman Brothers because I had insider information, and I knew they were going to crash. Everyone wondered why I moved money, but they only understood when the crash happened. Do you see? Sometimes you need a crystal ball to tell why something happened."

Desdemona waved her hand in casual dismissal. "Then thou canst make an educated guess."

"But I can't guess. I'm only a financial advisor. They could be moving money cause they're planning an act of terrorism."

"Excuse me?" Portia said. "That sounds important. Care to elaborate?"

Jacqueline let out a sigh. "You know September eleven?" The Vigiles nodded. "It was planned entirely by mortals. Shocked the Imperium as much as the rest of the world, except for High King Jin. He knew about it beforehand."

"Really?" Portia asked. "Why didn't he stop it?"

"Please, they were only mortals," Jacqueline sneered. "But Jin invested hard in preparation for the attacks. He knew the World Trade Centres were mostly law firms and investment agencies, so he invested into all of their competitors. After the attacks, all business and clientele went to their competitors, and Jin made a king's ransom."

"How very shrewd," Portia drawled.

"This is what I mean, though. What if the Royalists are preparing an attack like that? I won't be able to find anything just from looking at their financial records."

"Thou need only find the pattern," Desdemona said. "We will handle it from there."

"But I'm not a military strategist."

"Thou hast twenty-four hours."

"What?!"

Desdemona calmly stood to her feet and marched out of the boardroom without another glance or word at the financial advisor. Portia stood slowly and stretched, letting out a girlish sigh. "Thank you for your time, Ms Rothschild. It's been a pleasure." She strolled casually after her mistress, leaving Jacqueline with her head in her hands.

"I think that went well," Portia said as the teleportation spell ended and they arrived back at their base.

Portia collapsed into her favourite office chair and scanned her computer screen for updates. Nothing important.

"She will do as requested," Desdemona said. "Now that matter is tended to, thou and I must find Dorin."

"I thought so. My trace is still on him. I should be able to get us there in a few minutes. Shall I begin preparations?"

"At once."

Portia rested back in her chair, closed her eyes and began to reach out with her power. She could feel Desdemona sitting nearby, calmly and quietly waiting. Portia tried not to think about the fact she was being watched, and instead concentrated on finding the trace.

A little piece of her mind was in another place, tugging at her, trying to reunite with the rest of herself. It felt impossibly far away. Yet, she began to force her Will onto reality itself and pull the two distances closer together. The further the distance, the harder the magic. This trace was already coming into reach. Dorin was probably somewhere in Europe. She began to pull and fold space around them.

The trace suddenly slipped out of her reach.

Portia let out a gasp and her magic dissipated. She opened her eyes. "Mistress. Something happened. I lost the trace!"

"Explain."

"It… fell out of my reach. Like something yanked it out of my grip. Surely, he cannot know it was there. No one can find my trace."

"Stay calm," Desdemona ordered, and it helped to slow Portia's rising anxiety. "Now take a breath, and reach out again. Can you still find the trace?"

Portia took a full minute to calm herself. She reached out, and within moments, found the trace again. "It's still there," she said with a sigh of relief. "It's just… harder to find. No, wait… it's further away.

About twice the distance."

"He has been teleported," Desdemona said. "He must be working with someone."

"A High King?"

"Let's hope not." Desdemona gave her a pat on the shoulder. "Reach out to him again when you're ready. He will not escape us this time."

"It may take some time to focus my Will. The sudden shift rattled me, and he's further away now."

"Take your time. We will find him."

Portia took a long breath. Then, she began to summon her magic.

Chapter 11

"One more time, from the top," Jason said as he slid a robe over his head.

His hands already wanted to shake with nervousness. He forced himself to channel that fear into determination and focus for the task at hand.

Everyone had crowded together in the lounge room of Edward's mansion. The room was buzzing with activity as each member of their team worked to make their final preparations for their mission.

Leslie tapped the chalkboard with an ivory walking cane, bringing everyone's attention to them. "We have chosen our three infiltrators. Mr Turner, Miss Romanov, and Miss Al Khalifa."

"Poor bastards," Freddie said with a salute.

Jason grinned at him.

"Everyone else stays here to avoid suspicion. Too much movement around the Library will draw attention. So, only three will enter." Leslie pointed at the chalkboard again. "Stage one, you all must drink your potion to ensure you look like me. I have also prepared your identification papers that will grant you access. Do not forget them."

"We're not that stupid," Khadija growled.

Silvana had her robe on and tied up around the waist. "I still think it's risky if we all look like Leslie. Surely they'll notice three doppelgangers."

"That's why you're going in at the start of the work day," Leslie said. "They'll have four entry stations where people will line up. If you all go through separate queues, no one will notice. It's not like they have computers that scan your face."

Freddie checked three small go-pros that had arrived that morning. He'd ordered them through fake ID accounts, a rerouted ISP, and had them delivered to a drop box in Swansea town. He was certain they would be untraceable, yet Jason feared the assassin would have noticed it anyway, somehow. The cameras felt like the biggest risk of the whole thing. *Come on, Freddie, don't let us down.*

"Once you're through the first checkpoint," Leslie went on, "stop in the bathrooms and take Edward's second elixir, which will force you to throw up and return to your normal selves."

"Fun," Khadija groaned.

"Second checkpoint, Miss Al Khalifa will down her third elixir from Edward to make herself inebriated. That's when I will activate my focus spell. With two powers enhancing her own, she should be able to force her way through the wizard barrier and get all three of you through checkpoint two. Stay close to each other so no one gets cut off."

"Fucking risky," Khadija muttered.

"Don't tell us that!" Jason said. "Tell us it's going to work flawlessly. You need to believe it for your magic to be strong enough, right?"

"Don't tell me how to do magic, boy."

"The third checkpoint," Leslie said, "is entirely up to Miss Romanov and her vampiric powers. Which, I understand, you've had a breakthrough on recently?"

"Broke through my walls," Edward grumbled. The alchemist was laying out seven vials of elixirs and carefully labelling each one.

Silvana blushed. "I've figured it out. I can trigger the power at will.

I'm certain."

Jason knew her well enough to know she was telling the truth. Yet, he couldn't help the feeling of doubt lingering in the back of his mind. Something wasn't adding up about her power. She had only found it twice, and both times didn't seem like they had much in common. He didn't know if she could actually use the power with any consistency. If she failed, they would be caught, and the assassin would find them.

"And that will get you inside the Library of Alexandria," Leslie said. "From there, use the mortal devices provided by Freddie and film as many books as you can. Gather that data."

Freddie instructed them, "You can turn pages pretty quickly, but make sure they're totally motionless for about one second per page. We don't want hours of blurry footage."

"Remember," Jason added, "we're looking for anything to do with the big Immortal houses. Anything that might reveal what they're up to now. Anything to do with history about to be repeated."

"And anything relating to Dorin," Silvana reminded them.

Khadija asked, "Are we sure the witch cannot give us more clues than that?"

"Certain," Leslie said. "I cannot betray my order. But I'm beginning to have my suspicions about what you're looking for. I am feeling confident that you can find what you need."

"What about getting out again?" Silvana asked. "This is very important to me. My uncle Nicholas once showed me this Alfred Hitchcock film about a prisoner who tried to escape from jail." She shuddered. "She didn't get *all* the way out. It ended very, very badly. My point is we must be able to get out the same way we came in."

"Relax," Leslie soothed. "There are no security measures while exiting. You literally just need to walk out."

"You better be right about that," Silvana said.

Jason looked at his team. Himself, Silvana and Khadija were

wearing Middle Eastern robes of blue and brown wool. Khadija had insisted they were authentic and would help them fit into the city of Alexandria. The two women had their hair and faces covered, except for a thin slit around their eyes. "Still feels like cultural appropriation," Jason murmured.

"It's dressing appropriately. Stop being so sensitive," Khadija said. "Mortal, hand us the cameras."

Freddie twisted his lip. "First of all, I don't like being called mortal. Second, they're not cameras, they're Go-Pros." He handed one to each member of the away team. "They each have two and a half hours of recording time. So make them count, and for God's sake, don't fiddle with the settings. Simply press the big button to turn it on, and the red button to record. It's fool proof."

"Hang on. Why only two and a half hours of recording time?" Leslie asked, an edge of concern in their voice. "You should be able to stay in the library for eight hours."

"That's literally the best a Go-Pro can do," Freddie said. "I paid an arm and a leg for these. Especially since they're the plastic model, so they won't show up in metal detectors. This is some expert level spy gear."

Jason nodded. "Good job, Q." Jason winked at Freddie. "Besides, I don't want us to be there much longer than that. The more time we spend in the open, the more likely the chimera assassin will locate us."

"I seriously doubt they could find you in less than eight hours," Leslie said. "This is our second day here without a sighting."

"We covered our tracks well, getting here. It'll be different in the Library of Alexandria when we're out in public. Two and a half hours is already too long for my liking."

"Agreed," Khadija said. "We've already exposed ourselves to enough risk, by doing this. Let's not overstay our welcome."

Leslie looked like they wanted to argue more, but they held up their hands in surrender. "I only worry you won't find the information you need with such time restraints. You better be quick and efficient in your search."

"The Go-Pros will work," Freddie said. "Just hold the pages still to get a clear image. Or take photos individually, if that helps."

Jason nodded. He collected his identification papers from Leslie, then two vials from Edward, and a Go-Pro from Freddie, stashing all his equipment within the folds in his robes. Silvana and Khadija did the same. All three of them stood ready. Jason took a deep breath.

"Does anyone have any last minute concerns? Anything at all? Cause this is the perfect time to speak up if you think we've missed something?" The room was silent. "Are we all sure about this?"

"Hell no," Freddie mumbled. "Jason, are you sure you should be the third person? I know Khadija and Silvana are essential, but you're the all-rounder. Surely someone else—"

"Do you want my place?" Jason asked.

Freddie gave him a helpless shrug. "I don't know. I just don't want to see you get hurt, Bro," he seemed to add as an afterthought. He cleared his throat. "You're a normie like me. I know you're better trained, sure. But you're still sneaking into the lion's den."

"It has to be me," Jason said. "Leslie will be spotted too easily. And out of the three guys left to choose from, I'm the most combat ready."

"About that," Silvana said. "I do have one question. If Leslie can't go because the assassin will find them, why are we all taking a potion to look like Leslie?"

Leslie grinned. "Because only I have legal permission to enter the Library. You three can negate that risk because you only have to look like me for the first checkpoint. Then you vomit and return to normal. I agree that it's a risk, but by using Edward's elixirs the risk becomes minimal." Their grin broadened. "Besides, Miss Al Khalifa didn't want me there."

"I stand by that," Khadija said bluntly. "If you can perform your focus spell on me from anywhere in the world, then there's no need to be right next to me. One less threat to keep an eye on that way."

"Oh we'll be best friends before you know it," Leslie sneered. Khadija gave them a fake smile in return. Abruptly, Leslie cleared their throat and spoke in a serious, sombre voice. "I must make one request. When you take the potion to look like me, please respect my body. And… my privacy."

Jason was taken aback by the seriousness of the question. Leslie was putting themselves in a vulnerable position, sharing their body with others like this. Jason nodded and matched the solemn tone. "I promise, we will be respectful."

The others agreed. Even Khadija showed solemnity. Leslie simply nodded in thanks.

Jason looked around the room once more. "Anything else?" This time, the room was quiet, and he felt the wild urge to make up some problem to try to slow things down. Which probably meant it was time to begin. "All right," he said, hiding an internal sigh. "When can we start?"

Leslie checked their watch. "It's seven fifty-five in Cairo, which means you can go now and enter any time within the next hour."

"Gives us time to get in position," Khadija said. "Let's go."

She reached out her hands. Silvana and Jason each took one, then held on to each other to complete the circle. Silvana gave his hand an extra squeeze, and he matched her strength of grip in return.

"Good luck, you guys," Freddie said. His face was whiter than normal, and he looked between Silvana and Jason with open concern. "Be safe," he whispered.

"May the stars watch over you," Leslie said.

Edward only gave a nod.

"Ready kids?" Khadija asked.

Before either could reply, the wizard's power swept over them. The room began to bend in unnatural ways, the walls folding up and down, the roof dropping to the floor, and a black expanse with silver stars appeared in the gaps. Jason clutched onto the Immortal hands holding him as the ground fell away from under his feet. He felt the sensation of falling. Or at least, his brain told him he was falling even if he couldn't physically feel it.

The patterns around them began to change. The folding pieces of the world showed parts of brown structures, multi-coloured rugs, and a plastered grey ceiling. All the fragments started falling into one cohesive shape and within seconds they all converged into a single empty room. Jason suddenly felt the hard ground beneath his sandals again.

Khadija let go, and Jason had the urge to snatch her hand back for his safety.

"Where is this?" Silvana asked.

"Prayer room," Khadija answered. "It's between sunrise and Duhur, so no one will be here."

Oh right, it's a mosque, Jason thought to himself. He recognised the prayer rugs on the ground. "Oops!" he cried as he stepped off the one underneath his feet.

Khadija was shaking her head. "They really shouldn't leave the rugs out like this."

"Is that a… sin? I don't know the word," Jason asked.

"No, it's not *haram.* It's just bad etiquette. You should keep the rugs folded when they're not in use so they don't collect dust. They should be treated with respect."

Jason blinked. "I didn't realise you… uh… practised your religion."

Khadija shifted under her gown. Her face was covered, but Jason had the impression she was blushing. "My family think I'm a good little Muslim girl, and I play my part when I must. Honestly, I don't know if I believe, exactly. I'm just proud to be Arab. A lot of people seem to think that to be Arab means you must be Muslim too, but not necessarily." Khadija shook her head. "I'm getting nostalgic. I just brought us to the mosque because I knew it'd be quiet at this time of day. The Library entrance is only one street over from here." She gestured to the mosque door. "Jason, you should lead the way."

He walked carefully to avoid stepping on the rugs. As he approached the door, the bustling of moving people grew in volume, including several car horns beeping in a high-pitched nasal sound. Jason lifted the long wooden latch on the door, and a wall of noise and sunlight poured into the once quiet space.

Outside was the modern city of Alexandria. A two-way street ran between the tall buildings, yet pedestrians were walking all over the road as vehicles honked their horns to create a path through the crowd of people. The buildings appeared to be apartment blocks, with clothes hanging on lines from little windows and air conditioners stacked on top of each other in big clusters.

Jason noticed everyone was dressed in non-traditional attire. Every male wore jeans and a t-shirt, or business pants with button up shirts. The women wore long, flowing dresses with beautiful silk head coverings over their hair. Not a single person wore robes, and there were no women with faces fully covered.

"Ladies," he said, "I think we stand out."

"I thought you said this is what the locals wore!" Silvana hissed.

"They did," Khadija snapped, then in a softer tone added, "the last time I was here."

Jason took the lead, and they joined the flow of the crowd. Within seconds dozens of eyes were turning towards the trio.

Jason groaned. "And when exactly were you last here, wizard?"

He didn't have to see her face to know she was blushing. "It was just after the war."

"I assume you mean the *world* war?" Jason growled. "Should I even bother asking which one at this point, or is that unlikely to make a difference?"

"Blame the witch! Leslie let me make the decision on clothing," she growled. "Sweet Allah, they were even smiling when they did. That damn crook!"

Jason smirked. "Well, if Leslie thought it was funny, then it's probably not a big deal. Let's just hurry."

Khadija muttered something in his direction that sounded like an Arabic curse.

The streets were far less crowded than Jason expected, and the people walking around them seemed in no great hurry. Three times he stepped around a slow moving pedestrian just to get stuck behind another. He wasn't even walking that fast. Jason breathed in slowly to keep calm. He could feel everyone's eyes on him, yet rather than staring back, he tried to keep his own eyes focused straight ahead. It was just his anxiety making him impatient. They had time to spare.

No one in their trio spoke. The hustling city street made it too difficult to be heard anyway. The dirt and dust from the road flicked over his sandals, getting under the soles of his feet and between his toes. The heat of the morning sun made sweat roll down his back, despite it being early in the day. He tried to imagine his couch, TV, and favourite beer instead.

"This way," Khadija whispered and tugged on Jason's arm.

He followed her gesture towards the crossroads of streets and turned right. It was surreal walking through an unfamiliar city. Each street was completely different, and yet had the same designs and décor as the one before.

Jason spotted a small flow of people walking up a set of white stone steps towards a building built entirely of old bricks. His instincts immediately told him something was unusual, but he couldn't say what exactly. Several columns ran up the length of this building, with white bases and a red brick pillar. If he hadn't been looking for the Library of Alexandria, he never would have noticed anything special. But something…

"That building," Silvana said. "It looks English." Jason nearly clapped his hands in realisation. *That's what it was. Different architecture.*

"Correct," Khadija said. "This exterior was built by order of the English High King. That's where we're headed."

Jason felt an inward chill. *She means Reynold the First.* He still remembered that chilling smile on the old, wrinkled face, and that air of utter confidence he seemed to exude. His mind flashed with the image of another man hanging suspended in mid-air, ripped apart by invisible hands, and utterly crushed into a ball of meat. That bloody execution was done by the same man who owned this building. *"I'll be keeping an eye on you,"* Reynold had said. Now Jason had travelled halfway around the world to find Reynold had gotten here first, hundreds of years ago, and was now waiting for him to step inside his fortress.

I am not prepared for this. He wanted to turn back then and there, yet he knew the chimera assassin would find them soon if he did. The only way out was forward. *Relax,* he told himself. *Reynold doesn't know you're here.*

He kept his cowl up as he ascended the stairs. A natural gap appeared between the people around him so he stepped into the line. The team had already agreed they needed to line up in separate queues, so there was no need to keep together any longer. Without a backward glance, Jason left Silvana behind.

She'll be fine. This going to work out.

His eyes remained focused on the ground. The person in front of him wore long black trousers and formal black shoes that tapped loudly with each step against the old stone. Jason simply followed behind them. They reached the top of the stairs and stepped inside the doorway, and Jason immediately sighed with relief as the sun was blocked and the coolness of the shade rushed over him.

He reached inside his cloak for the two vials of elixir. He grasped the larger of the two and discreetly held it up to his face to check its shape and colour. It was labelled, *Metamorph,* for shape shifting. With his thumb and forefinger, he popped the cork and sipped the contents down. The taste was sour like a grapefruit long past ripe.

The elixir immediately took effect. He could feel his flesh and bones shifting with a will of their own. It was like a rumbling in his stomach, spontaneous and uncontrollable, but not painful. He kept his hood down until he felt the magic settle over him. Jason recognised the extra tightness in his joints and weariness in his muscles as the effects of aging. His eyesight became less focused. When he finally felt the last changes take effect, he looked up and was relieved to confirm no one had noticed.

People were still bunched together in line, but movement had slowed. They were inside the large foyer that matched Leslie's descriptions of a grand open theatre with tall alabaster columns holding the roof above. But there was open space all around Jason. He frowned. *Shouldn't there be multiple queues?* He leaned to the side to glance up the line.

There was a wall of security archways with an officer's desk up ahead, similar to airport security. But out of four kiosks available, only one was open.

Jason froze. There was supposed to be four. It was the only way that he, Silvana and Khadija could all enter with the same face. But if there was only one, they'd be spotted for sure.

He tried to turn around and signal the others, but there were at least twenty people in close proximity to him. It was too risky to call out. *Fuck.* Who knew what would happen if they got noticed? Would they call High King Reynold directly? No, that was ridiculous. But his Vigiles would be just as dangerous.

His mind raced as the line moved with agonising slowness. Maybe he should use the other elixir to vomit, then try to get through the checkpoint looking like himself? No, his ID papers showed Leslie's picture. That was the whole point of the elixir. He growled to himself. Maybe he should step out of line, that way at least Khadija or Silvana would get through, since only they could get through barriers two and three. But that didn't fix anything. The team needed both of the women to get all the way through to the Library, so even if he left, one of them would be caught.

He waited until he was next in line. The little security guard stood behind his desk, looking at papers and checking everyone's facial ID. *I should turn around. I'm the least important of the trio. It'll add to their chances if I turn around.*

"Next," the officer called. Jason stood motionless, unable to decide upon his next move. "Next!" the man called again, more insistent. Jason knew what he had to do. He turned to walk away.

"Come on!" the person behind him growled and gave Jason the slightest push on his shoulder. And just like that, Jason felt himself obeying as he stepped up to the checkpoint without thinking further.

"Papers please," the officer said.

Jason handed them over, then tried to relax his features into the calmest expression he could manage, hoping no one could hear how loud his heart was pounding. The man behind the desk read through the papers for some time. Jason forced himself not to talk, lest his nervousness make him start rambling.

"Reason for the visit, Mx Toussaint?"

Jason stammered, "I uh… work here?" He was relieved to hear his voice sounded like Leslie.

Great potion, Eddie.

"I know, Mx Toussaint. I have to ask everyone that question," the officer said.

"Right, of course."

The officer looked up, and Jason resisted the urge to smile. The officer stamped the form. "Have a lovely day, Mx Toussaint."

"Thank you, sir," Jason said and stepped towards the archway.

Only now that he was past the checkpoint did he recognise the archway. It was a metal detector. And he remembered the mini camera in his robes. He froze in place. Freddie said he had chosen plastic Go-Pros for this very purpose, so they could get through the metal detectors. But what if it didn't work?

"Toussaint?" the officer said.

"Sorry," Jason replied and stepped through.

Nothing happened.

Good job, Freddie. I should never have doubted you.

On the other side were a series of elevators with people waiting to get in. He started looking for the bathrooms and spent a full minute scanning the room before he remembered they were on the floor below. He'd forgotten the order of events in his frazzled state. He had to calm down and think clearly. So he resigned himself to being Leslie a little while longer and found a place off to the side to stand before turning to look back at the queue.

It was another two minutes before he could finally see another hooded figure close to the checkpoint. *Was it Khadija, or Silvana? What were they planning on doing?*

The elevator arrived, but Jason didn't board it with the others. He waited to see what happened. The hooded figure reached the checkpoint and removed their cowl.

Jason blinked. "What the hell?" he muttered. It was Khadija, still looking like herself. Why hadn't she taken the potion to look like Leslie?

He watched as she talked back and forth a few times with security, neither her nor the guard showing any signs of a problem. The officer abruptly picked up their stamp and placed it on Khadija's forms. She walked through the archway without a problem.

Was that magic?

Khadija walked straight to the elevators. Her eyes fell to Jason, and her face twisted with rage.

"Jason?" she hissed. "You idiot! What in Allah's name are you doing here?"

Jason frowned. "What do you mean? How did you get through?"

She rolled her eyes. "I'm a princess, fool. My name carries a lot of weight in these parts. I thought if I banked on it, Silvana could get through as Leslie. I thought for sure you would leave. I never thought you'd be stupid enough to just walk through! You're not even necessary!"

"I'm sorry! I panicked."

"How is Silvana going to get through now? How are we going to get through without her? God above, this was all…"

"Next!" a woman's voice shouted. Jason and Khadija spun around.

A Library officer had just appeared at another kiosk and opened a second queue. A hooded figure – who was clearly Silvana – appeared at the head of the line as if by magical teleportation. Within a minute, Silvana walked towards the elevators with a perfect copy of Leslie's face.

"Oh my god!" she hissed. "That was really fucking lucky."

"I'll say," Khadija said while glaring at Jason.

Silvana reached for Jason, and he reached back. But in the same second, both of them seemed to remember they were undercover and stopped themselves.

"Sorry," he said. "It's probably too conspicuous, us all standing together." He noticed someone walking towards them.

"Right," Silvana said and stepped away, preparing to take a separate elevator.

The elevator closest to them opened, and there was space enough for everyone. So all three piled in and Khadija rolled her eyes. There was only one button to press. A stranger joined them at the last second, and the doors closed.

The lift moved down silently. Jason kept his face aimed at the back wall. He knew both he and Silvana looked like Leslie, and this stranger could notice. It would be fine as long as they didn't turn and face them.

The stranger turned around.

Damn it. There was a beat of silence, then the man spoke. Jason couldn't understand what he was saying. *What language is that?*

Khadija answered him. *They must be speaking Arabic.* The man replied, and Jason could hear the light-hearted tone of voice. Khadija responded. She sounded like she was telling a joke. Sure enough, the man chuckled in response, and Jason relaxed.

The doors opened. The man and Khadija exchanged a farewell and they exited the elevator. This floor was a long corridor filled with shops, of all things. Jason recognised a type of food court where people were eating breakfast from various cafes and vendors. There was a bookstore, a place for wines and alcohols, and even a clothing store. The trio began to wander.

"Nice job with that guy," Jason whispered. "What did he ask you?"

Khadija grinned. "He asked if he'd missed the memo about dress codes. I said it was for keeping off the sun. Then he asked if you two were foreigners who had not seen the sun before. So I said you were just Americans who were ashamed of your ugly faces."

"That's pretty rude," Jason said. "How dare you call me American."

Khadija smirked. "Don't worry. I was insulting Leslie's face, not yours. I consider that insult especially rewarding."

"Bathrooms," Silvana announced. Jason followed her gaze and saw the signs in the far corner.

"Meet you back here," Khadija said.

Jason walked a few steps away from Silvana. The group had already spent too much time close to each other, but after the scare at the first checkpoint, everyone seemed to need the reassurance. As Jason went to the men's room, he turned to Silvana. He saw Leslie's face looking back. He gave Silvana a nod and a smile, and she returned it in kind.

The bathroom was way fancier than it needed to be with mosaic tiles covering the walls and roof in elaborate patterns. Jason found all the stalls were empty, so picked one right at the end. He whipped out the second vial and downed it before he had time to dread the experience.

The reaction was almost instantaneous. Jason regretted everything for a few minutes. Soon, he felt his body begin to shapeshift back to a more familiar shape as his muscles filled out, his eyesight sharpened, and his heart began beating with greater ease. The shifting ended and Jason touched his face with relief.

A bizarre thought occurred to him, and he pulled up his robes to check. *Ok good, penis still there.* He chuckled at his own boyish reaction. He cleaned up the splatter and flushed away the vomit, before washing his hands and heading back out.

He spotted Khadija sipping a coffee mug at a table. He went to the bookstore across from her and pretended to browse, even though most of the books were in Arabic. A few minutes later, he saw Silvana return from the bathrooms. He glanced across the corridor to Khadija and as she stood to leave, he did the same and started following the general flow of foot traffic further into the complex, confident that the others would copy him.

A sudden tingling sensation rippled across Jason's skin, like someone brushing him with a feather. He recognised the feeling of magic. They must be coming up to the second checkpoint.

The corridor opened up into another amphitheatre, though smaller and relatively empty compared to the last one. A currency booth and some sort of information outlet stood to one side. The room was designed for transit through, not stopping. The air itself shimmered like the heat off a road on a hot day. *That must be the barrier*, Jason thought. *The magic is so thick here even I can see it.* As he moved towards the checkpoint, he started to feel heavy, like he was trying to walk through water as it pushed against him. He wouldn't be able to go much further on his own. He stepped to the side, off the pathway and waited.

Khadija appeared at his side, pulled out a vial and swallowed the contents. Jason remembered the 'alcohol' elixir Edward had prepared to help her lower her inhibitions. Now, Leslie's spell would help Khadija focus, and she should be able to force her way through the barrier.

"You can do this," he said to her.

"I know," Khadija replied. He smiled. That much confidence meant she was summoning her Will. "Stay close to me," she said and turned to acknowledge Silvana as she appeared on her other side.

They approached the second checkpoint with shoulders brushing against each other.

"Leslie," Khadija said. "I'm ready."

A sudden look came over Khadija's face, like she was an actress pretending to be someone else. *No, not pretending. This is Leslie's expression. They are blending with her.* Khadija was silent, yet her eyes burned with intensity as she faced the barrier.

Jason felt the weight against him start to shift. He walked normally, with the weight of magic no longer pushing against them. Khadija had beads of sweat rolling down her forehead, but despite her straining, they continued without issue. It was working.

Khadija suddenly let out a gasp and her eyes widened. A heavy weight slammed against Jason, and it was all he could do not to fall over.

"Are you ok?" Silvana asked. "What happened?"

"Something's wrong," Khadija said. "I don't feel drunk."

"Is the elixir not working?" Jason asked.

Khadija groaned, "*Min 'ajl Allah,*" and shook her fists in helpless rage. "The Library's spell! The one that cancels out existing spells at this checkpoint. It's cancelled out my elixir. I'm no longer drunk"

Jason nearly slapped himself on the forehead. "God, I didn't even think of it."

"What do we do?" Silvana asked. "Should we turn back now?"

"Fuck that," Khadija growled, a look of determination flashing in her eyes. "I have just enough Will to do this without the elixir. With Leslie helping me, I won't need the alchemist's help." She huffed a deep breath. "It'll be enough."

Jason understood. She wasn't trying to summon a vague, unknowable amount of power. She was setting a firm goal to help shape her Will. *Exactly enough.* Jason pushed down the urge to ask, 'Are you sure?' in case it threw off her concentration. It had to be all or nothing. That was the only way this would work.

"Walk forward with me," Khadija whispered.

They began to press against the force of the spell. It didn't seem to shift at all. Jason felt like he was dragging a weight on a chain behind him. It was hard not to squat and lean forward in an obvious posture to pull at the weight dragging him down. Silvana had no trouble. Khadija was straining, but the pressure wasn't improving as they got closer to the barrier.

Jason blinked. It wasn't getting lighter, but it wasn't getting *heavier* either. Khadija was actually holding off the increasing power as they got closer, maintaining the same pressure. *She might actually do this.* Jason didn't say or do anything that might ruin it for her.

The core of the barrier was only ten steps away, where the shimmering air was at its thickest. Khadija's jaw was clenched and veins began to stand out on her face. Jason and Silvana walked slowly, deliberately, matching Khadija's pace. Seven steps. Khadija's face shook with effort. Five steps. Khadija's eyes squinted as if in pain.

At three steps, a gasp escaped her mouth, and a sudden onslaught of weight hit Jason all at once. He nearly groaned out loud. Khadija froze in place. Silvana's eyes darted between them, unsure what to do. A stranger stepped around them and passed through the barrier with ease.

"Khadija?" Jason asked. "You can do this. We're almost there."

"Excuse me?" a woman nearby asked with a German accent. "Are you ok, miss?"

"She wasn't feeling well this morning," Silvana said, then turned to Khadija. "Come on, you can keep going."

"Miss?" the woman repeated, stepping closer.

Khadija's head snapped up. "Three is too many," she hissed in a strained voice. "But, I can do two. Get going!"

Jason felt the pressure shift and tremble slightly. It wasn't much, but he thought he could push through it if he gave it everything he had. He looked at Silvana.

"Go!" Khadija hissed.

"Uh…" the German woman stammered, then shouted, "Security!"

Jason didn't wait. He left Khadija behind, dropped his shoulder and pushed with all the strength he had. The last steps felt like he was dragging a car behind him. Silvana wrapped an arm around his waist and pushed him along with her vampiric strength.

Then, with a sudden jolt, they both staggered through the checkpoint. Jason barely kept himself upright. He forced himself to walk normally as if nothing were wrong, giving a casual glance backwards.

Three guards surrounded Khadija in seconds. "All right! God!" she cried in a nasal, high-pitch voice. "I just wanted to test my power. I wasn't actually doing anything." The guards started to restrain her hands. "Hey, get off me. Do you know who I am? I'm Princess Al-Khalifa. Do you know how much wealth my family has? When my father hears about this…"

The guards led her away as she continued her tirade.

Jason kept his head down. "She plays the part well," he whispered.

"Let's hope it's good enough to keep her out of trouble," Silvana said. "Damn, we can't go back for her without exposing ourselves. We've lost her completely now. How will we get back to England!?"

"Fuck!" Jason hissed. He looked over his shoulder again, but Khadija was already gone. "The chimera might hear about this. What if it finds her?"

"What if it finds *us*?"

Jason swallowed. "Right. She sacrificed herself to get us here. We better make this work."

Chapter 12

Silvana walked on, trying to supress the onslaught of dark thoughts about Khadija's arrest and her unknown fate. Khadija had told them to go through the barrier. It was her choice to make the sacrifice. Their best hope at this point was for Khadija to resolve things with the guards on her own, probably relying on her famous name. Maybe she'd get out on her own before word passed through the Immortal community and the assassin came for her. Silvana clenched her fists. It was up to herself and Jason now to get into the Library.

She had to use her vampiric powers at the third checkpoint, or Khadija's heroism was all for nothing.

Silvana focused on that spark within her. She had felt it with Jason during their lovemaking and she could still sense it now. It was in the blood she had swallowed already, but it was more than that. She knew she could activate that power at will. She just knew it.

The final checkpoint came into view while the previous one was still in sight behind them. It was another barrier stretching across a wide corridor. Yet, unlike the wizard's barrier that was almost invisible apart from the slight shimmer in the air, this one stood out. It appeared to be a physical wall made of some sort of glimmering red, crystalized substance. Silvana almost shuddered. This barrier had been made by empowered vampires more than two thousand years ago at the height of their power. *What was this made of? She thought. Was the crystal wall like those death crystals made from compressed bodies? Was it red because of blood?* She dared not think about it any longer.

"Are you ready, sweetheart?" Jason whispered.

She nodded without speaking. Strangers were walking alongside them, librarians and scholars in black robes and suits, moving as if this was an everyday occurrence. Silvana blocked them from her mind and focused on that inner spark. All she had to do was touch it, and move it outward from her, just like she did against that wall in Edward's house. Just move that power out against the barrier.

Ahead of them, people held up red diamonds that allowed them passage through the crystalline barrier. They stepped through the solid wall without any resistance. *I just need to do that myself.* Silvana walked right up to the barrier and laid a hand on its cold crystal surface, noticing thousands of twisted shards that refracted the light in a kaleidoscope of broken images. Silvana's face reflected back one hundred times – all of them nervous. She took a deep breath and let it out slowly. She felt the power inside her, grasped it, and with a force of will, shifted it outwards.

Power flowed out of her and into the wall, allowing her hand to sink into the barrier. She let out a relieved laugh and stepped forward.

She was forced to stop almost immediately. The barrier only gave way a few centimetres around her hand. The rest of it remained completely solid. Even her hand didn't pass all the way through. She had only made the barest of impacts.

"Damn it," she hissed and tried again. But the power was gone. There was nothing left inside her. Had she… used it all up? It didn't make sense.

"Silvana?" Jason said.

"Hold my hand," she replied. "Pretend we're having sex."

"What?"

"Whatever you think during sex, think it now. I need to try again."

Jason gripped her hand. She tried to summon the power again to push through, but the barrier wouldn't give. She nearly screamed in frustration. She knew what was supposed to happen. She knew how to use that power. But nothing was coming.

"Hey!" someone shouted. Silvana's eyes stung with tears of frustration. Everyone was depending on her. She had been so sure. *Why isn't this working? WHY!?*

Someone placed a hand on her shoulder and spun her around. A guard with a long bushy beard and brown eyes stared at her. "What are you doing here?"

"Something's not working," Jason answered calmly. "We could partially get through, see?" he pointed to Silvana's hand still frozen part way into the barrier.

The guard frowned. "Miss, do you have your diamond? Can I see it?"

Jason looked to her nervously. Silvana's mouth opened and closed, but no words came out.

This is it. It's all over. We'll be imprisoned until the assassin comes for us. I can't find a way through this. Oh, Jason...

"That's all right, sir," a male voice said. "They're with me."

A handsome man with piercing blue eyes appeared beside them. He was dressed in a loose, white shirt and pants embroidered with colour on the sleeves and shoulders. And he was... intensely familiar.

Then, she remembered. The world's tallest building, the dry air on a balcony one hundred stories high. A man demanding her name. An explosion, and a fall...

"Dorin?" she whispered.

"In the flesh," the man said with a charming smile. "I'm so sorry I was late, Silvana. Shall we?" He stepped around her and Jason with the grace of a vampire's movement. Dorin waved a hand to the barrier and started to step through. He smiled back at them all. "Well? What are you waiting for?"

Silvana glanced at Jason, and saw her own uncertainty and fear mirrored back at her. She had only met Dorin once, however briefly, and he had been desperate to know who she really was. They'd searched for him for nearly a year. All they had managed to find was a hint that he was a Royalist, trying to destroy the Imperium and bring back the monarchy so that Immortals could rule the world in the open. They had even come to the Library in the hopes of finding clues that led to him.

And now somehow, he was right here in front of her, holding open the barrier. *Does he have a death diamond? How can it work for all three of us?*

"Hurry up," the guard said. "You're holding up the line."

Dorin smiled gently, as if trying to reassure her. His eyes were… pleading. He had that same desperation from the first time they met. It terrified her. Why was he so eager to talk to her? What did he know about her past? There was only one way to find out.

Suddenly, all her fear fell to the side, replaced by hardened determination. Whatever Dorin knew, she wanted to know too.

"Sorry about that," she said to the guard. Then she took Dorin's hand, held onto Jason, and the three of them passed through the barrier without a hint of resistance.

As soon as they stepped over to the other side, Silvana dropped Dorin's hand and started walking as if nothing had happened. Dorin fell into step beside them. Other people were glancing in their direction, curious at seeing someone take so long to get through the barrier. Silvana walked with her head forward, ignoring the strangers' stares and whispers. Yet, she couldn't help glaring at Dorin from the corner of her eye, and found him smiling back. She refused to look away.

So did he.

"What are you doing here?" she whispered so only he could hear.

"I was going to ask the same thing," he said.

"Not your business."

"Relax, Silvana, I won't tell anyone. I came because one of my informants saw you enter the building. I came as soon as I could. I just want to talk."

She glanced at Jason. He was watching the people around them with a relaxed expression, but she could feel the readiness in his stance. He was a knight protecting his lady. "I think it's that way," Silvana said, nodding to the approaching archway.

"Is he coming with us?" Jason asked in a polite tone, but he eyed Dorin with open distrust.

"Depends. Do you need more protection?" Dorin asked.

"I don't…" Silvana cut off. She had utterly failed at the third checkpoint. Like it or not, she had needed Dorin. She wasn't going to fail the rest of the group simply because of her pride.

"I mean you no harm, Silvana, I swear it," Dorin said, hand over his heart.

"Then who are you?" Silvana hissed.

"Not here." Dorin's eyes scanned the crowds. "But I swear I will tell you everything the first chance I get to do so safely. Please, Silvana. Trust me."

Silvana knew she could never trust him. He had found them so quickly, so easily. It could not be a coincidence. He must have been here already, waiting for them. Which could only mean he knew they would be here.

Because he must have sent the chimera assassin after Leslie.

It was the only explanation. He had ordered the hit, planning for Leslie to go to Jason and Silvana as independent detectives. He knew they would have to start their investigation at the Library of Alexandria. That was how Dorin had been able to get through the third checkpoint. He was prepared. The real question was why? Was it a recruitment tactic for the Royalists? Or something worse?

"Silvana?" Jason asked. They had nearly reached the Library's entrance. Time was running out to make a decision.

She glanced at Dorin once more. Even if this was a trap, it didn't explain everything. And running away now would not call off the assassin. The only way out was to walk even further into the belly of the beast. Besides, like it or not, they were in his debt now.

She could always feign ignorance. Pretend she was going along with whatever Dorin wanted, only to find a way out eventually. She could get him to lower his guard.

"OK," Silvana said. "You can come with us. But keep a low profile."

Dorin bowed his head. "Lead on, mistress."

They reached the archway just as he finished speaking, and Silvana nearly gasped out loud. There was a colossal amphitheatre on the other side.

At first all she could see were giant rows of shelves spread throughout the colossal room. It was too much to take in. Yet the longer she stared, she began noticing the pattern of isles running crisscrossed across the massive space. The far wall looked to be nearly a kilometre away. The shelves were stacked in rows almost ten metres high with ladders on wheels stretching to the top of each one. From where Silvana stood, she could see the contents of those shelves were in an assortment of different formats of books, scrolls, and loose parchment stacks leaning against each other. A sheer wall of fine sawdust, the intoxicating smell of ink, and the strong scent of cleaning products and chemicals used to keep it all preserved overpowered Silvana's hypersensitive nose.

"Don't stare," Dorin whispered. "You'll stand out."

Silvana closed her gaping mouth without a word of thanks.

"Where do we start?" Jason mumbled.

"There's topics listed at the start of every aisle," Dorin said. "Or there's a catalogue section over here. That's a good place to begin."

Silvana was relieved to see the names were written in English. *Makes sense, it's the official language of the Imperium.* She noted several topics. *History of Magic. World Religions. Imperium Law. Royal Houses. The Vampire Wars. Global Economy. Fae History. Ancient Languages. The Physically Enhanced.* She was beginning to feel overwhelmed. "I think the catalogue would make sense," she murmured.

Dorin put a hand on her shoulder and guided her towards a collection of desks tucked to the side of the entrance. Each one held a mighty tome with a chain running through it. People were flicking through similar ones nearby. Dorin lead them to the closest table. "So, what are you looking for?" he asked as he sat before the book.

"That's not your business," Jason said flatly.

"Just give me the topic," Dorin said. "I'll get you to the right section at least."

Jason raised his eyebrows towards Silvana, but she had no idea what to say. Could she warn him of her suspicions about Dorin and the assassin? Or had he already figured it out?

"Good Lord," Dorin said. "You two have no idea what you're looking for. This is a shot in the dark."

"Shut up," she hissed.

"I'm not judging. Just let me help. You must be pretty desperate. At least tell me what you're up against."

Silvana clenched her fists. She wanted to scream *'you know damn well what we're up against!'* But she kept her calm. Instead, she looked up at the ceiling for the first time, and let herself be distracted by the white alabaster stone that made up the structure. Built by vampires, in a time before the Imperium even existed. In a time where powerful vampire lords kept humanity in chains and drank oceans of blood. Were the wizards of the Imperium really that different today? She couldn't bring herself to answer her own question.

"Silvana?" Dorin asked.

Jason shushed him.

"The High Kings," she said. Both men looked at her. "All of them, past and present."

Dorin shrugged and started flicking through the tome. "Uh… ok. The High Kings are all in different aisles. But I can give you the grid numbers."

"Perfect." Silvana took up a pen and notepad that was clearly left on the desk for this reason.

"Present day High Kings are in Grid A, isle 12, section 23. Then Reynold is in his own section, Grid A, aisle 1, section 1." Dorin chuckled. "Pretentious ass, has to be in the first space chronologically. Then King Jin Yu Qing has his own section too. Grid D, isle 9, section 5." Dorin paused while Silvana wrote it all down. "If you want past High Kings, you have to look them up individually. But if you're just looking for a list of names, you could look up Imperium Law. The law changes every time a king is added or removed to the Imperium itself. You could get a list…"

"Tell me," Silvana insisted.

"Grid A, aisle 8, section 19."

"Jesus Christ," Jason sighed. "That's so much to search through. I don't know how we're going to find anything."

Dorin chuckled. "On the contrary, my friend, you're going to find everything. But I suspect the problem will be finding what you actually need. Are you sure you don't want to tell me?"

"Tell us exactly who you are, first," Silvana said.

Dorin paused, as if considering.

"Come on," Jason said. "We don't have a lot of time. We should start searching straight away."

"Wait," Dorin said. "I can't say who I am. Not here. But I can show you, if you're willing." He held out his hand to Silvana. "Taste my blood."

"What?" Jason growled. He slapped Dorin's hand away. "We're not doing that here. And vampires don't produce their own blood. Hence the whole vampire thing!"

"The blood was given to me, so it *is* mine now," Dorin said. He looked back at Silvana. "There is microscopic traces of my unique vampire venom in my blood. Taste it. I swear, you will understand."

"Silvana," Jason whispered. "You know it's against Imperium law to take blood from more than one person." Silvana eyed him. "Ok, I know I've never supported that law, but it's still dangerous to break it."

Dorin whispered, "Please. Just a drop. Here." He put a finger to his mouth as if biting a nail. When he held his finger up, a single red drop glistened on the tip. Silvana stared at it with a strange sense of longing. She'd never tasted a vampire's blood before. *What would happen?* He clearly knew more about his powers than she did. Maybe it truly would explain something. Or maybe… it would give him power over her in some way. Maybe this was the whole purpose of the trap with the assassin and Leslie leading her here, to this moment, all to trick her into consuming his blood.

"Put that away," she hissed. "If you want to help us, then help us find these sections." She held up the paper.

Dorin glared as he wiped his finger on his trousers, a hint of frustration in his expression. "Fine. But I still want to talk to you when we get some privacy. I don't intend to leave you until then."

"Fine," she said and started walking to the library shelves.

She could see the letters at the top of the aisles to indicate Grid A.

She found the first aisle nearby, mostly empty of people, and stopped at the first shelf. She grabbed the first book. *Reynold's family line.* She pulled out her Go-Pro and began to discreetly film the pages in front of her. Jason sat beside her and started flicking through another document. Dorin stood watch nearby, falling into the role of lookout without a word.

Silvana grimaced as she fumbled the camera. She hadn't considered that people might see them trying to film. She had to keep her camera covered up. This was going to slow them down considerably. She flicked through the pages a bit faster and tried to hold the camera at her hip to keep it covered. Her eyes scanned the page. It was a list of names and dates, mostly from the 10th century. There was no point reading it now; it would only slow her down. She just had to get the information on film.

Her camera vibrated. She looked at the screen and saw a red logo flashing at her. A battery, with a hollow inside.

"Jason," she whispered. "I think my battery is low."

"What?" Jason looked at her camera before frantically checking his own. "What the hell?" he groaned. "The battery is nearly empty. Oh my god... I think Freddie forgot to charge them."

Silvana's heart thudded with anxiety. "How long do we have?"

"I don't know. I've never used this thing before." Jason's voice was strained. "It doesn't give a time. It's probably only minutes."

Dorin cleared his throat. "Take pictures instead of filming." Jason and Silvana eyed him. "It will make the battery last longer."

"He's right," Jason said. "We better hurry."

Silvana began touching the screen randomly, trying to change the settings. She found a camera icon and swapped to individual photos, snapping one page at a time. *Damn it, Freddie. You had one job!* She knew it was an easy mistake to make, but in the moment, she let her thoughts run dark with fury.

"Maybe we should split up," Jason said. "I could go look at the other High Kings. Since we're low on time, it would cover more ground."

Silvana glanced at Dorin. "I don't think we should split up."

"Relax," Dorin said, shifting on his feet. "You two stay here. I'll go get some books about the other Kings and bring them back here. You wrote down the grid numbers, yes?" He held out his hand. Silvana hesitated, before she gave him the notes she'd written with the information and he dashed off at inhuman speed. Silvana supressed the urge to growl. *What if he's going off to betray us? Or call his assassin?* But it was their best chance to trust him this time.

"I'm doing two books at once," Jason said. He had two books open side by side, taking one picture of both of them. "Just don't let the picture get blurry."

Silvana started calling on the power in her blood to increase her speed, yet no matter how fast she went, the camera couldn't keep up with her. So many pictures were blurry, forcing her to take them twice. The lens took so long to focus. She nearly crushed the device out of sheer frustration.

"Here you go," Dorin said, laying a stack of books next to them. "Imperium Law. Should have a history of all the High Kings in there somewhere."

"Damn that was fast. Thank you," Jason said reluctantly. He started going through the new books straight away.

"Law was only a few aisles over. I'm going for Jin Yu Qing next, in Grid D. Might take a few extra minutes."

"Thank you," Silvana said.

Dorin's tone had a certain solemnity. "Thank you for not running off without me. It's important that we talk, Silvana." Dorin's blue eyes were full of conviction, before he ran off again.

"You ok?" Jason asked. Silvana only hummed before returning to her photos. "Do you want to have that talk with him?"

"I don't know," Silvana said, swapping to the next book. "But I think I must. He claimed to know about my past. I need to know."

"Your aunts said it could be some sort of scam."

"My aunts were determined to keep me away from him. There's a chance they were hiding something from me."

Jason was quiet for a moment. She caught him glancing at her, his face full of concern.

"I know what you're thinking," she said.

"You do?"

Was that nervousness?

"Dorin hired the assassin to bring us here. He set up this meeting."

"Oh." Jason relaxed. "Yes, I thought that too. Better keep our eyes open."

Silvana focused on flicking through pages, but her eye snagged on something and she leaned forward. She read, "Reynold's mortal brother William was tasked with ensuring the continuation of the wizard line. His wife Matilda had ten children, though many other illegitimate children were denied rights to the house and teachings of the House of Normandy."

Her mind latched onto the idea—*Wizards cannot sire children, just like vampires, but their mortal relatives continue the line.* Silvana knew she had to keep photographing the books, but her intuition held her there. She couldn't let go of this line of thought. Then it all came to her in a rush. *William the Conqueror was the King of England. Everyone knows the current royal family are his descendants. And Uncle Nicholas is their cousin. So... am I related to High King Reynold?*

The thought made her queasy. She hoped to never see Reynold again, or even hear of him. The thought of a real connection was sickening, even if it was only through her adoption. She shook her head. It probably didn't matter that much. The Immortal Houses were constantly giving children away in marriage. There were relations everywhere. What was one more connection, in the sea of complex family trees? It was probably nothing.

"Delivery," Dorin said with a chuckle and loaded another pile of books onto a nearby table. "Jin Yu Qing, High King of China and most of Asia." The stack of books was huge. Dorin patted the top of the pile. "That guy has been busy." He looked at Silvana. "Anything else you want?"

"Shit," Jason growled. "My camera screen just dimmed. I've probably only got seconds left."

"Here." Dorin began to set out some of the new books for him.

"Cheers," Jason said as he started taking photos.

Silvana checked her screen. It hadn't changed yet, but it wouldn't be long until it did. She stayed on the book about William the Conqueror's family tree and kept taking photos until she had gone through every last page.

"Damn it," Jason growled. "There it goes. Battery's dead."

"Sorry, my friend," Dorin replied. "Silvana, your friend here has already photographed this pile, ok?" He started stacking some books to the side.

"I'll just read some manually," Jason said. "You keep going, Silvy."

Her camera lasted another ten minutes. The boys were quiet to avoid distracting her, and she used her vampiric speed at a slow burn to get through the Reynolds section and about half way through the books on law. Finally, the camera flashed low, and died a minute later.

"I'm out too."

Jason sighed. "Remind me to go easy on Freddie about this. I have a feeling Khadija will give him enough shit for all of us."

"Khadija?" Dorin asked. "As in Khadija Al Khalifa?"

"No, a different Khadija."

"We were at the same party," Dorin chuckled. "The Burj Khalifa. I can put it together pretty easily, my friend." Jason grumbled, causing Dorin to smirk. "I didn't think you had many connections. Al Khalifa is pretty impressive."

Silvana spoke before Jason lost his temper. "I suppose we should just try to read as much as we can. We've only been here about twenty minutes. We planned to stay for two hours. Want to read for the remainder of the time?"

Jason nodded.

"Two hours?" Dorin cried. He looked around to check no one else was within earshot, then leaned forward to whisper. "I can't stay that long. I'll need to go soon. Silvana, can I please just talk to you in private?"

"We've gone through a lot to get here," Silvana said. "I'm not giving this time up."

"Look, I have to keep moving. Someone's hunting me. If I stay in one place too long, they'll find me."

"Well, someone's hunting me too. I can't afford to hurry."

"Oh really? Is your hunter a Vigile?"

Silvana blinked. "The Vigiles are after you?"

"Yeah, two women. Older lady with dark skin and long braided hair. The other white with…"

"Red curly hair," Jason finished. "Desdemona and Portia. They're dangerous enemies. I wouldn't mess with them if I were you."

"I'm not trying to!" Dorin cried, exasperated. He looked back at Silvana. "Who's after you? Maybe I can help."

Silvana decided to test his reaction. "A chimera assassin."

Dorin's eyes widened. *"Dracu pula!"* It sounded like a curse. "Maybe your enemy is worse than mine. But I can help you. I could take on a chimera for you."

I bet you can, you lying fuck.

"We don't need your help," Silvana said. "We already have allies."

"Oh, allies with magic? Cause let me tell you, Silvana, magic will do nothing against a chimera. You need a physically enhanced fighter."

Silvana remembered how Leslie's spell had bounced off the chimera. *Another thing Dorin planned for, perhaps.*

She asked, "Why are the Vigiles after you?"

Dorin sighed. "Please. Just come with me. I have a safe location in this city. We can speak freely there. I promise I'll tell you everything. But if I say it here, it could get us all killed."

"How convenient," Jason said. Then he blinked. "Not the getting killed part. You know, the part where you lure us into a dark alley because you have a special secret."

Dorin groaned. "How can I make you trust me?"

"I don't think you can," Jason said. "But perhaps you should just send me a friend request on facebook?"

"You know I'm trying to avoid Imperium detection, right? So how is an online message any better?" He turned to Silvana again. "It's now or never, Silvana. I can tell you about your past. About your powers. About why you weren't able to get through that checkpoint with your abilities."

Jason huffed loudly. "We have to keep reading. There's so much we haven't touched on yet. The royal houses, for one. Silvana, we have to stay."

"And keep clutching at straws?" Dorin asked. "I don't know how reading these books is going to help you fight off the assassin. But if you come with me, I can keep you safe. Please, I'll swear any vow you want. Any promise you need to hear. On my life itself. Please, Silvana."

Silvana stared at him without speaking. There was something in the back of her mind screaming at her. Something that wanted to lash out violently at this vampire. But that wasn't all. There was some part of her that wanted to… hug him? Cling to him? Never leave his side again. They were just vague images flicking through her mind, no real conscious thought behind them. Just emotions. But strong emotions.

"I'll go with you," she said.

"What?" Jason cried, and Dorin's face lifted into a massive grin.

"I'm sorry, Jason. You can stay here and read if you want. But I need to speak to Dorin. I would prefer if you came with me."

"Silvy," Jason hesitated. "I don't think you're making the right decision. I hate to say it, but I'm not sure you're in the right frame of mind for it."

"This isn't an emotional decision, Jason."

"I don't think it's emotional." He stammered again. "Look, I should have spoken about this earlier. I'm sorry. But sometimes you act... a little strange."

"Is that a bird?" Dorin asked.

"I... what?" Silvana cried.

"A bird," Dorin said, pointing upwards. She followed his gaze.

A tiny pigeon was perched on the top of the shelf above them. It ruffled the grey feathers on its wings before cocking its head to one side, revealing a blue tinge around the neck. Its black beady eyes were focused on them.

"Oh shit," Jason groaned.

The chimera launched at them.

Chapter 13

The figure dropped towards them, morphing into a massive shape mid-fall. For one millisecond, Jason considered shielding Silvana with his body. *No. She's stronger than me.* Instead, he dived out of the way of the attack.

The action saved his life.

A fully grown African elephant landed on the ground, cracking the stone floor with its immense weight where Jason had just been standing.

Patrons were screaming at the sudden barrage of noise and destruction around them. Jason looked up at the elephant's black eyes. The creature lunged at him. He scrambled backwards, but not fast enough. Its trunk seized him by the ankle and yanked him forward. Jason screamed as he landed underneath the elephant's chest. It raised up a massive foot to crush him, but just as it came down, a figure caught the foot. It took Jason a moment to realise who the figure was.

Dorin?

The male vampire hugged the elephant foot to his chest. He roared as he jerked his body and let the foot drop beside him. The creature stumbled. Dorin grabbed the elephant by the tusk and yanked it down so it collapsed onto its knees.

"Jason!" Silvana appeared at his side and helped him stand. Jason's knees shook. *I'm going into shock. That's dangerous. Focus up.*

"Let's get out of here," he cried.

Dorin went flying into the shelves with enough force to shake them in their racks. The elephant stood on all fours, faced Jason and Silvana, and brayed. The sound echoed loudly through the Library halls. Jason knew what an elephant sounded like, but he never realised how much noise such a large creature could make in an enclosed space. His ears were ringing painfully. The assassin was blocking the aisle exit, preventing their escape.

"Run!" Silvana yelled and nearly yanking Jason nearly off his feet.

They ran down the aisle, past Dorin's prone body. If Silvana was conflicted about leaving him there, she showed no sign. *He can probably handle himself.* A second later, the thudding footsteps of the elephant came from behind them.

Terrified voices shouted from beyond various aisles nearby. Jason focused on sprinting to the far end. He could hear the elephant smashing shelves apart as it gave chase down the narrow pathway. The sound of destruction seemed to only be getting closer, no matter how fast they ran. Jason didn't risk glancing over his shoulder as he ran.

The corner finally came into reach, and Silvana got there first. She snatched the corner shelf in one hand and Jason in the other, then spun him around hard enough to make his neck feel like it was going to detach from his spine. Not a half second later, the assassin barrelled past them like a freight train. It had too much momentum to stop. One of its limbs morphed into a gorilla arm and tried to snatch at them, but its hand fell short. The creature smashed into the next rack of shelves, turning priceless books into debris.

"Come on!" Silvana pulled him again, and Jason wondered once more how useful Mortal Knights were supposed to be.

A small crowd of Immortal folk were running back towards the Library entrance, their faces twisted in abject terror. *They can't do violent magic cause of the spell on this place, so they can't fight back. They must be terrified.* Jason couldn't stop the grin spreading on his face. *Now they might know how it feels to be mortal.*

A wild shriek filled the amphitheatre as a big cat on four legs hurtled towards them. Jason looked back for only a second, but he could already see it gaining on them.

Fuck!

"Dorin?" Silvana called out, looking around the amphitheatre. "Dorin!"

Why is she calling for him? A second later, he understood. They were moving towards the blood and diamond wall of the third checkpoint. Dozens of staff were racing through ahead of them with their dark red diamonds held forward to grant them access to the other side.

Leslie had said they could just walk out, but clearly that wasn't exactly true. If the locals were holding up their diamonds, it meant they needed the blood diamonds to get back through again. Leslie may not have even realised it. They must have just walked out every day and assumed it was easy going out. Or, they assume Silvana could do the same vampire trick twice. Either way, it didn't matter now. It was unlikely they could slip through in someone else's wake. They needed Dorin's help again, or they would never escape.

Jason checked over his shoulder. The four-legged assassin was already too close, and the checkpoint was too far away. The assassin would reach them again before they got there, even without Dorin.

"Get behind me, Jason," Silvana said and spun around, shielding him with her body.

He saw the creature coming in the form of a leopard. He looked around for some sort of weapon. He found nothing.

The leopard didn't leap. It ran straight for Silvana. Its teeth gnashing towards her legs, avoiding her teeth and fists. She reacted too late. Its claws wrapped around her ankles and she fell. It sank its teeth into her heels. Silvana screamed, the high pitch sound echoing through the chamber.

"No!" Jason growled, kicking at the leopard. His heel struck its forehead, but it didn't move. It kept biting down on Silvana's calf. Jason stomped over and over with the heel of his foot, trying to break its grip or cave in its skull, if that were even humanly possible. Silvana curled up and punched the thing in the jaw. Jason heard a loud crack. Silvana had clearly broken something.

The creature howled and shifted suddenly. Its back half turned into a massive anaconda's tail and struck Jason in his middle, knocking all the air out of him and sending him flying. He hit the ground and doubled over, unable to voice his pain out loud. The assassin was now holding Silvana down with its tail, blood pooling under its jaws and pouring out of her ankles. Her hands were pounding down on the snake's flesh, but to no effect.

A crack rang out and the creature was lifted off the ground and thrown a dozen metres away.

Jason gasped. *Her vampire power! It finally activated!* He raced forward and grabbed Silvana, lifting her up. "Silvy, you ok?"

"Oh, yeah. I'm just terrific."

Silvana tried to stand, but hissed in pain when she put weight on her feet. Blood was still running down her heels and smearing over her foot. She'd lost her sandals somewhere during the run. "Jason, I..." she stuttered.

"I know," he said as he reached under her thighs and lifted her off the ground. He took off at a run. "You were amazing! You really showed that thing."

They were one of the last people to reach the checkpoint. "Here, do what you did to the assassin!" he insisted.

"Jason… that wasn't me."

He blinked at her, uncomprehending. She nodded and winced. "Then what the hell?" Jason muttered between puffs of air. He looked up at the massive, impenetrable wall looming over him. "Oh shit, now what?"

He looked back at the assassin, its teeth red with Silvana's blood and growling like a beast as it struggled to its feet. Out of the aisle came Dorin, walking casually towards them, unconcerned of the monster nearby.

"Thanks for waiting," he drawled. "I suppose you want my help again?"

"If it's not too much to ask," Jason barked back.

"Well it kinda is. Do you know how rare my help is?"

"Yes, yes, now shut it and help already."

Dorin actually grinned at Jason as he strut past him. He held his hands up to the diamond wall, but they didn't pass through. "Hmm…" Dorin mumbled. "It's different on this side."

"What?" Jason cried.

"Relax. It's not a problem for me." Dorin pressed his hands against the blood red wall and the crystalline shards started folding back like paper origami, creating a passage way. It sounded like someone walking over gravel.

A low growl made Jason look back. The assassin had now taken on a lion's form and was barrelling towards them at full speed.

"Jesus, fucking hurry!" Jason yelled.

Dorin kept pushing and the diamond barrier shifted, before completely moving apart and creating a gap big enough for a person to pass through.

Two women – wearing black suits and satisfied smiles – waited on the other side. Desdemona and Portia.

"Oh crap," Jason cried.

He spun around as the lion sprinted at them. Jason clutched Silvana closer to his chest and backed up against Dorin until they stood all pressed together.

"Dorin, move!" Jason roared. But the vampire wouldn't take a single step towards the Vigiles. They were trapped. Silvana gripped his arms tightly.

At the last second, the lion slowed its approach. It stopped two metres from where Jason stood. This close, he could see the individual strands of fur on the big cat's face, and the blood that stained its canines red. It bared its teeth at Jason with an ominous deep growl, and he couldn't help picturing those massive teeth piercing his flesh.

He glanced over his shoulder. Dorin had frozen in the middle of the diamond wall, glaring at the Vigiles with cold fury. Beyond, Desdemona stood like an iron statue, her long individually braided strands of hair hanging motionless to her waist. Her lips were pressed together in a smile. Portia's burning red hair clashed with her cold black suit, her eyes glinting equal parts fire and ice.

"Well, what a fortuitous coincidence this be," Desdemona said. "My partner and I were just in the mood for a good book. And look who we should'st stumble into, but thee. I must say, thou lookest equally surprised."

"I hope we're not interrupting," Portia said with a sweet, childish tone.

"Let us be," Dorin snapped. "We didn't come here looking for trouble."

"And neither didst we. Yet here thou stands, as the fates hath provided."

"Honoured Vigile," Jason said, searching for the formal language required. "My charge and I are but passers-by in this situation. We are fleeing a chimera assassin who stands before us." Jason gestured to the creature looming behind them. "My lady has been wounded and can no longer walk. Please, by your grace, let us pass to safety so I can find her medical attention."

"I see no reason why we should'st grant thy boon, oh knight. Thou art consorting with a known enemy of the Imperium. And unless my guess is mistaken, thou art no librarian."

"Naughty, naughty," Portia cooed. "A police officer breaking and entering? Surely, you of all people should know better."

Jason clenched his jaw, and said nothing. The lion began to prowl slowly, stepping to one side before turning and circling to the other. The creature was clearly smiling. Jason glared back. He finally noticed something. The fur was slightly crooked, and the face wasn't symmetrical. A scar was just visible on the side of the lion's face. *Ah, Freddie's acid has left a mark.* These Immortals were not invincible, nor all powerful. They were vulnerable even to mortals. Jason felt his resolve return. There was still a chance.

"Then I wish to surrender," Jason said. "Take Silvana and I into custody, and we will come quietly. If that will spare us from the assassin."

"No!" Dorin hissed. "You fool. I must speak with Silvana. We will never get the chance if the Vigiles take you."

"Thou art correct, vampire," Desdemona said. "We are not in the habit of allowing known conspirators to share… social visits."

"I don't care," Jason growled, turning to face Dorin, knowingly exposing his back to the assassin. "What good will it be if we don't escape alive? Get out of my way, Dorin."

"Don't you get it?" Dorin snapped. "They're powerless out there. That's why the Vigiles haven't attacked already. The anti-violence spell of the Library prevents them. They're trying to lure you out so they'll be able to affect you again."

Jason hadn't considered that, and chided himself for not paying attention. "That doesn't matter. I have to get Silvana out."

"I cannot let you," Dorin hissed. "I've waited too long to miss my chance now."

"Why?!" Jason hissed back. "Tell me what's so important?"

Dorin simply pointed at Silvana. "She is."

What?

Silvana clutched at Jason's arm. "Let me down. I think I can walk now."

Jason lowered her, and she placed weight on her feet without issue. Her wounds had healed enough to function again. She looked ready to run, or fight, as needed. The lion prowled in wait. Was it slowly moving closer?

"Enough," Desdemona called. "Ye three will step through the checkpoint and surrender thyselves, lest I permit yonder beast to have its way with thy flesh. I doubt the beast will give thou so generous an offer."

The lion growled in response, yet for whatever reason, it seemed content to wait. It must have been unwilling to challenge the Vigiles for their prize.

"We cannot surrender," Dorin said.

"Dorin," Silvana growled in warning. "It's our only option."

"No! Fight alongside me! Together, we can overcome them all."

"You're mad," Jason said.

Dorin grinned. "No, I'm merely aware of my own strength. Haven't you figured out what I am yet?"

Jason frowned at him. "You're a vampire."

Silvana shook her head. "He's not just a vampire. He's an *empowered* vampire."

Dorin nodded in confirmation.

Jason's mouth fell open. No, it was impossible. He'd *seen* an empowered vampire twice before. Both times they glowed with a red aura. They floated in mid-air and moved objects with their mind. There was no…

Then he understood. Dorin had thrown the assassin off Silvana before, using telekinesis. He had opened the checkpoint that could only be opened by the blood diamonds of empowered vampires. He didn't need a diamond because he was the real thing. And the Vigiles would be chasing him for no other reason than the Imperium had outlawed the heightened vampire state because of the threat to wizard dominance. It was the whole reason for the laws surrounding vampire marriage. Perhaps Dorin had enough control over his powers so they weren't visible? He must have incredible control to be walking around with it all hidden away.

But Jason knew Dorin was a Royalist, and he had seen Royalists seeking the old vampire ways before. They had gained their power through murder, bloody and brutal. If Dorin was truly empowered, then who knows how many innocents he had killed to come this far. This only made Dorin more dangerous than ever.

"How many people have you killed?" Jason growled.

Dorin glared back at him, and for an instant, his eyes flashed red. "As many as were needed."

A chill ran down Jason's spine. *Oh my god. It's just as I feared.*

"Now, you two will fight alongside me," Dorin said, his voice full of command. "I've come too far to let this opportunity escape. Together, we can take all of these enemies…"

Silvana launched herself at Dorin in a sudden burst of speed, striking him hard.

She was so fast, Jason barely saw what happened. Silvana was so fast. In half a second Dorin was on his knees with an arm twisted behind his back. Silvana spun around him, placed her foot on his back, and kicked him towards the lion. The creature launched forward the second Silvana moved, and it caught Dorin between its paws.

Jason didn't have time to see what happened next. Silvana grabbed his arm and *yanked* him hard enough to nearly dislocate his shoulder. They slipped through the diamond wall as the gap snapped shut behind them.

They stood before the two smiling Vigiles as a lion roared behind them, and Dorin began to scream. The sound was so terrible, Jason found his heart pounding in blind panic. *It's the traumatic stress. I'll go into shock if I'm not careful.* Somehow, he forced his mind to disconnect from the awfulness occurring behind him.

"We surrender," Silvana said, holding up her hands. Jason mimicked her as the screaming continued behind them.

Desdemona merely squinted her eyes. "Thou expects us to be grateful, after thou denies us the prize we seek?" She stepped forward, holding her palms pointed up in front of her. Jason saw the air above her hands shimmering with heat, yet no flame was visible. *It's hotter than blue flame. Oh my god.* Desdemona shook her head. "I am afraid that thou art a poor substitute."

"But, the anti-violence spell?" Silvana cried.

"Vigile privilege," Desdemona sneered.

Silvana growled, "You traitorous bitch," as she crouched low, ready to strike.

Jason glanced at Portia, his eyes clearly pleading for help from his old ally. Portia only shrugged, as if to apologize.

"Fucking wizards," Jason spat.

The screeching sound of metal being ripping apart made Jason cover his ears.

The wall of diamonds had been shredded open with such force that shards broke away from the main structure. Dorin appeared in the gap, floating in the air. He was covered in blood and glowing with an aura of red much larger than any Jason had ever seen. His face and neck bore multiple thick gashes of torn flesh. And Jason could see the slightest white of his bones through the wounds. Yet, he still emanated raw power.

"Well, how fortunate," Desdemona purred. "It seems thou art a persistent—"

A crack ran out and Desdemona was thrown across the hallway with enough force to *bounce* off the opposite wall.

Chapter 14

"Mistress!" Portia screamed.

Jason's jaw hung slack. Dorin had just swatted Desdemona aside. "Fucking…" he started.

Then everything happened all at once. Dorin rushed at Silvana, pushing her head and shoulder apart, then bit down on her neck. Silvana screamed.

"No!" Jason roared.

Portia let out a shriek of rage, just as Dorin was smashed backwards by a blast of power from the wizard. Silvana fell away, clutching at the bite on her neck while a trickle of blood ran between her fingers. Jason gripped her shoulders and cried her name. She waved him off. The bite was not severe. Jason was ready to murder Dorin, empowered or not.

But Dorin no longer paid them any attention. He stared intently at Portia. The wizard gripped her hands into tight fists at her side and simply stared back at Dorin. A shockwave ran out from the air between them, sending cracks into the walls and dust clouds racing in all directions. Their faces were strained. Jaws clenched and eyes wide, though nothing visible moved around them.

They must be in a magic duel. I have to get Silvana out of here.

Jason grabbed Silvana, who seemed to be staring at Dorin in

fascination. "Come on, Silvy! We've got to run!"

Silvana couldn't turn her eyes away from Dorin. Jason yanked her arm and startled her out of her daze. All of a sudden, she sprinted with vampire speed, pulling Jason down the hall with her.

A cloud of darkness rose up from the ground with black tendrils seeping through every crack of stone. Desdemona floated in the centre, her lips pulled back in a snarl with her dreadlocks and open jacket billowing behind her. She was drawing the black cloud into a tight ball of darkness between her hands. She shrieked and thrust out her hands.

"Down!" Silvana tackled Jason to the ground. The roar of power flew over their heads. Jason glanced back and saw the ball of darkness slow before Dorin's outstretched hand. His eyes flared red as he strained to hold it back. Portia flicked her wrist, and the stones ripped out of the wall, launching at him.

And out of the Library came a full grown lion, dashing through the carnage, heading straight for Jason and Silvana.

"Fuck! Assassin!" Jason roared.

Silvana hurled Jason back up onto his feet. They could hear the deep thudding of an animals' feet pounding behind them as they ran, explosions of magic echoing through the tiny space.

Something struck Jason in the back with a burst of pain. *It's on me!* Yet he wasn't knocked over. Shards of stone scattered on the ground from behind. *It was just stones from the wall.* Silvana grabbed his hand to keep him from falling and he regained his balance. He glanced over his shoulder. The lion had slowed down and crouched low. Why was it—

Jason looked up to see Desdemona flying over them, her eyes black with rage, racing towards the fight. *Thank god she's not coming for me.* A wave of power ran out of her like a shockwave, striking at Dorin and sending dust clouds throughout the building.

"Come on!" Silvana yanked him forward. Jason ran, but they had paused too long. The lion had caught up and growled from right beside them. It was running, its jaws snapping at Jason's heels.

With vampiric speed, Silvana side-stepped around Jason and caught the lion by the mane, dragging its head down. Its face hit the ground with the thud. It's paw lashed out towards Silvana, swiping at her legs.

The wall burst in front of them, and Jason had to duck for cover. Portia had been thrown at the wall, but the force of her magic had cushioned her landing, leaving a crater in the solid rock behind her. She dusted the front of her jacket, flicked her long red hair over a shoulder and floated back towards the sounds of the explosions.

"Run, Jason!"

Silvana was wrestling with a fully grown lion, using every last piece of her vampiric strength, and somehow, she managed to hold it in place. She had her legs wrapped around its neck, holding a single paw in both hands.

"RUN!" she screamed at Jason again as he stood motionless wondering if he should help.

The lion changed shape and the motion threw Silvana backwards. In its place, a hulking grizzly bear reared up on hind legs.

A loud bang came from the direction of the magical battle and Dorin was thrown into the wall opposite Jason, crashing into stone and breaking off shards just like Portia had moments before. Jason ignored them, instead searching frantically for Silvana. The bear turned to face Jason and its eyes settled on him. Suddenly, the wizard Portia was next to him, firing lightning out of her hand. Jason thought she was saving him. But her magic bypassed the assassin, flying at Dorin.

I am an ant next to these giants.

The vampire raised a hand, and seemed to *absorb* the lightning into himself. Dorin saw the bear standing over Jason and thrust out a hand, throwing the lightning into the creature and knocking it aside.

What the hell? He just saved me? After he bit Silvana?

Jason didn't have time to consider Dorin's motives here. Silvana was lying on the other side of the hall. Jason ran to her.

"Burn, thou bastard!" Desdemona shrieked, and suddenly the entire hallway seemed to turn into an oven as the air shimmered with heat. Jason pulled Silvana up, and seconds later they were running again. Light flashed briefly against the walls as someone screamed.

"Keep running! Almost there!" Jason cried. He could see the faint outline of magic emanating from the second barrier. If they could just get through…

A bird flew overhead, morphing in mid-air as it dropped before them, standing once more as a grizzly bear on hind legs.

Silvana roared and crash-tackled it around the middle. The bear fell backward, swiping and gnawing at Silvana with tooth and claw. "No!" Jason screamed. He needed a weapon. Then, he saw a large clump of stone. He grabbed it with two hands, straining to lift it over his head. He took two steps forward and brought the stone down on the bear's head. It cracked against the bear's skull, splitting the stone in two. The creature seemed to immediately slow down. Silvana leapt out of its arms, blood running down her forearms.

"I told you to run!" she screamed.

"I heard you," he growled as he took her hand and they started running again.

Even though they were moving at top speed, Dorin sprinted past them. The flames on his clothes leaving a smoky trail behind him.

But if he's here...

Jason tackled Silvana to the ground, just as a wall of flame filled the hallway. He shielded her with his body as an intense heat scorched his arms and the back of his neck. The fire roared around them like a howling wind, but it did little to drown out Jason's painful screams.

"NO!" a voice rang out, and the flame disappeared as suddenly as it came. Jason looked up. The hallways were flickering with the orange light of a blazing fire. Where was it coming from? He saw Dorin, drawing all the flame *into* himself, and wielding it from within his chest. The flames circled around him in spinning torrents of amber and red.

The roar of the bear made Jason spin around. The assassin was shifting between multiple forms and screeching as all of its fur burned. It looked like a creature from hell. The shifting seemed to put the fires out. It turned to face Jason, and its bloodied chimera face and burning skin was still not as menacing as the expression of hate.

"Thou art no match for the Vigiles," Desdemona cried as both of them floated towards Jason and Silvana. He watched the assassin shift forms again, then emerged as a huge rhinoceros. It shook its head and clopped its hooves, ready to charge.

Dorin shouted, "You're right. It is no match." He glanced towards Jason and Silvana, gave them a wink, then Jason felt himself being thrown aside by an invisible force. He landed on top of Silvana in a crumpled heap by the corner.

The empowered vampire roared as all the flames he held in his core suddenly burst free, racing towards the two wizards. They didn't even flinch as the power split in two and perfectly parted around them. Yet somehow, Dorin lashed out with a separate act of magic and struck the rhino just as it started to charge, causing it to trip and crash to the ground.

"He's protecting us," Silvana cried.

A counter force of power came from the wizards and rushed into the flames. Shards of ice exploded across the room. The icicles gave a deafening hiss as they turned to white, hot steam. The room was enveloped in a pale cloud as the air turned into a steaming sauna at nearly burning temperature.

Jason felt his eyes begin to water from the sheer force of heat permeating the hall. The humidity in the air was so thick, he struggled to breath. It felt like something was caught in his airway.

A person burst out of the mist. Silvana screamed. It was Dorin – his back to them – as two flashes of light flew overhead. Another ball of darkness shot from Desdemona's hands and rushed towards him. Using his superspeed, Dorin dropped and managed to dodge underneath the Vigiles magic. A second dark attack came, and this time, Dorin sprinted up side of the wall to jump and flip like a martial artist. He dived into the steam cloud once more.

"Come on." Silvana dragged Jason to his feet.

They passed through the second barrier to the Library of Alexandria as the sounds of explosions rang out behind them. Silvana looked back over her shoulder as she ran, but Jason focused on the exit. The elevators were just ahead.

Silvana reached them first and frantically pressed the up button. Jason looked back towards the wizard brawl. The huge steam cloud still covered most of the hall, but flashes of red flame and white shards of lightning still shot through the mist. They had been lucky to get through alive.

How the hell was Dorin keeping up with the two of those Vigiles? That shouldn't be possible. Everything he knew about magic – as little as that was – still said that Desdemona should be untouchable to all except a High King. So how was one vampire standing up to her *and* her ally? How...

"Khadija!" Silvana cried. Jason couldn't believe he had forgotten. "They took her into one of these side doors. Do you think we should—"

A figure burst through the mist. The rhinoceros was charging straight towards them.

"Shit!" Jason cried. He started smashing the elevator button, as if that would summon it quicker. The rhino covered the distance *fast*. It was going to reach them well before…

Ding. The doors opened. Silvana pulled him inside and started banging the close door button. The rhino let out a loud bellow as its hooves thundered like explosives being set off. There was no way to stop such a massive creature with that much built up speed. The doors started closing, but Jason knew the flimsy steel wouldn't make a difference. He grabbed Silvana and huddled in the corner. She wrapped her arms around him and shielded him with her body. The doors closed in the rhino's face.

The impact never came. The elevator moved, and in the sudden quiet the only sound was the rapid rise and fall of Jason's chest. Silvana stood at the ready.

"That was strange," Jason said. "Do you think it's—"

Something burst through the floor. Metal howled as it was ripped apart. Jason cried out and leapt back as his eyes struggled to make sense of what he was seeing.

It was… a gorilla's fist on the end of a giant tentacle.

"What the fuck is that?" he screamed. The arm disappeared back down the newly created hole.

Silvana screamed, "It's coming again! Watch—"

A second blow smashed the floor opened even further. Now Jason had to clutch the railing to keep from falling into the darkness below. More tentacles reached into the cabin, latching onto the floor and pulling the bulk of its mass upwards. Silvana roared and began punching and kicking at the tentacles to make them lose their grip, but thick suction cups held it firmly in place.

A flailing limb lashed out at Silvana, catching her around the middle. She pounded on the appendage with her fists but couldn't break free. The assassin lifted her off the ground.

"No!" Jason screamed and grabbed Silvana around the middle to weigh her down. She snatched the tip of the tentacle and unwound it from her core. More limbs reached up. Jason saw the mass of a giant squid underneath them, its maw gaping at them like a hungry kraken.

Silvana broke free and they both dropped onto what was left of the floor. A second later, another giant fist smashed through and Jason went flying back. He found himself on the corner of the elevator with less than a foot of space beneath him. Silvana was on the opposite side of the carriage. Jason felt horribly exposed on his own. If it grabbed him…

A half dozen limbs shot out, and they all converged on Silvana. She screamed as some pushed her down and others slammed into her again and again, the deep sounds of heavy thuds filling the room. Jason didn't hesitate. He jumped *off* the elevator, through the gap in the floor, and landed on the creatures face. He screamed as he stomped down on its eye. The creature made a strained noise before dropping away into the darkness. Jason lurched and fell. He reached for something to grab hold of.

A hand snatched at his wrist, and Silvana groaned with effort as she pulled him back into the elevator.

The assassin dropped into the darkness below.

The doors suddenly opened with a pleasant ding.

Jason panted heavily. A cut streamed from Silvana's forehead and she clutched her side in pain. Her eyes were squeezed shut as she winced, but she remained alert.

"Come on," he said and helped her off the elevator.

The last of the crowds were still fleeing the Library. A perimeter of guards stood at the first checkpoint, rushing people through. Jason hobbled towards them with an injured Silvana leaning on his arms.

The guards waved him through without a second glance, allowing them to slip in amongst the crowd of people moving towards the exit.

The elevators dinged again, and Jason glanced back. He saw a single humanoid figure stepping off the same elevator. They were dressed in tight leather clothes that clung to a lean, muscular form. Their head was shaved bald, and their face covered in bruises. It was the assassin, in human form. Jason turned around before they saw him looking at them.

Outside, the sun was scorching hot. Locals still walked the dusty streets, unaware of the panic felt by the Immortal community in their midst. Jason stepped down the pathway and followed the road away from the Library of Alexandria.

"We have to blend in," he whispered. He pulled his cowl over his head again, then realised it had been severely burnt in multiple places. Silvana struggled to stand and cover her face once more. "Let's lose the robes." He pulled his off entirely, revealing his combat trousers and a plain black t-shirt underneath, already soaked in sweat. His sandals had fallen off long ago. Silvana struggled to disrobe, so he helped her pull the gown over her head. She had tight exercise gear underneath and a loose shirt.

"Should we run?" she asked.

"It'll look too suspicious. Just move slow and steady."

They walked in silence, keeping their heads down. The hustling of a mortal city felt surreal, after fighting a shapeshifting monster and witnessing wizards and an empowered vampire throwing magic around with reckless abandon. Jason wanted to check his surroundings every two seconds, but knew it would only make him seem nervous. He had to keep moving. They passed a public bin and disposed of their robes.

"Jesus…" Silvana groaned. "Khadija brought us here. How the hell are we going to get home now?"

Jason felt like the ground was tilting out from under him. He was exhausted. All he wanted was to be back in his own bed, in his own house, but they couldn't go there with the assassin on their tail. "We can't fly home," he muttered. "The assassin will be able to track our names. We can't get into England without our identities being noted. And I don't want a shapeshifter to show up on the same airplane as us. Can you imagine that *thing* in a tin box above the ground? He'd crash the whole plane just to take us out."

"Jason, you're rambling."

"Right." He shook his head. He was coming down off an adrenaline high. He was probably going into shock. "Do you have some way to contact Freddie?"

"I don't know his number. I think he has Facebook? We could borrow someone's phone and try to reach him there."

"It's risky to go online." Jason sighed and tried to stay calm. "All right. Let's go back to the mosque we arrived in and wait a little while. Khadija might find her own way to us."

"And if she doesn't?"

Jason shrugged. "Then we'll have to find her."

Chapter 15

Silvana felt like every eye was watching her. She knelt on a prayer mat like every other woman in the mosque. No one could critique her performance, since her posture during prayer time was perfect. Yet she still felt like an imposter. She wasn't Muslim. She felt certain she was going to offend someone by being there, even though she had already seen several other Caucasian women, and everyone had been welcoming so far. Still, she pulled her makeshift headpiece a bit tighter just in case someone tried to talk to her afterwards.

All she wanted was to be at home. Strangely, for the first time in her life, home didn't mean the family mansion in Plymouth, or her fancy bedroom with the four-poster bed and attached ensuite with its hundred year old décor. Home had become the simple, modern house she rented with Jason and Freddie. That was all she wanted right now. To cuddle on that couch, away from monsters and wizards and creepy vampires who wouldn't leave her alone.

Who is Dorin? Why does he feel familiar?

Maybe she should have tasted his blood. Maybe that would have meant something to vampires. After all, he was powerful enough to match Desdemona and Portia. He knew far more about vampire magic and abilities than she did. But then, why did he bite her? The wound had healed, yet she could still feel the itch of the bite marks on the nape of her neck.

The call to prayer ended, and the other women started to rise and move out of the mosque once again. A few of them bumped into her as they moved toward the door. Silvana kept her head bowed and eyes averted, allowing the crowd to manoeuvre her outside. She waited to the side and watched as the men came out of a separate entrance. She could track Jason by his scent and knew he wasn't far. He was one of the first out. They made eye contact, but stayed apart as the majority of worshippers passed. Once the crowd had dispersed, Jason appeared at her side, brushing her shoulder gently in reassurance.

"It's getting dark," she whispered. "I'm not sure how much longer we should wait for Khadija."

"Honestly, sweetheart," he grumbled. "I think we would have to wait here for days."

She sighed. "I was afraid you'd say that."

He sighed too. "You know what I can't stop wondering? How the fuck did that assassin find us?" The crowd had moved all the way past them, so Jason allowed more of his frustration to show. "We were on a different continent, in one of the most secure buildings in the world, and it just fucking appears right in front of us. That's bullshit."

Silvana couldn't help laughing at his word choice. "You're not wrong."

"And if it could find us there so quickly, how come it didn't find us after two days in Edwards's house? How come it hasn't found us here?"

She brushed his hand slightly. "Come on, let's go back inside."

They moved towards the mosque door just as an older man with a long white beard appeared, swinging the door shut and locking it with a key. He turned towards them, and Silvana pretended to be looking elsewhere. The man spoke to them in Arabic. His tone was soft, so she simply nodded to pretend she understood, then moved away from the mosque. The man didn't follow.

"Damn," Jason said as they walked down the street. It was dusk, and the setting sun was right at their eye level. The streets were emptier than before. "We're going to have to loiter somewhere nearby. Can't have Khadija coming back and not finding us."

"Who said she's coming back?" she muttered. "She might have already gone back to Edward's place on her own."

"Oh I hate that thought." A thin man wearing ragged clothes glanced in their direction, so Jason lowered his voice as they walked past. "Let's just find somewhere to sit down."

They walked down a side street towards a main road, crowded with several lanes of traffic, powerlines and bus stations on every corner. After the calm of the alleyway they came from, the hum of vehicles and the scent of spiced meats from street vendors shocked Silvana's senses. Several tall housing complexes lined the street with old air conditioners at every window and paint that cracked and peeled away with age. Despite the overwhelming scents wafting from the meat and traffic, the air was cleaner here. Silvana could smell salt water from just over an incline. They were *that* close to the Mediterranean Sea. She almost wanted to walk over the rise just to see it, but they had to stay near the mosque.

Silvana became aware of Jason's silence and the tension in his step. His mouth was turned down and he stared at the street with a glazed look in his eyes. He was thinking about something.

"Jason? You ok?"

It seemed a silly question when she said it aloud. Things were not exactly going well. But something about his mood suggested this was different. Personal.

He just shook his head. "I'm just stressed."

"Wanna talk about it?"

He huffed, sounding like a grumpy old man. She waited patiently.

"It's just… today I remembered how incredibly outclassed we are in this world. Everyone is so much stronger. That fight nearly killed us, and it was all we could do to escape."

Though he spoke the truth, something seemed off. Was he… deflecting?

"Yeah it's scary," she said, validating his concerns. "I wished I had super vampire powers again, you know?"

"Yeah. That would've been something." His tone was brighter, but he went silent again.

There was definitely something on his mind. Silvana was tempted to let it go, but that's what the old Silvana would have done. Now, she was better at speaking up, asking for what she wanted, and it had worked so well last time they had sex. Jason had proved time and again that he respected her. Still, she had to work up the courage to ask. "Is that all?"

He turned to look at her with a glimmer in his eye. "You're pretty sharp. What gave it away?"

"You walked funny."

"Walked funny?"

"Please, Jason."

He sighed. "All right, look. It's just that Dorin claims he knows you. And it just makes me think of something Nicholas said to me once."

"Oh." Silvana felt a sudden tension in her stomach.

They had barely spoken of her Aunts and Uncles over the last six months, and she was happy to go on ignoring them. It hurt her that not once had they reached out to her. Not even to thank her for paying off the family debt, or for the extra money she'd sent to help them repair the family home. An acknowledgement at least would have been nice. "I see why you didn't say anything." She finished.

"We can talk about it later," he offered.

"No, it's all right. I'm ok. Please. Tell me what Nicholas said."

Jason hesitated. He began to open his mouth before it froze in place. It looked like he would launch into a story, but instead, he shook his head. "Honestly, sweetheart, I'd like to talk about it later."

"Oh, ok."

"But everything's fine. Really. You don't need to worry."

Silvana squeezed her lips together in annoyance, but she didn't say anything. Sometimes she had to be assertive, and maybe sometimes, she had to be patient. There was a time and place for both. She let the conversation drop off.

They walked in silence around the block of buildings. Shops were closing down for the day, though a few places serving coffee and hot meals were still open. Silvana could feel her own natural hunger for human food rising. Jason must be starving. But he made no comment at the smell of cooked meat wafting down the street. They didn't have money on them anyway.

After they walked a few blocks, they took a turn back towards the street where the mosque was located. Silvana's senses were on high alert for signs of movement from any type of animal that could be a shapeshifter, but the city streets were overflowing with people. There was no sign of any animal.

Silvana realised she was still thinking about the conversation with Jason. She had tried to be patient and wait for another time when he was ready to talk, but the stress of the day had taken a toll on her patience. She blurted out, "What do you mean I act strangely?"

Jason blinked. "What?"

"Before, in the Library, you said I was making an emotional decision to go with Dorin, and that sometimes I acted strange."

"I... I'm surprised you remembered."

"I'm not an idiot, Jason."

"I didn't say you were."

"Well, sometimes you act like I am." She felt her temper rising, but she made no effort to stop it, relishing in the release of her own adrenaline and tension. "I thought I was just imagining it, cause that's how my family always treated me. But you do it too, sometimes. You act like I can't be trusted to make my own decisions. You of all people should trust me. So why don't you?"

"Silvana, I trust you with my life."

"But you don't trust me with *my* life."

Jason gave a long sigh. "Because I'm scared for you. I'm scared of losing you. I'm scared of pushing you away."

She had to bite back her sharp retort. Jason had opened up. Admitting his fear was a confession, and it couldn't have been easy. She had to reward him for being honest, not punish him, or he wouldn't open up next time.

"You're not going to lose me," she said. "But, if you're not careful, your fear will push me away. You need to show more trust in me."

"Ok." He nodded several times. "You're right. I need to trust you properly. The way you deserve." He brushed her hand with his. They stayed clear of public displays of affection, to avoid any potential cultural taboos, but she knew what he was thinking. He wanted to hold her close. "Silvana, I want to tell…"

'Jason?'

The word seemed to come from everywhere at once. Silvana spun around. And from the look of confusion on Jason's face, he'd heard it too. But no one was standing within speaking distance. Come to think of it, had she even *heard* anyone speak? It felt like the word had appeared in her mind.

'Silvana? Khadija? Are you there?'

"Jesus Christ!" Jason cried out in alarm, flinching with battle readiness. "What the hell?"

'Jason! There you are, thank the stars! What's going on?'

"Um… God? Is that you?" he murmured.

'It's Leslie. I'm using telepathy.'

"Oh. That makes more sense." Jason blinked. "Wait, no it doesn't! How are you doing this?"

'Where on earth are you? It's been ten hours since you left.'

Silvana looked around. There were some people on the street ahead, looking in their direction. She nudged Jason to the side of the road and spoke in a lower voice. "We had trouble. The chimera assassin found us."

There was a pause. *'The chimera? Are you certain?'*

Jason barked a laugh. "Uh, yeah. I think we can be pretty certain. I remember seeing an elephant, a lion, a bear, and a giant squid. What about you, Silvana?"

"You forgot the hawk."

"I did?"

"It was only there briefly."

"In my defence, a lot was happening."

"What with two wizards having a fight right over the top of us."

"Oh yeah. I'd almost forgotten about that too."

'All right!' Leslie cut in. *'That's enough sarcasm, children.'*

"Wait, you were being sarcastic?" Jason quipped, and Silvana snorted with laughter.

'What happened to Khadija? Why isn't she with you?'

Jason grumbled. "She didn't have enough power to get all of us through the second barrier. She got us through, while she stayed behind and was arrested by guards."

'What? That's absurd. My spell of concentration was on her, and I didn't feel a problem. I admit, she strained harder than I thought she'd have to. But I sensed her breakthrough.'

"She only got us through," Silvana said.

'But she had the alchemists' elixir in her. She should have been—'

Jason cut in loudly, "Ok first, the elixir's effects were wiped out by the Library's anti-enchantment spell. And second, can you help us get home or not? We're stranded in Alexandria and there's an assassin nearby trying to kill us."

Leslie was quiet a long time. Finally they said, *'Par les estoiles. I did not consider the neutralizer. Foolish witch.'*

"Leslie?"

'Oui. My power can get you home. But I'll need you to activate the spell with your Will, not mine. You ever seen The Wizard of Oz?'

"Oh my god. If you tell me what I think you're about to tell me..."

'Click your heels three times and say...'

"For God's sake..."

'There's no place like home.'

Silvana had the biggest smile on her face. Jason rolled his eyes at her. "I saw that film when I was a kid," she proudly told him.

"We all did."

"Yeah, but it was new, then." She grinned even more at Jason's expression. "Leslie, are you ready?"

Oui, mademoiselle.

Silvana held Jason's hand and closed her eyes. She clicked the back of her heels three times, and heard Jason do the same. Somehow, she could hear the reluctance in his clicks.

"There's no place like home."

The streets of Alexandria shifted faintly, as if the light was playing tricks on her eyes. Buildings expanded and compressed in her peripheral vision, yet seemed normal when Silvana looked directly at them. She began to wonder if anything were actually happening, but the movements increased rapidly until she could truly comprehend what was occurring. There were tiny wisps of light that zipped all around her like little fireflies. They sped up until they covered her entire field of vision and she could see nothing but spinning lights.

Moments later the lights slowed and faded, revealing a carpeted room with lounge chairs and hideous green wallpaper. Her disorientation faded and she could finally make out a man with shaggy hair and a thin frame. *Freddie!* She saw Edward's long robe and slightly chubby cheeks. And Leslie's weathered face squeezed in concentration as the spell finally ended.

Silvana's feet touched down on the carpet. She'd never realised she'd been lifted off the ground. *Witch's teleportation is much smoother than wizards.*

"Guys!" Freddie cried and ran forward to throw an arm around each of their necks and pull them in close for a hug. He planted a long kiss on Silvana's cheek, which made her laugh. "Holy crap, that was the most anxious day of my life! I kept thinking, no news is good news. No news is good news." She heard another kiss sound. *Wait, did he just kiss Jason on the cheek too?*

Freddie kept rambling. "I was like, 'Freddie, if you haven't heard from them, then everything's worked liked it should.' But man, it sucks sitting on the sidelines!"

"Freddie," Jason said in a soothing voice.

"I know, I had the easy part, I'm sure. But next time, you try sitting to the side all day and see how you like it."

"I'm sure it was a very difficult day, buddy," Jason said.

"Shit, I'm sorry." Freddie pulled back finally, but kept his hands on each of their arms. "I know I'm freaking out way too much. You probably want to tell us all about it. I mean, come on! It's the fucking Library of Alexandria! That's some real epic ancient shit, right? I was—"

"Where's Khadija?" Edward said.

His flat tone cut through Freddie's nervous blathering. He looked side to side. "Oh shit. I didn't even notice. Where is she?"

Silvana glanced at Jason, waiting for him to explain. Instead, he moved to a chair, collapsing into it with and exhausted huff. He stared blankly at the wall for a second, both eyes drooping and his mouth wide open, before glancing at Silvana. She offered him a nod and spoke for him. "We encountered a lot of problems. Let me explain."

"Yes," Leslie said as they sat down opposite them. "I too am curious regarding the full story."

Silvana couldn't explain it, but there was a slight tension to Leslie's movements. Something was just a little too controlled, deliberate, for the simple act of sitting down. They were clearly stressed about the results. *Fair enough, it's a life and death situation.* Carefully, Silvana adjusted her footing so she could move quickly, if she had to.

"We lost Khadija at the second barrier," she explained. "We forgot to account for the anti-enchantment spell. It washed Edward's elixir out of her, so she wasn't powerful enough to break through."

Edward gasped. "I should have known that." Then he made a loud grunting sound, and suddenly slapped himself hard in the forehead and screamed, "Stupid! I should have known that! I should have known that!"

Freddie jumped forward. "Whoa man! Eddie, calm down. It's ok." Edward tried to slap himself again, but Freddie held his arms. "It's ok. We all forgot about that."

"But I'm the alchemist. I should have been the one to think of it." He tried to yank his arms out of Freddie's grip.

"Don't be concerned, my friend," Leslie said in a calming voice. "The wizard and I were still able to get them through the second barrier. Besides, you were the one who came up with the disguise to make them look like me. Without you, they never would have even made it through the first barrier! And you got through that one without any problems, right?"

Silvana resisted the urge to glance at Jason. "Yep. No problems. First barrier was the easiest," she lied.

"Excellent. Thank you, my alchemist friend. We are still indebted to you," Leslie finished.

Edward nodded several times and relaxed his arms enough for Freddie to let go. "I still could have done better," Edward murmured.

"Hey, you did better than I could have," Freddie said. "You're awesome, buddy." He rubbed Edward's arm, and the alchemist accepted it well. Edward still twitched his hands in agitation, rubbing his thumbs and forefingers together, but he seemed to have his agitation under control.

"So Khadija was still able to force the two of us through the barrier," Silvana went on. "But she couldn't get through herself, and was arrested for trying."

"Were you unable to go back for her?" Leslie asked.

Silvana hesitated. She didn't want to tell the witch about the empowered vampire who claimed to know about her past. But she couldn't think of any other way to tell the story. Jason seemed to guess what she was thinking and offered her a helpless shrug. She sighed, and nodded as if to say, 'fine then'.

"All right listen. I couldn't get through the third barrier — the vampire barrier. I couldn't activate my power."

"What? You mean you didn't get through at all?" Leslie said. Their voice became a near shout, and Silvana bent her knees slightly, ready to attack if necessary.

"Another vampire approached me. His name is Dorin."

"Dorin?" Leslie asked. "Isn't he the one you were going to the Library to investigate?"

"The very same. He used his vampire power to get through the barrier. He accompanied us through the Library and helped us on our search." Leslie tried to interrupt again, but Silvana held up a hand to silence them. "That's when the chimera assassin appeared and attacked us. Dorin helped us fight it off until the Vigiles showed up and attacked him."

"Vigiles!" Edward cried. His hand movements sped up in an attempt to calm himself.

"Desdemona and Portia," Jason murmured.

"Jesus. Why is it always those two?" Freddie moaned.

"It was an all-out brawl to escape," Silvana finished. "We were in the Library for only an hour. We never got a chance to go back for Khadija. We barely escaped alive."

"Wait," Leslie said. "So you've spent the last ten hours… hiding in Alexandria?"

"Yep," Jason drawled. "Thinking every spider was about to become a bear and eat our faces."

"Which raises my question," Silvana asked, turning to Leslie. "How'd you contact us?"

Leslie shrugged. "Magic, of course."

"No no, don't give me that," Silvana said. "You contacted us telepathically and teleported us without physical contact. I would have thought that impossible, or at least extremely difficult. So you must have put some sort of tracking spell on us, didn't you? The Vigiles did it to us once before, six months ago. I bet it was the same spell you put on Khadija so you could add to her power and speak to her across distance. Except, you did it to us without our knowledge."

Leslie held up their hands. "Alas, I confess. No offense was intended, but yes, I put a tracking spell on you. And if I had not, you'd still be in Alexandria."

"That doesn't matter," Jason started. "You didn't ask our permission first."

Leslie nodded. "You're correct. It was still impolite of me. I

185

apologize. From now on, I will ask permission. Satisfied?"

"Is there a spell on us now?" Silvana asked.

Leslie winced and waved a hand. "No longer. I have removed the tracer spell. However, I would like your permission to put it back on until this situation is resolved."

"You can put it back on if we ask for it," Silvana said.

Leslie held up their hands in surrender.

"But how did the assassin find you?" Freddie cried. "You were on another continent! And you had only been there for what… an hour or two? How the hell did it know you were there?"

"Has anyone in this house been in contact with someone else?" Leslie asked. Their eyes scanned the room as everyone shook their head. "Then I hate to say it. But there's a possibility Khadija's arrest notified the Imperium. A royal princess like herself would have raised suspicion. The assassin could have heard it from there."

Jason sighed loudly. "Jesus… if that's true, then that's the reason why the assassin wasn't chasing us all day. Because it went back into the Library for Khadija. It was silencing a witness."

Silvana's eyes went wide. "Oh my god. Leslie!" She whirled towards the witch. "Can you still trace Khadija? Can you bring her here?"

"Sadly, no. My trace was wiped from her shortly after she broke through the barrier. I assumed she took it off herself once my help was no longer needed. In hindsight, the Library guards would have removed it. Upon arrest, they would have checked her for spells."

"Then we have to go back for her," Silvana said. A sense of dread settled over her, but she knew it was true. She could see it on everyone's faces.

Jason closed his eyes for a second, and when he opened them, they flashed with determination. "She's right. Khadija is in danger because of us. We owe it to her."

"With respect," Leslie said in their gentlest voice, "I don't think that's a good idea."

"Agreed," Edward said, before speaking quickly in a flurry of words as if worried about being interrupted. "Khadija is in a secure location after an emergency event. The area will be in lockdown and flooded with Imperium officials. She is also a princess of the Al Khalifa family. In a political situation like this, she can claim amnesty and bank on her diplomatic immunity granted by her family name. It will be more effective than her magic."

Silvana blinked at him. Edward sure had some moments of brilliance.

"Eddie, dude," Freddie said. "I'm not the biggest fan of Khadija. But even I think she's too exposed there. The assassin could still find her, diplomatic immunity or not. Hell, I could see that thing killing her and saying, 'just been revoked' for good measure." He looked to Jason with raised eyebrows, and Jason shook his head, wearing a bemused smile.

"It's a possibility," Leslie said. "But right now, Khadija will be surrounded by officials. There'll be too many people around for a secure assassination. Trust me. I know the Library procedure on matters like this. At this moment, Khadija is safer than all of us."

Edward nodded vigorously. "Any movement between here and Alexandria will only increase the likelihood of the assassin following us back to this location."

"I see," Jason said, looking at Leslie. "So all that talk about creating a fairer world. That was only as long as it's convenient."

Leslie leaned back in their chair, a grim look on their face. "Jason, there's no need to make accusations regarding the quality of my character. I am not abandoning Miss Al Khalifa to certain death. I am making an informed, ethical decision to trust her safety to circumstances I can confidently predict. She will be fine. I promise you."

Silvana felt the urge to defend Jason, but the truth was Leslie and Edward made a good point. Khadija was surrounded by people and she was well connected. She would find her own way out of this mess. Hell, she'd even put on the spoilt princess act the moment she was caught. Silvana hated to admit it, but Khadija knew what she was doing.

Leslie went on, "Our time would be better spent reviewing the information recorded on your cameras."

Silvana couldn't hide her wince. She couldn't bear to break the news to Freddie. She knew how this would crush him.

"I'm sure with even one hour in the Library, you will have found useful information. You can cover a lot in one hour."

"Actually," Jason said, "it was more like fifteen minutes."

Leslie blinked. "What? You said one hour? I don't understand what you mean—"

"The batteries died," Jason cut in. "The cameras were both low on battery when we got there. They each died after about fifteen minutes." He looked to Freddie. "Sorry, mate."

Freddie's face had gone completely slack. "I don't... what? Flat? I..." he shook his head. "They should still be going now. Let me see!" he rushed forward, and Jason held out his camera. Freddie fiddled with it, then let out a gasp. "Oh... oh god! Oh no..." He reached for Silvana's Go-Pro.

"Is this a joke?" Leslie said, their voice laced with tension.

Silvana handed over her camera. Freddie snatched it and started mashing the power button. Nothing happened. "Come on!" he cried, his voice straining on every syllable.

"You didn't charge their batteries?" Leslie hissed. "I cannot believe this."

"I thought I did! I don't understand why..."

"I'm eight hundred years old, and even I know you have to charge technologies. You claimed to be an expert."

"I claimed to be Asian! It's not the same thing." Freddie was still looking at both cameras. Silvana noticed his hands had begun to shake. "I can't believe this. I know I charged them." He ran from the room, and Leslie sighed as they followed him out. Silvana was right on his heels.

Freddie ran into the kitchen and snatched up a power board near the wall socket. "Yes! The board is right here. It's switched on still. It should have charged them both! I don't..." he trailed off. Slowly, he lifted the charger out of the board and held it up.

"Was it not plugged into the wall?" Silvana asked, using her softest, least accusing voice.

"Not that," Freddie said in a near whisper. "The USB plug. It wasn't all the way in." He gave it the slightest push, and Silvana heard an audible click as it fell in place. "It was enough for the green light. But not enough to actually charge the cameras." Freddie looked up at her. His eyes were starting to water, and his lip trembled. "I'm... I'm so sorry, guys." A tear fell down his cheek.

"Unbelievable," Leslie said.

"That's enough, Toussaint," Silvana warned.

Leslie spun on her. "We spend two days planning one of the most dangerous heists imaginable, and this moron couldn't charge a camera."

"Hey!" Jason snapped. "It was an easy mistake to make."

"A mistake that may cost us all our lives!" Leslie retorted with a raised voice. "We needed that information. We thought we would have two and a half hours of footage *per camera*. Now we have fifteen minutes?" They turned to Freddie. "You had literally the easiest job out of all of us."

"I know," Freddie whispered. Another tear spilled from his eye, and he furiously wiped it before it could fall. "Jase, Silvy, I'm so sorry."

"You can apologise to all of us, while you're at it," Leslie said. "This entire venture was wasted because of your incompet—"

"SHUT IT!" Jason roared, and the entire room went still.

Silvana's heartrate spiked. She had never heard Jason raise his voice like that. It was the sound of a furious man at the height of his anger, and it made her feel small. The face of Arthur – her late husband – flashed in her mind.

Yet she could see Jason, standing still and focused, his face schooled into a calm expression. He was furious, but still in control. He was not an aggressor. He was a defender.

"That's enough," he said in a much softer voice now. "Leslie Toussaint, you were a stranger that showed up at Freddie's front door in the middle of the night, and forced him to get involved in a life and death matter he had no stakes in. Since then, he has done nothing but help you in your mission to stay alive. Now I would think that deserves a little more respect from you. You are our *guest*." He emphasised the word. "I expect the proper courtesies to be observed."

The whole time he spoke, Silvana had been ready to attack and rip the head from the witch before they could speak a spell, just in case. She could never be too careful with the mentally enhanced Immortals. Yet, Leslie's body posture had completely relaxed. They cupped their hands together and bowed their head.

"You are correct, of course," Leslie said. "My deepest apologies to you all, for my boorish behaviour. And especially yourself, Freddie." Leslie offered him a bow. Freddie was still fighting back tears. His face was red and his eyes wet, so much so that it broke Silvana's heart to see him like this. "Freddie, my words were cruel and undignified to one who's shown the highest loyalty and integrity. Please, forgive me."

Freddie gave a small nod, and the movement caused another tear to fall. He furiously wiped it away. Silvana reached for him, but he shifted back out of her reach.

"I don't know anything about technology," Leslie said. "But by the sound of it, this was an easy mistake to make. I'm sure the footage we have will be sufficient. If I showed any frustration, it was only at the situation itself and not at you. I apologise once more, to all of you, for my behaviour."

Jason gave a nod. "Thank you, Toussaint."

"I..." Freddie's voice trembled, then he cleared his throat. "I'll put these on charge now. We can..." a sob burst out of him. His lips quivered as he squeezed them shut, as if trying to smother any other cries from escaping. He steadied his voice and said, "We can watch them in a few minutes once they've charged."

"Thanks, Freddie," Jason said gently.

"Yes, thank you, Freddie," Silvana echoed.

The young man nodded, put the cameras on charge, and hurried out of the room without another word. Silvana heard his footsteps run upstairs. A moment later, her vampire ears picked up the sound of Freddie's muffled cries.

"He wants to be alone right now," Jason said, as if speaking to himself. Silvana nodded. She had to stay back from Freddie, even though the sound of every sob was like a wound to her heart.

Chapter 16

Jason sat down in front of a large TV. A bitter scent drifted from his mug of coffee on the table next to him. He'd just enjoyed an absolutely delicious pile of sausages, mashed potato and sauerkraut that Edward had prepared for dinner. Everyone had let Jason eat Khadija's portion without a word. After skipping lunch, he was bloody hungry. Now that he was showered and wearing clean clothes again, he felt his brain shifting back into gear.

He hadn't intended to snap at Leslie like that. He didn't regret anything he said; Leslie was out of line and Freddie needed his friends to have his back. But the lack of control was scary. In the moment, he'd thought of his mum facing a barrage of verbal abuse from his father, and something inside Jason had snapped.

Still, the group spoke freely, if a little subdued. Leslie had been genuine with their apology. Only Freddie still seemed dejected. *I would be too, if something that stupid had gone wrong for me. Poor Freddie.* Jason would have to find time later to talk about it with him later.

"Ok, Jason, I believe this was your camera," Freddie said. A second later, shaky footage from a hand-held lens appeared on the TV. A dusty old book was opened by Jason's hand, and the words came into focus. Freddie hit pause.

"Just to reiterate," Leslie said. "I can only explain things that are common knowledge within Immortal circles. I cannot give away historian secrets."

"Right, cause of your all-important vows," Jason sneered. "Sorry," he added immediately in a softer tone. "Didn't mean to sound snappy. Long day."

"Quite understandable. And yes, my vows and my signet prevent me from revealing Library information. I will still do my best to answer your questions."

"Thank you." Jason took a sip of coffee and began to read.

The words were a little crooked and Jason tilted his head slightly so they appeared straight. This book used plenty of outdated words. The sentences were long and often circular, so it said everything a few times with a whole bunch of useless phrases like, 'be that as it may' and 'that being said'. Jason's eyes were glazing over. *God, it's only the first page.* He focused his mind on the words.

The writing was about some English duke and the rate of taxation. Jason couldn't tell what year it was, and there was clearly a lot of context that the author expected the reader to already know. "We all done?" Freddie said. Then he let the tape roll until they could see the next page.

They spent the next forty minutes going through this one book. From the little Jason could follow, it was a detailed list of one family line's approach to exerting financial control over the people of their area. The family was careful to tax at the highest rate possible without inciting a rebellion. They controlled the prices of all food and products in the area and paid the peasants a considered, precise amount.

"Huh," Freddie said. "So the whole point of this book is Duke Harold wanted the peasants to give him back every cent he paid them for their work. Essentially, it all came back to him anyway."

Jason could only shake his head. He hadn't understood half of that from what he'd read. But then, Freddie was attending university and was clearly more academically skilled.

"Very astute of you, Freddie," Leslie said warmly. "That is exactly the point. The Duke monopolized every necessity of the people and controlled the costs, so that even the money he paid them was still his."

"My god," Silvana said. "It looks boring on the surface, but the truth is actually pretty dark."

"Indeed."

Jason stared at the dusty old book on the screen. "I can't help but wonder how many lives were lived under this system. How many people were effectively slaves to the one who wrote this book. Never had a chance to do anything else with their lives because they were too poor."

"And *kept* too poor," Freddie said.

"Come on," Leslie prompted. "I know it's hard to accept, but we have a lot to get through. Next book?" The room gave assent, and Freddie rolled the tap to the next text.

This one was filled with religious language that made Jason feel strangely nostalgic. He'd spent years going to an Anglican church with his foster parents and had been rewarded for reading the scriptures. Even years later, he could still quote the book, chapter and verses these passages came from. He read the line, *"All Scripture is given by inspiration of God, and is profitable for doctrine, for reproof, for correction, for instruction in righteousness"*. Jason chuckled to himself. *Second Timothy, chapter three, verse sixteen. Well done, Jason.*

"What is this book meant to be?" Silvana asked.

"I think it's some sort of instructional guide book for priests," Freddie offered.

"Indeed," Leslie confirmed. "This text was for religious leaders on how they should handle teaching the Bible."

"Oh crap," Freddie groaned. "This is going to be some fresh horror."

"You're not wrong."

The text instructed the reader to emphasise the virtues of faith and endurance in their sermons. If the people were filled with hope for the future, they would be happier. The more inspirational, the better for their purposes. Like the text before, it said many of the same things over and over.

Why's it repeat itself so much? Jason thought. Ironically, the very next page held an answer.

"Belief comes from repetition. Doing the same action, hearing the same words, will instil a sense of familiarity, which in time, gives birth to comfort and acceptance. Thou need not convince them of every finer detail. Simply hold true to your message, never wavering, and with enough time and consistency, the people will believe everything you say."

"Well," Freddie said with false cheer. "I hated that."

"How many more books are on this tape?" Leslie asked.

"Well, there's about ten minutes of footage left. So… maybe four books?"

Leslie's lip twitched like they wanted to speak, but kept silent.

"I don't understand," Jason asked. "We were in the first aisle. We were looking for information on High King Reynold. Why is all this information on economy and religion in his section?"

Leslie could only shrug.

"Cause these are his tactics," Silvana answered. "His methods for ruling."

The room fell into silence, and Jason sat back in his chair. He slowly sipped from his coffee cup with a scowl. Every time he thought of the Imperium, he felt like there must be some way to change things. To stop the Immortal society ruling from the shadows. Then he saw just how deeply entrenched their power was, and it nearly overwhelmed him with hopelessness.

An image came to mind. Himself, ducking low and running full speed through the Library with duelling wizards and an empowered vampire hurling lethal magic just over his head. A killer shape-shifter chasing him and the woman he loved. And not having the power to do a damn thing about it.

He forced his thoughts back to the task at hand. "Let's keep reading."

The next book was on education. It highlighted the information that had to be taught in schools, churches, universities, and government training programs while still emphasising the divine right to rule as granted to the monarchy. The book taught the role of every person in a functional society, and the ongoing work to organise all of history to emphasise the importance of English culture.

"Wait a moment," Silvana cried. "What is that? Bottom of the page. Does that say… Vlad the Impaler?"

"Oh!" Leslie made an excited noise, then quickly went silent again.

Jason gestured, "Next page, dude." Freddie ran the tape and they all read the words in silence.

"…the influence of Vlad III the Voivode was widespread, and his assaults on Anglo-Saxon townships unacceptable. His power was only growing until High King Reynold issued a new commanding tactic to change the history. Europa faced the influx of tidings reporting stories of atrocities, impalings en masse, mothers impaled towards their babes on the very spike. It led to public outrage and a unity of nations against the Ottoman invader, the ensuing counterstroke effectively ending the uprising."

"Am I reading that right?" Jason whispered. "Vlad the third… is that Vlad the Impaler? The man who inspired the legend of Dracula?"

"The very same," Leslie said.

"But… this implies that Reynold just made up all that shit about him. He did it to turn the nations against him. That can't be real, right?"

Leslie kept their face blank.

"Hey, I know this one!" Freddie shouted. "Even in regular history – you know, mortal history – there are some historians who claim that the stories about Vlad were falsified to turn him into a villain. There's actually no evidence of his impalings other than the written word of historians who may have been lying. Some think that the Western Europeans were just being racist and that Vlad was a decent guy. You know Vlad is a national hero in Romania."

"But was he really a vampire?" Jason asked. He turned to Silvana, who could only shrug. "Wait a minute!" Jason was nearly shouting as he leapt across the room and pointed at the screen. "Look at this. Vlad was growing more powerful. He was attacking Reynold's land. Do you see what this is?" He pointed at the screen insistently. "It's an uprising! Vlad was leading a rebellion! A vampire rebellion against the *wizards*."

"Oh my god," Freddie murmured.

Jason continued pointing at the screen. "And Reynold didn't have to fight back with magic or armies. He just smeared Vlad's reputation." He looked around the room and found everyone staring back at him. "I can't believe this. Has the Imperium lied like this before? How many people from history were made into villains by the High Kings?"

"Probably most of them, mate," Freddie said. "They say history is written by the victors. The High Kings are sure as hell the victors."

Jason looked back to Leslie. "Tell me, is this what you wanted us to find?"

Leslie's face was an emotionless mask. "Unfortunately, no. But young Freddie is right. History is written by the victors. This information about Vlad is…" they bobbed their head in thought. "…not exactly common knowledge. But common enough. Every Immortal knows they should distrust their history books just a little, even if they don't know specifics. Many reasonable Immortals will suspect this about Vlad, even without confirmation."

"I knew," Edward said, speaking up for the first time in a while from his couch in the corner. "The history books are written by Imperium agents. It's not objective fact." He shrugged and repeated, "I knew."

"So it's nothing we had to break into the Library to find out?" Jason asked.

Leslie smiled. "Only if you wanted proof."

"Ok, but still," Freddie chimed in. "Is the truth about Dracula recorded somewhere?"

"Possibly. It's a big Library. It might be somewhere."

"But why?" Silvana asked, her feminine voice sounding high-pitched after Jason and Freddie dominating most of the conversation. "Why was Vlad leading an uprising in the first place? Was it just about his country of Wallachia? Or was it about destroying the Imperium?"

Leslie sighed. "I cannot answer that. But that is perhaps the most important question of all. Still, I must advise that we get back on task."

Jason curled his hand into a fist. He had just learnt a secret truth about history, but it changed nothing. He still had a pit of overwhelming helplessness gnawing at his stomach. He sat back down on his couch and took a long swig of coffee. The drink was still steaming hot. Had Edward done something to keep his drink warm? Jason found he didn't mind.

The rest of the book continued its lesson on education. It discussed attempts to keep history focused on the Anglo-Saxon culture in order to give greater significance to Reynold's rule. Other kingdoms had their deeds overlooked or smeared outright. The book gave many examples of events Jason had never heard of. He couldn't tell if it was because his own history education was lacking, or if the history referenced was entirely different to what mortals knew.

"This is whitewashing," Freddie said.

"I'm unfamiliar with the term," Leslie said.

"Means rewriting history to favour white people. Cover up their mistakes, exaggerate their accomplishments, that sort of thing."

Leslie grinned. "Yes. Perhaps an oversimplification, yet more or less accurate."

Jason kept reading in silence. His fingers went white as they gripped his warm mug, his fury boiling even hotter. He forced himself to relax. Reynold was such an asshole. The worst part was he thought this was all justified because he was powerful.

The book went on for some time, but Jason found his attention waning. Leslie was clearly hiding their impatience, so Jason knew this was not why the assassin was trying to silence the historian. Or at least, not according to Leslie's suspicion. But it made Jason wonder what truth Leslie knew. How could only Leslie know a secret if this information was available in a Library that other historians had access to? What did Leslie know that was unique to them?

"This is why I'm self-employed," Edward said with a smug grin. "The Imperium control the flow of information. Whenever I worked with them on alchemy, someone was telling me what experiments I was allowed to try. The only way to be true to the craft was to work outside their influence."

"Like what, buddy?" Freddie asked.

Edward shrugged. "Well, the resurrection elixir, for one. Imperium alchemists are adamant that it's impossible. I refuse to believe it. Anything is possible. We just have to find out how. I cannot think inside their box."

They kept reading in silence. The sounds of thunder rolled in from the distance, and soon, a steady pattering of rainfall danced on the mansion roof as the night grew darker outside their lounge room.

Lightning flashed in the window and the lights in the room flickered for an instant, but still the group continued to study long into the night.

Silvana was always the first to reach the end of the page. Towards the end of the book, she called out, "What's that mean? An Act of God?"

Jason answered, "It's like a spontaneous freak accident. House burns down, car struck by lightning. It's a common phrase for police." He grinned. "And for insurance agents."

"I know that, my dear. But why is it in an Imperium book? What does an 'Act of God' mean in Immortal circles?"

Leslie held up their hands. "I'm sorry, my friends. That is against my signet. I cannot say."

"But it doesn't make sense," Freddie said. "There are wizards who can do things like that. Hell, we were in Norway fighting the Gluckbergs when Samantha Kennedy created a firestorm and hurled lightning at us. By all accounts, that was an Act of God."

"Ah," Silvana said in understanding. "I think you're right, Freddie." She pointed at Leslie. "If the Imperium re-write history, isn't it possible that every time a wizard has a tantrum and blows up a town, it gets reported as an Act of God?"

Leslie only answered with a polite smile.

"Oh my god," Freddie cried. He pointed repeatedly at Silvana. "Oh my god! How did I not realise that sooner?"

"Freddie?"

"Japan!" he shouted, leaping to his feet with a sudden burst of energy. "Twelfth century. The Mongols had just conquered China and were planning to attack Japan next. But when they were crossing the ocean, a freak hurricane sank all their ships."

"Ok?" Jason asked, confused.

"You really know your history, son," Leslie said, sounding impressed.

Freddie gestured at his face. "Uh, hello! Huge Asian nerd over here. But that's not even the best part. It was like twenty years later when the Mongols tried again, this time with a much bigger army. And the exact same thing happened *a second time!* Another freak hurricane destroyed most of their ships! That's where the Japanese got the word *kamikaze* from. It means 'wind of heaven', like the hurricanes that saved their country from invasion. It's considered one of the luckiest coincidences in history." Freddie pointed at Leslie. "But it wasn't a coincidence at all, was it?"

Leslie merely held their hands out in a helpless gesture.

"An Act of God indeed," Edward said, a smile on his face.

"Huh," Jason murmured.

"But that's not all! You guys heard of the Lisbon earthquake?" Freddie's face was alive with excitement now. It made Jason smile in shared joy. Freddie was *cute* when he got like this. Freddie waved his hands with excess energy.

"Ok, so late seventeenth century. Lisbon is having a big religious party when a massive earthquake hits the city. Destroys a huge amount of it. Then just a few minutes later, a tsunami fucks up what's left. And that's not all! The religious party they were celebrating involved lighting candles. Suddenly, thousands of candles are overturned, and a huge *fire* burns the rest of the city! It's like earthquake, water and fire all at once. Historians say that ninety percent of the city inhabitants died! *Ninety percent!*"

"Jesus," Jason cried.

"The Portuguese could see the irony too. They're in the middle of praying to God, and God is just like, 'fuck you in particular!' It led to a massive swing away from religion. It's unbelievable."

"Interesting," Silvana said in a polite tone while waving her hands at Freddie as if to settle him down.

"But that's not all!" Freddie went on, and Jason couldn't help laughing at him. "No seriously, there's more! Shut it, Jase, I'm still going!" Jason laughed even louder. "Portugal was in the middle of colonising several other countries. They were in a big race with a few other European nations to colonise the Americas. But this earthquake absolutely wrecks Portugal's biggest port. They had to completely stop colonising. They literally never started again."

"Huh," Jason said. "Almost makes me want to believe in God again."

"Right? Karma's a bitch."

"I can add something here," Leslie said, and all eyes turned to them. "We have seven High Kings now, but there weren't always seven. And the thrones didn't always represent the same kingdoms they do now. They have changed position several times in history. For example, it was replaced in the 17th century."

Freddie gasped. "You mean, after the Lisbon earthquake?"

"Indeed. There were four primary countries competing in colonisation. England, France, Spain and Portugal. They represented the four High Kings of Europe at the time. However, Portugal no longer has a High King today."

"What?" Jason cried.

"Wait, wait, wait," Silvana called. "Are you saying that a High King was killed? Actually killed?"

"Not truly. No High King has ever been killed. More like they were defeated and their power broken. Demoted back down to a regular king."

"But who did it?" Silvana asked, sitting up straighter in her chair. "Surely it must have been another High King, or several of them working together. The destructive power involved…"

"Was it Reynold?" Jason asked calmly.

Leslie's face was unreadable, but Jason could see through their guise easily. "I see. Reynold destroyed a rival, and incidentally, ninety percent of a city's population at the same time. All in an Act of God."

The room went totally silent. Jason was lost in his own thoughts as he struggled to comprehend the scale. Reynold had destroyed an entire city. He was the equivalent of a nuclear bomb. *Oh god, were nuclear bombs made by wizards too, somehow?* Regardless, he knew they might as well be. The High Kings had a power he'd never really appreciated until this moment. Reynold could destroy London, New York, Beijing. All on a whim. And there would be no police to arrest him, no judge to make him stand trial for his crimes. *God, the thought seems so silly. Arresting Reynold?*

"Is this what we're looking for?" Silvana asked in a deathly whisper. "Is the assassin trying to kill you, Leslie, because you are one of the few people who know about 'Acts of God'?" Silvana leaned towards the old historian. "You couldn't tell us about them, so they must be pretty secret. That's why you sent us into the Library, to find a book about them. To warn us." She paused, as if the words were too awful to even consider. She forced herself to go on. "Leslie, is someone planning to… repeat history?"

"Oh my god," Jason whispered. "The High Kings are about to go to war. And someone is trying to remove those who might stop them."

At that moment, a flash of light came through the window, and the mansion rumbled with a low roar of thunder.

Chapter 17

"Settle down, everyone," Leslie said with a wave of their hand. Their voice was louder, more confident, and it cut through the growing tension in the room. The old witch adjusted their posture in their chair with a slow, strained movement, but their voice remained firm.

"First of all, the High Kings are always fighting each other. But they have many tactics other than blowing up cities. We've been reading all evening about how they work. Economy, religion, and education. There are many ways they can fight each other without using magic. You don't have to fear mass death and destruction just yet. And second, yes, I must keep this... particular topic a secret. But I'm also not the only historian who knows about it. Anyone else working in my field has access to this information too. So why is the assassin coming for only me?"

Jason scratched his chin. "How sure are you of that they're only coming for you?"

Leslie grinned. "Because the Library of Alexandria was still open today. If the historians were being slaughtered, they'd shut that place down. But it was business as usual."

"Still," Jason said. "I'm not willing to skip past the theory of High Kings going to war and causing mass destruction. Can you tell us more about them? Whatever you can?"

"I'm sure it's not the best use of our time," Leslie said. Jason waited, and the historian sighed. "As you wish, sir knight. Edward, would you be so kind as to use your chalkboard once more?"

Edward nodded and pulled the board into the centre of the room. He flipped over their plans for the Library heist and quickly dusted off the alchemy notes on the back. Then, he stared and waited patiently for Leslie to begin.

"Seven High Kings," Leslie said. "We have Reynold the First, the English." Edward started writing it down. "Then Louis the Third, and Alfonso the Third, kings from France and Spain, respectively. These three kings have an alliance. They may not be friends, but an understanding exists between them."

"Question," Silvana asked. "Is there a hierarchy between High Kings? I know Reynold is considered the strongest of them all."

"There's no official hierarchy. But unofficially, yes, there absolutely is. It actually comes down to language." Leslie shrugged as if they knew how odd that sounded. "Each king speaks their native language and makes those in their territory speak it too. You can tell who controls more territory by how many people speak the kings' language. Technically, Reynold is first as the English king. The second most powerful is High King Jin Yu Qing, ruler of China." Edwards started writing. "Though Jin more or less rules over most of the Asian region. Japan, Korea, Thailand, much of that continent comes under his influence through lesser rulers."

"Son of a bitch," Freddie growled.

"Indeed. Jin also is unique among the High Kings. His is the only throne that has endured consistently since almost the beginning, when Immortals were first born from Zapharahleous himself. The Jin family line has ruled for nearly seven thousand years. Even Reynold is only a second generation ruler, having inherited the throne from his uncle, the original Anglo-Saxon ruler in Denmark. By comparison, Jin is a twelfth generation High King. The oldest line."

Jason couldn't find the words to speak. The concept seemed too vast for him to comprehend. Edward had finished writing and tapped the board to signal his readiness to write more.

Leslie continued, "We have High King Mohammad Al Siddig, ruler of most of the Middle East and the Arabic nations. His centre of power is Dubai."

"Really?" Freddie asked. "Dubai? Not Baghdad or Cairo?"

"Many of the High Kings prefer the more modern cities. After all, Al Siddig is the youngest High King. You might call him progressive by Immortal standards. In fact, he is closely connected with the Al Khalifa family."

"Khadija," Jason murmured to himself, thinking of his friend lost in some Alexandria facility.

"Indeed. Al Siddig probably knows Khadija by name. Like I said, she is well connected." Edward was tapping the board again, and Leslie smiled. "Sorry, my friend. Next we have Serfoji Singh, High King of India." Edward started writing. "Singh was king in exile after the English took over most of India and occupied it in 1858. Singh managed to maintain his position throughout British rule and after. Though, he is considered one of the weaker High Kings and has all but sworn allegiance to Reynold."

"Oof!" Freddie moaned. "There's a dark bit of history."

"Indeed. And the final High King is Alexei the Fourth from Russia."

"I know him!" Silvana cried. "He was the Immortal benefactor that supported the Romanov family when they ruled Russia. He was the power behind their throne."

"The very same. Alexei is the newest High King and is certainly the weakest of the seven. His throne has only existed for about eighty years."

"Oh crap," Freddie said with a groan. "Eighty years, huh? Let me guess. This is because of World War Two."

"Your maths is correct, my friend."

"Oh God," Jason groaned too. "I know I'm going to regret asking this but… what happened in World War Two?"

Leslie gave a pained sigh. "It was a war between High Kings. A new alliance was formed between Germany, Italy, and Russia. They planned to replace the three European High Kings, Reynold, Louis and Alfonso. In truth, they were only convinced they could win after seeing the success Japan experienced in challenging Jin, the second strongest of them all."

"That was the Japanese invasion of China in the 1930s," Freddie chimed in.

"Yes. They thought if Jin could be beaten, maybe Reynold could be too. The alliance in Europe might have succeeded too had not Russia betrayed them. Alexei changed sides mid-war and, in doing so, secured his rank as High King."

"You're joking," Jason cried. "So this guy literally used World War Two to secure himself… a promotion? And he got away with it?"

Leslie nodded. "He wasn't the first. The Great War was very similar, but with the Ottoman Empire trying to replace the European Kings. Many wars were little more than Immortal conflict that used mortal soldiers as fodder."

"So all those who died in the world wars," Silvana said in a soft whisper. "The millions of soldiers, civilians, the victims of the holocaust and all those displaced refugees. That was all caused by the greed of the High Kings?"

"With respect, my vampire friend, you are incredibly incorrect," Leslie said. Jason flinched and prepared to defend Silvana, but the old witch held up their hands in defence. "Mortal or Immortal, it makes no difference. Every individual was responsible for the atrocities they committed, or permitted. Do not think for one second that someone was tricked into committing evil. Wizards did not force soldiers to shoot the innocent, or for people to turn on their neighbours, or for generals to target civilian populations. We are all human, and as such, have the capacity to commit the same evil. We must remember that truth because it is our duty to remain vigilant against evil's next move."

Jason nodded. He wholeheartedly agreed with Leslie. And yet, something didn't feel quite right. He couldn't put it into words. Yes, mortal and Immortal were all capable of evil. But at least the Immortals knew what they were choosing. The mortals were deceived. They didn't have a fair chance to make the right decisions. They didn't know all the facts.

Edward tapped the board again. "So that's all you need?" he asked. They all studied the list he'd made;

Reynold the First – English
  Louis the Third – French
  Alfonso the Third – Spanish
  Jin Yu Qing – China – Oldest Throne
  Mohammad Al Siddig – Middle East – Youngest Ruler
  Serfoji Singh – India – Weak
  Alexei the Fourth – Russia – Weakest/Newest

Edward also wrote a list of those combatants who had challenged the existing kings in the world wars and failed. He also wrote Portugal, which he promptly crossed off.

"I was displaced," Silvana said softly, and Jason could have slapped himself in the head. He'd forgotten all about Silvana living through the World War. She went on. "I was separated from my family during the war. I was a young vampire with no memory before my change.

I was found by my Aunts and adopted." She pointed at the board. "I never knew my real family because of those assholes. I would have had a completely different life."

She lowered her voice even further, and her whisper held the hint of a growl. "I was a *child*, and you tell me I was responsible."

Jason felt a chill spread down his spine. For a moment, he thought Silvana was about to change. That other look had come into her eyes. But her face didn't change any further. Silvana just sat back, her eyes squeezed shut. So, Jason reached out and took her hand.

"I'm sorry, sweetie."

She gripped his hand back. "I'm grateful I got to meet you. That wouldn't have happened otherwise. But I hate that's how it happened."

"Of course. I hate it too."

"Silvana," Leslie said. "If I caused any offense..."

But she waved them away. "I understand what you meant. No offence was given. It's just a hard truth to accept."

Jason went quiet and looked back at the board again. "I know you don't think the assassin is targeting you regarding the High Kings," Jason said. "But I can't ignore my instincts. Something about this feels significant. Especially when we consider the Royalist's activities in the past year. Peter Erikson, The Gluckbergs, Hana and Mikeru of the Japanese imperial family, Yamato. These people were trying to bring back the monarchy. And they were moving money around to do it. Is it possible that they're trying to rally behind a High King in another attempt of conquest? Which of those kings are most likely to push the world back to the age of Kings and Queens?"

No one answered him, but Jason had a growing feeling of certainty. It had been eighty years since the High Kings had challenged each other for power. Things were overdue. Another World War? Or conflict in a different form? He couldn't be sure. But he knew something was coming.

"It's possible you're right," Leslie said. "But even so, I don't think it relates to the matter of my assassination attempts. You might be facing two separate problems. You may consider me selfish here, but I recommend dealing with the one you're facing today."

"Yeah, you're right," Freddie said. "Come on, I want to go to bed at some point tonight. Let's keep reading."

Another two hours passed with little more conversation. Everyone was subdued after such heavy topics. The Library books they read didn't help much either, focusing on topics of academia and law. They finished the last of Jason's film and switched to Silvana's. Thankfully, her recording was over twenty-five minutes long. They started going through the next books. After only a few minutes of reading, Leslie cried out, "Wait. These books are about Jin Yu Qing."

"That's right," Silvana said. "Dorin carried a stack over for me from another section of the Library. We knew we weren't going to be able to cover more ground before the batteries ran out."

"So, the rest of the footage is all Jin's work?"

"Yeah, I believe so. Why?"

Leslie slumped down in their chair and shut their eyes, going quiet for a long while.

"I see," Jason said. "The information you wanted us to find. It was in Reynold's area. Whatever it was we needed, we didn't find it."

"You know I can't answer that," Leslie whispered with obvious dejection in their voice.

"You don't have to," Jason said. "So, we didn't record it. Both of us read through other books while we were there. It's possible we covered it the old fashion way. Silvana, do you remember anything noteworthy?"

"I do, in fact," Silvana said. "I was looking at the genealogy of Reynold."

Leslie shifted ever so slightly, and Jason noticed. There was something there. Something they were trying to act casual about. *Here we go, at last.*

"Go on, child," Leslie replied flatly.

"Well, I noticed that William the Conqueror… that was Reynold's younger brother?"

"Correct. The eldest child inherits the magic. The second inherits the house and name."

"William had about ten children, and the Windsor family are his descendants. And I'm related to that line through the adoption of my Uncle Phillip. So… am I related to Reynold?"

Leslie's mouth hung open for a few moments, and Jason noted them struggling to speak. *Is that disappointment?* Leslie shook their head slightly. "I'm sorry, I'm just surprised at the question. My dear, everyone is related to one High King or another. That's just how Immortal family trees work. They're one big entangled network. It's so complex. There are historians like me whose entire career is spent just comprehending it. Though I am sure you're connected to Reynold somehow, I doubt there's any real significance in that connection."

"Oh," Silvana trailed off. "Well, I guess that's a relief. I wasn't exactly hoping for a connection."

"Could you imagine?" Freddie said with an obvious grin. "Reynold showing up to your family's Christmas and birthdays?" He laughed. "Wouldn't that be terrifying? He'd be like, 'Merry Christmas. Here are the heads of your enemies.'"

"And their children," Jason said, and Freddie groaned in mock horror. Jason grinned back, but couldn't help noticing everyone else slumping down in their seats, no longer watching the screen or the chalkboard. Even Edward put down his chalk and sat back in his couch. Jason could sense a feeling of dread and hopelessness settle on the room. He cleared his throat. He had to say something before the mood spiralled any further.

"Ok, so…" he struggled to think of something to say. "So genealogy. Everyone's connected to Reynold in some way, but it doesn't matter much. So then, what would it take for it to matter?" He shrugged at Leslie. "What is a serious connection?"

Leslie scoffed at him in good humour. "What do you think is a serious connection to a king?"

"Oh," Jason said. "Inheriting the throne."

Suddenly everyone reacted at once, and the room came alive with excitement. "Holy shit," Jason said. "Is that what this is all about? Reynold's throne?"

"An heir to the throne?" Freddie cried.

"Who's next in line?" Silvana nearly shouted. She had leapt to her feet. "Leslie, is that your specialty? Inheritance? Do you know who's going to be the next High King? And someone's trying to kill you for it?"

"It would make sense," Jason said, standing next to Silvana and nodding in agreement. "Someone is hoping to put their own candidate on the top throne. Or themselves!" He pointed at Leslie. "So you need us to find out who's trying to take Reynold's job, because they're the ones trying to kill you. And you were hoping that the book on genealogy would point us to the right person. Leslie, is that right?"

"Brilliant, Jase," Freddie cried, cutting off Leslie's answer. "We solved it. Well, mostly. But at least now we know what we're looking for. Ah!" he sighed. "That's such a relief! I thought I'd fucked it all up with the damn cameras."

Leslie, however, was silent.

"Leslie?" Jason asked. "Is something wrong?"

"Oh, god no," Freddie said. "Are we wrong? Oh, please don't tell us we're wrong."

Leslie smiled. "I cannot say. But perhaps I can get away with saying…" they looked at the signet on their outstretched arm and whispered. "I think you're close enough." The signet didn't react, and Leslie sighed in relief.

Freddie cried out with a loud whoop. But Jason couldn't help a sense of foreboding. In his mind, close enough was still risky. Especially when dealing with such high stakes.

"Then we've still got a lot of work to do," Jason said.

"Who's Reynold's heir right now?" Silvana said. "Is that common knowledge? Maybe we should warn them. And Reynold too." She held up her hands as every head spun sharply to face her. "I know! He scares me too. But it could make us an ally, and I'll take anything right now."

"It wouldn't help," Leslie said, and let out a long sigh. "This part is common knowledge that I can share with you. My friends, Reynold doesn't have an heir. He has never had one! He's the only High King who hasn't named his heir. There are many of us in the Imperium who are terrified at the danger presented here. He has the most powerful throne, and with no heir, it could very easily turn into a massive conflict. Such a power vacuum has not been seen in centuries. Everyone will want a piece."

"Why hasn't he named an heir?" Edward asked. "He should do that. Every king's responsibility is to secure the line after them."

"Yes. But he hasn't. We don't know why."

"That doesn't make any sense," Edward said. "Why isn't someone else doing something about it?"

"You have to remember, Reynold has been a High King for most of his life. He ascended young and has enjoyed nearly seven hundred years of rule. He has never once named an heir in that entire time. This is an *old* problem. Everyone's sort of forgotten about it."

"But Reynold is old now," Silvana said.

"Indeed, nine hundred and eighty-two years old. One of the oldest Immortals to have ever lived. Older than Methuselah. No one has ever lived more than a thousand years, so we can expect Reynold will die before that time too. In the very best-case scenario, Reynold will die within the next eighteen years. Likely, sooner. And when he does, there could very easily be a new World War to claim his throne."

"My god," Jason whispered. He paused in thought and began a slow pace around the room. "So Leslie, you know who the heir is, don't you? Or at least, who Reynold might name as his heir. And you want to find them to stop the war for Reynold's throne. Only someone else is trying to kill you in order to let it happen?"

Leslie only held up their hands, but Jason could see it again. The witch's poker face needed work. Or, they were deliberately letting their emotions show. Either way, Jason knew he had just guessed Leslie's motivation. *Bingo.*

"Then, this isn't about surviving an assassin anymore," Jason said. "This is about stopping Reynold from dying and letting war break out in his absence. We have to find this heir."

"Agreed," Silvana said, and Edward nodded as well.

"Well, kinda," Freddie said. "I don't know about you, but I'm still invested in surviving the assassin." The room filled with quiet chuckles.

A loud knock came from the front door.

Everyone froze. Jason's adrenaline surged with sudden readiness as he clutched the gun at his waist. No one did anything. Everyone waited for someone else to make the first move.

"Eddie," Freddie said in a fake cheery voice. "I don't suppose you're expecting any visitors and you just forgot to tell us?"

"I don't get visitors."

"Ah. Too bad."

The knock echoed through the house again. A little louder this time.

"Jesus Christ," Jason whispered. "All right, Freddie and Eddie, stay here. Everyone else, cover me." He drew his handgun and a flashlight and moved to the hallway. Silvana and Leslie flanked him on either side.

They crept down the long hallway towards the front door. Outside, they could hear the patter of soft rain and the distant rumble of thunder. The mansion hallway was pitch black, with only shadows coming from the lounge room light behind them. Jason focused on steadying his breathing and relaxing his grip on the gun. He held the flashlight up and kept the gun aimed slightly towards the floor.

They reached the door. Jason faced Silvana and nodded towards the handle. She gripped it gently. He nodded again, and she flung the door open with vampire speed. Jason shoved his light and gun into the doorway.

A single man stood on the other side. He was dressed in a white shirt with gold embroidery that swirled up the sleeves. The rain had made his clothes cling to his muscular form, and his wet hair dripped into his eyes and down his face. But they recognised him immediately.

"Hello," Dorin said, flashing them a wide grin. "At the risk of sounding like a cliché vampire, may I have permission to enter?"

Chapter 18

Silvana was stunned.

Dorin stood before her. In the doorway of Edward's mansion. In Swansea, England.

He had surprised her before in in Dubai and Alexandria, but those were gathering points within the Immortal community. Here, was her private life. He had appeared in a place he didn't belong, as if no time had passed and distance meant nothing. He was... inescapable.

She remembered the incredible power he had shown, fighting two Vigiles at once, overpowering her easily to bite her neck, back flipping off walls and wrestling the shapeshifting assassin when it morphed into an elephant. She was helpless against him. And now he was here again, in a place she had believed was safe.

"What the hell are you doing here?" Jason growled. He kept his gun aimed at Dorin's chest.

Dorin tilted his head sideways. "Is that the thanks I get?" he growled back. "As I recall, I saved you from your assassin many times. You!" he pointed at Silvana and she felt her heart jolt, "threw me into the lion's jaws, fully expecting me to die. And still I saved you after that."

"For your own reasons, I'm sure," Jason said.

"How did you find us?" Silvana whispered.

He pointed at her neck. "Your blood. I'm sorry I had to steal it from you like that. I never would have done that under any other circumstance. But I couldn't let you get away again. I knew if I had your blood, I could find you anywhere in the world."

Silvana stared at him. *What the hell?* She wanted to slam the door in his face, but she knew he was only being polite. If he wanted to break his way in, or even kill them, he probably could. She really should try to be more amenable, but the way he had just taken her blood without her consent made her skin crawl.

"Ah, so this is your empowered vampire?" Leslie asked, eyeing Dorin. They stepped forward, forcing Jason to lower his gun. Leslie extended a hand. "The one who defies Imperium law."

"Who are you?" Dorin asked.

"Leslie Toussaint, witch of the Imperium, and historian." Dorin eyed them blankly. "And a friend," Leslie added.

"Ah. Then it's a pleasure to meet you." Dorin shook their hand.

"Likewise. Now, why have you come to find us? We weren't exactly expecting visitors."

"Well, I'm glad someone here remembers their manners." Dorin offered the witch a nod. "I was hoping to speak with Silvana in private. However, I'm willing to speak in your presence if Silvana vouches for you. Silvana, do you trust…" he frowned. "Pardon, is it Mr or Mrs Toussaint?"

"Just Toussaint, thank you."

"Of course. Do you trust Toussaint with your life?"

Silvana couldn't just go along with this. She tried to find some way to resist his entry. She spoke the first idea that came to mind, "There are others in the house."

"Oh. Well if you trust them too, I'll happily share my information with all of them. May I come in?"

Jason's hands shifted as if he was considering raising his gun again.

Instead, he looked to Silvana for permission. She didn't know what to say. The thought of Dorin entering this home was repulsive.

And yet, she wanted to know. She *had* to know. If he knew anything about her past…

"If you promise to do no harm," Silvana said. "You may enter. We will hear you out."

"I swear it," Dorin said with a bow, and graciously stepped inside. Jason stood his ground, not making any room for Dorin inside the doorway, but the vampire casually stepped around him. "Where is this place? Is it yours, Toussaint?"

"I too am a guest here," Leslie said. "This is the home of Edward, a talented alchemist. If you'll follow me." Leslie led Dorin down the hallway, with Jason and Silvana watching their back.

Jason leaned down to whisper, "Are you sure you're ok?"

Silvana couldn't bring herself to answer. There were too many emotions to put it into words. She simply nodded back and kept following Leslie and Dorin down the hallway.

"Everyone," Leslie said in a warm, reassuring voice. "This is Dorin, our vampire ally from the Library. Dorin, this is Edward, the owner of this mansion. And our mortal friend Freddie."

Silence was the only response from the other side of the doorway. Silvana followed them into the room and saw the wide-eyed stare on Freddie's face. Edward was staring at the ground, though he clutched at his robes where he kept his vials of potions.

"Thank you for inviting me in," Dorin said. "I promise I am your ally in this. I'm eager to share my knowledge with Silvana. She assures me you are all her closest allies. I hope you will extend that honour to me as well, in time."

"Yeah," Freddie said. "Ditto."

Dorin glided through the room like a graceful tiger and sat on a couch. He leaned back on the soft leather, his arm thrown casually over the back of the lounge, as if trying to appear as non-threatening as possible. "I want to share what I know with Silvana." He looked at her with his piercing blue eyes. "However, I'm worried that you won't believe what I have to say. So instead, I want to offer you some of my blood."

"You already offered that," Jason said. "We said no."

"Please, listen to me," Dorin said. "You probably don't know much about vampiric powers. Which is not your fault, of course. The wizards of the Imperium have hidden much knowledge of vampire abilities for fear of an uprising. But I know these secrets. And I'm willing to share all of them with you. I couldn't explain this in the Library." He held out a hand to Silvana. "A drop of my blood will contain memories. You can see what I have seen. This way you will know I'm telling the truth."

"Is that true of all vampire blood?" Silvana snapped. "Did you steal memories from me when you stole my blood?"

Dorin merely smiled at her harsh tone. "I stole only the drop itself, and I used it up completely when I tracked you here. But this blood of mine is a gift, and I have wilfully placed my memories there. I am bearing my heart and soul to you. Please, accept this gift."

She noticed movement on his fingertip. A single bead of red blood oozed through the skin and formed a single drop that glistened on his index finger.

"Is this a trick?" Jason said. "Will that blood give you power over her?"

"Be at ease, sir knight," Leslie said, cutting off Dorin's protest. "The vampire speaks true. That blood will indeed hold memories, and it will give him no power over you if you take it."

"Is that an Imperium secret?" Jason asked, his eyebrow raised.

Leslie smirked. "Perhaps it is, but I'm referring to something I have seen with my own eyes. Do not forget my many centuries of life. I have seen things outside of my job that I was never sworn to secrecy on afterwards."

"Thank you," Dorin said with a nod of his head. He held the finger out to Silvana. "Please. You can trust me."

Silvana's breathing grew more rapid. Her legs started to tremble with nerves. Somehow, she knew Dorin was right. She could *feel* it. He was telling the truth, and that blood would show her the distant past. It would answer all the questions she had wondered about for nearly a century. And now it was right here in front of her… could she actually take it?

"Will this change anything?" she whispered.

Dorin nodded. "It will change everything. But I promise you, it is worth it."

"Silvana," Jason whispered. "You don't…" he seemed to stop himself with a sigh. "If you want to do this, I'll support you." He stepped forward and gripped her hand.

And she found the strength she needed. "Thank you, Jason," she whispered. She took a deep breath and spoke louder. "I will take it."

Dorin extended his hand slightly and Silvana bent down and kissed the edge of his finger, tasting the blood's bitter iron flavour as the power was absorbed into her being.

Immediately, images flashed to life.

Mother looks worried. She always looks worried now. I wish I understood why. Father has been talking about someone coming here, but we have visitors all the time. More visitors isn't a bad thing. So why is mother worried?

Velouette is at my side. She's only two years older than me, so she's the safest of them all. I wish I could say her name right. I just call her Velooy. Mother gets mad sometimes when I say it wrong, but I like the funny name.

It makes Velooy laugh anyway.

Mother is talking now. "This is really important," she says. "Today is the day Ana is going through her big change. Your uncle Grigore is here to help. So it's important that we all be very supportive to Ana and be extra nice to her."

"I don't want Ana to change," Velouette cries. "She was fine the way she was."

"Now, don't be silly, Velouette. You knew this change was coming. Ana is going to become very strong. We need her to inherit our family power." Mother looks into the distance. "Tough times are coming."

She walks away, and Velouette grabs me by the hand. "You're not allowed to change, Dory."

I giggle. She says my name wrong just like I say hers wrong. It's our little game. "You too, Velooy."

"Good. Cause I'm never going to change."

A horrible noise comes from down the hallway, and I cover my ears. It's really loud and sharp, and I hate it. The sound is wrong, so very wrong, but I don't know why. It makes my head hurt. It sounds like a person. But how can a person make those noises?

"Ana!" Velouette cries out and runs towards the sound. She disappears, leaving me standing in the hallway alone. I hear the sound of mother yelling and Velouette screaming back at her. I hear loud slaps, and Velouette howls even louder. The awful sounds keep going. Mother yells again, and a door slams. I can't bear to be alone anymore. I move forward, even though I'm more scared than I've ever been in my life.

I find Velouette. She's crying and slamming her fists against a wooden door. "Ana! Ana!" she screams over and over. I watch her, unsure what to do. After a long while she seems to calm down. The awful sound was still going behind the door, but Velouette doesn't seem mad anymore. She starts to cry. I hate watching her cry.

I walk up to her and hold her hand. "I'm still here," I say. "You won't lose me."

Mother and father are arguing in the next room. I can hear every word, but I don't understand what they mean. Something about a bad man very far away. I hear the name over and over, but I have no idea who Barbarossa is.

"You know what Grigore is going to ask," father says. "And if he does, we won't be able to deny him."

"It's still wrong. She's our daughter."

"For all intents and purposes, she's Grigore's daughter now. If he asks us for permission, it's merely a courtesy."

Mother raises her voice louder. "She still needs our blood. She still feeds on us. God, she's so young! What difference could it make whether a ten year old fights in Barbarossa's war?"

"You know it doesn't matter. The High Kings have given the order. If Grigore answers the summons, we need to suffer this with our heads held high. For the children's sake."

I panic when they mention children. It must be a sign that they know I'm listening from behind the door. I run away as quickly as possible.

Velouette finds me later when I'm hiding under my bed covers. She always finds me, no matter where I hide. She sits next to me on the bed and pats me through the covers. "You shouldn't listen in on mother and father. It's adult talk."

"Ana is going to visit," I say.

It doesn't make my sister happier like I thought it would. She is acting strangely. "I've heard the other kids at school," she whispers. "Some of them think there's going to be another war. That's why the Germans have been in the city. They're planning to take over. That's why mother and father are so scared."

"Will father have to go fight?"

"No, he's too old now. But, I think Ana will have too."

"Kids don't fight in wars."

"Ana does. She's a vampire now. They need her super powers."

I feel scared for Ana, but I feel more scared for myself. I snuggled up to Velouette and put my face against her arms. "I'm glad I didn't change, or I'd have to fight too."

"Yeah," Velouette said. She wraps an arm around me and it makes me feel safe. "We'll always be together. We'll always take care of each other."

"Good. I'd like that."

"Dory! Ana's here!"

I come running at the sound of Velouette's voice. Now that I'm eight years old, I can run across the whole house in no time. Soon I'll run faster than father.

The foyer is full of people. Mother and father are greeting my uncle Grigore. He wears a long black coat with the collar pulled up high. He looks scary. There's a woman standing behind him. She's holding a long gun and a sword. I want to touch them, but she looks too scary to talk to.

Velouette is waiting for me to stand next to her. I hold her hand as we look at our eldest sister.

Ana looks really different now. She is twelve years old and she's much taller. Her skin is so much whiter and her eyes brighter. She's not smiling, like she used to do all the time. Instead, she looks like she's very angry. She's wearing a shiny necklace with a big red stone in the middle. The necklace is extra sparkly against her pale skin.

"Hi Ana," Velouette says. "How are you?"

"Fine," she says. Her voice is quiet now. She sounds mean.

"You look taller."

"That's because I'm older now."

Velouette seems embarrassed for some reason, so I talk to help her out.

"Hi Ana. It's me, Dorin."

"I know who you are, Dorin."

"Oh. Ok, I was worried you had forgotten."

"I'm not an idiot."

I'm confused. "I didn't say you were an idiot." Ana just rolls her eyes at me, so I keep talking. "You've changed a lot. I like your necklace." She doesn't say anything back to me. Why isn't she talking?

"Hello, children," Uncle Grigore says. "I'm glad you've had a chance to get reacquainted. We've just stopped by to tell you the news." The lady with the long gun stands behind him like she's ready to shoot us.

"Grigore," my father whispers, even though we can hear him clearly. "We're not telling the children about conflict."

"Nonsense. They'll find out soon enough. Better they hear it from you instead of the air raid sirens when the bombing starts."

"Bombing?" Velouette asks.

My parents seem angry when my uncle starts talking. "There's going to be another war. The mortals haven't figured it out yet, but the New Kings are determined to go through with it. Louis and Alfonso have refused to make concessions, and Reynold has done absolutely nothing at all. The Kings have no choice left but to start the invasion. It'll be a week, at most, before it begins."

"My god," mother says. "The three New Kings fighting the High Kings? The conflict will cover the whole world."

"Especially if Japan joins in," father says.

"Exactly," Grigore replies, but for some reason he seems really happy about it. "This may be the start of an entirely new order of rulership within the Imperium. It's our best chance for our country to advance. That's why myself and Ana will be joining the war effort."

"No!" Velouette cries.

Our parents get angry at her straight away.

"Quiet, girl," father yells. Ana watches all this without moving like she's

become a statue.

"Fear not, child," Grigore says. "I suspect we shall be much safer than you are about to be. The war will be hell on the mortals. You better hope your leaders surrender quickly because you cannot hope to win a protracted war. The Germans have spent years preparing, and you have no defences." He looks at my parents. "That's why I'm here, not to announce my intention, but to warn you. If you are planning to flee the country, now is the time."

"Absolutely not. This is our home," father says. "I am a king in waiting. And Dorin after me. This country belongs to us and no other." I get nervous at hearing my name spoken, but no one looks at me, so I'm not in trouble.

"You'd be better off as a king in exile. Because here, you're more likely to be a king in memory."

"We are staying," my father insists.

Grigore shrugs. "As you wish, brother. Come on, Ana. Say your goodbyes."

I look at my oldest sister, waiting, and hoping she would say something nice. I look again at the shiny necklace with the red stone that she wears. Is the necklace a magic necklace that makes her angry? Or maybe Ana will say something very kind since she is going away for a long time. Instead, she simply says, "Goodbye," in an icy voice.

She follows my uncle and the woman with the gun as they leave our home.

Velouette runs from the room. Mother and father talk to me for a little while, but I don't really hear anything they say. Eventually, they let me go follow Velouette. I find her in her room, crying into a pillow. So I sit next to her and rub her back until she's finished crying.

"I'm still here," I say. "We'll never lose each other. You'll see."

The airplanes have been flying above us for hours now. I'm still hiding under my bed even though I'm ten and should be braver. After all, those planes are flying over me towards the enemy. But I can't stop thinking. What if they dropped one bomb by accident? What if it hits my home, but I'm not killed in the blast? What if I get set on fire? I don't want to burn to death. I don't want that.

Velouette finds me again. "Dory, you've got to get out from the bed. If father sees you, he'll get angry again."

"The planes," I say, feeling miserable.

"You know those are German planes. Remember, we're on the German's side now. Why would they bomb us? They're flying towards the Eastern front. They're not coming here."

"I don't like the Germans."

"I know, Dory. But they're the best chance we have to free our country."

"The Germans made us get rid of our king. How does that help?"

Velouette sighs. "I don't know, Dory. Just come out from under the bed, all right?"

I know she's right, so I crawl out. I try not to listen as more planes pass overhead, carrying all their bombs to the front line.

We have dinner as a family every night, but no one talks. We sit together in the living room with all the lights off, just in case someone sees our house. Father has been ordering us to spend time together, even if we're not talking. I don't mind being together, but I'd prefer to just have me and Velouette. She is the only one who actually listens to me.

Someone knocks on the front door. Father tells us to be quiet as he gets up to answer. Voices start muttering in the other room.

Suddenly, Father is yelling. I clutch onto Velouette to stop my hands from shaking. Are the Russians back, somehow? Have they pushed the Germans all the way back to our home?

Mother hasn't moved off her chair. Maybe she's not worried. But then, she had been growing more and more quiet lately. She doesn't move all day and spends a long time staring off into the distance like her mind is somewhere else. So I hold Velouette closer.

A tall figure enters the room. I recognise Uncle Grigore, even though it's been years.

"Hello," he says. He's wearing the same black coat, except this time, it's covered in strange brown streaks. His face is dirty. He smells funny.

"Grigore," father says. "Do not speak to the children. I want you to verify what you've told me first before you risk upsetting them for nothing."

"I cannot afford to indulge your denial, brother," Grigore says. "Times are desperate. Alexei's betrayal has thrown the whole war into jeopardy. We may very well lose everything if we don't commit every resource available."

"You've already taken Ana," mother yells suddenly. "Haven't you done enough?"

Grigore looks sad as he shakes his head. "I've come with terrible news. There's no easy way to say this, so I'll just say it plainly. Ana is dead."

I hear the words, and they mean nothing.

"What?" mother says in a flat tone.

"She's dead. We were on the Eastern front and a coterie of wizards surprised us. It was a small battlefield, it shouldn't have warranted such an extreme response, but I suspect that's why they did it. We were completely unprepared for such power. Many of the Axis Immortals were killed. My own knight, Yetta, was blown to pieces." He gestures to the red marks on his coat, though I don't understand what he means. "And I saw Ana die with my own eyes."

"Ana died?" Velouette cries. "How? She is powerful now. She is a vampire. You said she was Immortal. How can she die?"

Grigore shakes his head sadly. He reaches inside his pocket and pulls out a strange, silver string that glitters in the candlelight. There is a flash of red. Grigore takes it with both hands and holds it out so we can all see a silver necklace with a red ruby in the centre. It looks familiar. Have I seen that somewhere before?

"Immortal does not mean invincible," my uncle says. "Ana was killed in battle, just like many Immortals are killed. I recovered this heirloom from her corpse. Regrettable, and yet, I have little time to debate this." He puts the necklace in his pocket, and his face takes on a serious expression. His voice becomes stern like father when he gives orders. "I need another vampire heir. Right now."

Mother and father start shouting. Velouette suddenly hugs me really tightly, though I don't realise why any of them are acting this way.

"How dare you?" father roars in his scary voice. "You wasted the life of one child, and now you want to do that again? You disgusting pig!"

"You cannot have her! You hear me? You cannot have her!" Mother shrieks.

"It's not a debate," Grigore says in a calm voice. "It is my right. It is the law of succession that has existed for thousands of years. I will not be denied my prerogative."

"You get out of my house right now," father yells. "And don't you ever step foot in here again. Don't ever pretend to be our ally, and don't ever call me brother."

I want to tell father to stop. He is yelling too much, and Grigore is being so calm and polite. But I don't want father to yell at me instead.

Grigore's face changes, and suddenly, I'm terrified of him. "I will take her now. If you stand in my way, I will strike you down."

Everyone goes quiet. Mother starts weeping. Even Velouette is crying. Should I be crying? What are they talking about?

"She's too old," father says. "You said yourself. A vampire has to be changed when they're seven. Any older, and the change could kill them. Velouette is twelve, Grigore. This would kill her."

"You'd rather I take Dorin? Your heir?"

"You're just killing her. It would accomplish nothing."

"She will survive. I'm sure of it. And she'll be all the stronger for it. When she finishes her change, she'll be able to crush entire armies with her

ferocity. If she gets enough mortal blood, she could probably even challenge a wizard."

"I don't want to kill mortals," Velouette cries. "I want to see Ana. I want to stay with Dorin."

Grigore only shakes his head. "You don't get a say in the matter, girl. You will become a vampire. It is your destiny."

Suddenly, I understood just enough of what was going on. I stand in front of my big sister and say in my loudest voice, "You can't have her. She needs to stay here."

My uncle smiles at me, and I wonder if he's going to agree with me. "I hope you are that fearless if you become king. But I cannot indulge you, boy." He shouts in a loud voice, "Remove your boy, brother, or I'll do it for you."

"Don't call me brother!"

Grigore looks at me, then suddenly he's right up in my face. He's so big. I cry out for help, but something grabs me and moves me so quickly. Pain explodes in my head and I start to cry, but no one comes to me. Velouette is screaming. I have to get up. Somehow, I'm on the ground on the other side of the room. How did I get here?

I can see my sister being dragged away by Grigore. But there's blood in my eyes. I don't know what's happening.

"Get off her, you bastard!" father roars and tries to shove Grigore off. But Grigore slaps him aside and father falls over. How did that happen? Father is the strongest person in the family. But then I remember, he is only mortal.

"Daddy!" Velouette cries.

I can't stand to hear my sister crying. I have to do something. She is the only one who makes me feel safe.

I rush at my uncle. I screamed and wildly slammed my fists down on his legs. Then father is gripping Grigore around the throat. Velouette breaks free of uncle's grip, and she starts punching uncle too.

I feel pain again. It's the worst pain in my entire life. I find myself on the ground. Everyone else is lying down, except Uncle Grigore, who stands over us all.

"Pathetic mortals," he growls. "You should be grateful that one of you has the chance to make something of your wretched existence. I'm offering you godhood, and you dare—"

A gunshot blasts through the room, so loud it hurts my ears, and Grigore jerks to the side.

Mother has entered the room, holding the family revolver. She is crying as she stalks across the room and fires again, and again, and again. Each gunshot creates a bright flash of light that makes it hard to see. I cover my ears from the loud noise until it finally stops.

I look up. It takes time for my eyes to adjust to the candlelight. When I can see again, I see my uncle on his knees. There is red liquid coming out of his chest. That's blood. He's bleeding. Even though he's really strong, he can still bleed.

"Don't you fucking touch my family!" mother cries. She walks up to Grigore and puts the revolver against his head. I look away.

I hear a thud and a squishing sound. I had been expecting a gunshot. I look up.

Grigore is still on his knees, but he has his arm inside mother. His fist is somehow behind her, coming out of her back. There is blood everywhere.

Everyone is screaming. I can't move. I can only scream and scream. Mother is bleeding out of her mouth. Grigore puts his face up against her belly where all the blood is, and he starts making drinking sounds.

My father attacks him, but Grigore does something to him really quickly. I hear another awful sound and father collapses to the ground.

I can't move. I can't scream anymore. I just watch as Grigore starts eating blood from my mother, and then my father. They both lay on the ground. Their eyes are blinking, but they aren't saying anything. Grigore just keeps eating and eating for a long time. Then he stands up and he looks perfectly strong again.

"I'm sorry, brother," Grigore says. "It had to be done." He searches around the room. His eyes fall on me, but he looks away again as if he never noticed me. Then he sees Velouette nearby. She is huddled into a ball in the corner of the room. Grigore moves towards her, and she starts screaming.

"I'm not going to hurt you," he says. "I need you."

"Get away from me!" she shrieks.

Grigore grabs her by the hair. He lifts her up in the air as she cries. He takes the silver and red necklace from his pocket and locks it around her neck. Velouette looks at me. We can't say anything to each other. But we share one last connection between the two of us.

Then Grigore bites down on her neck and she cries out in pain.

I start crying. I can feel more tears streaming down my face, but I can't do anything else. There is nothing I can do. I'm too scared to do anything. So I watch as my closest friend in the whole world is attacked by a monster, and turned into a monster too. She starts twitching really quickly all over her body. She screams and kicks with her legs. Grigore only holds her in place.

Her noises change. They go even higher. Her eyes become red. Her fists start making even louder thuds as she slams them repeatedly against our uncle, and he winces in pain now when they land.

"Stop it, girl," he growls. But she only attacks him more. With a sudden crack, Grigore's arm bends in a way that looks wrong. He cries out as he drops her.

Velouette hits the ground and shrieks like an animal. She looks at her parents bodies and makes a loud, monstrous sound that somehow seems sad.

She looks at me. I think she's going to eat me. "Velooy," I cry.

She twitches again, and starts running on all fours like a dog. She runs out of the house and into the night.

A few seconds later, Grigore is swearing as he leaves to go chase her. He never even looks back at me. He doesn't see me kneeling between the broken bodies of my parents and crying for hours and hours. I cry for my parents, my sister Ana, and my sister Velouette most of all.

I live with my cousins now. One of them used to be a king, but isn't a king anymore. Apparently, a group of soldiers kicked him out of power, and the Immortals were too busy fighting the war to come back and help him get his throne.

I don't talk to my cousins very much. I've only been with them a few weeks. They've been nice to me and have given me lots of food, clothes and other things, but they only want to ask about my family. I don't want to talk about that.

The war has stalled. They told me that High King Alexei is proving a stubborn opponent, and King Barbarosa is having a hard time beating him. King Yamato has finally joined the war on our side. But now Reynold has joined in fighting against us. The war is the biggest war ever.

"Dorin," my older cousin says. I think of her as my aunt because she is so much older, but she insists she is still just a cousin. "Someone has come to visit you."

"I don't want visitors," I say.

"Dorin," my cousin says as she sits next to me on my bed. "It's your uncle Grigore."

I feel a horrible fear inside me. The very thought of Grigore makes me shiver and shake. I have nightmares about my uncle. I never want to see him again.

"Please, don't make me see him," I whisper.

"Dorin. You need to be brave. Your sister has disappeared. We've been searching for months, but she's gone. We can't find Velouette."

"Good. That means she's free."

My cousin sighs. "It means she's lost her mind. She will wonder around the world killing anyone she finds until she's either killed, or dies of starvation. I'm sorry, Dorin, but she's not living in a paradise somewhere."

I can't help it. I start crying, even though I know I should be brave. My cousin puts her arm around me, but I wish it was Velouette instead.

"This means you will become the next vampire of the family."

I begin to scream. I jump away from my cousin and run for the door, but she has already locked it. "No! I don't want to be a vampire! Let me go!" I scream.

I smash at the door with my fists and cry as much as I can. No one listens to me. No one ever listens to me. That's why I need Velouette. She is the only one who ever listens to me. She is alive somewhere. She wouldn't kill people. She's a good person and they're lying about her. I just know it. They are lying about everything.

"It's ok," my cousin says. "You'll be a strong vampire. A good one. You will help to save our country. We need you."

"I'll be a monster," I cry. "Like Grigore. He murdered my parents."

"That was just in self-defence. It was an accident."

"I don't care."

"Dorin, that only happened because of the war and because the king was taken from his throne. If you have the power of a vampire, you can bring the king back. You can make the whole country safe again."

I stop crying. "What do you mean?"

"You can use your power for good. You can protect the small families. You can stop wars, and stop military coups against the king. Your job will be to keep everyone safe."

"Can I kill Grigore?"

"No, Dorin. He will be your teacher. He will make you strong."

"I don't care. I don't want that."

"Dorin," she sighs. "You don't understand how many people need you. Our whole family needs you. Can you do this for us?"

I think to myself, the only one I'd do something for is Velouette. *Then an idea occurs to me. If I became a vampire, if I become strong, I can find Velouette. I won't save a whole country. I will just save her.*

"Ok," *I agree finally.*

The whole family gathers around. Grigore is there. I hate him, but I don't let myself be afraid of him anymore. I don't listen to anything my uncle says, or any of my cousins. It is all lies anyway.

"You're ten years old," *Grigore says.* "It could be dangerous. You could go mad like your sister. But your odds are better because you're younger than she was. The truth is, I don't know what it'll do to you. But it has to be you. You're our best hope now."

I let Grigore take my hand and let him bite down on my wrist.

It feels like fire is inside his hands. It spreads all up my arms and into my head. I grit my teeth and don't let myself make a sound. The fire floods into my chest like burning hot needles. I can't help thrashing with each new wave of pain. I gasp for breath between gritted teeth. Little tears come out from under my squeezed eyes. But no matter what, I don't scream.

For you, Velouette. I will find you.

A long time has passed. I am tall now, no longer a boy, but a man. I am wearing my country's traditional clothes, even to such an important occasion. Especially now, since I know it will piss off the Imperium.

The room is full of people from all over the globe. Pretentious, phony, self-absorbed Immortals at the top of society. They have no idea how many orphans were born from the wars they waged, all so they could have a little more power, a little more money.

I smell something. A strange scent that makes me think of my old family bed. My first family, my first bed, before I became a vampire.

I see a woman dressed in blue and silver. She is beautiful and regal, like the queens of old, and clearly a vampire. I follow her at a distance trying to be discreet, and yet, I can't help staring. Something about this woman in blue and silver calls to me. Is that where the scent is coming from? Why does she smell familiar, yet foreign? My instincts are telling me something, and I intend to find out what.

"Begging your pardon, good sir," says an old man. I can tell this is an old mortal knight, judging by his suit and accent, a British man married to a vampire. Was this the woman in blue's husband? No, I can see another vampire behind the knight. A tall, stern woman with short black hair and a hard face. That was this man's wife. "You seem to be following that woman there," the knight says.

"Who is she?" I ask.

The man scowls. "That is no concern of yours, zounderkite. Now, I suggest you find another to deploy your charms on."

I glance at the old knight a second more, then simply walk away.

"Excuse me, miss?" I call out.

The young woman spins around to face me. Her eyes are crystal blue, her face a soft white, fitting perfectly with her blue and silver dress. A young mortal man is at her side, lean and angular, yet handsome enough. I can feel the old knight try to seize my shoulder, but I shrug it off easily.

"Young lady," I say. "What is your name?"

She looks concerned. A moment later a certain glint of mischief enters her eye. "First give me your name, stranger, then I shall give you mine."

It feels like a reference to something I don't know. I grow impatient. "Dorin. Now yours!"

"Excuse me, sir," she snaps. "You have no right to demand anything."

I know I'm being pushy, but a strange certainty is coming over me. I force myself to be calm and not scare her off. "All right, I'm sorry for pushing. Please, just tell me your name. It's important." I reach forward without meaning too.

The mortal knight has his sword out and at my throat within a second. Damn. That's one loyal knight. "Your behaviour is threatening, sir. Stand down," the young knight orders.

"You cannot hurt me. There's an enchantment."

"And it will not save you if you threaten her again."

I can't help an impressed grin. I sense the older knight and vampire behind me, growing tenser by the second. I have to reassure them all. "I'm not going to hurt her," I start to say, but the words burst out of me with sudden desperation. "I would never hurt her. Especially if she is who I think she is. Please, miss." I whisper desperately, "Can you please just tell me your name?"

"She will tell you nothing!" The older vampire lady says.

But the young woman has a look of rebellion. "My name is Silvana."

And I know it. She is exactly what I thought. The way she says the last part of her name. Silvana. Ana. It is the same inflection, the same tone, that unique accent she'd always used when she said the name Ana when we were children. The name of our eldest sister. No wonder she smells familiar, yet different. I haven't smelled her since I was mortal.

"You," I whisper. "It's the wrong name, but it is you. I'm sure of it. It should be impossible. I've searched for years, yet here you are. I don't understand."

"You stay away from my daughter!" the older vampire hisses, "or I'll tear you to shreds."

"She is not your daughter," I say on reflex. The words are coming out of me with no control, my emotions being all over the place. I look at this adult woman, Silvana.

"Who are you?" she asks.

That's when I realise, she doesn't recognise me. Does she even remember me? I have to find the words to explain it to her. Oh, I have to tell her everything! Even with all the risk it would bring to my life. She has to know the truth. I open my mouth to speak just as a loud bang comes from underneath me.

The ground drops away. Something hits me in the side of the head. I start falling from the side of the building.

It takes a few precious seconds to comprehend what is happening. An explosion has destroyed the balcony. Silvana is falling. I can save her, but only if I expose my empowered vampire state. If I use my powers now, the entire Imperium would know what I'm capable of. It would ruin nearly a century of planning.

But I don't care. I have to save Silvana.

I start summoning my Will in the middle of my fall. I see Silvana and her knight just ahead, rapidly approaching the ground. I begin the spell just as two shapes appear. I recognise the Vigile uniform as they catch Silvana and her family. She is safe.

Instead, I use my powers to save myself. I draw on the blood inside me and shift through the world itself.

Ten minutes later, I appear again at the bottom of the Burj Khalifa. Silvana's family is there.

She is not.

I wait, but there are too many Vigiles. Too many officials of the Imperium on full alert, and a strong possibility that one of them noticed my use of vampire magic. They will certainly find me if I wait around. I have to leave.

But I know now. For the first time in eighty years, I have seen her with my own eyes. After all these endless years of searching, I finally have hope.

Velouette is alive. And I will find her again.

Silvana opened her eyes. The taste of Dorin's blood was still on her lips. If felt like an hour had passed, but everyone was still in the same positions. Dorin waited on the couch, Jason at her side, and Freddie, Edward and Leslie standing around the room of Edward's mansion, with the rain coming down outside.

And she knew. Without a doubt, she knew who this man was.

"Dory," she whispered. "You found me."

Dorin had tears welling in his eyes. He tried to offer her a smile, but the strain broke through on his face. "I didn't want to change," he whispered. "I never wanted to be a vampire. But I had to find you."

And now, Silvana was crying too. "I'm sorry. I broke my promise. I said we'd never lose each other."

They moved at the exact same time and pulled each other into a hug. Now she could smell everything she remembered. The scent of honey. The musk of wooden boards and bedsheets. His dark hair like oak.

He was sobbing. "I'm so sorry!" It came out like a desperate moan. "I'm so sorry I lost you! I didn't mean to lose you!"

"Oh, Dorin," she wept, sobs breaking up her words. "You've found me. I can't believe you found me." She pulled back and looked at his face again. A face she was beginning to remember. "You won't lose me again. I promise."

He crumpled against her, burying his face in her shoulder like he had in the memory. It seemed he had eighty years of grief and pain that finally came to the surface. As his loud sobs wrecked against her chest, and hot tears poured from her own eyes, she saw Jason looking on in confusion. She couldn't help laughing even through the tears.

"It's ok," she said. "Dorin is my little brother."

Chapter 19

Portia checked her suit in the mirror for the ninth time. She knew it was perfect. She knew she was stalling.

"Art thou ready, my love?" Desdemona asked patiently.

Portia straightened the collar one more time. Her face had none of its usual lightweight makeup, so nothing was framed with colour. Her eyes were flat and her lips less red and full than normal. Her fiery hair was tucked firmly into a tight bun in perfect symmetry. She missed the feeling of it bouncing over her shoulder and brushing her back, but it was better this way. Now she looked less feminine. Hopefully, she would look as unappealing as possible.

"Do I look beautiful?" she whispered.

"Always, my love," Desdemona replied.

Portia glared back. "I'm trying not to, Mistress."

A soft hand traced up her spine and over the back of her neck to cup her cheek. "I'm afraid there is not enough magic in the whole world to achieve such a feat."

"If you say so. I was thinking a razor for my hair, and some facial wounds might also do it. Some light burns, perhaps?"

The hand on her cheek spun her around, and Portia looked into her mistress's dark face. "I will be with thou the whole time. Be brave, and be steady. He will see any uncertainty. Best just be a wizard, a rock, immoveable."

"Yes, mistress."

Desdemona took her hand, and with a force of Will, she began the process to teleport them across the world. Portia gripped her mistress tighter than normal.

I am a wizard. I am a rock. Immoveable.

They arrived inside a vast castle hall lined with giant portraits, golden pillars and marbled floors exactly where one would expect to find an Immortal High King. The room was filled with other Immortals, all mumbling in a low volume. Portia recognised more Vigiles in their suits. There were several witches with long robes and pointy black hats, and dozens of Fae servants with faces of ethereal beauty. Everyone waited in this glorious throne room for their audience to begin. A resplendent golden throne stood at the far end, and an enormous portrait of Christ and his apostles loomed above. Currently, the throne was empty.

"It won't be long," Desdemona said. "Thou need not much patience."

Portia put on a fake expression that allowed her eyes to relax and shine with the hint of a smile. She wore her mask like armour.

The hall displayed several banners that hadn't been there on her last two visits. Reynold saved these for official judgement days. One depicted a blood-red coat of arms with two golden lions that had clearly been drawn by someone who had never seen a real lion before. Another banner portrayed a pyramid surrounded by four obelisks pointing towards the sun. More showed eagles with outstretched wings and golden crowns on their head. These were old symbols. Most people knew them at a glance, though Portia would be hard pressed to name a single one of them.

"Hear ye!"

A voice announced from somewhere behind the throne and the room went quiet. A young herald emerged from behind a curtain. He was Caucasian, dressed in red robes, wearing a puffy circular crown with a feather plume, and reading from a large tome in an orator's voice.

"Presenting the illustrious High King of the English, Keeper of the Seals, Wielder of the Crown of Christ, the Sceptre of Joseph, and the Holy Grail, the Slayer of Vlad the Impaler, Peter the Third of Portugal, and King Phillip the eighth of France. I give you the Ruler of the Imperium, Reynold the First!"

The room filled with shuffles as everyone bent to one knee. Portia kept her head low as faint sounds of movement came from the stage. It took a painfully long time for the old king to make his way to his throne and sit down. Yet, his voice was deep and strong even with its raspy edge.

"Court is in session," Reynold said.

Everyone stood, but refrained from talking. Portia knew the laws. They were all on Reynolds property seeking his favour, therefore, they were all in his control. He could do whatever he wanted on his land, and it was entirely legal. No one dared speak out of turn.

"Who doth beseech the great king," the herald said. "Who cometh before the throne of heaven to beg a boon of his greatness?"

Several voices cried out, "I do!" at the same time. But one repeated themselves over and over, growing louder each time and drowning out all others by force of will. "I have come with a request. I demand that Reynold hear me!" The voice was male and spoke with a slight Russian accent.

"I know that voice," Portia whispered.

"Thou wouldst. That is Alexei, High King of Russia."

Portia tilted her head in surprise. "Surely not. A High King in another's courtroom? He must be desperate."

Desdemona sneered. "Indeed."

Reynold had a half smile on his face as he whispered to his herald. The announcer's eye grew wide and his voice shook as he said, "His illustrious grace has requested to hear from… one of his Vigiles first."

"Der'mo!" Alexei shouted. "Don't snub me, Reynold. I've come on your terms. Now grant me the honour worthy of my title."

Reynold continued to stay silent. The herald steadied themselves with visible effort and asked, "Is there a Vigile here with a claim?"

Despite the hundreds of occupants, the room was unnaturally still as none dared to interrupt a waiting High King. But Desdemona raised her hand. *Damn it.*

"Thy Majesty," she said in her own stentorian voice. "Vigiles Desdemona and Portia, of the British Isles."

Portia nearly rolled her eyes. Desdemona was rolling her r's like an actress. *Bloody palaver!*

Reynold gave a nod of approval.

"You may speak," the herald said.

Desdemona paused a moment as if waiting for Alexei to disapprove, but the High King was silent. Many knew Desdemona by reputation. Some said if she wasn't sworn to the Vigiles and therefore banned from claiming land and titles, she could one day claim the throne of a High King—such was her power. Everyone knew Alexei, while mighty, was the weakest of the Kings. It was likely Desdemona spoke now, only to point out the narrow gap between their power. And they both knew it.

"We have encountered a fully empowered vampire," she said.

Shocked murmurs rippled through the audience. No one could stop themselves from talking, even with two High Kings in one room and the fear of death for interrupting. Portia felt a smug grin spread over her face. How many wizards could say they'd gone spell to spell with an enemy like that? She was still sour that they hadn't captured

Dorin outright. But they had forced him to flee. And now, their reputation would skyrocket around the world.

"How certain are you?" the herald asked. "There hasn't been a fully empowered vampire in nearly six hundred years. Surely you encountered only a rule breaker. A petty criminal with limited power who had killed a dozen mortals at most."

Desdemona kept her cool. "I summoned the black death," she announced, and several attendants muttered in awe. Portia had seen it herself, and it had terrified her. "The vampire touched it, and absorbed it into himself."

The murmuring turned into open discussion. Portia nearly laughed out loud. She'd never seen Immortals so flagrantly disregard the sanctimony of a High King's courtroom. Reynold's face was a mask of calm, but Portia could *sense* how pissed off he was that he had lost control. *Suck on that, you bastard.*

"How convenient," Alexei shouted, and the room quieted down again. "I come to see Reynold on important business, and we suddenly have a world crisis the likes which hasn't been seen in half a millennium. This is nothing more than a stalling tactic. Would the court please recognise the true seriousness of the international state?"

"The ego on that man," Desdemona whispered. "Thinks we found a great enemy just to spite him."

"Didn't we?" Portia quipped.

The herald shouted to quiet the hall, "Vigile Desdemona. His Highness, the great King Reynold, wishes to hear your full report."

Desdemona paused dramatically, and Portia got the impression she was doing it just to piss of Alexei further. "We hath been tracking the movements of known Royalists for over a year now. We took several into custody and have been *suggesting* that they name their conspirators. One finally named Dorin, a vampire. We put a description of him into circulation and got a notice from within the Library of Alexandria."

Portia hid her smile. Her mistress had completely omitted their failed attempt to apprehend him at the government meeting. That was probably for the best.

"He was working with two accomplices. However, it is my opinion that they were merely bystanders who he may have been trying to recruit to his cause. When we confronted them, his companions turned on him and claimed to know nothing about his dealings. They fled the scene and offered no resistance. Meanwhile, Dorin demonstrated the full range of abilities of an empowered vampire. We witnessed spell absorption, spell redirection, and a Will to nearly cause us difficulty." She shrugged as if it had not in any way been a close match. "It was his physical prowess that enabled him to slip away. Now, I wish to recruit more Vigiles to aid in our search, and notify the heads of government to be on the lookout."

Everyone had watched Desdemona as she spoke. Now, heads spun towards Reynold to see his response. The old King raised his chin.

"Who were his companions?" he asked in a raspy voice.

Now she was under his scrutiny, Portia felt herself growing more uncomfortable. Would he recognise her from her last visit here? Would he want to touch her again in front of all these people? She could remember the feeling of his old, wrinkled hands, and his fingers trembling from the effort. *No! I am a wizard. I am immoveable.*

"His companions were Silvana Romanov, the vampire, and her knight, Jason," Desdemona answered. "Though begging thy forgiveness, majesty, but I am confident they are not allies of Dorin. It was they who have opposed the Royalists twice now. They are responsible for the fall of wizard Peter Erikson and the knight Mikeru Yamato. It is likely Dorin sees them as enemies and has a vendetta against them for the harm they've done the Royalist cause."

Reynold seemed to smile now. "Interesting. We should get their testimony, don't you think?"

He stretched out his hand, and every wizard in the room seemed to feel the incalculable power of the greatest High King being brought to bear. Those in the front row leapt back in fear. Yet, it became clear that he wasn't attacking anyone. A sphere of magic began to warp in the centre of the stage, at the foot of the throne. Space folded itself according to the Will of the great king. Painted walls and marbled floors bent around themselves, and stars and planets shone through vacant space. Then, in the midst of that chaos appeared two screaming figures, dumped on the floor at the High King's feet with a loud thud.

The throne room was eerily silent, save for the frantic panting of the two victims of the High King's Will. Portia couldn't help feel a wave of sympathy for the poor fools. Her mistress had been right. Those two would never work with Dorin. But now they had to convince Reynold the First of that fact. *God rest their souls.*

It was the knight who seemed to figure out what had happened first. He dropped to one knee, the vampire half a second behind.

"Your Highness," Jason said. "How can we be of service?"

"We are yours to command," Silvana echoed.

It was surreal seeing those two in this context. Jason was a taller-than-average, athletic man in the peak of his youth, and to mortal eyes, he looked like he could easily beat up the old man on the chair. Silvana was beauty and grace personified, with long black hair, silver skin and blue eyes. She would have looked like a queen in any other age. Now, she cowered like anyone else.

Reynold gave a dark chuckle. "What's this, I hear? You have been consorting with empowered vampires, known Royalists and enemies of the Imperium. And now you claim you are mine to command? And I thought I knew audacity."

The couple looked at each other, utterly petrified. Unfortunately for them, fear made them look guilty, even if fear before Reynold was the appropriate response. The vampire spoke very slowly. "Your Highness, our wish is to serve you. How can we…" she stumbled and had to gasp for air, "…serve you?" she finished awkwardly.

Reynold chuckled again. "Oh, well said." He tapped his finger on the armrest of his throne several times, and the soft taps reached across the soundless hall. "What is your relationship to the vampire known as Dorin?"

The couple were perfectly still. Silvana spoke in a flat voice, like reading a newspaper aloud. "He helped us recently in the Library of Alexandria. He assisted us in our research since he was nearby. It was a coincidental meeting."

"Sir Knight," the herald asked. "Is this the truth?"

"Absolutely," Jason said without hesitation. The herald gave the High King a nod.

Portia recognised the spell the herald had used; a truth tester. She had used the same spell on Jason one year ago, in the Romanov mansion. If someone lied in its hearing, it would cause them incredible pain. Unfortunately, it only worked for mortals. That's why the herald had checked with the knight, in case the vampire was lying.

"When the Vigiles arrived," Silvana went on, "they attempted to capture Dorin. We removed ourselves from his company."

"Yes. We are not his allies."

Interesting. That was definitely not a lie. So if they're not allies, what are they instead?

Reynold tilted forward in his chair, and the couple shifted under his gaze. "What were you researching in the Library? I was not aware you had access."

They exchanged a glance again. The vampire started to say, "With respect, sire, I cannot…"

"Your Highness," the knight cut in. It was a terrible taboo for a mortal to interrupt an Immortal, even one married into the society. "We can answer your question if you will it. We only wish to state… if we reveal what we were researching, in front of all these strangers, it very well may cost us our lives. Naturally," he laughed, "we desire to live!" no one laughed with him. "But if you ask it of us, we will tell you everything here and now. Is that…" he took a deep breath, "…your will, oh High King?"

Reynold exhibited a curious expression, a raised eyebrow and a smirk. *Does he… approve this display?*

"Very well," Reynold said. "If it would mean your life, I will not require you to answer regarding your business in the Library."

Jason and Silvana bowed low in thanks. "We are in your debt, great king," the vampire said.

"However," the king cut in, and the hall went silent once more. "You should know something. This Dorin was hunting you. He is a Royalist, and you have killed two of his allies now. He is, in all likelihood, planning your deaths."

Jason gasped, "No!" in disbelief.

Portia smiled briefly. Her instincts told her Jason had faked his shock. But by saying *no* in a broad sense, he had not triggered the lying spell. Though, by design or sheer dumb luck, she couldn't tell.

"Thus, I would not aid my enemy," Reynold said. "By bringing about the deaths he desires. You may live. But be warned. He will find you again."

"Yes, your majesty," Silvana said.

"Very well. I shall return you to your origin." Reynold stretched out a hand.

"Wait!"

Jason's shout echoed through the hall and brought on a muttering of shocked voices. Even Reynold seemed surprised.

"Your Highness, may I be so bold as to ask a question of you?"

There was an audible gasp from the hall, including one from Portia's own mouth. *Stupid boy! You were so close.* Reynold's face became a chiselled stone of hard lines and weathered skin. Jason seemed to realise he'd said the wrong thing, yet still, he spat out his words in a mad rush.

"Forgive my impertinence, your majesty. I am new to Immortal customs. I am a mortal born from an unnamed family. Only a year ago, I did not believe vampires were real!" His voice raised in a bright tone for a second, till he thought better of it. "I only wish to be blessed by your wisdom and guidance, oh great King." Jason bowed his head and waited.

Reynold was motionless for nearly a full minute. No one spoke. No one breathed.

"Ask your question," he said. His tone was masked, so Portia could not tell if it was welcoming or filled with fury.

"Your majesty, this may be a delicate question." Reynold's face was impassive, so Jason seemed to just blurt out, "How come you don't have an heir?"

Good lord, child. Just when I thought you couldn't be more dense.

In the stunned silence of the hall came the sounds of a deep throated laugh. Everyone spun to see the High King, Alexei of Russia, clutching his large belly and roaring obnoxiously. Now, Portia had a good view of him through the crowd. She could see the man's thick beard and round face. He appeared like a mortal in his mid-forties, dressed in a traditional ushanka headwear and a long embroidered gown, with jewels and medals on his chest. All his ornaments were either silver or gold, and his clothes a dark brown, so he lacked all the colour of Reynold's regalia.

"The lad asks the question of the day," Alexei roared in amusement.

"Now it has been broached— yes, Reynold—let us all hear your answer. Your subjects wish to know, High King. Why don't you have an heir? And who will you name when the time comes? Pray tell."

Portia felt her own interest pique. She leaned in closer and watched as Reynold addressed the assembly.

"I," he said slowly, methodically, "have no need of an heir this day."

His words cut down the mood of the room. Alexei said nothing in response, and it seemed like the issue would disappear as quick as it came.

"Begging your pardon, your majesty," Jason said.

Eejit boy! Just shut up!

"I understand that you may not need an heir. But, your kingdom does. The world does."

The silence of the hall could not be any louder. No one could believe that a mere mortal had just corrected the High King.

"Thou art a fool, boy," Desdemona muttered, "Even if thou art correct."

Reynold stared at him for a long moment, his face blank, unreadable. Then he gestured with his hand, and Jason was suddenly lurched off the ground into mid-air. The crowd let out a collective cry.

"Jason!" Silvana screamed.

Jason was yanked towards the High King. His arms and legs floated outstretched just before the throne, suspended right in front of Reynolds face in the shape of a tormented X. The old man tilted forward in the throne, so much that the herald nearly stepped forward to balance him. Reynold smiled, revealing a broken grin with gaps in his teeth.

"If the world needs an heir," he whispered, his voice carrying in the silence of the room, "then God will provide one."

He released his magic, and Jason dropped to the ground with

a grunt of pain. Still, he bowed low multiple times as he backed away from the throne. Silvana made no move towards him, simply matching his bow. They were the perfect picture of submission.

"Regardless," Reynold said. "I am satisfied you are not working with this empowered vampire. Vigiles," he commanded, and several wizards in black stood to attention around the hall. "Pass on my command. The empowered vampire known as Dorin is to be hunted down with extreme prejudice. I want his descriptions listed at every Immortal building in the world. However, I do not want the mortals notified at this time. And, I want to know how he's getting his power. Vigile Desdemona, I charge you to find his source and cut it off."

"Yes, thy majesty," she answered.

"Oh, Great High King," the voice of Alexei said with a sneer. "I believe I can assist you in this matter."

Somehow, that was the one interruption that finally got under Reynold's skin. The old king turned a contemptuous glare towards his peer. Several people scurried away from Alexei. Portia summoned her Will, ready to throw up a shield at a moment's thought. Reynold had fought Alexei once before, in the year nineteen hundred and eight. It was known as the Tunguska event and it had flattened an entire forest for seventy miles in all directions. It was nothing more than a show of strength from Reynold.

"I need no assistance," Reynold said coldly. "Not when God sees to my every need already. Do you think you are greater than God? He who is the source of all your power? Tell me you are not so foolish."

"Where do you think my assistance would come from," Alexei said. "If not from God himself? Truly it is His divine hand we see in all things." He chuckled, as if unaware of the shoestring that his entire life hung by. "I have information on this Dorin. I would gladly share it with you." He grinned. "However—"

"Do not," Reynold ordered, his voice going deeper, "dare to bargain with me. You will give me the information you claim to possess."

"You know what I want in exchange. What is already owed to me. I am only adding incentive for you to proclaim justice be done."

"Justice," Reynold sneered. "You want to be gifted land without the expense of claiming it for yourself. I should think it fortunate you are not in my position as you can barely grasp the concept of justice."

"You swore," Alexei growled, real malice entering his tone now. Immortals, wizards and witches alike stepped back further. "You gave your word eighty years ago. The lands of Eastern Europe do not come under jurisdiction of any High King. They have been uncontested since the second Great War. All this time, I have been waiting for the treaty that we agreed upon to be recognised. Give those lands to me. It will bond us together as brothers and end bloodshed in those territories for the entirety of my rule. It is within your power to do this. Do not deny me any further."

The young vampire and her knight exchanged a glance now. Obviously, they had caught on to what was happening here. Reynold paid them no heed. He tapped his finger on his throne idly, as a certain glimmer came into his eye.

"I see no reason to bow to your demands," Reynold said. "You have already been invading these lands without my permission and have made absolutely no progress whatsoever. You, a High King, have been turned back again and again by the lower courts of local houses."

"Only because you backed them," Alexei growled.

"Is such the limit of your might? That a simple collection of farmers and peasants can turn it aside with a fraction of my support? I should hardly think I need listen to you at all. Your information on Dorin must be just as… impotent."

Desdemona rolled her eyes. "A phallic reference?" she whispered. "Are these High Kings, or little boys?"

"I suspect both, Mistress," Portia answered.

Alexei was growling under his breath. He looked ready to lose control and attack, yet Portia felt the shift of power in the room. Reynold was no longer playing around and ignoring Alexei for amusement. Reynold was in control now, and he was unassailable. Alexei had to know it.

The Russian High King merely said, "Then there will be bloodshed anew every day for the next hundred years until I claim what is rightfully mine. And know that you could have changed all of that with a word. I can only hope we avoid another Great War." He sneered. "And may God be with you in your search for the empowered vampire. By His grace, may he cause you no harm." Then, the world warped around Alexei and a mere heartbeat later, he was gone from the throne room.

The herald then proclaimed, "High King Alexei is cleared to leave the Royal Sanctum."

Portia couldn't help snorting. *A little late for that, herald.*

Reynold looked sharply at his herald, and the poor wizard seemed to quiver where he stood. He hadn't done anything wrong, per se. He'd just drawn attention to himself at the worst possible time. Portia braced herself for an explosion of meat and blood.

"Your majesty," Silvana spoke up. Her tone was polite, but her volume was loud enough to be heard across the hall. "By your grace, may we part ways?"

The herald looked like he was going to throw up. Reynold merely glanced down as if remembering the vampire and her knight were still there. With a simple thought of Will, the two were wrapped up in a turret of magic and disappeared from the throne room. Portia couldn't help a sigh of relief on their behalf.

The herald stood up tall. "Who else doth beseech the great king?" he asked. "Who comes before the throne of heaven t—"

He exploded.

There was a split second where Portia recognised the blast of Will from the High King, before the herald literally burst apart with a loud crack. Several screams went up from the crowd as a spray of blood and bone fragments were splashed across the room. Yet, all the gore flew away from Reynold, and his throne remained unmarked. The picture of Christ loomed behind him, unblemished except for the bloodied holes in His hands.

"I had not finished," Reynold said calmly.

He looked back in the direction of Desdemona and Portia. *Oh god, please don't recognise me now. Please.*

"If any Vigile," Reynolds announced, "discovers news of this Dorin, you are to report it to Vigile headquarters immediately. After which, report it to me personally."

"Yes, thy majesty," Desdemona called back.

"Very well. You are dismissed. Now, I shall hear petitioners myself. You all may approach my throne and speak with me directly. Consider yourselves blessed by God Himself to speak with His representative without any intermediary."

Desdemona and Portia each offered a low bow before they began to teleport away from the room. As they did, they noticed several petitioners also leaving, having abandoned their requests. Portia couldn't blame them.

Portia breathed a loud sigh of relief when they arrived back in their home. She immediately pulled her hair out of its bun and let it dangle around her shoulders and upper back once more, flicking her head and neck back and forth to loosen it up.

"Art thou... well?" Desdemona asked.

"Fine, mistress. Thank you." Portia let out a sigh. She'd kept it together. There was nothing in her mind that felt panic or unease during that entire exchange, at least not for her own safety. Which meant she had successfully kept her fear in check. She was a wizard. Strong. Immoveable. "Let's get to work."

Desdemona turned towards her instead. She leant forward and suddenly kissed Portia on the mouth. And Portia let her. Her scent was rich and earthy like sandalwood, and her lips warm and soft. It was all she could think of in the moment.

They broke the kiss. "Art thou certain?" Desdemona said, noticeable coyness in her tone, her eyebrow raised in question.

Portia couldn't help blushing and grinning. She knew they didn't really have the time to play, and it was not a serious offer. But she drew reassurance from it all the same.

"Thank you," she whispered.

Desdemona cupped her cheek and offered a smile. *That woman can be so terrifying when she wants to be. How few have seen this side of her. She can be so sweet.*

"It vexes me," Portia said as they drew away from their embrace. "The High King tasked us to find where Dorin gets his power, but the vampire has broken my trace."

"That was no fault of thine. Our foe is cunning. Thou was astute enough to lay a trace on the assassin instead. That may yet prove useful."

"Thank you, mistress. But, Dorin's power makes no sense. Surely he would need a lot of blood to grow this strong. Someone would have noticed if there were mass killings. How have we not heard of anything? It doesn't make sense."

Desdemona moved towards their wall of bookcases. "A vampire's power is not spoken of in the Imperium, for the danger of an uprising. Suffice to say, there's more to it than mere blood." She pulled out an old grimoire and walked back towards her. "This is a closely guarded secret, even among Vigiles. Only those with three centuries of service are privy to this knowledge, and the High Kings themselves. Although, by Imperium law, the information can be shared when an empowered vampire appears. Knowledge of their power will aid in their defeat."

She handed the book to Portia. "Read, and know why vampire laws are so strict. Why the boundaries on their power are so enforced. Know why they are not allowed to experiment with blood beyond their spouse. It will help us with our investigation." Desdemona let out a heavy sigh. "It is time thou learnt the true secrets of vampirism."

Portia took the book and felt her curiosity rising. She smiled. "Thank you, Mistress." She sat at her office chair and began to read.

Chapter 20

Jason ran to the sink and began to vomit.

Chunks of Edward's freshly made porridge splattered over the porcelain sink. Jason could even taste the honey. Edward had been so proud of his creation. It was his German family recipe from the 19th century. Now it was mixed with burning hot bile.

"Jase!" Freddie cried, appearing at his side. "There you are! What the hell hap—oh."

Jason ran the tap and splashed water over the corners of his mouth. "Reynold," he growled by way of answer.

"Fuck me! Uh… where's Silvana?

Jason stood up with a jolt. "Silvana!" he shouted. He scanned the empty kitchen, but Freddie was the only one there. "Silvy! Where are you?"

"Jason!" her cry came from across the mansion.

He sprinted towards the sound of her voice. Leslie appeared in a doorway, and Jason all but shoved the old historian aside. Silvana ran downstairs with Dorin a step behind. Jason had eyes only for her. They leapt into each other's arms with an audible thud. She squeezed all the breath out of him, and it was just what he needed. The physical reassurance of knowing she was there.

"I got sent to where I was standing when I was taken," Silvana said.

"Of course," Jason replied. He'd been eating breakfast when the magic had seized him, so that's where he went back. So stupid of him to think they'd go back side by side. He was clearly rattled.

"What happened?" Dorin asked from nearby.

"They didn't say," Leslie answered.

Freddie added, "Jase just said the name Reynold."

Everyone began to talk over each other in a big rush. Even Edward had appeared now and was chattering as insistently as everyone else. Jason finally loosened his grip on Silvana, but kept an arm wrapped around her shoulder. He couldn't bear to let her go out of reach. She was clearly thinking the same thing and held an arm at his waist.

"Was Reynold alone or with others?" Leslie asked.

"Was it his throne room? The one with the big Jesus painting above it?" Dorin asked.

Silvana shushed them all. "Let us sit down first," she ordered, and the others settled.

She led the way back to the lounge room where they'd had all their recent meetings. She let go of Jason to gracefully sit on the three-seater, leaving room for him to settle next to her. He tried to relax, though his heart was still pounding. His stomach gave another gurgle from the movement of sitting.

Together, they repeated the story of Reynold's courtroom and his interrogation regarding Dorin. They did their best to repeat the argument he'd had with Alexei, the Russian High King. And they mentioned how Reynold had been furious when Jason asked about his heir.

"I couldn't believe you did that," Silvana said, annoyance lacing her voice.

"By the stars," Leslie muttered. "The fates consider you fortunate, sir knight. Forgive my impoliteness, but I cannot imagine a more foolish thing to say! Nor a more dangerous person to say it too."

"Yeah, I know it was risky," Jason drawled, as if it were obvious. "But I figured there was a crowd of people. He would look bad if he didn't answer, since the question had been asked so publicly."

Leslie scolded him. "You underestimate the vanity of the High Kings. They have no need to worry about public opinion when they can kill on a whim, and their very word is law." Leslie ran a hand through their short mane of white hair. "I know you mean well, Jason. But you are too used to democracy and the belief in human rights. Monarchy has no such qualms."

"Leslie's right," Silvana added. "Reynold nearly killed his announcer for speaking at the wrong time. I had to interrupt, just to save that man's life. But for a second, I thought he was going to kill me instead."

"I'm sorry, Velouette," Dorin said, and Jason frowned at hearing Silvana's birth name used so casually. "I should have been there to protect you. I just found you again after decades of searching, and already I'm failing to keep you safe. I thought about going to Reynold's palace to rescue you, but that would only put you in greater danger."

Silvana shook her head and patted her little brother on the arm. "It's not your fault, Dory. None of it was. Not today, and not the last eighty years."

Jason wondered at that too—the use of the familiar nickname of Dory. What had she seen in those memories to make her suddenly feel so close to this stranger? She'd told the full story to Jason, so he knew the facts of the situation, but something was missing. There was an intimacy that seemed… rushed. *Or maybe I'm just jealous. Or it's because I don't have siblings.* Jason tried not to let his feelings show.

"I'm curious, Dorin," Jason asked. "How did you know it was Reynold's palace?" He immediately cursed himself for asking such a suspicious question.

Dorin sighed. "There are few Immortals capable of summoning

someone at a distance like that, so the odds were it was him. Reynold's palace is in Hastings, the site where his family's conquest of England began. I've been there before, incognito."

Jason nodded in acceptance. Dorin knew so much more than he did, and now that he had been proven as Silvana's true family, Jason no longer had a right to be suspicious of him. *He's family. Would you relax?* He had to make space for Dorin in his life. Silvana had spent the entire previous night telling Dorin about her life in Plymouth with her aunts and uncles. And Dorin had shared all about his search for her over the last eight decades. Meanwhile, Jason had fallen asleep on the couch with nothing to add to the conversation. It was hard not to be a little insecure about it.

"Well, we've been strangely fortunate," Leslie said. "When Reynold asked why you were in the Library, he very nearly doomed us all. You were wise to beg his allowance, Silvana. And I'm sure the flattery helped too." They smirked. "Although, Jason's blunt question afterwards could have undone that." They held up their hands. "Forgive me, I should not repeat my complaint. Our real concern now is the focus of the entire Imperium falling upon our new ally, Dorin."

"Yes," Dorin growled. "If only I could have finished off those two Vigiles. But they were a force to be reckoned with. That Desdemona especially."

Jason studied the empowered vampire. "Would you really have killed them?" he asked.

Dorin sneered. "No, I would have made tea with them." Jason bristled at his tone, but Dorin went on without pause. "Desdemona is nearly as powerful as a High King. I don't know how they measure these things, but if they did, there wouldn't be much of a difference between her and Alexei. I think Reynold is still several leagues above that. It's no wonder I couldn't beat her."

"She has a fearsome reputation among the Imperium," Leslie said. "I heard she didn't come from a wizard family. Rumour has it that she was a mortal who discovered magic on her own, such was the force of her will."

"I'd believe it," Dorin said. "She is formidable."

"Wait," Freddie said. "Is that possible?"

"If it's true," Leslie said, "then it's only happened once. I do not like your chances, my friend." They offered Freddie a smile, but the young man couldn't hide his disappointment.

"Well, I shouldn't keep regretting what's done," Dorin said to himself. "I couldn't beat Desdemona, and that's that. Now the whole Imperium knows there's an empowered vampire once more. My timeline has just dramatically shifted." He looked at Silvana with an intense focus. "My dear sister, I apologize for asking this so soon. But I need your help."

Everyone was watching him now. Jason felt yet another wave of suspicion for Dorin, and he forced it back down again. *He's Silvana's brother. You're just insecure.*

"Not to be rude," Freddie said. "But we're kinda in the middle of something already. A life and death situation, you know."

"My need is just as dire as yours, if not more so." Dorin stood up and began to pace, but with passion and zeal. "Velouette, I need you to come to our home country. To the place where I am fighting for my kingdom, to free my people from oppression." He smiled. "They are your people too."

Silvana gave a soft, joyful sigh.

"Wait, what am I missing?" Jason asked. "What people?"

"Romania!" Dorin said with a proud smile. "The great country of vampires. Perhaps the last."

Silvana's eyes glistened as she clutched Jason's hand. "It's true, Jason. I'm… Romanian." She let out a happy laugh. "I always thought

I was French."

"You should be so lucky, mademoiselle," Leslie said in their thickest French accent, winking as they did. Silvana smiled back.

She's Romanian. And she just... forgot to tell me?

Dorin knelt before Silvana and took her hands in his. "I have been working for most of my life to bring freedom to the people of my country. To truly break away from the control of the High Kings and establish our independence. But now that the Imperium know of my powers, they'll do everything they can to stop me. I must act quickly, or my country will face decades more of Imperium oppression. Our window of opportunity is narrow indeed. Please, Velouette, I need your help."

Silvana looked at the others for their opinions. Jason was quick to offer his.

"What about our mission?" Jason asked. "And the assassin? We've made so much progress. We finally know that we're looking for Reynold's heir. And we have Khadija to think about too. We need to resolve this before any harm comes to her."

"Velouette," Dorin insisted. "There are twenty million people in our country, and they all need us."

Silvana pulled a face. Jason knew what she was thinking. If Reynold did not have an heir, there could be global war. The number of lives at risk was higher.

"I sympathise," Leslie said, standing alongside Dorin. "I believe you are a good man, and it's precious and rare for an Immortal to care so much for the mortals of their lands. But we have our own mission of extreme importance. We were just starting to make real headway. We cannot afford to get distracted now."

"Fine," Dorin said. "You can all stay here and keep working on your cause. I just need Velouette."

"Ok, hang on a minute," Freddie cried, raising his voice louder than the others. "Can you please call her Silvana? I'm sorry, I'm not the only one getting bugged by this, right?" Dorin was glaring at him, but Freddie went on. "I know she was your sister Velouette. But that was like a hundred years ago or something? It's just polite to call her Silvana."

Inwardly, Jason smiled. *Finally, someone said it. Thank God for you, Freddie.*

Dorin merely shook his head. "Silvana is the name given her by her aunts. It's the name she used for her life of obedience to her family and her High King. But Velouette is her true name. Silvana is a prisoner, Velouette is free. I will call her the name that gives her power."

"She's not a prisoner," Jason said, but Silvana cut him off before he could go on.

"It's fine. I don't mind either name," she said.

Jason had to bite his tongue to avoid arguing with her. She was trying to keep the peace. Which name did she actually prefer? Did she even know?

"My point still stands," Dorin said. "Velouette can come with me. The rest of you can stay here and work on your own cause. I think that's a fair compromise. We are allies. We should work in partnership."

"Why just her?" Jason said, and Freddie nodded vigorously. "Why don't you want any of us there?"

Leslie grumbled their disapproval. They clearly didn't want more of the group leaving now.

"You can come if you must," Dorin said casually. "But you would be useless. I need Velouette. There is no one else in the world who will do."

"Why?" Jason insisted. "What do you want her for? Tell us what is so important."

Dorin took a breath like he was forcing himself to be patient. "I need to explain the secrets of vampire magic. She is the only vampire among you. It's as simple as that. This will help my people."

"I think you've skipped a few steps in that, buddy," Freddie grumbled.

"No one's asked me!" Silvana snapped, and the room went quiet. Only now did Jason realise they'd all been talking over the top of each other, and that he'd been speaking on Silvana's behalf. *Idiot.* He had to show her more respect than that.

"I'm sorry, Silvana," he said. "Please tell us. What do you want to do?"

"Yes," Dorin said. "Do you want to come with me, and learn the secrets of your power and save your country? Or stay with the witch here, and work on your great mystery?"

Leslie and Dorin stood side by side, opposite Silvana, and her eyes flicked back and forth between them. Jason stood at her side, supportive, willing to accept whatever she chose. He clenched his fists in helpless frustration. No one was talking about how Dorin's powers had incurred the wrath of the Imperium. Whatever his plan was, it was by far more dangerous. But Silvana was smart. She would know. And it was her choice.

"It's ok," Silvana said at last. She looked her brother in the eye. "I trust Dorin. I will go with him."

Jason had to hold back a groan. He tried to catch Silvana's eye, but she was only looking at Dorin. So he clenched his fists at his sides again. "If Silvana's going, then I'm going," Jason said.

"No!" Leslie cried. But Jason ignored their protests and collected his sword and his gun holster, attaching them to his belt in readiness. He put on his thickest coat so that it hung low enough to conceal his weapons, except for the lowest part of the sword's sheath.

"I'm coming too," Freddie said. "This is a huge thing for Silvana. I want to be there for you."

Edward said in a quiet mumble, "If Freddie's going, I'm going."

"Oh, come on!" Leslie cried. "All of you? This is absurd. Don't you understand how serious our situation is?"

"It's just temporary," Jason said.

"But the assassin found you the last time you left this mansion. This is the safest place."

"We've sat in this mansion long enough," Jason said. "The assassin could still find us here. I'd prefer to go on the move to avoid it."

"All right," Dorin said with a nod to Leslie. "Out of respect to my witch friend here, Velouette, you may only bring one person."

"Jason," Silvana said, turning to him. "I want you to come with me."

He sighed in relief. "I'll be there."

Dorin nodded. "Good. Now, we must hurry. If you two take my hand, I can teleport us there. I trust you have some way to stay in contact?"

Jason looked at Freddie. "My phone's fully charged."

Freddie was staring at the ground. "I got you, man. I'll actually take it off silent for once." His tone was filled with forced joviality.

"I'm sorry you have to go through that for me."

Freddie gave a dark laugh. "Take care of her, mate." It sounded like a simple pleasantry, but Jason understood his meaning. Freddie was frustrated he couldn't go, and he was clearly sceptical of this whole situation. Jason could only nod and hope that conveyed his understanding.

"Keep us informed," Leslie said, unable to hide their disappointment either. "Our time is also short. If you are able to re-join us as soon as possible, it would be ideal. We must find Reynold's heir before the assassin silences us."

"Thank you, Leslie," Jason said, but couldn't think of any other way to offer reassurance. He glanced at Edward, and saw the discomfort on his face. The alchemist seemed to hate the situation, but clearly wasn't going to say anything. Jason suddenly realised how much he didn't want to do this. He wanted to stay with Silvana, but he didn't want to go with Dorin into an unknown place.

"Come on," Dorin said. He was holding Silvana's hand and reached out for Jason's. They locked hands and Jason felt the vampire's cold skin and powerful grip as Dorin's power began to envelop them.

It was exactly like a wizard's power. The room folded around them in geometrically impossible shapes. Empty black space and white stars shone between the gaps, and Jason felt the ground lift underneath him. *He's a vampire. How is it working the same way as a wizard?*

They arrived in a small one-room apartment.

Jason felt disorientated as he tried to take in what he was seeing. He had expected a palace, for some reason. Instead, this was a cramped living space. The apartment was surprisingly modern. New lino flooring that looked like brown wood gave it an antique vibe. A stylish lounge room with Ikea couches stood opposite a compact kitchen with a floating island ideal for serving guests. It looked so mundane. Like the living quarters of any regular mortal.

"Welcome to my home," Dorin said as they looked around. "It's humble, but it helps me blend in with the mortals. That's why the Imperium hasn't found me. They assume an Immortal would be so vain they would need a palace. Or they'd be so radical they'd live underground. But how do you hide a leaf?"

"In a forest," Jason answered.

"Exactly. Here, I blend in like a mortal. Besides, our destination is not far. We should walk the rest of the way." Dorin opened the apartment door and held it open for them.

He led them down the narrow stairways and towards the street. Jason felt a little overwhelmed. It was the third new place he'd travelled to within twelve hours. He missed his real home, with its couch and beer fridge.

Outside, it was very early morning. The sun was only peeking above the horizon, and many of the people on the street were exercising before they started the day. The strangers paid them no mind, so Jason tried to ignore them as well. Yet, he couldn't help noticing… there were a LOT of beautiful people. Men and women. They all looked like they could be models walking around during their off-hours. Jason tucked his coat tighter to hide his weapons.

"Romania is a proud country," Dorin said as they began to move down the city streets. "But in many ways, we still haven't recovered from the Second World War. Our country was financially ruined. Our leadership shattered. We have been divided ever since."

"Forgive me for asking," Jason said. "But didn't Romania… join with the Germans?"

Dorin gave a dark chuckle. "It's complicated."

The city air was surprisingly clean. The entire street was lined with healthy green trees planted the length of the footpath and the main road had very little traffic, leaving plenty of space for pedestrians. The buildings looked like any other modern civilisation. Yet, there was a certain disrepair to their exteriors. The signs of a weak economy were everywhere. If Jason looked for them. Several businesses on the street had closed signs hanging in their windows, and those that were open looked like their signage had been made forty years ago.

"I'm unfamiliar with Romanian history," Silvana said. "I didn't even know they… we… joined with the Axis."

"Romania tried to remain neutral during the war," Dorin explained. "Our king was still ruling then. He asked France and Britain to protect us. We hoped the combined might of the two great High Kings would guarantee our safety, but both kings lost territory quickly. Reynold was reluctant to commit himself fully. Romania became expendable." Dorin sighed. "And despite our neutrality, Germany signed a deal with Russia without our consent, to let the Russians use our land for their troops. We were occupied by the Russians, who were known for their cruelty. We lost huge portions of our land.

"Then, in the second year of the war, there was a military coup. Our good king was removed from power and the Romanian military set up a new fascist government. That's when we joined the Germans and the other Axis. It was all done without public approval." Dorin gave a dark laugh. "I know the fascists took over our country and sent us into war, but many Romanians were quietly understanding. Many of us were bitter that we had been abandoned by France and Britain, and occupied by Russians. At least the Germans paid us any attention. We began to hope they would lead us to freedom, eventually. Romanians didn't think of ourselves as Nazis. More like... freedom fighters. We genuinely thought we were the good guys." He shook his head. "Then, when Russia changed sides in the war, many Romanians were eager for a chance to fight against the people who had occupied us and oppressed us."

Several locals walked close by them, and Dorin drifted into silence for a time. Silvana asked when the coast was clear, "What about the Holocaust?" She steadied her voice as if the question were physically painful. "Did Romania participate in that?"

"A tough but fair question. To some extent... yes." Dorin sighed and spoke the word with heaviness. "We participated. Romania was responsible for the deaths of a quarter of a million Jews, mostly in other countries. But we also protected the Romanian Jews as best as we were able. We weren't like the Germans, who were much more thorough in their purges. We at least tried to protect our neighbours."

Dorin stared into the distance. "But it was different for the fascist Romanians. They participated eagerly in the Holocaust. They hunted down Romanian Jews, even as many of us tried to hide them. Those were dark days.

"Then, the Allies began to bomb us in nineteen forty-three. By the time the Russians invaded again the following year, we were too weak to resist them. The people finally saw the error of fighting alongside the Germans. A new king rose up, and he led a coup against the military regime. He freed our country again, and in doing so, Romania was finally able to turn on the Germans and change sides for good. Unfortunately, this meant the Russians returned." He shook his head. "It's been eighty years, and High King Alexei still believes that our country belongs to him. You've seen what he's been doing to our neighbours. Meanwhile, Reynold does nothing."

"That sounds like Reynold," Jason growled.

"So where are we going?" Silvana asked.

Dorin gave her a grin. "There's a certain museum I need to show you. It's similar to when I showed you my memories. I probably could just tell you. But you need to *see* the truth for yourself."

"I'm sorry... a museum?" Jason tried to keep his tone light. "I thought our timeline was short."

"Trust me. This is essential."

They turned down a side street into a section of town that had no roads for cars at all. It was entirely designed for foot traffic. Everything here seemed significantly older. Cobblestone walkways, old oven-brick buildings and no street lamps.

"Welcome to the old town," Dorin said. "This is in the centre of Bucharest, our capital. Just north of here is our Jewish Neighbourhood. We give them a place of honour in the city as a way to ask forgiveness for failing them in the past." He gestured to the old stones. "This place is ancient. We keep it here to remind each generation of our heritage. Romania is a small country, surrounded by giants. It's important for us to remember our own pride too."

He led them across the courtyard of old cobblestones and ancient stone buildings. Jason noticed several plaques in front of the statues, explaining the history of each place. The plaques were written in English and Romanian. "Does everyone speak English here?" Jason asked.

"We have to. But many of us are trying to push for our language to gain greater use. It's just one more way we keep ourselves independent from the High Kings. We're here, by the way."

They had reached a tall museum entrance with stone pillars out the front. Posters advertised the Crown Jewels and history of the Romanian royal family as a special exhibit.

'Must leave in six weeks!' The posters advertised.

The trio walked up the steps. Silvana had been unusually quiet, and Jason knew she was trying to take it all in. He let her stay silent and figured she would talk when she was ready. He held her hand, and she squeezed back.

Dorin led them to a reception desk. He spoke in Romanian to the clerk, handed over cash, and got them three tickets in exchange.

"Have a good day," the clerk said in English, and Jason thanked her.

They followed a small crowd of senior citizens shuffling slowly down the walkway. At first chance, Dorin overtook them and moved straight towards the Royal family exhibit. Jason was relieved he didn't have to check in his weapons, yet at the same time, as a police officer he was always uncomfortable with a lack of security in public places.

On the wall were black and white pictures of people dated one hundred years ago. One man in the photograph wore a suit emblazed with emblems and medals, and his wife and children with heavily embroidered clothes and white vests. Nearby was a picture in full colour and high definition. A group of people in their fifties and sixties dressed in bright clothes and waving at the camera.

"Velouette," Dorin said. "This is our family. Our cousins. You saw them briefly in my memories. They were the ones who raised me after our parents were killed."

"The current royal family?" Jason asked.

"Eh… technically they are in line for the throne, but have no power now. The royalty was dismantled in the fifties, despite the fact that the king singlehandedly saved the country from fascists. These are the royal line in waiting."

Silvana read through the information silently. Dorin and Jason followed her and let her set the pace. She didn't ask any questions, so Jason had no clue what she was really thinking. Dorin was happy to commentate on each picture and display.

"Dorin," Jason asked. "We heard some time ago that you were one of the Royalists."

"Ah yes," he smiled. "I was wondering when you'd get to that. Yes, I did have an affiliation with the Royalist that you've fought in the past. I knew of Peter Erikson and his coterie. But I am not like them. Many Royalists are nothing more than young naïve Immortals who dream of power and control. Or they are older Immortals who dream of the 'glory days' of their family's supremacy." He looked at a picture of a king. "I am a Royalist. But in the sense that I believe it the royalty's sacred duty to care and protect for their people. Like my uncle, Michael the First, the last king of Romania who saved the country from the Nazis. Kings are meant to be the servants of the people. That's what the High Kings have forgotten. As Christ said, 'To whom much is given, much will be required.'"

"So, you're not trying to rule over mortals?" Jason said. His tone was light, but his question was serious.

"I want to free them," Dorin said, turning to face Jason with his piercing blue eyes. "Surely you want the same thing? You know he is a taint on this world hoarding all wealth and power. Don't you want mortals to live free from his rule?"

"I do. I actually agree with you about serving the people. You know I'm a police officer. That's what I do."

Dorin scoffed. "A police officer." He shook his head. "Jason, you are the Vigiles of the mortal kingdoms. You speak of serving the people, but you merely uphold the power structures of the mighty."

Jason blinked. "I joined to help protect the innocent. To uphold justice."

"Please, Jason," Dorin said, though his tone was respectful. "What justice is there if a rich man can steal as much as he wants through exuberant rent, but a poor man can't steal food to survive? That is the myth of the Imperium, that desperate thievery is worse than systematic thievery, even if the latter is born from nothing but greed. I believe the civilised thief is more evil than the uncivilised."

"I believe all thievery is bad."

"Oh, sir knight. Which is the worse crime? To steal a dollar from a billionaire? Or to steal a dollar from a homeless man?" Jason didn't answer. "Because if you think there's no difference, then you are on the side of the High Kings, not justice."

"Dorin?" Silvana called, and the male vampire turned away from Jason without pausing, as if Jason's angry scowl had no effect on him.

"Yes, Velouette?"

"This board here. It says the family line can be drawn all the way back to…" she stumbled. "Vlad the Impaler."

"Ah!" Dorin grinned. "The English would know him as the Impaler. The Imperium went to great lengths to make him infamous and defame his name and works. Here in Romania, we teach the true history. That man is a national hero."

"The inspiration for Dracula, right?" Jason asked.

Dorin shook his head. "He *was* Dracula. Dracul is literally Romanian for 'The Devil'. It was the name his enemies gave him, but he claimed it with pride."

"We were just talking about him," Silvana said. "Leslie was explaining that Reynolds invented crimes to slander Vlad's name."

"Yes! I'm surprised you know this." Dorin was smiling now, and his voice grew louder as he spoke. "Vlad of Wallachia was a great man who challenged the might of Europe and made massive reforms for his people. Education went up, human rights improved, quality of life and distribution of wealth was more fair and just for everyone. Naturally, the High Kings hated him for it. But that's not his worst crime." Dorin leaned in and whispered. "Vlad was an empowered vampire. The last of the old vampire lords."

"I don't understand," Jason said. "Vlad was a mortal ruler. I thought only firstborn children became Immortal?"

Dorin's voice grew louder in the quiet, empty museum halls. "Vlad was the eldest of the family, so he inherited the Immortality. But he *also* ruled the family house, which is the role of the second-born. He defied tradition and Imperium law to become both an Immortal and a ruler because he knew that he could make a difference." Dorin laughed darkly. "History remembers him as a monster, but that couldn't be further from the truth. Vlad was literally the nicest person you could ever meet. He cared about *everyone*. The lowest servant had the same rights as the greatest king. He was a humanitarian of the highest quality."

Silvana turned around. "Are you saying what I think you are?"

Dorin smiled. "Yes, Velouette. He is our ancestor. You and I have the same power. The same vampire venom now flows through our veins. And you are the eldest out of us two. Do you understand now what I'm trying to show you?"

He leaned in and whispered. "You are the heir of Dracula, the greatest vampire of all."

Chapter 21

Silvana couldn't believe what she'd just heard. The heir of Dracula? *The* Dracula?

It seemed too grandiose for the quiet, simple life she'd always lived, sheltered behind her aunts and forced into arranged marriages to mediocre men who resented their small lives. Through Nicholas's adoption, she had always been royalty as a Romanov even though it was a useless title for a fallen house. But here she stood, heir to an ancient house with a powerful, famous name. Heir to the greatest vampire of all time.

But I'm just... me.

"You probably don't know this," Dorin said. "Vampires take on the characteristics of our predecessors. It's just like how mortals have the genes of their parents and inherit traits through their DNA. Vampires are influenced similarly by our venom, which means you probably have a lot in common with Dracula. Tell me, have you ever stood up for the rights of the little people?"

Silvana gasped. "Yes. In Dubai, on the night we met. I ran to the kitchens to help the wounded after that explosion."

"And you saved that girl," Jason added. "Aakriti. The one who was being tortured for information on the bombing. You were ready to fight a wizard to save her!"

"Exactly. That's your vampire nature," Dorin said. "That is the heart of Dracula. You are destined to care for the oppressed, just like your forefather. You are a born liberator. Velouette, you were destined to be the saviour of our people."

Silvana's mouth fell open. It seemed so crazy. Yet it made total sense. It explained why she'd always been frustrated at her small life that made no difference, and why she'd always fought with her family when they encouraged her to do nothing in the global community. It wasn't about being rich and famous. It was about helping to make a difference. She was meant for so much more.

As she turned to Jason, he had a concerned look on his face like he wanted to say something. She didn't mind. He was always worried about something. They'd face it together when they had a moment alone. He would always be family to her, just like Dorin.

"Wait," she said. "Family. Is our family in here somewhere?"

Dorin paused before giving a sad nod. "Would you like to see a picture?" he asked. "See what they looked like?"

"I mean, I saw them in your memories."

"Yes, but that was also through the eyes of a child. It's also what they looked like during the most difficult time of their lives. Come, I want to show you what they looked like when they were happy."

They marched through the museum, skipping past much of the display. Silvana barely glimpsed artefacts behind the glass cages, rare items of jewels, clothing, old diaries, and several swords. None of that mattered now. She was jittery with nervousness. She just wanted to see her family. Her *true* family. *God, why are there so many other pictures here?*

"There they are," Dorin said. "Velouette, these are our parents on their wedding day."

Silvana paused, then she held her breath and moved to where she could see.

The couple in the photo were young, maybe early twenties or even late teens. The man had a grim face, hard lines and angular jaw. Yet, he was also beautiful in a very masculine way. His bright blue eyes and strong appearance would have been the envy of many. The woman next to him was even more gorgeous in her gown of white. She had the biggest smile, perfect teeth and full lips. Her face was soft in every way that the man's was hard. Her entire aura was bright and overflowing with joy.

Mum. Dad.

"They look so happy," she whispered.

"They were. They married for love, which can be very uncommon for Immortal Houses."

Silvana finally noticed there were other people in the photo, beside the bride and groom. She saw faces that looked slightly similar, and others with no resemblance. She didn't recognise any of them at first. Until one face made her blood run cold.

"Grigore," she murmured.

"Yes, that's him. Our uncle. The one who ruined our family, killed our parents, and caused Ana's death."

Grigore was standing beside the happy couple, his face hard as chiselled stone. All the joy in the room seemed not to touch him. At his side was the tall woman Silvana had seen in Dorin's memories. Grigore's mortal knight was a woman who wore trousers and a vest with a barely concealed sword to a wedding.

"What happened to him?" she asked. "Is he still alive?"

"No," Dorin said. "Don't worry, I had nothing to do with it. I know why Ana died in the war. Grigore was far too reckless. He was convinced if he went where the fighting was heaviest, he could consume lots of mortal blood and grow in power. Ana died when he attempted it once, but he still tried again. He died on the battlefield. Shot dead by mere mortals. It was a most inglorious end for one with such high hopes." Dorin's eyes were like two glittering orbs of blue ice as he growled, "He got what he deserved."

Silvana couldn't help feeling disappointed. Perhaps on some level she'd been hoping for revenge. But the one who destroyed her life had been dead for eighty years. There was nothing to avenge anymore.

"Is there a picture of us?" she asked.

"Over here." He led her down a display of the family timeline from the late twenties to the start of the war. There, she saw a black and white photo of a young family with three children.

She recognised herself from Dorin's vision. Here, she was a little girl. She'd never seen herself at that age before and had never been able to remember it. It gave her the most uncanny feeling of déjà vu, even though it was a new image. Looking at this child, she could see hints of her face as it was today, like a glimpse of the adult she became. The girl was smiling for the photo, but in the awkward way of a child who knows they're being photographed and is trying to smile on purpose. There was too much of her bottom teeth to be a natural smile. It only made it look more adorable.

She saw Dorin next to her. She hadn't actually seen him in his memories, since they were through his eyes. Now, she saw this tiny boy barely older than five with bright blond hair and blue eyes looking away from the camera in embarrassment.

"You're a cute kid," she said with a laugh

"Yeah, I was shy," he groaned.

She looked at the oldest girl. "Is that... her?"

"Yeah. That's Ana."

Silvana leaned in to look at the little girl. She had clearly already been changed into a vampire at the time of the photo. She was no more than ten years old. Her face was cold and beautiful like a master artist had created a perfect doll, but shadows had darkened its appearance. Ana was staring at the camera with such intensity it sent a cold shiver down Silvana's spine. It was like Ana was looking through time, straight into her eyes, like she knew her little sister was watching her in the future.

Silvana felt a wild urge to start shouting. There was an energy that burned inside her, rising up to the surface. She wanted to laugh. She wanted to *scream*. Something was yearning to come out and make a lot of noise. Noise. All the sound and the feelings in the world had to come out. Silvana threw back her head and let out a loud laugh.

Ana opened her eyes with a happy sigh. "That's better," she said. She was looking at a stupid photo of her family from a few months ago. Blegh, they all looked so happy. What was wrong with them? No one cared if they were happy or not. That's why they were all dead. Cause they were useless idiots.

She turned around. A man was staring at her. "Who the fuck are you, pretty boy?" she snapped at him.

He blinked. "Excuse me?"

"You heard me, cunt. What the fuck are you doing in my face? Do you want me to bite your fucking throat out?"

The pretty boy frowned in confusion. What an idiot. Another man appeared at his side and stood with his hands between them. "Hold on, it's ok," he said.

Ana smiled. "Oh, I remember you. Pussy knight."

He eyed her with distrust. "Hello again."

"Surprised to see me?" Ana said.

The knight maintained eye contact with her. "No. Just surprised to see you now. There's no danger."

"I am the danger," she said, running her tongue along her teeth. "I can come and go as I please. Now, who the fuck is this asshole? You better tell me."

"I'm… Dorin," he said.

She put on a dumb voice, "*I'm... Dorin!*' Are you even sure? Do you not know your own name, moron?"

"Velouette?" he asked. "What are you doing?"

"I am NOT Velouette!" Ana shrieked. "That stupid bitch is dead." She shoved at Dorin. "But you can at least recognise her sister."

His eyes and mouth widened into the stupidest face she'd ever seen. "You think you're... Ana?"

"Fuck you!" she snapped. "Don't treat me like I'm crazy. You're the fucking moron. Fuck this, I'm getting out of here. I want food. Where's some pizza?"

"Come back," the knight called. "We'll get you some food. Just come with us."

"Piss off," she swore and stormed out of the boring museum, past the old bags that were staring at her in horror. She thought about yelling 'Boo' just to scare them, but she was too hungry to care. The sun outside was hotter than she expected. The city was completely unfamiliar. She'd never been here before in her life. She turned around and saw the two men chasing her. "Where the fuck am I?"

"Bucharest," Dorin said. "Romania. We came here together... Ana."

"Well, I didn't want to come here. Take me back."

"But don't you want pizza?" the knight said. "We can get you pizza. You won't be able to pay for it yourself."

"Why the fuck would I pay for it? I can just fuck up anyone who gets in my way."

"No, Ana, you can't do that," the knight said.

She turned to the knight and leapt at him with her vampire speed. She snatched him around the neck and gripped him tight. The knight gasped. He had a gun at his belt, but he didn't reach for it.

"You aren't gonna fucking stop me, bitch. I tell you what to—"

Something gripped her hand and wrenched it free. She saw Dorin staring intensely at her, and she could feel power—vampire magic—

coming from him. "You're not attacking anyone, Ana," Dorin said calmly. "Now come on. We'll get you food, and we'll go back to my place to eat it. Then, I'll take you home."

She scoffed. "Fine. But the pizza can't be too cold. I hate that cold shit."

"All right," Dorin said, holding out his hands. "Come on. I know a good place." He started walking, and the knight hesitated as if he feared turning his back to her, which was the only smart thing she'd ever seen him do. But the knight followed the other vampire. Bored and with no other option left, Ana followed too.

The vampire was honest, at least. He found a pizza place and ordered a whole box straight out of a glass case. "It's always shit when it's not cooked fresh," she moaned.

"It'll take longer to get a fresh one. Besides, look how much cheese is on this one." She grumbled cause he was right. She really wanted to eat that cheese.

"Give it to me now."

"Not yet. We'll eat at home," he insisted.

"I don't want to fucking wait. Give it."

"No."

She screamed and tried to snatch the box, but the vampire restrained her again with his power. So she grumbled and let herself be led back to his apartment. As soon as they were inside, she snatched the box out of his hands and started chewing.

The pizza wasn't hot enough. But the cheese was good. Ana ate, and ate, and slowly she felt her mood mellowing out. When she finished the pizza, she just wanted to sleep. She wanted to lie down on the couch and cuddle this pillow. She wanted to shut her eyes.

Silvana opened her eyes.

She felt a strange stickiness on her fingers, and her stomach was bloated. She was so tired. She sat up and found herself in a strange place. *No, not strange. This is Dorin's place.* She scanned the room and saw Dorin and Jason sitting at a table opposite her. They both watched her intently.

"Did we just teleport?" she asked.

"No," Dorin said.

"Silvana?" Jason asked.

"Yes," she replied, confused.

He let out a sigh of relief. "Ok, good. Glad it's you. I was a bit worried there."

"What do you mean, *'you're glad it's me?'* What are you talking about? How did we get here?" The men exchanged a loaded glance. "Hello? Am I the only one here? Why are you both looking at me like I'm crazy?"

"Ok, sorry," Dorin said. "We didn't want to alarm you. But there's no avoiding it now." Jason looked like he was about to interject, but Dorin ignored him. "Velouette, something just happened to you. For a little while there, you were acting like you were another person."

Silvana blinked. "What? Acting like someone else? When?"

"It seems you don't remember it," Dorin said. "That can happen sometime. Sister, I think you just showed another personality."

"Personality?" Silvana said. "I don't understand."

Jason chimed in, "You were looking at your family picture. Your older sister, Ana, was in the photo. Then suddenly, you started acting like her. You called yourself Ana. You didn't recognise Dorin. It's like you were a completely different person."

Silvana stared at them, wondering when the punchline would come, but they looked completely serious. "Is this some sort of joke? I don't remember any of this."

"It's ok," Dorin said. "I've seen something like this once before. A friend of mine from years ago had this happen. Apparently, they had three different personalities, and they'd all take turns being in charge."

"Wait," Jason cried. "So it's not a vampire thing?"

Dorin screwed up his face. "What? No it's not a *vampire* thing! It's a mental health thing. You thought this was about her being a vampire?"

"I…" Jason stammered, but couldn't answer.

"I can't believe this," Silvana said, attempting to stand. A pizza box and half-eaten crusts covered her lap. "Where the hell did this come from?"

"That was your pizza," Dorin said. "Well, Ana's pizza. It was the only way we could calm her down. She tried to attack Jason at one point."

Silvana looked at the palms of her hands. They were covered in pizza grease. Now she understood why she felt full. *I ate this entire pizza. But I don't remember it at all.*

"I can't believe it," she whispered. Her stomach was full of food she didn't remember eating. She had to admit that maybe this was real. *How can this be real? I'm not crazy!* Out loud, she said, "This has never happened before. But then, how would I remember if it did? But no one's ever said anything."

"It's ok, sweetheart," Jason said. "Nothing bad happened, and we're all ok."

"Oh my god!" she cried louder. Her heart was racing and her hands shook with nervous energy. "I was acting like my dead sister? That's so fucking *wrong!* I didn't even remember she existed till yesterday. Is that was this is? My brain is trying to bring her back to life?"

"Uh… no, you didn't bring her back," Dorin said, a slight smile on his face. "Ana was nothing like… how you were acting."

"Then what am I doing?" she cried.

Dorin held up his hands. "I do have one theory." She nodded

for him to continue. "That person I knew who had the multiple personalities. They had three, which I understand is pretty common, though you can have more. One personality was their default, who they were most of the time. We thought originally that this was their 'normal' personality, but it was actually the 'good person' personality. The one who behaved themselves all the time and was always nice and polite. Then, they had their child personality, who was the youngest and most emotional. And third, their 'dark' personality." He shrugged. "It was a little nasty, yes. Foul-mouthed and angry. But it's not evil. It's more like a protector personality. The angry one is the guardian who protects you and keeps you safe."

"Ah," Jason said. "So Ana was probably the protector personality."

"I hope so. But she was also pretty childish. She wanted pizza and had a nap."

"True. But if Ana is the protector personality it would explain…" Jason trailed off.

"Ok," Silvana said. "So now we think I have *three* personalities? Not just the other one?" She could feel herself growing more out of control, but it was impossible to stop. She stood abruptly, letting the pizza crusts fall to the floor. She started pacing to burn off the nervous energy. "And you're telling me I just don't remember the other two at all? How am I going to stop them taking over at the wrong time? What if I stand before a High King and angry Ana starts swearing at him? Would I even recognise friend or foe in that state? Did I even recognise you?"

"Well, you didn't recognise me," Dorin said.

"Exactly. So what's to stop me attacking you if it happens again during a fight? I can't…"

Silvana stopped pacing. She slowly looked at the two men. They both stared back with blank expressions. "What did you just say?" she asked.

Dorin shuffled in his seat. "You didn't recognise me?"

She nodded. "That's right. You said me. Not *us*." She turned to Jason. "That means my other personality recognised you. And that means you've met them before. Haven't you?"

Dorin turned to stare at Jason as well. Her beloved knight shifted his gaze between them. He let out a long sigh. "Yes," he said. "I've met Ana, twice before."

"You're joking," Silvana gasped. "I can't believe it. You knew?" She let out a fake laugh. "You knew about this? And you said nothing?!"

"Hang on, I can explain." Jason held up his hands.

"What the hell, Jason? How could you keep this from me?"

"I'm sorry!" He cried in panic. "I didn't understand what was happening at the time. I mean, both times. It was very confusing."

"What times? When did this happen?" Silvana could feel her temper rising, but she didn't care. Jason had never lied to her before. It made her furious.

"Ok, ok, the first time was when we were fighting Peter Erikson," he said. "You took my blood and you got very strong. You were savage in that fight. It looked like you became… I'm sorry, but you became like an animal. I thought it was just your vampire powers at full strength." Dorin groaned loudly, but Jason kept talking. "You didn't speak at the time, you just fought the wizard. I didn't think there was any personality to it at first."

"And the other time?"

Jason sighed. "When we were fighting Hana and Mikeru. I got stabbed and you went savage again. You beat Hana. That time… you talked to me. And it was really scary. You said you were no longer Silvana, and that you weren't there to help me. You were only there to save Silvana. So I made a 'deal' with you to work together to save Silvana. Then you—Ana—bit me. It was against my will too. She said she had to take more of my blood for the fight."

"Why didn't you say anything?" she cried.

"Cause I had no idea what to say," Jason shouted. Then he forced himself to speak softer. "Look, I'm sorry. I was wrong. I should have said something. But it only happened during two dangerous, life or death moments. I thought it was just a savage side to you. Like an animal."

"An *animal?*" she screamed.

"No! Like a vampire thing," he scrambled.

"Oh, so you think vampires are like animals? Is that it?"

"No! Please, Silvana. I should have said something, I know. But I was scared. Because I'm just mortal." She rolled her eyes at him. "Everything's new and bigger than me and scary as fuck. I have no idea what magic can do. And I thought it was a weird magic thing that I didn't understand."

She glared at him. "Did you tell my family? Did you tell Emberline? Nicholas?"

Jason hesitated. "No. I told them nothing."

Yet, he had paused just a little too long. Silvana eyed him until the line of thought clicked into place.

"But they told *you* about it, didn't they?" She saw the flicker in his eyes, and knew she was right. "They already knew." She wanted to scream in fury. "They knew all along, and they never said anything. But they had the fucking audacity to warn you about it. Those… gaslighting fuckers! No wonder they always treated me different. They thought I was crazy."

"Velouette?"

"What?" she snapped.

Dorin spoke gently. "Do you want to ask Jason what they told him? Rather than speculating?"

She glared at Jason. "Right. Tell me everything." Jason looked so uncomfortable. *Damn right he should.*

"After your fight with Peter," he said. "I asked Nicholas and Phillip about your behaviour. They knew about it, but encouraged me not to say anything. Apparently, you were in that state when Emberline and Lisbeth found you."

Silvana frowned. "They told me they found me in a refugee camp during the war. They took me to England and nursed me back to health."

Jason looked at the floor. "Nicholas said that's what they told you. The truth is… you weren't in the refugee camp. You were outside of it, preying on the mortals inside."

"Oh my god," Silvana moaned, clutching at her head and collapsing on the couch.

"They said you had killed people. Mortal soldiers had tried to stop you and failed. Your aunts went hunting, and they said when they found you, you were feral. Like a wild animal. They adopted you and took you to England. It took four years for you to settle down. During that time, they told me that you… that you killed Emberline's husband."

Silvana let out a soft cry. "Oh Christ… so that's why she's always hated me. For something I don't' even remember doing!"

"They said you hadn't had a single relapse since then. That's why they told me not to bring it up. They thought it could upset you, and ultimately cause you to revert back to that stage."

She was breathing deeply, trying to keep herself calm. "Did they say how many people I killed?"

"No," Jason said, then added, "It's because they don't know." She let out a groan.

"I heard of that camp," Dorin said. "Northern France. After the Germans had taken over, I went there looking for you. There were hundreds of thousands of displaced people just living in camps, guarded by the Germans." He shook his head as if to dispel the memories. "One camp had a monster preying on them. People assumed it was German soldiers, kidnapping victims for rape or torture. But there were bodies drained of blood." He looked up at Silvana, and she saw his eyes starting to glisten with tears. "I searched for you there. I must have missed you by mere *days*. I never considered that someone would have adopted you. And if you were unsettled, they would have hid you away from the public eye. No wonder all traces of you disappeared there."

Silvana couldn't help it anymore. She gritted her teeth as a loud sob burst out of her. She clutched her face in her hands and let the tears flow. They continued for several long minutes.

Her true family had been that close. And her aunts had stolen her away from them. They had lied to her for all her life. They had trusted Jason more than they trusted her. And Emberline. *That bitch!* She had always treated Silvana like there was something wrong with her. Always treated her like a spoilt child, like nothing she'd ever done was good enough. Now she knew why. Her other personality had killed her husband, and Silvana couldn't even remember it.

She was supposed to have lived in Romania. She was supposed to be the heir of Dracula, the mightiest of vampires. She was supposed to be helping her people here. Instead, she'd spent her entire life behind closed walls in a prison built by the people who claimed to love her.

She had thought Jason was coming to set her free. He didn't want to marry her right away because he wanted her to be independent. He treated her with respect and encouraged her to be her true self. He had been different. But in the end, he had sided with the rest of her family. He was scared of her. Scared that she would be dangerous if she was free. She looked at him, and there it was plain as day on his face. He was scared of her, even now.

"Jason," she said. "I think you should go back and help the others.

Dorin and I can handle this from here."

The look of horror on his face was worse than anything she'd ever seen. He had not looked this upset when he stood before Reynold, or a furious Desdemona. This was his biggest fear. Something in Silvana nearly broke and relented at seeing his expression. But she wanted to get back at him for this. Maybe in a few days they could talk about it. Right now, she was mad. And he needed to know it.

"Silvana," he whispered, tears glistening in his eyes. "Please don't do this. I swear I love you. And I never meant to hurt you like this. I... I was just so scared of losing you."

"Just go, Jason," she said, giving him the coldest look she could muster. "We'll talk about this later when I'm done here. For now, I need you to leave."

She watched as Jason and Dorin exchanged a glance, both of them clearly uncomfortable and reluctant at first. But Jason gave a nod of agreement and held out his hand. Dorin took it and began to transport them away.

Jason looked at her one last time, and his mouth opened, but he didn't say anything before he disappeared.

Silvana sat down in the empty apartment. She felt a strange relief at having finally learnt the truth. Now she understood why her aunts had never trusted her and why her uncles still treated her like a child, even though they had both been younger than her. And why Jason had always been overprotective. But she would show them. She was the heir of Dracula. She was a powerful vampire. Dorin would show her the lost secrets that the Imperium had hidden from her kind. She would show them all.

As for those things in her head, this Ana, or whatever other personalities that still might be in there, she could handle it. She *would* handle it. Because she was stronger than anyone thought.

Dorin appeared a moment later. She could sense him standing

perfectly still, waiting. She didn't look up. "I think I need a minute," she said. "But then we can continue."

"Good, sister," he said. "Take all the time you need. When you are ready, I will teach you the true secrets of vampire magic."

Chapter 22

"I told you this would happen."

Portia wished she could let out a long, dramatic sigh, no matter how improper it would be for a Vigile of the Imperium to behave with such little decorum. If only she could blow something up.

Meanwhile, Jacqueline Rothschild, arguably the Imperium's greatest financial expert, was being no help at all. She sat opposite the two Vigiles in a blue business suit that had been stitched by hand using rare fibres of vicuna wool harvested in South America. Portia had googled the brand to check. The price tag was over one million euros. It still had lower value than Jacqueline's Rolex, her blue diamond earrings and the surplus surgery she'd undergone to remain young in appearance. The woman exuded opulence.

Desdemona growled, "Thou saidst thou wert the greatest financial expert of our time. Hast thou been misleading me?"

Jacqueline Rothschild clicked her tongue in exasperation. "I told you very clearly that I was an expert at money, not strategy. Certainly not criminology. I have fulfilled my part of the bargain exactly as I promised. You were the one who refused to hear me."

Portia traced her fingers along the room's mahogany table. This whole situation was the opposite of what she expected to happen.

Why had everything become so complicated all of a sudden? The room's fluorescent lights glared, and her face reflected back at her in all the blank TV screens around the conference room. Desdemona was the only one of the three women who refused to sit down. She loomed over Jacqueline like a dark shadow.

"Art thou questioning my intelligence?" Desdemona whispered.

"I'm telling you that you refused to listen."

"Let's go over the numbers again," Portia said, cutting off her mistress before the tension grew any further out of control. "You said you can account for every dollar the Royalists own. So where is it all?"

Jacqueline let out a long, dramatic sigh, exactly like the one Portia was thinking of. *That bitch stole my sigh.* "The Royalists have seventy-eight million dollars invested across one hundred and ninety-seven companies, spread among forty-three industries. They have a pool in banking, telecoms, transport and freight, engineering, infrastructure, and even Netflix."

"Why so many companies?" Portia asked.

"Because that's standard practice for good investment," Jacqueline snapped. "Everyone knows that. Don't put all your eggs in one basket." She picked up the stack of sheets in front of her and slapped them back down on the table. "This looks like literally every other investment portfolio I've seen a thousand times over. I couldn't improve on this."

"Thou couldn't?" Desdemona sneered. "Is someone better at this than thou?"

"I have an entire company of experts working under my command. A small army. No one could challenge us. So if I say this portfolio couldn't be improved, you can believe it."

Portia raised her eyebrow. "A small army?"

"The Rothschild banking group. We're the best at what we do.

Don't worry, they're initiated into Immortal society. They would not have leaked your precious information."

"And you're… what? The CEO?"

"What's your point?"

Portia let out a chuckle. "We've been talking to the wrong person. You're not the financial genius you claim to be. You're a manager. And you're a credit stealer, taking the praise for the people under you."

Jacqueline's face turned stony. It would have looked intimidating if Portia could see anything of the woman's original face still there. *It's like fighting with Barbie.*

"You have no idea what you're talking about. You came to me for help because you knew nothing on your own. I'm the one who manages Reynold's trillions. I'm the expert here. You think I have time for all the grunt work? The endless paperwork? Do you know how bloody long it takes to write computer code? I'm far too important for that bullshit. That's why I have people beneath me."

"I bet you didn't even do this work yourself," Portia said, pointing to the pile of papers. "You had your lackeys do it all for you?"

"I oversaw the work."

"You're just the company figurehead," Portia said. "You're a fraud."

"Fraud? I'm the culmination of a millennia of banking practice. I am the queen of capital."

"Enough," Desdemona said. Her calm, flat voice cut like a blade. "Regardless, I trust this work was done with the highest competency?"

"Of course."

"Good. Then thou canst continue to investigate this matter further."

"What? But I already—"

"Thy team is most effective. I trust their ability to find a link between these investments."

Jacqueline's voice became shrill. "It's not my field!"

"Then let me give you some suggestions," Portia said. "Look at these one hundred and ninety companies you mentioned. Which High King owns them? Is there a High King they've invested with more than the others? Or less? Where are their locations? Do they have buildings near each other in a group? What about their competitors?"

"Well, that's easy. They have almost none with Reynold."

"Reynold?" Portia asked, frowning in suspicion. "Isn't he the richest of the Kings?"

"No, that's Jin. But Reynold is second."

Portia exchanged a glance with Desdemona. "What if that's their plan? Target Reynold in some way that affects his economy. They then profit when his competitors rise."

"They wouldn't dare be so foolish."

"Unless they were being backed," Portia said. The implication was clear between the Vigiles. They suspected another High King was involved.

"What are you saying? Who is backing them?" Jacqueline asked.

Portia ignored her question. "Where are all these companies located? The ones the Royalists chose. I want a chart of their worldwide locations."

Jacqueline sighed again. "I'll get one made."

"Send it to me once it's finished," Portia said. "You have my contacts."

Desdemona started to teleport right away, unannounced and on the spot. Portia had to hasten to reach the magical sphere in time to join her. It was a most undignified scramble. Portia could feel her mistress' patience for the whole situation growing thinner by the minute. She caught a glimpse of Jacqueline's relieved expression before the scene changed entirely.

They arrived back in their main headquarters, and Desdemona immediately stalked towards a computer desk and sat down. Portia sensed her tension and took a stance before her, feet together, back straight, hands at her side. "How can I assist you, mistress?"

"Portia," Desdemona soothed. "Thou hast no need for formality. I am not wrathful."

"You are disappointed."

"In the situation, not thyself. Please, be at ease." She lowered her voice to a whisper, "my love."

Portia startled. She had thought Desdemona was tense. Portia sat down opposite her, tapped her computer screen to wake it, and tried to adopt a relaxed pose in her chair. "You left rather abruptly."

"It was my own impatience."

Her own impatience? That sounded strangely like admitting fault. That was very unlike her. Unless… "Wait. Do you think it was a mistake to see Rothschild?"

"It didn't exactly help."

Portia studied her for some time. Desdemona always kept her thoughts closed off, even to her most significant life partner. Yet, there was something Portia was missing here. Some mistake that her mistress was trying to avoid talking about.

"You didn't realise she was just a figurehead," Portia said, understanding in her voice. "You believed the myth. That Rothschild was the brains behind her operations."

"It's what they all claimed," Desdemona said flatly. From her, it was as good as an admission of fault. No wonder she was frustrated. She had taken so long to admit she needed help investigating the Royalists finances, only to ask for help from the wrong person.

"Rothschild's position is not uncommon. She is the top of a pyramid and takes credit for everything created underneath. You shouldn't feel bad for believing her. People like her spend all their efforts on creating the perfect reputation."

"I am not a fool. I am practised at seeing through lies."

Portia offered her a smile. "I saw through her, and you trained me. You can still count it as a victory of yours."

Desdemona eyed her and smirked. "Thou art being generous. But I am grateful. I am… unused to such situations."

"Oh, well put," Portia purred. She sat back in her chair and stretched her arms overhead, before tilting her neck to crack it. "But this leaves us back to guessing. Rothschild may yet provide something of use. Meanwhile, what else do we have to go on?"

"Dorin. The High King tasked us to find the source of his power. We could switch targets for a while. Where wouldst thou search for him?"

"The Romanovs. I'm sure they knew more about Dorin than they revealed to Reynold."

"I concur. Though the Romanovs have their own trouble. What of their assassin?"

Portia huffed in frustration. "My trace is still on the shapeshifter since our encounter in the Library. But it hasn't changed. I still cannot teleport to their location. Some powerful magic is blocking my trace."

"Canst thou attempt to overpower it?"

Portia winced. "It would be unwise to test myself. I fear the power involved is significant."

"Another mark of the High King?"

"Tis possible."

Desdemona let out a low breath that was in equal parts a growl. "We grasp at straws. If we could only interrogate a High King, we could begin to make progress. One of them is guarding Dorin, and either they or another is protecting this assassin. We are tangled in a web woven by greater powers, and I fear we shall not escape without finding the weaver."

Portia studied her mistress closely as she closed her eyes and began to meditate. She knew Desdemona's mannerisms enough to know when she needed to think in silence, so she gladly waited. The older Vigile was silent for several long minutes.

"It is possible," Desdemona said, her eyes still shut, "that speaking with the Romanovs will lead to answers regarding Dorin. Yet, I am loathe to seek them out and essentially ask for their help. Not unless there are no other options."

"I understand, mistress."

"Therefore," her eyes snapped open, "I would like to attempt to locate this assassin. You will pass the trace to me, and I will find it."

"Understood."

Portia summoned her Will. With a thought, she took the piece of her mind that was locked to the assassin, then she placed that piece in the palm of her hand. It was all metaphysical, there was nothing tangible to touch, but the act was sufficient. Desdemona took Portia in her hands and absorbed part of the power. It worked without a hitch, and Portia nearly let out a childish giggle. Swapping magic was a rare ability, even among the mighty. It required an intimacy between the two users that few others had. The fact that Portia could pass her mind over to Desdemona was a magical certainty that their bond was strong and intact.

"So, thou hast not withdrawn from me," Desdemona said. "That is as it should be."

Portia frowned. "Withdrawn? Why would I…" she stopped and studied the look on her mistress's face. "That was a test. You wanted to see if we were still bonded."

"Thou hast been withdrawn for six months. I should think it prudent and wise to show some concern at this point."

"That has nothing to do with you. I've told you this many times. I just…" she trailed off.

"My love," Desdemona grasped her hand, this time clutched between her two. "I was merely making sure. I could not bear it if thou wert to leave. Thou knowst thy worth in my heart."

Portia's train of thought faltered. Desdemona was being… vulnerable. She was bearing her heart and emotions to her. It wasn't unheard of, yet it was a rare thing indeed. She must really be concerned. Her sincerity seemed to melt away the wall of ice Portia had built around her own heart. Desdemona deserved something in return.

"You've been patient," she said. "I really appreciate it. And I will be ready again soon. Just… not yet. I'm sorry."

"No apology is necessary," Desdemona said. Then she bent down to kiss the back of Portia's hand. "I will always be here when thou art once again willing."

Portia felt the slightest stirring of that old flame within her. It wasn't much, but just enough to remind her that she still desired this woman and would continue to desire her no matter what. Even a small spark was enough to prove she was healing. Maybe if she tried fanning the flames a little now, a fire would ignite.

Her computer made a soft chime. Portia glanced away on impulse, but Desdemona took it as a sign and released her hand. Portia almost regretted to see it go. She checked the notification on her screen to help dissipate the awkwardness.

"It's from Rothschild," she said, then let out a short bark. "Apparently her team could put the information together quicker than she expected. Sounds like she has no idea what goes on in her company." Portia clicked on a link and brought up a map of the world. There were nearly two hundred red tags marking different locations. She hovered her mouse over one to bring up information on the company. She began to read through the information.

"Curious," Desdemona murmured. "One would think a list of

investment companies would have a bigger cluster here." She leaned over Portia's shoulder and pointed to the eastern coast of America. "New York. That's where Reynold keeps the majority of his banks. It's usually a hotspot for finance. Yet the Royalists don't have anything in this area."

It was true. There were multiple clusters of red tags around several major world cities, particularly in Asia and Eastern Europe. Yet North America had a certain sparsity.

"Well, Rothschild mentioned this," Portia said. "It seems the Royalists are avoiding any investment tied to Reynold and his accounts."

"Finally."

Portia blinked. "Mistress?"

"We have one more piece of the puzzle. We can safely say *who* the Royalists are targeting, even if we don't know where and how exactly."

She blinked again. "Surely you don't mean… Reynold? Who would be crazy enough to challenge him?"

Desdemona turned to face her. "Someone with the backing of another High King."

Chapter 23

Jason arrived back in Edward's mansion in Swansea, England, once again, in the empty lounge room. Dorin relaxed his grip on his arm and cleared his throat, avoiding eye contact.

"Thank you," Jason said, still feeling numb.

"It's ok," Dorin replied. He shuffled a few steps back. "You know, I'm going to take care of her. She'll be perfectly safe with me. I'm sure she'll feel better soon, and I'll encourage her to talk to you when things settle."

"Thanks." Jason let out a long sigh. "I just wish I'd told her. I tried to tell her several times, but I always lost my nerve."

Dorin frowned at him. "If I may offer some unsolicited advice," he said. "She's a vampire. You are her mortal knight. She will always be stronger than you. Your job is to watch her back, not to coddle her."

"I know," Jason snapped. "I've been the one telling her that for the last year."

"Really?" Dorin drawled. "Then why didn't you tell her the truth?" Jason had no answer, but he could see the satisfaction in Dorin's face. "See you around, knight." Dorin stepped back, and the world folded around him once more until he was gone.

Jason stood alone. It was the first time he'd been alone in days. He waited a moment to see if anyone would walk by the lounge or notice his return, but the house was devoid of activity. He listened for sound, finally registering a faint clamour of voices coming from Edward's lab. Leslie, Freddie and Edward were clearly doing fine on their own. So, he sat down on the couch for a moment.

The tears started to flow, unbidden.

He buried his face in his hands and let himself cry. He hated this. He hated everything that had happened. And, most of all, he hated that he was responsible. He'd been too scared to tell Silvana the truth, too insecure that something would go wrong with their relationship. He should have been honest with her, no matter the consequences. Let her make her own choice. That was the only way for love to be real, when everyone gets to choose it for themselves. *What an idiot. I've been telling her I believe in her. Then I hide the truth because I clearly didn't trust her enough. No wonder she's mad at me.*

The sobs slowed down at last. Jason wiped his eyes with the back of his hand and gave a loud sigh. He had to do something to fix this. All he wanted was to find Silvana and just explain himself again. Maybe, if he used different words, she would understand. If only he could get back to Romania and talk to her again. He pulled out his phone. Maybe he should call her. Text her. Beg her to listen to him.

"No," he said.

He knew he was still being insecure. He was scared of losing her, like he'd lost his mother, and it was exactly the fear of losing her that had *caused* him to lose her. He had become so afraid that he'd acted stupidly. He needed to show her more trust.

So he sent a single text, calmly worded, doing his best to be respectful.

"I'm so sorry I didn't tell you the truth. I was wrong. Please let me know if you'd like to talk. I'm here for you. I love you, Silvana." And hit send. He would have to hope that was enough.

Now, to do something practical. There was no point wallowing any further, even if he felt emotionally exhausted. He forced himself to stand up and move towards Edward's lab.

The low mumble of conversation became clear-cut as he climbed the stairs. Edward spoke in an animated tone, excited about something. Jason stood in the doorway, taking in the sights of Edward's stacked shelves filled with bizarre contents, all neatly ordered according to colour.

"...if we mix the sample into the elixir," Edward said, "we should be able to scent its duplicate for up to an hour. If we use it before a public gathering, we could literally sniff out our target."

"Like drug dogs at the airport," Freddie said.

"A colourful yet apt description," Leslie replied a little dryly.

Jason knocked on the door and watched as all three occupants jumped out of their seats. "Sorry!" he called. "I'm back early."

"Jesus fucking Christ, mate," Freddie yelled while clutching his chest. "Thought we were all about to die a painful death."

"I just knocked on the door."

"Well, next time, think first!"

Jason blinked. "Ok sure." He crossed the room to their workbench. "What are you working on?"

Leslie chimed in before Edward could explain. "I think the priority question is… why are you back so soon? And where's Silvana and Dorin?"

The names brought a fresh stab of pain to Jason's heart. *Should I tell them that I'm a horrible boyfriend, and she's better off now with her brother?* At least Dorin treated her with the respect she deserved. *Stop it, you're moping,* he told himself. He looked them in the eye and told them the truth.

"Silvana and I had a fight, and she asked Dorin to bring me back."

Their faces reflected the exact emotion he didn't want to see. Pity. He brushed past it and launched into a full explanation. He was always going to tell the truth now, to everyone, no matter the risks. "Silvana's family line are descended from Vlad the Impaler. She is the heir of Dracula, and heir to the royal house of Romania."

"You're joking," Leslie cried, frowning in thought. "The heir of Dracula? But that line was finally broken in the Second World War. Ah!" Leslie nodded to themselves. "But she was a war orphan. I guess it makes sense." Leslie laughed. "What are the odds?"

"It is pretty cool," Freddie said. "I always knew she was special."

Jason went on. "Then Dorin showed her some family pictures, and she had a mental breakdown. She started acting like a different person and called herself Ana, like her dead older sister, Ana. This persona attacked me and got violent until we calmed her down."

"Whoa," Freddie said. "Silvana has multiple personalities? That's kinda cool." He blushed. "I know that's not PC to say, but I think it's cool. How long has she had it? Did she know about it, or was it a surprise?"

Jason felt like the wind had been knocked out of him. Freddie had accepted it already just like *that*. As if it was the most natural thing in the world. And suddenly, Jason understood the depths of his mistake. He'd been selfish. If he hadn't been so focused on his feelings, he could have reacted just like Freddie. With acceptance. How much more could he have helped and supported Silvana, if he had just thought about what was best for her?

Maybe she should be dating Freddie.

"Jase?" Freddie asked.

"Sorry. I just can't believe how accepting you are. I wish I'd reacted that well." He grimaced. "To answer your question, no. Silvana did not know she had it. But she figured out that I knew. I'd seen it happen twice before, and her family warned me about it too."

"Wait," Freddie said. "You didn't tell her? Not once? Dude!"

"I know! I'm very aware that it was the wrong thing to do. I was just scared. I didn't realise it was a mental health thing. I thought it was a vampire thing."

"Oh boy," Leslie said with a groan. "I bet she hated that."

"Yeah."

Leslie let out a sigh. "Ok, this isn't the end of the world. You and Silvana are married, and you have a strong relationship. After things cool down, I'm sure you'll work this out. Also, forgive me if this is somewhat calloused of me to say, but she needs your blood. She'll be back eventually. Meanwhile, we've got some ideas we could use your help with. Are you ready to get back to work?"

Jason grumbled. "Yeah. Sure." Freddie put an arm around Jason's shoulder and clasped him tight, and Jason gripped the hand there for a moment, nodding in thanks.

"It'll be ok, buddy," Freddie said in a soft voice. "You and Silvana are an amazing couple. You'll work through this, I'm sure."

"Thanks man. I just feel like shit right now." He noticed Leslie watching him, so he let go of Freddie's hand and cleared his throat. "So, what's going on here?"

Leslie smiled, but it didn't reach their eyes for some reason. "Edward here has thought of a brilliant way we could track down Reynold's heir," Leslie said. "Apparently, if we had a drop of Reynold's blood, we could mix it with this elixir—"

Edward cut in, "It's a scent amplifier! It makes your nose extra sensitive to another of the same scent. So if you put a bee in the elixir, you could smell another bee from a mile away. It's a great way to search for something. So if we put someone's blood in there, we could find them through smell." Jason found himself nodding along with a smile. "If we put in Reynold's blood, we could smell someone with his blood type as well. We could smell his descendant. It would help us find his heir. Isn't that great?"

Jason frowned. "Doesn't Reynold have like… a million descendants? How do we smell which one is the heir?"

All three of them exchanged glances.

"Oh," was all Freddie said.

Jason looked at Leslie. "You signed off on this?"

Leslie grumbled. "We were somewhat desperate."

"Oh boy." Jason sighed. He rubbed his face with his hands. "Ok, well sorry to be a big downer on your day. Can I just… does anyone mind if I go eat something? I threw up my breakfast and have been teleported four times already today. A bit of food will help me think of what to do next."

"I'll come with you," Freddie said and he left without another word.

The two Immortals stayed in place, Edward continuing to work on his elixir, and Leslie sitting with their hands in their lap and a thoughtful expression. Jason followed behind Freddie without a second glance back.

"Do you ever feel hopelessly outclassed?" Freddie asked.

Jason was standing by the kitchen bench, building an absolute mountainous pile of sandwiches. He wasn't sure how many of these he was going to eat, but it would damn well be a lot of them. He still wore his sword and gun around the house, just in case. "Constantly, mate," he grumbled.

"It sucks being a mortal on a team of Immortals," Freddie said, sitting at the table. "It's like being the only white person in a room full of Asians."

"You're Asian!"

"I know. That's how I know what it's like." Jason smirked and didn't answer. "I had one job in the heist. Those damn cameras. We all know how that worked."

"Honestly, it kinda did work. We figured out we're looking for

Reynold's heir. The cameras got us far enough in the end."

"You're being kind, mate. But I know I fucked up pretty hard. We still have no idea how to find this heir, and I'm sure if the cameras had worked, we would have found the information we needed. I don't know what I can do anymore. I'm on this team and I'm trying my best, but I'm absolute deadweight."

"Trust me," Jason said. "I know how you feel."

"Come on, Jase. You? You're a cop and a knight. You've got firearm training, and combat training from two Knights Templar." He pointed to Jason's belt where his gun holster and sword hung at the ready. "You out-fought Mikeru Yamato, a literal ninja." Jason snorted. "No, seriously. You may be the underdog, but at least you can hold your own through sheer badassery. What am I, by comparison?"

Jason turned around sharply. "You're my best friend, Freddie. I couldn't do this without you."

"Jason…"

"I mean that. I would have died a year ago, on my first case in the Immortal world, if you hadn't saved me. I need you."

Freddie chuckled. "Yeah, yeah, I love you too, Jason," he drawled like it was a joke.

Then they made eye contact across the kitchen and the smile disappeared from Freddie's face. Instead, Jason found himself staring into Freddie's dark brown eyes as he stared back. The room went very, very quiet.

Jason cleared his throat and they both looked away. "So, yeah… um… you want a sandwich?"

"Oh, yeah. I was just… yeah. Sandwich is good." Freddie cleared his throat too.

Jason sat at the table, threading his sword around the back of the chair. He slid the massive plate of sandwiches into the middle of the table where Freddie could reach too, avoiding his gaze. They ate together in silence.

"So I was saying," Freddie went on. "Wouldn't it be great if I could become Immortal and find some power to help the team? That's why I got excited when Leslie said that Desdemona had found magic on her own."

"Yeah, I feel like there's a story there," Jason said.

Freddie only shrugged. "I've asked Eddie if he can teach me alchemy, but apparently there's a limit. I can mix elixirs and do basic herbology, but there's a magic component you need to be taught from birth, and I'm too old to learn it now. I think the only real option would be to get bitten by a vampire."

"Buddy, I don't think you need to go to that extreme just now."

"Come on. Wouldn't you want to become Immortal if you could?"

Jason shrugged. "If I were an Immortal, then Silvana couldn't use my blood."

"Ah. So you choose a mortal life for her, like in Lord of the Rings?"

"Yeah, I guess. I haven't really thought about it too much. I guess I see the Immortals commit so much evil through their rule from the shadows. I don't want to be anything like them."

"Even if you would use your power for good?"

"I think that power might corrupt me. Like if Gandalf took the ring." He winked. "Keeping with the Lord of the Rings theme."

"I appreciate that." Freddie shook his head. "Well, I respect your opinion. But that wouldn't be my choice. I would absolutely become Immortal if I could. Then, I could actually contribute something useful."

"Stop that." Jason lowered his sandwich and looked at his friend. "Freddie, I hate hearing you talk about yourself that way."

"Well, come on. What exactly am I going to do in this current situation? What's my contribution?"

Jason glared at him. "All right. Let's say you become a wizard as powerful as a High King. How would that fix this situation? How would more power help us find the heir, stop a potential war of succession and call off a murderous assassin?"

"Well, if I were as powerful as a High King, I would just slap them all in the face and say, 'Shut the fuck up'. That would stop the war pretty easily, wouldn't it?"

"Freddie…"

"All right," he grumbled. "It wouldn't really solve anything. But at least I wouldn't feel so powerless all the time."

Jason reached across the table and patted him on the arm. "Honestly mate, I think magic and power are like money. We all want just a little more. But at a certain point, it just becomes a bottomless pit that you can never fill, and it'll never be enough."

Freddie's eye narrowed, but his lips curled up into a smile. "Yeah, all right, Jase. You make a good point." Jason understood. Freddie had lost the argument and was somewhat mad about it. Freddie sighed. "This reminds me of my days with the Monster Hunters."

"Ah, yes. Those nut cases."

"They all thought they could fix the world if they found the big secret bad guy doing all the bad things. But it was just a front for all their rage and hatred. What they needed was therapy and weed." Jason couldn't help laughing. "I guess I still have the same proclivities. I tend to look for a quick, easy solution to a complex problem."

Jason gave him a sombre nod, then kept eating. He tried his best to cheer Freddie up, but the truth was he felt exactly the same. Maybe if he knew a little more about magic or had more wisdom or power or expertise, he would be able to make informed decisions about everything. Maybe, he wouldn't have screwed things up so badly with Silvana.

Freddie pulled out his phone and started scrolling in silence. Jason took the chance to think through their situation. He couldn't help

Silvana right now, so his sole focus needed to be Reynold's heir. He tried to think of who could be a contender for the throne, but he gave up on that pretty quickly. He didn't know enough Immortals to have any real idea about that.

So, he thought about Leslie. The witch had been pretty damn sure that they would find what they needed in the Library. That book on genealogy must have been the goal. It was convenient that they had found it at all. But come to think of it, the book had been placed strategically at the start of the filing system. It was from grid A, aisle 1, section 1. He wondered if Leslie had placed it there before coming to find them and asking for help.

Maybe… they should try to go back for it. Was that too crazy an idea? What other option did they have? A dark thought occurred to him that maybe they could tie up Leslie and just beat them until they broke their oath and told them plainly what they knew. Now that option had a certain grim appeal. *Stop that. You're just frustrated about Silvana. Don't blame Leslie.*

"Hey bro," Freddie said, drawing Jason out of his bleak thoughts. "Check this out. I was just googling multiple personalities."

"Oh. Yeah?"

"Well turns out, that's an old term for it. They call it DID now, for dissociative identity disorder. It's when you disassociate from something really traumatic, and you do it so well that you actually create another part of your psyche."

"Huh… is that like repressed memories?"

"Eh, a little. Apparently, repressed and dissociation are similar. Both go through something really fucked up, but they hide the trauma in different ways. Some brains repress it, and other split into pieces and put all the scary stuff in a different part of the brain to escape it." Freddie shrugged. "I'm probably explaining this badly. I'm just googling it."

"That's all right. What else did you find?"

"Apparently it's rare for the personas to be unknown to each other. That only happens in the most extreme cases. Most of the time there's some awareness, even a certain amount of control."

"How many personalities are there, on average?"

"Less than ten." Freddie read from his phone for half a minute. "Yeah, it's rare for there to be more than that. Although, there are some exceptional people who have thousands. But it's not like the movies. The personalities are usually in a state of flux. Some come and go, and others merge together. There's no cure, per se. But you can treat it and manage it to have better mental health. Hey," he sat up straighter. "They're called 'alters'. You know, alter egos?"

"Makes sense."

Freddie waved his phone at Jason for emphasis. "This says the alters often represent parts of you that aren't acknowledged. It's common for your alters to show sides of you that you hide away."

"That would explain Silvana's alter, Ana. She was so angry."

"Yeah, Silvana hides her anger a lot. But there can be child-like alters where you manifest your inner child. Sometimes they're different genders and races altogether. They're mostly fictitious people."

"But Ana was her older sister."

"Yeah, but Silvana doesn't remember her. It's obviously a version of her sister that her mind created to cope with her loss. I wonder if she has versions of her parents, or even a baby Dorin."

"Wow." Jason gave a nod. "Interesting. It's a lot less scary now we know what we're dealing with." He smiled. "Thanks man."

Freddie shrugged. "I just googled something. Wasn't hard."

Jason frowned as he looked down at the phone. "Hang on," he said. "Weren't we staying off the internet? So the assassin didn't track us?"

Freddie's eyes went wide. He looked up at Jason. Then, he laughed.

"Fair enough. I'll get offline now. But I'm sure nothing bad is gonna—
"

A thunderous crack came from the front of the house. Jason flinched and looked down the hallway just in time to see the front door smash open in a spray of wooden shards and a giant bear appear in the doorframe. Its powerful roar shook the house.

Freddie said in a strangely detached, calm voice, "Look, before we start running for our lives, can I just say, my bad?"

"Yeah, all good bro," Jason said in the same flat tone. "No harm done."

"Well, I think *some* harm was…"

The bear started running on all fours down the hallway.

"Fuuuck!" they screamed in unison.

Chapter 24

The distance between Jason and the bear disappeared *fast*. Jason hurled the table into the bear's path and ducked behind the cabinetry. Freddie was already moving into the next room. The sounds of destruction hit the kitchen as the bear smashed apart the table, sink and bench in one charge. Water sprayed from the broken taps. Jason drew his firearm and aimed at the hulking form. The creature shifted into some small rodent thing and scuttled into the debris. He fired two shots, and immediately realized he didn't have a chance at hitting it at that size. He ran after Freddie who was waiting for him in the adjoining library.

Freddie was at the door to the next room, holding it open. "Come on!" he shouted.

Jason leapt over an armchair to catch up before sliding through the door, and slamming it shut. The lock clicked into place.

Jason cried, "That won't hold him. Where are the stairs?"

"Opposite side of the house."

"Fuck. We need the others."

"You mean the Immortals?" Freddie drawled, a sassy hand on his hip. "Cause they're actually useful in this situa—"

A gorilla's fist burst through the door and Freddie shrieked.

Jason grabbed him by the arm and pulled him away. "Run now!

Bitch later!"

The gorilla arm reached for the handle and unlocked it. The door swung open, revealing a mighty silverback gorilla. Jason had already lined up his shot. He fired straight into its chest.

A bright flash of red light came from the assassin's skin, and the bullet reflected into the roof above.

"Oh no," Jason groaned.

The gorilla leapt at him. Jason turned to run, already knowing it was far too late.

The ceiling collapsed and something massive dropped onto the assassin with a loud crash. A cloud of dust coated the room, obscuring the impact zone. Great thuds of contact sounded over and over as two great hulking figures thrashed wildly in combat. Jason shielded his eyes and stepped back into the sitting room. Freddie stood at his side, and together they watched as the dust cleared.

Two titanic creatures wrestled against each other. One a gorilla with black fur and enormous arms. The other was humanoid, hairless, a great mass of skin and muscle. It slammed huge, meaty fists onto the gorilla's head and drove it to the ground. It stood over its enemy and roared.

Only then did Jason recognise Edward's face.

It was disfigured by massive growth and stretched to non-human proportions, but it was definitely him. The muscles in his arms and shoulders were bigger than an adult male's entire body. He gripped the assassin with these bulky fingers and pinned it in place.

"Holy shit," Freddie cried. "Eddie?"

"Yes, it's me," Edward answered. His speech was slurred, his tongue was too big for his mouth, and his voice was deeper, but he spoke in the same cadence and tone he usually did. He was fully conscious in this form.

"Is this what you meant when you said you could make yourself stronger? Because I don't think that was an accurate statement."

"I am stronger," he answered simply.

"Yeah, sure, I guess that's my bad."

Leslie dropped down from the hole in the roof, floating gracefully on a glowing orb of light and landing soundlessly. "Great work, Edward," they said. "The assassin's magical protection can't protect them from physical attacks like yours. Brilliant. Now, hold them still."

The witch began to wave their hands in slow motions as they muttered ancient words. The gorilla tried to thrash, but there was no breaking Edward's solid, monstrous grip. The assassin's skin lit up again with a flash of light. Jason could see the magical barrier protecting it. Then, slowly, a piece of it seemed to break off and float away before disintegrating altogether. Leslie kept working, and the shield came apart piece by piece until the last of the light was gone.

"There, that's better," Leslie said. "Now reveal your face, assassin. I would prefer not to force you."

The gorilla growled with enough menace to make Jason take a step back. Yet the creature shifted at Leslie's command. A second later, a small, lithe human form lay under Edward's grip.

The assassin had short black hair with a slight fringe. They were surprisingly thin, not muscular or athletic at all, but more like someone who didn't go outside much. As they lifted their face up, Jason saw it was a young woman. She looked to be in her early twenties. She was Caucasian with bright blue eyes and small, pouty lips. She was also quite beautiful. It was almost annoying to find his attempted killer attractive. Her hair was messy, and her face was covered in lines of dirt.

"Hello there," Leslie said with a warm smile. "So nice of you to join us. Perhaps you'd like to talk?"

"Fuck off," the woman spat. "You know I'll die before giving you information, so don't waste my time." She spoke with a high societal British accent.

"Well," Freddie declared as he clapped his hands together and strode confidently towards the centre of the room. "That's certainly a relief. I was worried I'd get us all killed, somehow. But this worked out just perfectly. We stopped the assassin." He patted Edward on his giant muscular shoulder, and Jason couldn't help laughing. "Great work, Eddie. You're the man! And assassin lady, sorry about the acid in the face earlier. No hard feelings. But I'd say, overall, all's well that ends well. Great job team. We really pulled through when we worked together. Personally, I'd like to thank the academy—"

The room began to warp and bend around them. Jason recognized the effects of magic. Someone was teleporting in.

"I knew it," Freddie groaned. "For fucks sake."

Two women in black suits appeared in the room. *Of course it's fucking them.* Desdemona and Portia stood side by side, taking in the sights of the room with cold, impassive expressions.

"Well," Portia gave a high pitch, musical chime. "Isn't this the happiest of meetings? Jason Romanov. A pleasure to see you again."

Jason spoke clearly, "Good morning, Honoured Vigiles. We welcome you to this manor. As our guests here, I request that you join us in celebrating our victory this day as we have subdued our foe and narrowly escaped with our lives. Please…" he stumbled as they both stared at him. "Please do your uttermost to avoid bringing down the celebration?" It sounded like a question.

"Oh yes, your Imperium speech is coming along nicely," Portia drawled, flashing him a bright smile of glistening white teeth that complimented her blue eyes and red hair. "Don't worry, sweet knight, we wouldn't dream of interrupting. Though, you should know that Vigiles are exempt from guest laws. Just as a heads up for next time." She gave him a wink.

"Honoured Vigiles," Leslie said with a bow. "How can we assist?"

Desdemona raised her chin. "We placed a tracking spell on this one," she pointed at the assassin girl. "Yet, her magical protection was great enough to… slow our efforts to locate her. Until now, whence it were removed. I presume that was thee, oh witch?" Leslie nodded. "Our thanks to thee. Now, we would like to speak with thou, assassin."

Though Desdemona remained motionless and silent, the girl was yanked out from under Edward's grip and held suspended in the air before her. The assassin struggled against the invisible bonds that held her arms and legs pinned at her side.

"Oh crap," Jason said. His legs twitched on their own as if they wanted to run forward and intervene before someone was brutally murdered. Leslie saw him and shook their head in warning.

"Tell us, assassin," Desdemona said, "art thou in league with the empowered vampire? The one known as Dorin?"

The girl trembled in place. Her eyes were wide in obvious terror. "No, great Vigile," she said. "I… I tried to kill the vampire in the Library. He prevented me from reaching my prey several times. If not for him, I would have succeeded in eliminating my targets."

"Was this a ploy?" Portia said. "A feint agreed upon by the two of you to hide your…" she gestured idly at her victim, "…cooperation?"

"No, great Vigile. I swear, the vampire was my opponent in every way. In fact, I was planning to target him next until I saw the extent of his power. You know I cannot reveal who hired me. But I can reveal who didn't, and Dorin didn't."

"How interesting," Desdemona said. "And art thou aware of the penalty of lying to Vigiles?"

The assassin's eyes went wide. "Please, great mistress, I am hiding nothing from you. I would never dare challenge a member of the Imperium. You know our creed."

Desdemona said nothing, and Jason had a horrible feeling in the pit of his stomach. Was he about to witness a torture? Or a violent murder? He had no idea. He forced himself to watch. He would not show fear in front of the Vigiles.

A wave of energy seemed to pass through the room, and the assassin dropped to the ground. Desdemona let out a sigh. "That certainly is frustrating," she growled. She looked to Leslie. "Does this manor have… whisky?"

Jason blinked. "Did you say whisky?"

* * *

A few minutes later, Jason found himself in one of the strangest meetings he'd ever seen.

Desdemona and Portia were sipping red-brown whisky from crystal glasses. They sat on Edward's chairs where Jason and Freddie had been eating sandwiches only moments before. Except now, the table had been shattered into fragments that still lay scattered about the room. Kitchen debris was everywhere, though Edward had turned off the water mains to stop the taps spraying more water. Small puddles covered the floor. The assassin who'd caused the damage sat next to the Vigiles with her head down. Everyone else sat in their own chairs, their hands clasped together and sitting up straight, watching silently as the Vigiles enjoyed their drinks. Everyone just pretended the table was still there.

Jason caught Freddie's eye and pressed his lips together. Freddie mimicked the look. Leslie shook their head at both of them.

"Well," Portia said in her sing-song voice. "This has been a lovely break. I'm so glad we came."

"We should do this again," Desdemona said flatly.

Then, they resumed drinking in total silence. Jason couldn't help stretching his leg to alleviate the nervous tension. He remembered something. When he had been kneeling before Reynold, it was Desdemona who spoke in his defence. He probably owed her for that.

"Begging your pardon," Jason said. The Vigiles gave no sign that they'd heard him, and Leslie glared at him in warning. "I wish to thank you both for your aid and counsel when I was before his Majesty, Reynold the First. You advocated for me, and I am…" he struggled with all the fancy words, "filled with gratitude."

Desdemona gazed at him with her dark eyes. "I was merely assisting the King," she said. "Thy life was hardly the object of my efforts."

He couldn't help but smile. "Oh, of course. I didn't mean to imply that you cared about my well-being. I would never consider that for a moment."

Desdemona actually smirked in response. He was relieved that his joke had landed.

"My home is severely out of order," Edward said, changing topics rather abruptly. "I've had multiple parts of my home destroyed. A bedroom wall, my front door, my entire kitchen, my serving table, and the interior roof of my sitting room." He went quiet and added nothing more.

"My apologies, my friend," Leslie said. "When this is all over, I'll be sure to financially compensate you for your pains." Edward made no acknowledgement, so Leslie sighed and added, "And I'll assist with organising the repairs."

"Thank you," Edward said.

Desdemona finally finished her small glass of whisky and let out a sigh. "We came here to question the assassin about Dorin," she said.

"Though the matters appear unrelated. Still, I understand Dorin is known to thee." Jason kept his face neutral. "Thou hast interacted with him. I would like to speak with thee about this."

"Separately, of course," Portia said with a grin. "Best make sure your stories corroborate." She stood up from the table and eyed Jason directly. "Somewhere we can talk privately, hun?" she said with a wink.

"Alone?" Jason gulped.

"You can bring your mortal friend. Should make it interesting." She winked at Freddie, and his Adam's apple bobbed in response. Jason reluctantly stood, and Freddie joined him to follow Portia down the hallway.

"Be sure not to lie to her," Desdemona said with a bored tone, "or she'll set you on fire."

"Shhh, mistress," Portia cried. "Don't spoil the surprise!" She let out a sweet, high pitch laugh and swayed in a dance-like motion as she walked away. Jason and Freddie glanced at each other.

Portia led them upstairs, down the short hallway and into one of the bedrooms. The room was covered in loose clothes and unsorted items. Also, the wall had been blown down. *Oh right. This room.* Portia spun around with a bright smile and clapped her hands together.

"Now. Where shall we begin?"

Chapter 25

Silvana stood at the bathroom sink, having washed her face three times. She stared at her pale face in the mirror. Her skin was unblemished, except for the red around her eyes.

She gripped the sink and huffed. It was all she could do not to rip the sink off the wall and hurl it out the window onto the street below. But it wasn't her house. She shouldn't do that.

What she really wanted was to cuff Jason on the side of the head. In fact, if she could get her whole family together, line them up, and she could slap them all in turn. But she stopped that line of thought. *I would never hurt Jason. I'm mad at him, but I would never attack him.*

But… a part of her wanted to do just that. A part of her called… Ana. In fact, Ana had already attacked him twice. The thought filled her with revulsion down to the pit of her stomach.

"Are you there?" she said to the mirror.

Her face didn't change at all. It simply stared back as if searching for something behind her eyes. *And even if something did happen, would I even remember?* She sighed. She couldn't function this way, constantly second guessing her own mind and capacity. She had to move on and do something useful instead.

Silvana came out of the bathroom and found Dorin sitting at a barstool near the kitchen, leaning comfortably on the bench. He sat up straight when he saw her.

"I'm ready," she said. "Teach me the secrets of our power."

Dorin gave her a decidedly cheeky grin. "I thought you'd never ask." He gestured to the stool opposite, where she sat down. "Do you know the history of the Imperium?"

She nodded. "They formed in the year One AD. It was the first global government."

He shook his head. "First thing you need to know is that the Imperium lies. And they lie *a lot*." He growled under his breath. "You know how the mortals think BC and AD stand for—"

"I learnt this," she interrupted. "Among Immortals, they stand for Before Conquest, and After Dominion."

"Correct. We were taught that the Imperium defeated its enemies after a long heroic struggle. What you don't know is that the Imperium set itself up as a ruling body of *wizards*. The enemies they subjugated were the vampires. Year One marks the change of global leadership and the beginning of the oppression of our species."

She blinked at him. "Was it that extreme?"

"Absolutely. And here's how I know. Because when the Imperium took over, they implemented the marriage law. A vampire can only draw blood from their spouse, as a way to place a limit on vampire powers. They hid all the secrets to our powers. They hid them so well that even they don't remember anymore. But our family remembered. Grigore had kept the secret to pass on to me. And finally, I can pass it on to someone else."

He leaned in close and whispered so low that only a vampire could hear.

"Our power doesn't actually come from blood. It comes from *souls.*"

She stared at her little brother and saw the total sincerity in his eyes. "Souls?" she asked.

"You might call it life force, if that's easier. But that's what vampires take through the blood of mortals. Blood is only the vessel that carries the real power we use. It's like mortal medicine, where you swallow a pill with water. Well, blood is just the water. The real medicine—the real power of a vampire—comes from a mortal's soul."

She frowned in thought. "I don't understand how that works."

He grinned. "Ok, so the soul is not a literal, physical thing. It's like a well. A well slowly fills up with water over time. Then, a vampire comes and empties the well, so it can start refilling. We feed off the energy a soul creates."

"All right. What's so significant about that?"

"Ah, but this changes everything!" Dorin took a loud breath as if to calm himself down. "The issue here is consent. If someone gives you blood—surrendered willingly and with full consent—then they are willingly giving you a piece of their soul as well. But if a vampire takes someone's blood by force, they're not receiving the soul. The soul has to be *given*."

"Wait, so the soul isn't already in the blood?"

"No. Well technically, yes." Dorin held out his hands in surrender. "Ok, let me put it this way. The wellspring of the soul, the source, is somewhere deep inside the belly." He placed a fist just below his ribcage where it joined his stomach. "If a mortal gives you some of their soul, it comes from there. Now, there are little pieces of the soul that float around in the blood all the time. But they're more like spillage. Soul energy that leaked into the blood, or was left over from the last feeding. Does that make sense?"

Silvana thought it through for a moment, then nodded. "So if a vampire steals someone's blood, they're only getting the smallest fraction of soul power."

"Exactly. The true power has to be surrendered. That's why some vampires in the past would go on killing rampages to try to get their power, but it would barely achieve anything. They were trying to steal life force. They would kill thousands before they would get enough power from the tiny pieces of soul energy that naturally came in the blood. By comparison, a good vampire could be given the same power from as few as a dozen willing mortals. And it wouldn't hurt the mortals either."

Silvana nodded. "Ok, so the few times I was able to tap into my empowered vampire state, it was because I was using someone's soul?"

"Yes exactly. It wasn't about whether or not you chose to use the power. It had to be given to you first. And it had nothing to do with how much blood you had in you at the time. It had to be a soul, surrendered easily."

The pieces fell into place. The first time she had used her full power was in the fight against Peter Erikson. She had been on the verge of dying from thirst when she had taken Jason's blood, and she had exploded with power.

Because he thought he was going to die to save me. He surrendered his entire soul to me.

Her mouth fell open. At last, she understood. She had spent a year wondering about that night and how she had gained her powers, and now it finally made sense. It wasn't about Peter's magic or their true love, or the healing elixir, or anything else. Jason had simply given her the power she needed.

Because he gave her everything.

Oh my god... he loved me that much. Even back then. God, he'd only known me a week.

The image of his face came to mind. She remembered how he'd looked when she told him to go home to England and that look of heartbreak. *He really does love me. Oh Jason! Damn you, why didn't you just tell me the truth?*

"You're understanding now, aren't you?" Dorin asked.

She forced her thoughts of Jason away and nodded. "My second husband, Arthur. I swore there was something wrong with his blood. For fifty three years it was barely enough to sustain me. But it's because he didn't love me. So he never put his soul into it."

"That's awful, Velouette. And that's what the Imperium has done to us."

"But Jason," she went on. "I touched the power only two days ago while he and I were…" she blushed, "intimate. I thought I had just figured it out. That maybe I was in the right mind-set at that moment. But it was his life force. The entire time, he was giving his soul to me."

Dorin nodded. "Yes. The mortal doesn't have to understand what they're doing. They just have to feel it, and the soul energy responds."

"So, Jason's love gives me my power?"

"Oof, don't say it like that," Dorin said with a laugh. "You are currently receiving power from just one person. There's a reason why the Imperium limited us to one spouse. The limits of power almost disappear when you have multiple people giving you their energy. You should think beyond one person now."

She looked at him. "Who gives you their soul, little brother?"

"Ah, now we're asking the right questions. But we'll get to that in a moment." He gestured at himself. "So, now that you understand the secret the Imperium has guarded, you understand just how limited your power currently is. You're only getting blood from one person. You could be directly receiving a stronger dose of soul energy, and from many sources. Souls are just the fuel for your power. You have no idea the abilities you can use once you have enough fuel to reach the higher power levels. Let's talk about that."

He held out his hand. "Do you want to arm wrestle?"

She eyed him. "No."

"Oh, come on!"

"This feels like a trick."

"I'm your younger brother. I'm supposed to trick you." He chuckled. "All right, fine. If you did, you'd find I'm physically stronger than you. You are probably as physically strong as a mortal. I mean, an especially strong mortal. You could win a world's strongest man competition if you pushed yourself, but that's still within the realms of what is mortally possible. As for me? And the level I'm at?" He shrugged. "Honestly, I haven't had the chance to test it very thoroughly. I'd love to get into a lab and put some numbers on what I can do."

Silvana's eyes were wide. "What can you do?"

"Well for comparison, you could probably lift up a small car, right? I mean, grab it by one side and lift two tyres off the ground." He grinned. "I have picked up a truck and held all four tyres completely off the ground."

"A truck?"

"Ok, it was a light truck. But I also threw it about ten metres. I'm pretty sure I could have done twice that if I was really going hard."

She could only blink at him. "Wow."

"Yeah. I'm also a lot faster and more agile. You saw me jumping off walls in the Library. All of your physical attributes can increase as well."

She nodded. "What about mental attributes?"

"Oh, now we get to the good stuff." His smile widened until he looked like a model on a magazine cover. "Our great power is telekinesis. Moving objects with our mind."

"I've experienced that before."

"But at my level, you can move magic too. Other people's magic." He nodded at her shocked expression. "You saw me catch the wizard's spells. When you boil it down, a wizard's spell is just their Will, versus mine. That's how I go toe to toe with Vigiles."

"Can you cast spells?"

He laughed. "I don't need to. I can use their spells against them."

He paused for a minute and let Silvana just think it through. There was much to take in, yet she could feel her excitement racing with every new revelation. She nodded to show she was ready to hear more.

"I also have telepathic abilities. So, like psychic powers. In some circumstances, I can read parts of someone's mind. In fact, that's how I gave you my memories. I used telepathy to put those memories in your mind. There, that's a better example."

"Right. So mind powers."

"Essentially, yes. But there's one other power, and honestly, I've barely reached this one. I hardly understand it." He leaned in closer. "It's called psychokinesis. Instead of moving objects with my mind, I can *change* them. Literally alter the state of the object."

Silvana's mouth fell open. "So, you could change water to ice? Or lead into gold?"

He shrugged. "I could probably do water to ice. But lead to gold would be impossible for me at this point. Like I said, I can barely do this one. I think this is the highest tier of vampire powers. The ultimate ability. I've only managed to use it in a few instances. I was able to cool down some water when it came out hot from the tap. The truth is, I don't have enough followers to reach that level."

"But the possibilities."

"Exactly. We could reach the level required to challenge the High Kings. That's why they hid the secrets from us."

Silvana nodded. "Ok, where do you keep all these followers of yours? Are you like... a youtuber?"

Dorin laughed. "God no! Who would do such a thing? Sounds depressing." He shuddered. "Besides, that wouldn't do anything. It doesn't matter how many people 'like' or 'follow' me. Digital clicks don't give me soul energy. There has to be a physical connection to exchange life force. There must be touch. In fact… this is strange, but it usually needs to come in liquid form."

"Like blood?"

"Yeah. Or… you know… when you and Jason had sex and—"

"Ugh!" She blushed bright red and turned away. "Dorin, you're being gross!"

"Uh, hello? Little brother?" He said proudly and laughed.

"Wait… are you saying you're… *a prostitute?*"

He laughed even louder until she joined in out of the sheer awkwardness of the conversation. "Oh no, I'm not a prostitute. Although that is a way vampires have gained power in the past. You've heard of a succubus, right? A monster that gains power from sex. That's Imperium propaganda, but there is truth to it. Some vampires have used that method. But it's not my method. My power comes in the form of a kiss." He nodded his head graciously. "Come on. I think it's time you met my followers. I want to show you my organisation."

Dorin stood up, and Silvana followed before taking a step towards the door. Dorin didn't move. "Aren't we going somewhere?" she asked.

"I can teleport."

"Oh. Of course." She blinked. "Then why did we walk to the museum?"

"That's a public building in the middle of the day. We couldn't just appear in the open. But this place we're going is a little more discreet."

They held hands as the world folded around them and they dropped through space.

They arrived in the middle of a colossal warehouse. Silvana

recognised the huge shelves with multiple racks stretching to the roof some twenty metres high. Loud beeping came from dozens of forklifts, constantly honking at each intersection as they zoomed around the floor, each beep echoing through the vast empty space. The building was as big as an airplane hangar with a giant pile of pallets and crates stacked in one corner. She saw warehouse workers wearing high-vis shirts and talking in near-shouts over the noise.

"Any guesses what this is?" Dorin asked.

She saw further down the warehouse that natural light was coming through giant bay doors. Outside, she could hear the sounds of cars driving past.

"It's not an airport," she said.

"That's right."

She looked through the shelves. A lot of the contents were in boxes. She had expected flat-packs for furniture or something similar. She read a label. *Clothes, male.*

"Oh, a clothing store?"

"Not exactly."

She read a few more labels on the shelves, but was quickly confused by the system. *Clothes, girls. Shoes. Toothcare. Hair products. Hygiene. Handbags.*

"What the hell is this place?" she cried, and Dorin laughed. Then, she saw the one clue she'd been missing. Over by one of the entry doors was a bright red arrow on a sign reading, *Incoming donations.* She rounded on him. "Donations… This is a charity!"

"Exactly!" he cheered. "And a damn big one too. My life's work, in fact. This place is called *'Pentru Oameni'.* Don't suppose you remember enough Romanian?" She shook her head sadly. "It means 'for the people' because that's what this is all about."

He walked towards an office complex, marching with his shoulders back and his head high, and Silvana felt such a wave of admiration for him. This was her little brother. A powerful vampire from a famous house doing charity work for his people. It was everything she'd hoped her true family would be. She had to breathe deeply to keep back the tears before they could fall. This was everything she had wished for as a little girl. If only the rest of her family were alive to see it.

Someone shouted out in Romanian. One of the forklift drivers had stopped in the middle of his path and waved eagerly at Dorin, and when her brother waved back, the driver blew a kiss. Dorin laughed loud enough for the forklift operator to hear from his position across the room, and the driver zipped away with a big smile. *Blowing a kiss? That's a bit intense.*

They approached the office and more people on the warehouse floor started to wave at them. Most of them called out in Romanian. Silvana understood nothing, but their tone and body language were extremely positive. They were thrilled to see Dorin.

But nothing prepared her for when he opened the office door. One worker cried out Dorin's name, and suddenly a room full of workers had leapt out of their chairs and were cheering.

Silvana stopped in the doorway, almost frozen with shock. The amount of happiness on everyone's face was unmissable. Dorin was greeted like a family member or a beloved rock star. Almost every single person gripped him in a hug, then very deliberately kissed him on both cheeks. Silvana laughed softly at the sight. *Of course, cheek kissing. It's a cultural thing.* A few of them were giving her kind nods and smiles of welcome, though they were clearly more interested in Dorin.

That's when she noticed it. The kisses. There was a strange energy to them. She could feel an influx of power each time they touched their lips to Dorin's cheek.

Life force. She recognised it. With each kiss, these mortals were giving Dorin a part of their soul, knowingly or unknowingly. And Dorin was taking it in. Silvana almost started salivating with desire. Each kiss was giving him the same amount of power as Jason's blood gave her once a month. He was taking in so much energy. And it wasn't hurting anyone. This was all freely given.

It's love. They love him. And that's where his power comes from.

She almost laughed. The power of love. It was so cheesy.

Dorin held his hands up and waited for the group to grow still.

"Forgive me for swapping to English," he said. His voice was filled with joy and bounced around the room as each person hung on his every word. "You all know that I believe we should use Romanian as much as possible. But today, we have a very special guest. This lovely woman here, this beauty, is my older sister. Velouette."

He hadn't even finished saying her name when people started swarming her. Every one of them wanted to kiss both of her cheeks and embrace her as if she was everyone's long lost sister.

"So honoured to meet you, friend."

"You can consider us family. We're all family here."

"A sister of Dorin is a sister to all of us."

"Sorry if we're being a bit much. We're just so excited!"

Almost all of them said a variation of, "You're so lucky to have Dorin as your little brother. You must be so proud."

She told each of them that she was beyond proud of him, and she meant it too.

That's when she noticed something strange. When they each embraced her, they began to not grip her as tightly as they first did. Their kisses became more gentle, though they were no less enthusiastic. Were they being delicate on purpose? Were they worried about hurting her?

No. It's not them. It's you.

She could feel it now. The power in every touch, in every

interaction. She was absorbing life force too without even realising it. Her body grew stronger at an incredible rate. Her muscles burned with power. Her adrenaline rose and her mind became alert. She could feel it inside of her. That trigger to her mental powers had returned. She knew then that she only had to think it, and she could push everything in this office away from her.

Dorin appeared at her side. "Ok, ok, I think she's had enough. She's British after all. I think that's the most she's ever been hugged in her life."

Everyone laughed and gave Silvana some space. Dorin spoke a little more in Romanian to them in parting, then led her through the office. People still clapped them both on the back and offered well-wishes, but gradually, they all sat back down at their desks and resumed their work.

Silvana was led to an office room separate from the others. It had one large desk with Spartan furnishings and a computer in the centre. Dorin let her in, shut the door, and turned to face her.

"Ok, take a deep breath, sister," he said in a calm tone. "Another second, and you would have started glowing red."

"Shit," she cried. She flexed her hands and felt power emanating from her. "I could lift a car right now."

"I'm sure you could. This is a new power for you, so you can't get too excited. If you try to wield it now, you'll activate your empowered state too soon and lose control. Just let it sit inside you. Let it rest, and be confident, knowing you can draw on that strength whenever you're ready."

She was breathing rapidly now, trying to control the urge to burst with power and make the world shake. It was almost intoxicating. It was like she had taken a stimulant drug that made it impossible to stand still.

"You know," she said between strained breaths. "A little warning might have been nice."

"Well, to be honest, I had no idea that was going to happen. I didn't tell them I was coming today." He stopped and blinked. "Which, in hindsight, probably made the surprise visit all the more exciting for them. Then revealing you're my sister…" he frowned. "Yeah, I should have seen that coming. That's on me."

"It's ok," she said as she paced the room. She shook her hands deliberately as if trying to shake water off them. "My god, how do you handle this much power all the time? How do you just sit there without letting it out?"

He smiled. "Practise. But Velouette, you need to understand something. What you're feeling now? This is a vampire's *true* state. This is what you should feel all the time. The wizards have kept you handicapped all your life because they fear your power."

"Keep talking. It's helping me settle." She nodded more vigorously. "So these people give you their power. You don't have any power on your own. It has to come from someone else?"

"Exactly, yes. Wizards get their power from themselves. We need others. You know how mortals vote for politicians who they want to represent them? Well that's what vampires are supposed to be. People give us power when they want us to serve them, protect them, when we have earned their trust." He shook his head sadly. "That's what the Imperium has worked so hard to undermine. They create a belief that we are monsters who shapeshift into bats and sell our souls to the devil. That's why the word vampire is a slur now, meaning the same as parasite. But we are meant to be *guardians* of the people. We have to earn the good faith of the mortals in order to deserve our power."

She smiled, feeling herself settling at last. "We have to be worthy. Like Thor's hammer."

"Sure, if that works for you," he said with a laugh.

"But some vampires were bloodthirsty, right?" she asked. "There were some who committed massacres to get their power. Some were monsters, right?"

"Yes, they were monsters. But not because they were vampires." She eyed him, knowing that he was deflecting the point. Finally, he shrugged. "Ok, yes, there were vampires who led kingdoms built of blood. Europe in the BCs was basically a battleground dominated by warlords. We, as a species, lost our way. In some regard, we deserved to have the wizards take our power away. We should have done better. But the wizards were the same. They could have worked with us, helped us do better. Instead, they replaced us."

"Can you imagine?" Dorin cried in a grand voice. He turned to his office wall, and Silvana finally took in the details. Much of the walls were lined with maps of Romania, marked with distribution routes for charity goods. "What if vampires were allowed to serve their people once again? What if the mortals could choose their representatives? And the wizards could act as the check to our power? What if instead of them ruling, we ruled together? In balance, as it should be?" He reached out and laid a hand on his map. "Could you imagine how much better life would be for mortals, if Immortals were leaders instead of rulers?"

Silvana saw the dedication in his eyes and heard the sincerity in his voice. Finally, here was the morally good person she'd always wanted to find. Her aunts and uncles always taught her to obey the Imperium and keep her head down. Royalists and rebels were all about destroying the Imperium and revenge against the High Kings. But here was someone who wanted to *build* something. This was a real visionary she could follow.

In that moment, she felt sorry for Jason and the others. Working with Leslie to help find an heir for Reynold's throne to prevent a new war. How pointless that all seemed now. All they were doing was trying to keep the same system in place and minimise the fallout of Reynold's eventual death. No matter what they did, the petty High Kings would go to war again one day.

No, Dorin had a better plan.

"So, what do we do?" she asked. "You have this power, and now, I have some of it too. What can I do to help you?"

He turned around and beamed at her with a wide, approving smile. "Are you sure you're ready for this?" he asked. "Because I have to warn you, I've held off telling you this part because it's going to get dark."

"Dark?" she asked with a raised brow.

"There is no easy road to building a better world. If you look at every revolution, they have only ever been bloody. Tyrants never surrender their power. The only way to remove a tyrant is through violence. So this will be a long and hard road to peace and freedom. But, I believe this will work. Now, are you sure you're willing to make the tough decisions?"

"Of course," she said without hesitating. This felt right in her blood. This was what her lineage wanted. She was a descendant from the house of Dracula, and she knew she had to fight for what was right. She wanted to fight.

"Are you sure?" he asked. "Because—"

"I'm ready," she interrupted. "Tell me what you need."

He smiled. Then in a moment of raw emotion, he lunged forward and hugged her in a firm embrace. This time, she could feel how tight he was squeezing.

"I love you, Velooy," he said quietly.

She hesitated a moment, then replied, "I love you too, Dory." It felt awkward to say, like she was repeating someone else's words, but she still agreed with the sentiment. Dorin's body shook as he laughed in response.

When he let her go, he gave her a stern nod. "Let's do this." He turned to the phone on his desk and pressed a button. He spoke a few words in Romanian, and a woman answered on the other line. They exchanged a few sentences, then hung up.

"I have allies," he said. "It is time for you to meet them and hear the full scope of our plan."

The door opened then, and a short Romanian woman greeted Dorin with a nod. She said something in their language, then withdrew from the doorway, allowing two other people to enter the room.

The first was an Asian man in his mid-twenties. He was rather short, with a lean build and fine hair. His fringe covered part of his eyes, and his face was set in a permanent hard gaze. He was dressed in a pair of loose pants and a tight shirt.

The second was an older man who looked to be in his thirties with a larger, muscular build and a handsome chiselled jaw. This man looked like a soldier. It was then that Silvana realised, with a start, that she recognised him.

"I know you," she whispered. The eyes of the large man landed on her, and she recalled his name. "The knight, Wilhelm Glucksburg. From Denmark."

"Silvana Romanov," Wilhelm said.

His eyes scanned Dorin's office, then he and his fellow knight shared a nod. They spoke in their own respective languages to someone outside of the room, and two more people entered.

These people, Silvana recognised immediately. A wizard, standing tall and domineering with his black eyes and aura of power. The only difference was now he sported a long, thick white beard that reached his chest. And next to him, a short vampire woman with a beautiful, cold face and dark eyes that burned with pure hatred for Silvana.

"You," she growled.

Power from Dorin immediately flooded the room and pushed against everyone, keeping them from moving towards each other. They all glared daggers at Silvana. Dorin spoke in a calm, stern voice.

"My friends. You may know this woman as Silvana Romanov. But she is in fact, my sister. Velouette Tepes. The heir of Dracula." He smiled. "Velouette, this is—"

"I know them," she whispered. "Wizard Ingolf Glucksburg. And vampire, Hana Yamato. The Royalists."

Both sneered at her, and it took all of Silvana's self-control not to lash out at them with her new power.

"I understand there may be bad blood between us all," Dorin said. "But we are allies now, united in purpose. If you would all take a seat, we can get started."

Silvana looked at her little brother, and he offered her a smile in return.

Chapter 26

Jason struggled to keep his breathing steady. Portia would notice if he looked nervous. Then again, Freddie looked like he was about to throw up. Maybe acting calm wouldn't matter that much.

Portia sat on a lounge chair with both elbows on the arm rests, hands clasped together and her head reclined back on the high head rest. One leg was crossed elegantly over the other, and her suit jacket hung open, revealing a deep purple interior lining. Meanwhile, Jason and Freddie sat at the foot of the bed with nothing to lean on, sitting with their hands crossed in their lap. Jason had been told to put his sword and gun in the far corner of the room, well out of reach. He didn't mind. He suspected they wouldn't have done much against Portia anyway.

"So," Freddie said to break the silence. "You come here often?"

Jason looked up at the roof in despair.

Portia scoffed. "So this is the guy you wanted at your side? At least he's cute."

"Hey, Freddie's my closest friend," Jason insisted. "I mean, not that he isn't cute." He blinked. "Sorry, it just felt rude to leave that part unacknowledged."

"Appreciate it," Freddie replied.

Portia raised an eyebrow. "Are you two a couple on the side?"

"We're roommates."

"Oh, you think there's no overlap?" Portia laughed.

"What about you and the other wizard?" Freddie asked. "You're definitely a couple, right?"

Portia didn't move at all, but her eyes turned cold as ice. Jason's heart skipped a beat, and he couldn't help but wonder if they were about to die.

"Desdemona and I are just… roommates," Portia said, and her eyes twinkled with amusement.

"Oh!" Freddie laughed in obvious relief.

"What were you doing in the Library?" Portia asked casually.

The shift in topic was so abrupt, Jason nearly blurted out the first answer that came to mind. He grimaced instead. Portia was a damn good interrogator to put him on the back foot so quickly. Thankfully, he knew a thing or two about this himself.

"Technically," Jason said, "Freddie wasn't in the Library."

"Right. So he's just here to be pretty, then? For team morale?"

Freddie barked a laugh. "Pretty much. I was kinda useless at everything else."

"How sad for you. Now, Mr Turner," she snapped, her volume jumping up a notch. "Why were *you* in the Library?"

Jason didn't even try to lie. There was no point. But, he did resolve to hold back as much as possible. "Leslie Toussaint came to our house, asking for my help to stop a chimera assassin. That same assassin followed Leslie and tried to kill us all. I've been trying to investigate who sent them. Leslie came to me because they said Vigiles don't investigate hired killings."

"True," she said. "We only investigate illegal things."

"Oh, come on! How is that—" Freddie slapped a hand over his own mouth. "Sorry," he said.

Jason continued before Freddie made things worse. "Leslie said they were probably at risk because of the information they knew as a Librarian. But because of their vows, they couldn't just tell us what that information was. So, they helped us get into the Library so we could look up what they had been researching. Maybe we could find a topic or clue that would lead us to their hired killer."

"Really?" Portia said.

Jason opened his mouth to answer, but she cut him off with a wave of her hand. Instead of talking herself, she let them sit in a most uncomfortable silence. *Damn she's good at this.* Finally, she asked, "So, you thought Leslie had learnt some terrible secret… from a public library? Where anyone else could read it?"

Jason blinked. "Well… I mean…it's not exactly public. It was very restricted access."

"Oh really? Was the Library empty when you went there?"

"Uh… no."

"Was there a small number of people? Or a crowd?"

"A crowd."

"I see. So it's public enough to have a crowd of people who could all read the same information. But Leslie said only they knew the information that was worth killing for?"

Jason couldn't help frowning. He knew now why Leslie had suggested the Library infiltration. They wanted Jason to find the heir for Reynold. Should he tell Portia that? The Vigiles basically worked for Reynold directly. They might not take well to someone sniffing around in his business, so he chose another tact.

"Leslie is an eight hundred year old witch. They know a lot more than we do. I thought it best to trust them."

"Interesting. You don't think Leslie was setting you up?"

"No."

"Ah. Is that because Leslie was in the Library too? Right there helping you?"

"Uh… no. Leslie was back here the whole time. But they helped us with the plan. We couldn't have done it without them."

Portia raised an eyebrow. "Curious. Mr Turner, through most of our interactions over the past year, you've tried to convince me that you're pretty smart. Yet today, for some reason, you're trying to convince me that you're very stupid."

"I—"

"It's quite odd. Because only a smart person would try to convince everyone they're stupid. They see the benefit of being underestimated. So either you're so wise that you're doing this very thing now. Or you're just lucky you come across this way, in which case, you were always stupid."

"Definitely the second one," Jason insisted.

Portia's eyes twinkled with delight. "What a wise thing to say."

Freddie cleared his throat. "I'm lost. Is she saying you're smart or dumb?"

"Well, clearly, I don't need to ask the roommate which he is," Portia drawled, and Freddie's lip twisted. "So what did Dorin ask you about?"

Another fast topic change. I'm ready for you this time, wizard. "Oh, you know, what Royalists always talk about. Destroying the government and a vast conspiracy. Basic nutcase wackadoodle bullshit."

"Oh, I do love a conspiracy theory. Please, tell me everything. Be specific."

Damn. She's caught me again. Come on, Jason. "All right. He said he had a secret he wanted to tell us in private. But he didn't say anything bad about the Imperium. He implied that he was running from Vigiles and that we couldn't trust them. But it was just a scam."

"A scam? Whatever could you mean?"

"We met Dorin once before in Dubai, and he claimed to know

Silvana."

"Do you believe him?"

Jason kept his face flat. "Well, Silvana's aunts said it's a common scam tactic. Scammers pretend to be some long-lost relative, then embezzle you out of your wealth and titles. He was just trying that again."

"So is he a long lost relative?"

Jason spoke quickly before he could give anything away. "Probably. I mean, all the royal houses are connected in some way. Hell, I might be related to Reynold!" He laughed, but Portia didn't join him.

"Why would Dorin go to the Library and try to scam you again? Seems like a lot of effort to con a minor house."

Jason shrugged. "I'm not sure. I'm a beat cop, not a criminal psychologist."

"You said you met him at the party in Dubai. Weren't there families richer than yours there? For example, all of them?"

Jason pressed his lips together, and Portia gave him the hint of a smile. "Touché," he said flatly.

"So why try to get money from the poorest family?"

Freddie spoke up then. "Why do lions chase the oldest and weakest in the pack?" He smiled as if proud of himself, then glanced at Jason. "Sorry. Not that your family is old and weak."

"No it was a good point."

"Ok thanks."

Portia sighed through her nose. "I see. So you're just a poor helpless mortal way out of their depth?"

Jason blinked. "Yeah. Same as always."

"I see. Then I have one more question for you…" She uncrossed her legs, lowered her arms and leaned forward in her chair. Her face was simply gorgeous this close, and Jason felt his heart racing. *Now she's charming you. Play it cool.* She offered him a smile that lit up her whole face, and Jason was dazzled by her beauty. "Why did Dorin bite Silvana?"

"I…" he stammered for words. "I don't know."

Pain instantly clutched him in a vice. He let out a strained half shout and collapsed onto the floor. His stomach felt like it was burning as if someone had plunged a knife deep inside his gut, and he knew exactly what that felt like. This agony gripped him so hard that he couldn't scream. His breath caught in his chest. All he could make were little gargled sounds in his throat.

"Jason," Freddie shouted and clutched at his shoulder. "What did you do to him?"

Portia 'tisked' to herself. "Temper, temper, young mortal. Remember your manners when speaking to a Vigile. In truth, I did nothing to him. He chose to lie to me. Desdemona even warned him not to lie, didn't she?"

Jason half heard her. All he could see was the knight Mikeru standing before him once more like a ghost, ramming his sword into Jason's belly. The vengeful spirit gave a cruel smile and vanished, leaving the blade inside him. *It's not real! You're just delirious with pain.* He looked up through teary eyes to see Portia kneeling beside him, a look of concern on her face.

"*Make it stop!*" he howled.

"Please deary, it'll only get better when you tell the truth. Why did Dorin bite her?"

"Revenge! For turning on him…"

The pain suddenly jolted anew, and Jason could only rasp. The world grew dim as he struggled to stay conscious. It was horrible beyond his mind's ability to comprehend.

"Try again, honey," Portia sung. "Oh, please try. You know it pains me to see this—"

"He wanted her blood!"

The pain vanished. Jason sucked in air like a dead man that had risen to life and filled their empty lungs. He still clutched his stomach at the phantom memories of pain. But underneath his shirts were no wounds whatsoever. Freddie clutched him in relief and with tears in his eyes. Jason held him back for comfort. The simple reassurance of the touch helped the horror start to fade.

"I am so sorry, Jason," Portia said, and it sounded like she meant it. She reached out and stroked the top of Jason's head, and he didn't have the will to stop her. "I never wanted to hurt you. I had hoped we could have an easy conversation. But you chose to lie. At that point, it was the consequences of your own actions." She sighed heavily. Her hand cupped his cheek and chin, and her fingers were cold and soothing. "Please, finish telling me the truth, and this can all be over."

"Fuck you!" Jason roared, the sound all the more savage from his hoarse throat.

"Sssh," she whispered. "It's ok. I'm not going to hurt you again, I swear. Now, please be a good boy. Give me the information I need."

Jason looked at her face, so close to his. She was stunning and terrifying in equal measure. *Idiot! She's not some police investigator playing by the rules. She's the Spanish Inquisition! When will you learn the Imperium doesn't follow civilised law?* This time, Jason didn't even try to hold anything back.

"Dorin could track her," he whispered. "With a drop of her blood, he could find her again. He…" Jason trailed off when he realised he was about to confess Silvana's relationship to Dorin. That was too much. Jason paused in his confession and panted for breath. The pause made the sharp pain flash through his gut again, like a warning. Portia made a cooing sound and stroked his head again, coaxing the truth out of him. "He took Silvana. He just arrived at the front door. Then he took Silvana. I have no idea what he's planning. But I can't find Silvana now. I have no idea where she is, and I'm scared for her."

"Oh, sweetie," Portia cooed. "No wonder you tried to hide the truth. You were scared for the woman you love. And you were ashamed that you, her knight, were unable to protect her. I understand."

She leaned forward and before Jason knew what was happening, she kissed him on the mouth.

It was a quick kiss, neat yet sincere, and it made his blood rush. She leaned back only half a second later and smiled. "Don't worry. We will find her for you. But you have to tell me where they are."

Jason was confused. That phantom pain was fading, yet the terror of the event still burned in his mind. And that kiss. It had been so humiliating. It had been against his will, yet he enjoyed it after feeling such agony a minute before. He couldn't think clearly. Portia was doing this on purpose, and by God, it was fucking working. How the hell was he supposed to know how to handle something like this? He was a cop, not even a detective. He was mortal and overpowered in every way.

"Please, Jason, tell me where they are."

In that moment, in the utter depths of his helplessness, Jason couldn't help resenting Silvana. She had pushed him away because he wasn't perfect. That's why he was in this situation now. Because she told him to leave. After he'd done everything he could to protect her. *Well fine. She doesn't want my help anymore? That's her choice.*

"Romania," he whispered. "They're in Romania, somewhere in the capital city."

"Oh, really? What makes you so sure?"

"Cause that's where Dorin is from. He wouldn't shut up about it."

He already felt sick to his stomach. He regretted his resentment just as quickly as it had come. Silvana had been right to push him away. What was he thinking, lashing out and sabotaging her like this? *God, what an idiot!* He knew it was Portia, rattling him so he gave away information. Yet, he couldn't help blaming himself all the same.

"Interesting." Portia stood up and dusted off her suit. "That's all I need. Looks like this interview is done. Thank you for your cooperation." She moved towards the door.

"Wait," Freddie called. "I need to know."

She spun around with a wild expression and broad smile. "You need something of me? How quaint."

"Your partner. That's Desdemona, right? The famous Desdemona?" Portia just eyed him. "How'd she get her magic?"

"Freddie," Jason warned.

"The witch told us," Freddie said. "Desdemona isn't from a wizard house. She found magic on her own. That means it's possible. So how'd she do it?"

Portia was silent for a full half a minute, and Jason thought she was about to punish Freddie for his hubris. Yet, her face softened. When she spoke, it was with tenderness. "I am one hundred and eighty years old. I have seen a lot in that time working as a Vigile. Believe me when I say, I have seen the very worst of humanity." Her eyes became distant, and she looked past both mortals into the distance. "I fought in the Second World War. I saw the camps. The mass graves. The train carriages filled with bodies." Her face grew harder still. "I've seen occupying armies use widespread violence and rape on a defenceless civilian population. I've seen torture that lasted for years. I've even… participated. As both liberator, and captor."

She seemed to remember herself and looked down at Freddie again. "So trust me when I say, Desdemona found her powers in the darkest situation you can possibly imagine. She found her magic out of pure desperation and will, in the face of the most hopeless state." Portia offered another smile that seemed just as real as all the others. She wore that mask well. "Trust me, young Fredrick. You don't want magic at that cost." She turned to leave again.

"What happened to her?" Jason asked softly.

Portia spoke with her back to him. "She's a four hundred and thirty year old black woman from Nigeria, who now works for the English. What do you think happened to her?" Portia left the room without another word.

Jason finally picked himself off the floor. He stared at Freddie a moment, though he didn't seem to notice.

"What are you doing, man?" Jason said.

Freddie looked around. "Sitting on the ground?"

"You're asking everyone how to get Immortality. Can you chill out a bit?"

"What? You think I liked watching you dying in pain and not being able to do a damn thing about it? Well excuse me, buddy, but I'm trying to do something meaningful."

Jason glared at him. "You're not..." he stopped. He had been intending to argue with Freddie the way he would with himself. He needed a different strategy for this particular audience. "Ok, Freddie, right now, you're being like Anakin."

His face relaxed. "I'm listening."

"Ok, Anakin wanted to save Padme. That's a good desire. But he turned to the dark side and committed mass murder in order to do it. Bad action. You see what I'm getting at here?"

"This is different."

"No, it isn't."

"It absolutely fucking is! In my case, it's more like I'm just a regular guy, and I want to save Padme. I could be the Naboo Captain. But I'm not going to the dark side. All I'm trying to do is become force-sensitive. That's all!"

"Yeah, but Padme wasn't force-sensitive either. But she was still a queen, a senator, and she practically started the rebellion. I mean, that was in the deleted scenes, but they're canon now."

Freddie rolled his eyes. "Don't cite the deep magic to me, witch." They both stopped to laugh, and some of the tension left the room. Freddie spoke a little softer. "Look man, keeping with this metaphor—slash lawsuit waiting to happen—you're the Padme in this situation. You're the badass normal who's still doing awesome stuff. Me? You know who I am?"

"Oh no, Freddie! Don't say it. Don't you dare say it!"

"I'm the Jar Jar."

"Oooh!" Jason groaned. "I knew your self-esteem was low…"

"I mean it. I'm the comic relief who achieves nothing meaningful. We both know that's true."

"Yeah, but Jar Jar wasn't just comedy. He united the Naboo with the Gunguns—"

"But he also gave emergency powers to—oh, for fucks sake!" Freddie couldn't help laughing as he got up to leave, finally done with the conversation. Still, he paused by the door. "Look, I've heard what you're saying, Jason. Message received, loud and clear. Let's talk about it more later."

"All right," Jason said, trying not to sigh. Freddie was avoiding him, like he often did when it came to serious topics. Jason followed him to the door.

"But I appreciate the Star Wars references," Freddie said gently. "That was very thoughtful. Even if your metaphor game needs work."

Jason cuffed him on the shoulder, making them both laugh again. Then Jason remember his weapons, and went to retrieve them. But there was something different about them. They called to him, somehow. Was it instinct? Or was it the bloody callousness of the Vigiles making him feel defensive? Jason looked at himself. He was wearing casual pants and t-shirt. House clothes. It wasn't right.

He grabbed his weapons and rushed down the hall to the bedroom he'd been sharing with Silvana. He opened his backpack and pulled out a new set of cloths. "Avert your eyes, young child," he joked and stripped to his undies.

"What are you doing?" Freddie asked in a decidedly flat voice.

"Gearing up," Jason said grimly. "I'm not sure what's happening, but I want to be ready for anything." He put on his fighting trousers. They had extra flexibility in the thighs. He wore a tight black shirt and sturdy combat boots. He took up the sword and strapped it around his waist. He put his handgun in its holster on his opposite hip. He looked at himself in the mirror.

I look like a knight. But without the vassal I'm charged to protect. He grimaced. *I'm like a Ronin.*

"I'm gearing up too," Freddie said.

Jason eyed him. "You just put on a jacket."

Freddie grinned. "The jacket has a bunch of vials from Eddie inside the pockets. I'll contribute something, damn it." They gave each other an approving nod and fist bumped before heading downstairs.

Chapter 27

The mood in the kitchen was decidedly less jovial. Leslie, Edward and the assassin girl were still sitting on dining chairs positioned around the tattered remains of where the table had been an hour ago. All three avoided each other's gaze. The two Vigiles spoke in hushed tones at the far end of the room and looked up when Jason and Freddie entered.

"Ah, boys. Kissed and made up, have we?" Portia cooed before winking and giggling. Jason scowled back as he sat next to Leslie and turned to face the witch.

"What did you tell them?" he asked.

"The truth," Leslie said. "We were in the Library to find why the assassin was hunting me. Dorin's meeting was a chance. They don't know anything else about him."

Jason winced. "I tried to say the same. But I had to add that Silvana is with Dorin now, and they're in Romania."

Leslie gave a sympathetic smile. "I heard you screaming. I figured you had to give something up."

"Yeah."

"It's ok. Vigiles are extremely hard to deceive. You did well."

"What do we do now?"

Leslie smirked. "This is where mortals usually like to pray."

The Vigiles seemed to finish their hushed conversation and moved back towards the table. They paused dramatically and everyone squirmed for a minute. *They are enjoying this.*

"Thou hast been somewhat helpful," Desdemona said. "I would not think it smart to try to hide knowledge from Vigiles. Yet thou hast never shown thyself to be the smartest, witch." Leslie inclined their head as if it were a compliment. "We shall continue our investigation. And should we have further questions, we know where to find thou."

"Wait," Jason cried. All he could think of was Silvana and the risk of these Vigiles finding her. What would they do to her, if they found her working with Dorin? He couldn't let that happen. He summoned his best Imperium speech. "Begging your pardon, good Vigile. May I ask, are you going to Romania to search for Dorin?"

"It is no concern of thine."

"Yes, precisely. But I can't help think that Romania is a big place. It will take you a while to search all of it."

"You gave me the city, remember?" Portia said. "The capital, Bucharest. We shall start there."

Jason shrugged. "I only wish to help. Perhaps there's a way you could narrow down your search even further?"

They eyed him, both squinting in unison. "Did you have something in mind, sweetie?" Portia asked.

Jason racked his brain. He had to find some way to keep Silvana safe without lying to the Vigiles. In the back of his mind, he knew he couldn't afford to get distracted from his own quest. He had to find the heir of Reynold the First. At least the assassin was caught now. But what had that achieved if they still didn't know who sent them? This was all getting too complicated. He had to find a way to make it all start fitting together and to keep everyone safe. Was there even a way to do that?

"Thou art stalling," Desdemona said. "Merely trying to protect thy charge. We have not the time for thy childish prattle." She gripped Portia's hand and the room began to spin around them.

"The High King!" Jason shouted, only half aware of the idea forming in his head.

The Vigiles paused, their magic slowing as all the others in the room looked at him. "Dost thou truly suggest another meeting with Reynold? Thou art welcome to try thy luck with—"

"Not him," Jason declared. "I meant the High King Alexei."

Everyone was looking at him like he was mad. The Vigiles remained silent, so Jason took that as permission to continue.

"When we were in Reynold's court, Alexei claimed to know Dorin. But he kept that information in an attempt to bargain with Reynold. Well, why don't we go see Alexei ourselves? Have a chat with him about what he knows?"

"Impossible," Portia said. "Vigiles are not permitted to investigate the High Kings. The seven are above the law. Alexei would refuse an audience from us."

"Ah," Jason replied. "But what about an audience with *family?*"

Leslie clapped their hands together. "Oh, clever lad!" they cheered. "Jason has married into the Romanov family, the former royal line of Russia. He is related to Alexei and has grounds to request an audience with him. I believe that would help you in your investigation."

The Vigiles exchanged a glance. "Fine. But we will take just you."

"Not to be rude, but you misunderstand me," Jason said. Now his heart was pounding with terror, but he made himself continue. "I am not offering this as a gift. I am offering an audience with a High King as a bargaining chip. You have to do something for me in return."

Desdemona's face turned to stone. "Thou art in no position to make demands, mortal knight."

"Actually, he is," Leslie interjected. "He's offering you a favour. You need to respond with a favour of your own. You cannot demand anything of him."

Desdemona scowled at the witch. "Thou art a historian, not a lawyer. Thou—"

"Don't try it," Leslie snapped back. "You will not intimidate us. If you want this favour, you will acquiesce his request. Jason, please make your demands."

Jason paused just long enough to let Desdemona fume in the silence. "Khadija Al Khalifa. She was arrested in the Library of Alexandria. I want her returned in exchange for the audience with Alexei."

The Vigiles glared at him, but Jason knew he held the upper hand here. They would follow through on his request. He would just have to put up with their bluffing first.

"Ms Al Khalifa is a suspect in a crime," Desdemona said. "I cannot upset the course of justice for thy favour, mortal."

"The hell you can't," Jason said. "I know the great and powerful Vigile Desdemona does whatever she wants. So please, bring her here, now."

Desdemona's lip curled, but Portia laid a hand on her arm. "Mistress, we have been tasked by Reynold to find answers. I would consider this the highest priority in the Imperium at this time."

"But his audacity," Desdemona growled.

"There will be a chance to teach him."

"Thou taught him just moments ago. And look what he hath learned! The arrogance of this mortal man presuming he can take from me."

"Mistress?"

Desdemona had a wild look in her eyes. Something was going on behind that stare. This meant something to her. Suddenly she threw out a wave of magic that shook the mansion. Jason braced himself against the wall and reached for his gun. Desdemona simply teleported herself out of the room. Everyone breathed a sigh of relief.

"I hate to admit it," Freddie said, "but I kinda forgot about Khadija."

The assassin murmured, "I didn't."

"Quiet you."

Portia eyed Jason and shook her head. "My mistress is right. You have too much audacity, boy. Especially for someone I just tortured minutes ago. Have you learnt nothing?"

"I'd say he has learnt something," Leslie said. "He's learnt that magic is not the only power in this world. As the saying goes, 'the pen is mightier than the sword'. Jason has the power of words and wisdom, and he can wield his power effectively when he needs to."

Leslie looked to Jason and gave a nod of approval. Jason nodded back, though he wanted to hide from such high praise. He also noticed Freddie watching them with a thoughtful expression.

"Be that as it may," Portia said. "It is not wise to test Desdemona. She will find some way to get you back for this. Even if she has to act outside of legal channels. Hell, you may not even have to wait long."

The room swirled with magic, and Desdemona popped back into existence. She wasn't alone.

"Well it's about fucking time," Khadija Al Khalifa said, shaking her head so much her curls bounced about her beautiful face. "Three days I sat in that cell. And do I get so much as a phone call checking in on me? This is the thanks I get after a heroic sacrifice?"

"Khadija?" Jason said, holding up a finger.

She went on. "I literally took a bullet for you. I'm just saying, it would have been nice to receive a visitor. First my family refuse to take my calls, then you lot don't even try to find out about me. Well that's just perfect. I guess I chose my friends well. You're all a bunch of assholes."

"Look, before you say something that'll hurt my feelings," Jason said.

"Did we at least find—"

"The Vigiles are here," Jason cut in. "As our guests. They've been interrogating us." He gave her a fake smile, and she finally seemed to get it.

"Splendid," her tone instantly became happier. "To what do we owe the pleasure?"

Portia offered her a smile. "I'm sorry, are you feeling a little tense?" Khadija only scowled back, which made Portia smile all the more.

"Thy favour has been met, sir knight," Desdemona spat. "Now, thou shalt provide mine. A meeting with High King Alexei."

"Alexei?!" Khadija cried.

Jason gave a nod. He noted that Desdemona had reworded the 'favours' so it sounded like it was by her demand, not his. He decided to ignore it. "Right. Well, I'll place some calls. And I'll let you know—"

"Oh no," Desdemona said, a decidedly evil smile growing on her face. "I expect my favour provided in the same haste with which I provided thine."

Jason suddenly lurched forward as something shoved him from behind. He thought one of his friends had attacked him. But everyone cried out as the same force shoved them up against each other and pinned them close together. *Magic! It's Desdemona doing this!* The older Vigile indeed had a face alive with fury as power spread out from her like a hurricane. The entire room started to fold into space as everyone's clothes and hair began to ripple in the wind of her magic.

The ground dropped away and everyone lurched into freefall. Jason clutched at Freddie's shirt just as Edward clawed at Leslie's arms in desperation. Khadija threw herself at Freddie as the two Vigiles grinned in sadistic glee. Piercing screams were loud in Jason's ears before they began to fade in and out as the bending of space warped their sound.

Jason finally hit solid ground with a thud that reverberated painfully through his knees. He immediately began searching for people as they landed. He saw Freddie on his side, clutching his shoulder and grinding his teeth together. Edward's legs were twisted at awkward angles causing a spike of alarm that maybe they were broken, but a heartbeat later Jason could see his knees were just bent. Leslie, Khadija, and the assassin were all on their feet, stabilised by their magic and agility.

And of course, Desdemona and Portia stood comfortably and unaffected.

"You bitch," Jason growled. "You could have warned us. And you didn't have to bring everyone."

"My dear knight," she purred in a way that made Jason's blood chill in his veins. "Why didn't thou simply say so?" Her smile somehow kept getting bigger.

"Who dares enter my court uninvited?" roared a deep, echoing voice.

Jason froze. He slowly looked up and noticed they were in a grand hall surrounded by paintings, alabaster pillars and coloured tiles which had been worked into each surface. Soldiers dressed in army greens and ushanka headwear lined the room, each holding an assault rifle. But that wasn't where the mighty voice had come from.

Jason turned to find a large man dressed in royal gowns sitting atop an obsidian iron throne. A crown secured firmly on his head. It could only be one person.

High King Alexei the Fourth of Russia.

"Ah, great High King," Desdemona said, bowing to him alongside Portia as if they had just walked through the front door. "We come to request an audience with thy majesty."

"How dare you?" the High King growled. "I am above investigation. The Vigiles have no right to ask me anything. I demand you leave before I incinerate you where you stand."

"Why, thy majesty," Desdemona exclaimed. "This isn't an investigation. It's a family visit! This here is your relative. The mortal knight, Jason Turner, who married into the Romanov family." She gestured to Jason as he struggled to his feet. "Jason demands the right of blood to speak with you, don't you, Jason?"

Jason could practically feel the burning fury of the High King. Jason had frozen in place and almost wondered if it was Alexei's magic holding him there. But, Leslie shoved him forward towards the throne.

"Speak, man," they whispered. "You have a right to speak. Do not falter."

Right. Jason stood up and dusted off his shirt and pants. He tucked his sword to the side and bowed low. "Great High King," he declared. "We have not had the pleasure of formally meeting. But I heard you in Reynold's court just this morning."

"I remember a pathetic, cowering wretch," Alexei growled, and Jason had to steady his will to continue speaking.

"You may also recall I asked Reynold about his heir. I was not cowering when I asked such a bold question of your opponent."

Alexei seemed to rethink this. "What do you want, boy?"

"I want to ask you about the vampire, Dorin."

Alexei tilted his head to the side, and his large beard could not hide the smile in his eyes. "How interesting. Come, you should ask me. But be quick about it. I have another meeting after this one."

Jason looked to Desdemona, and she merely glared back, signalling she wanted him to speak. So Jason swallowed his nerves and began to interrogate a High King.

Chapter 28

Silvana glared at her brother.

"These friends of yours tried to kill me," she spat, pointing at Ingolf Glucksburg and Hana Yamato. "This vampire embezzled me out of five million dollars. She nearly ruined my family."

"Velouette," Dorin warned.

"Her knight literally impaled Jason on a sword."

"You have no right," Hana snapped back, her eyes literally glowing red with vampire magic. "No right to cry victim. You caused Mikeru's death! You cost me my knight and husband. I should have a blood feud with you."

"I simply exposed his actions. He was responsible for what he did."

"I must say," Ingolf said in a deep, gruff voice. "I thought you had better sense, Dorin, than to ally yourself with this pathetic house. The Romanovs are dead and destroyed. This child is the last vestige of a broken line."

Silvana snapped back, "And yet I beat you. How that must gall." Ingolf raised his chin and shifted his shoulders, and his knight Wilhelm put his hand on his blade. Silvana braced herself. She could feel the magnitude of power brimming inside of her. One move from Ingolf, and she'd let it all out. He wouldn't see it coming.

"That's enough," Dorin said in a steely voice. Ingolf relaxed at the command. "I told you before. This is not Silvana Romanov, this is Velouette Tepes. She is my sister and the heir to Dracula himself. You will speak to her with the courtesy you would show me. And if you have fought her in the past, you will apologise for the harm you caused her."

To Silvana's surprise, that's what they did.

"I beg your pardon," Ingolf said with a bow of his head, and a strained voice. "I knew not who you truly were."

Hana's scowl was venomous, but she too bowed her head. "Apologies," was all she said.

"That doesn't excuse the embezzlement," Silvana growled.

"Ah," Dorin interrupted. "If it's any consolation, sister, that may have been my fault. Indirectly, of course." He shrugged. "Please, take a seat. It is time you heard my plan in full."

Silvana managed to force down the shout that threatened to shred her throat. It was so hard to trust him right now, and yet, he was family. If she couldn't trust him, who else did she have? She calmly sat down at the far side of the room, facing his desk and avoiding the eyes of the other Royalists. The two knights stood behind their vassals, and Hana shifted her chair away from Silvana.

"We have been collecting money for some time now," Dorin said. "The money Hana took from you was just one tiny piece of the investments we have been accumulating for nearly a decade. The truth is we have a massive portfolio spread all around the world." He pulled out a binder and opened it to the first page. "One of our mortal branches is called Kennedy and Sons."

"I know them," Silvana said. "That's where I invested my money."

"They're the largest of several companies we own and operate. They have been investing money into all sorts of fields."

"How much money?"

Dorin smiled proudly. "It has a cumulative value of seventy-eight million dollars."

Silvana tried to maintain her poker face, but her eyes widened against her will. She couldn't imagine that much money in any one hand. That would change her life and her family fortune. But after the initial shock wore off, she reconsidered. It was a lot of money by her standards, but she was poor when compared to the rest of Immortal community. There were mortal billionaires with more money than that, and Reynold himself was worth trillions. How did they expect to topple the Imperium with seventy-eight million? It seemed far too small a sum for what they wanted to spend it on.

"And that's how you plan to destroy Reynold?" she quipped. She could feel Ingolf and Hana seething at her answer.

Dorin simply chuckled in response.

"Here's the truth," Dorin said. "Everyone thinks the power of the High Kings is in their magic. And yet, while their magic is significant, that's not their real power. There are two things that actually allow them to rule the world. The first is their wealth. It comes from huge territories of land they occupy, and the taxes and resources they can farm. In the Second World War, Reynold never had to fight because he had money. In fact, he increased his wealth substantially because of the war. His power is his business."

"The second reason they rule is information. They hoard information like the true powers of vampires. They hoard knowledge of magic and the ability to use it, so only their houses can become wizards. And they indoctrinate the world into their beliefs so that everyone accepts what they do as right."

"I understand," Silvana said, "but you haven't answered my question yet. What's your plan?"

"Insolent girl," Ingolf growled.

"Ingolf," Dorin replied in warning, and the wizard grimaced.

Silvana took note. *Interesting. Ingolf is four centuries old. Yet he defers to Dorin?*

Dorin sighed. "I'm sorry, Velouette. I will answer your question soon, but I'm merely explaining crucial information first." He smiled at her. "You know Germany spent a decade building its army before it invaded Poland. That's why they were winning the war for the first few years. They had prepared more than anyone else. Well, that's what we've done. Our money is all over the world in secure locations. Our knowledge is ready to be shared with other vampires so they can find their power. And now that you're here, we have three empowered vampires in this room alone."

Silvana looked to Hana. "You weren't empowered last time we fought."

She scowled. "Yes, I was."

Silvana remembered now. During that fight, there had been a brief moment where Hana's eyes had glowed red. It was just before Jason had hit her with a sword. It seemed he interrupted her the moment she was about to call on her powers.

"Why didn't you use them?" Silvana asked.

Hana's eyes were red now, like pools of blood floating around the dark iris. "I could not. I would have revealed my abilities too soon. You survived our encounter only because of my restraint." She scowled at Dorin. "You should have kept it secret too. I sacrificed Mikeru for the cause, yet you flaunted your power in a public place."

"I know," he said softly. "His loss is felt by all. But I used my power to save Silvana, and now we have another ally who will soon be just as powerful as myself. It was worth it. Now, let's move on."

He opened the binder to show a page of stats. "Our main competitor is Reynold. We want to hit his banks, and in doing so, cripple his power and prime him for a takeover. We will fight a war against him with no soldiers dying needlessly on battlefields. We will simply eradicate his source of power." He pointed at the page. "See? These are Reynold's companies. Ours are all competitors. When we eliminate his stocks, that entire cash flow will become ours."

She frowned at him. "I'm confused."

"I know it's a lot to take in. The maths can be tricky—"

"No, I mean how are you taking out his banks?"

Dorin's mouth hung open a moment. "Velouette," he started in a soft tone. "You need to understand. We're going to destroy these banks. And there will be casualties."

She stared at him a long while, waiting for some sort of punchline, but his face showed only sincerity. Surely she hadn't heard him right. Dorin was fighting for the freedom of his people. He was honest, sincere, and moral. There was no way he would do this. And yet, he merely continued staring at her in wait.

"Dorin?" she asked.

"I know."

"But… but you said no one was going to die on a battlefield…" she trailed off as she understood the implication.

He sighed. "Listen to me. Yes, there will be innocents in those buildings. But destroying them will finally remove Reynold's power and cripple the Imperium. It will allow every single country in the world to finally gain independence from the High Kings. We will set so many people free."

She held up her hands in bewilderment. "I'm sorry, you keep skimming over the details. You're going to destroy these banks? So, a terrorist attack?"

The others in the room scoffed at her. "It's only called terrorism," Ingolf growled, "when violence is committed *against* the High Kings. When they do it, it's legal. You see the hypocrisy?"

Silvana's mouth hung open as she looked at her brother. Her long lost brother—her one true family member—was making excuses for terrorism. "Dorin, how can you do this?"

"Technically, I'm not doing this," Dorin said. "We have one other ally we haven't told you about yet. You see, one of the High Kings is on our side."

She blinked. "You're kidding? Which one?"

"You'll see in a little while. This King will be performing a tactical strike and hitting all of Reynold's banks in one fell swoop. The entire economy of the English throne will be shattered, and our wealth will skyrocket by comparison. As simple as that, we will replace Reynold as the greatest economic power in the world. The rule of Imperialism will finally come to an end."

Her mind struggled to comprehend what Dorin was telling her. "You have seventy-eight million. How is that suddenly going to equal the power of trillions?"

"Because we've invested in Reynold's competitors. They will absorb all his wealth and our stocks will skyrocket."

"But that'll leave a paper trail. Surely the Vigiles will trace it to you?"

Dorin held out his hands, palms up. "Let them challenge me," he sneered.

"But who says you will become the dominant power? Why not Jin, Louis, or a thousand other investors? Surely, there are others in as good a position as yours."

"They all invest with Reynold, cause he's the best. We are the only ones who can anticipate his downfall and plan accordingly."

She shook her head. "You're guessing. You have no idea how this fallout will affect you."

"We are experts," Ingolf growled. "We know far more about this than you do. Didn't you almost lose your home last year on a bad loan?" He smirked when he saw her expression. "You are..." it sounded like he was about to say naïve, but he cut off with a glance at Dorin. "…inexperienced," he finished. "You can trust that we've done the maths on this. Our plan is truly foolproof."

Says the most arrogant man I've ever met. Like I'd ever trust him to be level-headed.

"What about this attack? You're planning on killing innocents. I'm surprised at you, Dorin. Your people love you!" She gestured outside the office door where the sounds of Dorin's staff could be heard chatting in the background. "They trust you. Have you told them you intend to commit mass murder?"

Dorin nodded along with her. "I fully anticipated this push back, Velouette. Your response is perfectly valid. But hear me out. What I'm going to say will sound offensive." He held both hands towards her, palms up in supplication. "You have lived under the Imperium all your life. You don't realise this, but you are essentially brainwashed. You have been bombarded with their propaganda and philosophy all your life, so it's hard for you to think outside the box they've set around you."

"Because I'm stupid?" she quipped.

"Cause you've been lied to. It's not your fault," he said gently. "The Imperium tells us that murder and genocide is wrong, unless *they* do it. Do you know how many genocides the Imperium has committed in the last two millennia? How many cities have been decimated, whole populations enslaved, and countries forced into economic submission? Reynold obliterated every indigenous population that stood in his way. Even now, he removes world leaders who disagree with his economic philosophy in case they become too successful."

Dorin stood up now and his voice rose with passion. "You know the saying, 'history is written by the victors'? Well it's not just history. It's the present too. Every day, the people who fight for Reynold are labelled as heroes and freedom fighters. The people who fight *against* Reynold? They're labelled as terrorists, barbarians and evil.

The world does not determine if you are good or evil by your actions. Instead, it's defined by whether we support Reynold, or oppose him. Sister, you know this is true."

Silvana's head dropped down as she stared at the ground. "But you're talking about killing innocent people." Her voice was growing weaker, and she was repeating herself in desperation.

Dorin appeared at her side with a gentle touch to her shoulder. His eyes brimmed with tears, and he studied her with such earnestness that she had to look away.

"Velouette, listen. Please listen to me," he pleaded. "I know how it sounds. Trust me. I've struggled with this decision a lot over the years. But I promise you there is no other way. Reynold has reigned for seven hundred years, Velouette. Seven hundred. Do you think his heir is going to be any better? I'm telling you, the world is *stuck.* Humanity is stuck beneath the High Kings. We can't progress or grow or do anything new because they are holding us down. And we will never move forward while they hold our chains. We have to break those chains. And trust me, there is no path to revolution that does not include violence. There has never been a non-violent revolution in all of history. We have to fight."

She stared at him. "But Dorin, there will be repercussions. If we destroy his banks, Reynold will come for us."

"And that, dear sister, is why we need you." He smiled as he cupped her cheek is his cold hand. "Another vampire at my level of power will be exactly what we need to match Reynold. You are the heir of Dracula. Your name has the power to rally others to your cause. The Immortals will rise to join you. I will teach you how to use our magic. Then, as soon as this attack on the banks is completed, I will announce to the world the secret of vampire empowerment. I will tell them of you. Our allies will multiply, and the Imperium will fall."

"Not bad," Ingolf said, "for four forgotten royal lines. Glucksburg,

Yamato, Tepes and Romanov. Houses that have fallen from power will now rise to become the new High Kings."

"All of us were beaten by Reynold," Hana said, her tone cold and menacing. "Glucksburg by a long battle of economic dominance. My people rose against Reynold in the World War, and in return, my house is stripped of all but ceremonial power." She spat the last word. "Tepes was all but wiped out. And the Romanovs were betrayed when they asked for help." She shook her head at Silvana. "We are all victims of Reynold's cruelty. Now, he shall know ours."

"We will win the freedom for our people," Dorin said. "Freedom for everyone. Soon, we will have an army of empowered vampires. We will teach the mortals to place their faith in us. We will be worthy of that faith. And with the power they give us, we will set them free from wizard rule. The vampires will lead, but only by the consensus of the people! The world will be free at last."

Silvana could feel the weight of five pairs of eyes watching her, waiting in silence, expecting her to agree with their plan. The power within her was boiling to the surface as if yearning to seize control and steer her towards the most violent course of action. Or maybe it wasn't the energy in her core yearning for that. Maybe it was Ana? That part of herself that seemed desperate to rage and destroy. *Hell, what am I even doing here?* Before she realised what was happening, the gentle trickle of tears ran down her cheeks.

She felt like such an idiot for trusting Dorin. She had a sudden urge to shout and scream at him. But she knew if she did that, he would assume she was brainwashed and that the Imperium had far too much control over her, and the world itself. That Reynold had too much control. Maybe she *had* been brainwashed by the Imperium. How could she be considering attacking her own brother? How could Reynold be right, and Dorin be wrong? But even then, how could she truly know what she wanted? She had other personalities in her brain, influencing her decisions. She couldn't even trust herself. How could she make a decision?

Just then, something in her mind began to shake, growing frantic and wild. She wanted to yell and scream and cry at the entire situation. *Oh my god, that's Ana! She's trying to take over.* Silvana gripped her head with both hands and dug her fingers into her scalp. *Oh God, I can't trust my own mind.* She turned to Dorin, his handsome face and crystalline blue eyes staring back at her.

He was the family she had waited nearly a century for. He was the little boy from the memories who clung to his sister when all seemed lost. He had searched for her for eighty years.

"You're the only family I have left," she whispered. "I cannot lose you, too."

Dorin gave Silvana a warm smile as he knelt before her, wrapping his arms around her shoulders. "You won't lose me. I promise." He held her tight. She squeezed him back, and the scent of him filled her nose with memories from another life.

Dorin stood up again. "Come on. It's time. We're going to take you to see the High King," he said.

"We can't bring her to that meeting," Hana snapped. "Our treaty is still fragile. I don't want her screwing this up—"

"She still has concerns. We need her to believe in the cause. If we show her our greatest ally, it will dispel any lingering doubts." He looked to her again. "Is that ok, sister?"

"Yes," she said.

Dorin let out a long sigh and smiled. "Excellent. That will be enough for now. Thank you, Velouette." He stood up and moved around the desk. "In that case, I suggest we all hold hands like one big happy family, and I can take us to our next destination. Everyone?" He held a hand out to Silvana.

She hesitated. Maybe she shouldn't go with them. Or she could talk to Jason first, and at least update him. She pulled out her phone as she considered her options. There was a text already there waiting for her.

"I'm so sorry I didn't tell you the truth. I was wrong. Please let me know if you'd like to talk. I'm here for you. I love you, Silvana."

"Velouette? Everything ok?" Dorin asked.

She stared at her phone screen. It seemed no one in her life ever told her the full truth. Her aunts and uncles, Jason, and now even Dorin was keeping things from her. *At least Jason is sorry.* But, she was still angry at being treated like a child. She wasn't a child any longer.

Silvana took Dorin's hand and stepped into the circle.

She was forced to reach towards Hana. The Japanese vampire glared back and moved so that her knight would take Silvana's hand instead.

They formed a circle, and Dorin sent out a wave of power. This time, Silvana had enough of her own to see how he did it. She could feel the waves of thought coming out of him and shaping the magic around them. She thought she could probably do it herself if she had to. *Interesting.*

A few seconds later, she found herself in a large throne room, much like Reynolds. Guards were spaced evenly around the room, dressed in soldier's gear and holding machine guns aimed at the intricately tiled floors. A large black throne stood against one wall with an imposing man lounging back in the plush cushions. He wore a Russian hat and long royal robes. Another group of people stood to the side of the throne room, and Silvana turned to face them out of sheer politeness…

But nothing could have prepared her for who stood at the head of the group.

Jason stared back at her.

The Vigiles Desdemona and Portia were at his side. In fact, the whole group was there. Freddie, Edward, Leslie, and even Khadija. There was also a short girl with black hair she didn't recognise.

"Silvana?!" Jason cried. He took a step towards her.

"Jason?" she called back.

"Halt!" Desdemona barked, and suddenly Dorin stood in front of Silvana, shielding her with his body.

"Don't you dare touch her!" Dorin roared.

His Royalist allies formed a line alongside him, and the other group formed a line of their own. The guards ran forward and aimed their automatic weapons at both parties.

Everyone started talking at once. Desdemona was shouting orders to surrender. Dorin roared his defiance. Jason and Freddie were backing away, though Jason had his sword and handgun drawn and aimed. Ingolf was floating in the air with a wave of rippling heat around his person. Hana had an aura of glowing red circling her body. Portia held a ball of fire in her hands, and her long red hair was standing on end like she was wielding electricity. Leslie and Khadija held hands to combine their power as a kaleidoscope of stars loomed above them.

"I will end you!" Dorin roared. "Do you hear me? I will fucking end you right here, Desdemona!"

"Thou *rat!* I will rip out thine innards!"

"Everyone just calm down!" Jason shouted. "Stand down! Do not fire!"

Silvana's mind quivered in fear. There was too much terror for her to function. All the people she loved were in this room. They were all going to die. She held her hands to her head and nearly started shrieking incoherently.

Her mind flashed with memories. Not the memories Dorin had shown her, but rather, her own memories dragged out of the depths of her mind at last. Her mother, dying with a fist through her stomach. Her father dead, broken form and bent neck. Young Dorin screaming her name. Hands gripping her and dragging her away from the only family she'd ever known. Here at last, in the hall of the High King, it was all happening again. History would repeat itself.

Stop! You're going to lose control! You can't do that here!

And above all the chaos, through all the panic in her mind and the terror of the moment, a deep male voice echoed over the entire hall.

The High King Alexei was laughing.

Chapter 29

Jason was relieved when the new group arrived in the amphitheatre. He had no idea how in the world he was supposed to address a High King. Both times he'd spoken to Reynold, he'd fumbled through his words like a child and wasn't looking forward to repeating that experience. He even laughed to himself and thought '*saved by the bell*' at the interruption.

Then, he saw Silvana.

Standing with Dorin alongside the other Royalists. His heart lurched in his chest.

Silvana! What are you doing with them? She was looking at him with the same expression of shock and terror like she too wanted to just run to his side.

Dear God... Silvana and I on opposite sides. How did it come to this?

Dorin and Desdemona seemed ready to kill each other with the greatest of magics when the laughter of the High King cut through it all. Everyone fell silent as his voice rang out through his grand hall.

"Alexei?" Silvana cried. She looked at Dorin. "That's your ally?"

Desdemona gave a short bark of laughter. "Yes, Dorin. Answer her. Art thou and Alexei conspiring together? I would dearly love to know."

"Stay out of this!" Dorin snapped at the Vigile. He turned to face

Alexei on his throne, high on the stage above. "Great High King. You knew of our appointment with you. Why would you allow Vigiles to witness a private meeting?"

Alexei simply raised an eyebrow. "Are you questioning me?"

Dorin glared back. "I think it's clear I was."

"We all are," Desdemona said, a look of pure ecstasy on her face. "Oh great High King, we would all dearly love to know, art thou consorting with known enemies of the Imperium? Art thou indeed a traitor?"

All eyes turned to the king on his throne, high above them all. He looked down with a sneer that was obvious even through his thick, bushy beard. "Whether or not I am a traitor," he spoke with slow, deliberate care, "depends entirely on all of you."

"What do you mean?" Dorin growled. "We already had a deal in place!"

"And I will gladly honour that deal," Alexei said. "Provided you can prove your power. Here, we have two Vigiles, including the famous Desdemona, the prodigy. And unless I misplace my guess, we have a formidable witch, another wizard, and their respective minor allies." Alexei leaned forward in his chair, his teeth visible in a broad smile.

"Destroy them, and I will join you."

Jason's blood turned cold. Silvana cried across the hall, "No! High King, that is my husband! I will never raise a hand against him."

"You won't have to," Hana replied. "Consider this fair payment. You killed my husband, I'll kill yours for you."

What the hell? What kind of arrangement do they even have? Is Silvana a prisoner?

"Thou art too much of a coward!" Desdemona roared at the High King. "Thou dares not face me thyself. Thou knows thy power is not my equal."

"Alas, we shall never know the truth of it," Alexei sneered.

Freddie stood at Jason's side. His hands were shaking, but his eyes were facing the Royalists like he was eager to fight. He gave Jason a nod. *He's a brave man, and a dear friend.* Edward waited a step behind, fidgeting with his cloak in agitation. And Khadija stood at Jason's opposite side. Her body language was clear. She would protect them.

"Look, I have no desire to fight any of you," Dorin declared. "Except maybe you, Desdemona. You've had this coming a long time." She only grinned back, like the comment made her happy, somehow. "But this would be a pointless fight. My sister on one side and my brother-in-law on another." He nodded at Jason in a show of respect. "This will only cause needless pain and suffering."

"Yet it is my will," Alexei growled. "You dare to challenge Reynold himself, yet cower away from his mere servant and her allies? How could I ally with you without proof of your power?"

"Enough!" Ingolf roared, the air around his hands starting to shimmer with heat. "Let's begin. I am eager to crush these bitches."

"Oh geez, mister," Portia chimed in her high pitch voice. "I'm just a pretty little thing. You wouldn't hurt such a beautiful face as mine?"

He growled in response.

Leslie stepped towards the front line and spoke with deliberate care. "Dorin, how do you plan to challenge Reynold? I am genuinely curious to know," they said.

"Art thou planning to switch sides, witch?" Desdemona hissed.

Leslie gave a coy shrug. "Maybe. If their plan is good enough."

"Thou damn traitor!"

"It's not an option," Alexei declared. "You will not learn our plan. You will fight or you will die. That is the only option I grant you."

"New York."

Heads turned towards Portia. The younger Vigile's eyes had grown wide and her mouth hung open.

I know that look. She's figured it out.

"I didn't understand at first," Portia said. "Until I realised you were working with a High King. I should have seen it earlier. After all, we've suspected a High King's involvement for some time now." She shook her head. No one on either side dared interrupt her. "You've been investing into all of Reynold's competitors. You want to destroy his economy so that yours grows in its absence. But you're not just going to destroy a few banks. You want to target all of them." She pointed at Dorin. "The entire city of New York is your target. That's why you need Alexei. To wipe out the whole damn thing."

"An Act of God," Leslie said. "Against Reynold. How poetic."

The blood drained from Jason's face. This was everything he had feared since learning of a wizard's true power. A scene of mass destruction on a populated area. That was exactly what Dorin and Alexei were planning. *My god. Surely, Silvana is not on board with this.* He saw the shock flicker over her face, and nearly sighed in relief. She had not known.

"Dorin?" Silvana asked. "Is this true?"

Dorin was glaring with murderous rage at Portia, and she only looked back with a smug smirk. "I got you now, didn't I?" Portia laughed. "Tell your sister the truth. Come on."

"You said it was a tactical strike," Silvana cried. "That you would wipe out the banks."

"It *is* tactical," Dorin said, avoiding eye contact.

Silvana gasped. "It's true then. You're wiping out the whole city. You... you deceived me!"

"You weren't ready for the truth!" he cried. "I'm sorry, Velouette, but you still believe Imperium propaganda. I knew you wouldn't stand for it. And after I revealed my powers in the Library to save you, I knew it was only a matter of time till our plans were discovered. I didn't have time to explain everything to you. I wanted to talk it through first, believe me."

"So you were going to involve me in mass murder, then tell me the truth once I was committed?"

"That's not it at all."

"You wanted to free your people. How is destroying New York going to help Romania?"

Dorin turned on her. "I will free our people from Reynold's control!" He snapped. "I told you, Velouette. There is no way to fight against Reynold without violence. You only think it's wrong because we're doing it against him. Do you know how many times Reynold has used an 'Act of God' against his enemies? Lisbon, Tokyo, Yangtze! And every time he did it, hundreds of thousands were killed. This justice is long overdue."

"Justice?" Jason yelled. "Don't even use the word. How many innocent lives are in New York?"

"Eight million," Freddie answered immediately, then cleared his throat in embarrassment.

"Exactly. You think killing eight million people will bring justice against one old wizard? It won't affect Reynold in any way."

"You're a cop, Jason," Dorin yelled. "What would you know about justice? You're an enforcer for the wealthy and nothing more. You pervert justice on a daily basis."

Jason growled under his breath and tightened his grip on his gun.

Silvana grasped her brother by the arm. "Dorin, do you realise who you're working with? Alexei helped to start the Second World War. Then, he betrayed his side and used it to become High King. He's the one who tore our family apart. He's the reason our parents are dead and why we were separated all these years. Do you really want to work with him?"

Her brother smiled and whispered, *"For now."*

Silvana gave a pained cry and turned away from him, facing the wall. She furiously wiped her eyes. "I thought..." her voice broke. "I thought you were family."

"Velouette," Dorin said, putting a hand on her shoulder. "I swear, I would never do anything that might hurt you. In fact, do you know what I want for you and our country?" He glanced nervously at the Vigiles, only to shrug in their direction as if he didn't care anymore. "I want to bring the monarchy back."

"Monarchy?" she cried.

"Yes!" his face lit up with excitement. "It was the king who removed the fascists from power during the War. And how did the country repay him? They exiled him!" Dorin shook his head. "This country hasn't been free since we had a king. That's why I want to bring it back. And now you're here as the first in line of our House. I can resume my original birthright as firstborn son." He stood up straight and declared, "I will be a king in waiting once more."

She stared into that face that was alive with manic glee. Her face grew sombre as she took a step away from him. "You're not trying to fight a Third World War," she said. "You're trying to go back and fight the Second."

"What?" Dorin said with strained joviality.

"Don't you see, brother? You're trying to go back to the way things were. You're trying to fix the past. You want to be the mortal king, and you want me to be the Immortal heir. Dorin," her voice lowered to a whisper. "It's a child's dream. And all it's going to accomplish is more wars, more bloodshed and more families torn apart. You're going to start the whole process all over again."

Dorin gave a cold glare. "I'm doing it differently this time. Velouette. I've learnt a lot from the last war. We're not fighting with soldiers, we're fighting with economy. Trust me, everything's going to go better this time."

"No, it won't!" she cried, her voice a desperate plea. "You're still just a little boy trying to bring his family back. You're stuck in the past."

Dorin's blue eyes flashed with anger. "I'm trying to fight the fascists."

"By becoming one of them," she answered.

Dorin's eyes flashed red. His lip curled like he wanted to scream back at her. But the moment passed, and he gave a long sigh.

"I forgot what it's like to have a family," he said coldly. "I forgot no one else can hurt you this much."

Silvana shook her head. "No, brother. I'm not hurting you. I'm just not willing to be manipulated by my family any longer."

At that moment, Jason nearly ran to her and hugged her. It had taken Silvana nearly a century to reach this point, but she was finally there now. He couldn't have been more proud of her.

"Silvana is right," Leslie announced as they walked into the centre of the room, placing themselves right in the middle between the two groups. Curiously, the shapeshifter assassin girl was at their side. "You have no idea what you're starting."

"We are prepared for Reynold," Dorin said.

"It's not Reynold I'm worried about. It's war." Leslie pointed at the Royalist leader. "Haven't you heard the saying, 'no plan survives first contact with the enemy?' From the moment the first shot is fired, you have no idea how many will die until the last shot. You lose control faster than you can imagine. Your enemies will fight back in ways you cannot anticipate. The death toll is unpredictable. You may lose nothing, or everything. War is a gamble of the worst kind, where the bet is humanity itself."

"I have seen war, my friend," Dorin sneered. "I am not some child to be instructed."

"You are to me," Leslie roared, and Jason nearly stepped away from the witch. Their fury was something he'd not seen before.

This was an Immortal with *righteous* fury, someone who had seen centuries of injustice and was sick of it beyond mortal comprehension.

"You've seen war," Leslie said. "Well good for you. I have seen hundreds of wars and *thousands* of battles. Do you think you're the first to believe their cause is just? That their moral outrage justifies anything? Or that their power will make any damn difference in the midst of conflict?"

"You've never seen my power."

"Fool," Leslie screamed. "They all say the same thing! You can't guarantee anything will improve even if you win. But I can guarantee a world of suffering in the meantime. That is a fact you are blinding yourself to deliberately."

"I've had enough," Ingolf growled.

"Agreed," Dorin replied.

Jason felt the moment approaching. He held his sword up and his gun ready for all the good it would do.

"You boys stay close to me," Khadija whispered. "I'll get you out of here."

Meanwhile Desdemona summoned thick balls of black mist in her hands. The room filled with the rushing of wind and the roar of flames.

"Wait!" Silvana cried and stood before her brother. Now she and Leslie stood between both groups. "Brother, please! I don't want to fight you. Please stop this!"

Dorin looked at her, his face visible to Jason, his expression being watched intently by the whole room. Jason had his gun at the ready. If it came to a choice, he would take the shot at his brother-in-law and hope it bloody well did something. Dorin kept staring at his sister, ignoring the growing powers of magic being summoned, while everyone paused in waiting for his decision.

"Fine," he said. It sounded like a declaration.

"Really?" Silvana cried.

He leaned over his shoulder, towards Hana. "Incapacitate her," he said simply.

Hana moved faster than humanly possible. Jason only saw a blur of movement before Silvana let out a scream. Her leg was suddenly bent at an unnatural angle and the bone jutted out from her calf as she dropped to the ground.

"No!" Jason roared and pulled the trigger of his gun, shooting twice at Hana.

His gun acted like a starter pistol, and within a second, a dozen explosions had filled the throne room. Something blasted Jason to the ground, and he fell with his hands over his head. The sounds of battle drowned out everything else. It was suddenly shockingly loud as deafening cracks of thunder and blinding flashes of lightning rang out in close proximity.

The face of the High King was lit up for only an instant, but there was no mistaking his broad grin.

Chapter 30

Chaos was unfolding everywhere Jason looked.

Desdemona was front and centre of the battle, her jacket unbuttoned and billowing behind her from the shockwaves of every spell. Her hands were clenched into fists at her side, and she snarled as blasts of black mist launched from her position and formed massive impact craters all around her. Portia stood proudly beside her, hurling flames in every direction. Everything beyond that was completely obscured by the explosive force of magic. Jason couldn't even see Dorin, let alone the other Royalists.

A blast of red sparks exploded in front of his face, and Khadija let out a scream as she blocked it. Her words were drowned out by the noise.

"Khadija!" he shouted, but she couldn't hear him. "Edward? Can you help her?" Jason cried. Edward was already in the throes of a panic attack. His hands were cupped over his ears, and he screamed between desperate gasps. Any elixirs he'd brought were forgotten in his terror.

Another blast hit their position. Khadija caught it but stumbled backwards from the shock. Both Jason and Freddie caught her and lifted her back to her feet. She stopped them both with a tight grip on their arms.

"Guys." Her voice exploded inside Jason's mind. *"I... I don't know about this. I might be out of my league here."*

Jason remembered Khadija could communicate with thoughts. The whole sentence took half a second to hear.

"Khadija! Can you get us out of here?" he yelled.

"I can't hear you or your thoughts, remember? Now, for some reason, I can't teleport away. I think Alexei is blocking me."

"That bastard!"

"We can try and see if the Vigiles beat them. Or we can try to take out at least one of their heavy hitters. Either Dorin, Ingolf, or Hana. Removing one would give the Vigiles a better chance. Also, I think Leslie is giving me a boost like they did in the Library. It's the only reason I've lasted this long."

A flash of red light came from Portia's hands as a wall of flame surged towards the Royalists. A second later it was deflected aside, redirected straight for Jason's group like a falling building.

Khadija roared in defiance and flung up her hands. The fiery blast hit hard enough to knock the whole group to the ground, scattering them like a bowling ball knocking down pins. Jason knew this feeling all too well. The feeling of being hopelessly outclassed. He started to scramble to his feet, trying to find Khadija and get her on the defence again, but another firestorm was already headed their way. He stared at the approaching fireball without a single idea of how he could avoid it.

The flaming attack abruptly swirled into a vortex and was sucked away into nothingness. A moment later, Leslie appeared at Jason's side. Their voice also filled his head.

"Sorry I took so long. The damn chimera assassin refused to fight with us. I fear they've used this chance to escape."

"Witch?" Khadija's mental voice said with a clear note of surprise.

"Ah, wizard. I thought you might be capable of this. I see two can play

at that game."

Khadija barked a sarcastic, mental laugh. *"Clearly we have more in common than we thought. I was just saying we have to help the Vigiles. You and I could focus fire one of their big three."*

"Ingolf is our best target. We better understand how a wizard's power works. I'll charge you up, and you deliver the killing blow?"

"Agreed."

"Wait!" Jason shouted. He had to wave his hands to be heard over the noise of battle. "Silvana!" he shouted.

Leslie shook their head. *"We cannot help her now. We have to win this fight."*

"Silvana!" Jason shouted again. He couldn't make any real argument, not with the cacophony drowning out his words.

"Jason," Leslie thought to him. *"You have to think like a leader now. Like a king! Silvana is not a priority target for either side. You need to leave her and focus on defeating the Royalists. If we fail, they will destroy New York. It's our only chance to save eight million lives."*

Jason let out a low growl, but he knew it was true. He gave the witch a nod. And Leslie gave him the weirdest expression in return. A satisfied smile. Was that pride in the gleam of their bright eyes? Like a proud parent? He couldn't tell. Leslie put their hand on Khadija's shoulder and the two started taking slow steps towards the carnage.

"Stay close," Leslie warned.

Freddie had one arm around a nervous Edward and a vial of green liquid in his other hand, which Jason recognised as the acid he had used on the assassin. Jason kept his sword and handgun at the ready as they advanced into the chaos.

The throne room had grown dark. Whatever lights that had been illuminating the hall were now blown out, but there was no chance for darkness to establish itself with the constant flashes of magical explosions. Khadija and Leslie were moving the group around the side of the battle, attempting to flank the Royalists. Jason found himself grinning. With all this noise and chaos from the battle, they might just be able to sneak up on their enemy.

A figure immerged from the darkness, holding a massive gun in two hands.

In an instant, Jason realised the Royalist knight had the same idea of flanking the battle. Wilhelm already had his assault rifle aimed on them.

"I've got this," Leslie mentally assured them. The gun burst with automatic fire, but Leslie was somehow making the air warp around them—similar to a teleporting spell—and all the bullets were absorbed into it. *"Now Jason! You've got a clear target."* Leslie's words screamed inside his mind.

Jason leaned over their shoulder and fired half a dozen rounds in quick succession. Most of them hit the knight in the chest, hip and shoulder. Wilhelm was definitely wearing a vest to spare them the worst of the damage, but the wounds on the hip and shoulder were enough to knock him down. Dead or alive, he was too incapacitated to be a threat.

"Excellent work, sir knight."

"That was the Glucksburg knight," Khadija thought to the group. *"Which means Ingolf is just ahead."*

"Our moment approaches. Prepare yourself, wizard, and wait for my command."

They crept further forward. Someone was still throwing blasts of fire and energy across the hall, clearly trying to hit Jason's group. But with no idea where they were, Jason and his friends had the upper hand. They had a chance to make a difference in this fight.

"There!" Leslie mentally shouted. Jason saw a figure in a long robe just ahead, lit up by a momentary flash of light.

"I'm thinking lightning," Khadija said.

"Agreed. Hit him with all you've got."

Khadija started to draw on her power. A hand clasped over Jason's shoulder, startling him, but it was just Freddie. The two men exchanged a nod of reassurance as Freddie gave his shoulder a firm squeeze. They might just get out of this alive.

Then Khadija let out a single bar of white lightning that rang out through the hall with a deafening crack. It was so bright that Jason could see everything in the room clearly for one full second. The lightning hit Ingolf square in the chest and passed through him, forking out into a dozen branches on the other side and striking the opposite wall.

"Yes!" Jason roared.

Then bright light flashed directly at him. It happened so quickly he didn't have time to feel any sort of fear before Ingolf's counter blast of lightning hit him in the chest. And he blacked out.

Jason's face was pressed up against the cold stone floor. Something was burning in his chest. *Shit, we were in the middle of a fight!* He tried to sit up but his head started spinning.

The others were sprawled out on the ground beside him. Some of them had smoke trailing from their scorched clothes from where the lightning had burnt through the fabric. Jason noted a similar burn through his left chest and shoulder, and he was vaguely aware of a deep pain radiating down his arm. The others were moving, so they were still alive. But the battle between the Royalists and the Vigiles was still going strong. Khadija's attack had not even made a difference. And Silvana was still somewhere in the middle of the unfolding chaos.

"Pathetic!" a voice roared. Jason covered his ears from the sudden volume. He recognised the voice of High King Alexei. It had been magically enhanced to be louder than all the sounds of battle. "You claimed you could challenge the other High Kings, *Dorin Tepes*. Yet, you can barely fight Desdemona to an equilibrium. I had hoped for so much more."

From somewhere in the midst of the magic came Dorin's shrill voice. "Power?!" he screamed. "I'll show you *power!*"

Dorin appeared amongst the waves of explosive magics, wearing his traditional Romanian white vest with golden embroidery. His eyes glowed red and an aura of power emanated from him. The two Vigiles targeted him with attacks that Jason couldn't even comprehend, yet all seemed to strike him without doing damage. Then, he sprinted at them with inhuman speed.

Jason heard a cry of panic, and he turned just in time to see Dorin appear before Portia and strike her right on the sternum. He punched her so hard she went flying back out of sight. Jason felt his mind shutting off from the trauma of such violence. Portia had probably just had multiple bones broken, if she had even survived the blow.

"*No!*" Desdemona roared.

Ingolf and Hana appeared on either side of her with a flurry of attacks. Even Dorin was already striking at her again. Desdemona held off all three of them, frantically waving her arms and uttering spell after spell. All the while, the laughter of the High King rang through his throne room.

"*Come on!*" Leslie mentally roared. "*She can't hold them all alone. We have to make another attempt, or we're all dead!*"

Leslie was picking up Khadija, the latter holding her stomach in pain as tears ran down her cheeks. Jason grabbed her other side and helped her to her feet. Freddie and Edward were holding each other. The team stood together, ready to make one final stand.

Then Dorin was in front of them.

"Oh shit!" Jason cried.

Dorin made no visible movement. Khadija held out her hands to summon a visible shimmer of magic to block him. But the power of his mind punched straight through her shield and into her body, knocking her back a dozen metres. He pivoted to shoot blue flames out of his palm across the hall towards Desdemona, not letting the pressure up on her for a second.

Jason took no chances and fired at Dorin several times, while Leslie waved their hands, putting a spell between Dorin and the group. The empowered vampire took the bullets to his chest like they were nothing. He punched at Leslie's spell barrier, and his hand seemed to disappear like it was passing into another dimension. Dorin waved his arms and the spell came apart instantly. Then, he hit Leslie with his telekinesis. The witch was blown away with just a thought.

Oh god, this is it. Jason swung his sword in a two-handed downward strike. Dorin *caught* the blade in his hand. It didn't even break his skin.

"You lying bastard!" Jason roared. "We trusted you!" Dorin sneered as he threw the sword aside and pulled back his fist to strike Jason's face.

A vial broke against Dorin's head. Green acid began to drip over Dorin's face, melting his skin.

"Fuck you!" Freddie screamed and threw a second vial at Dorin's chest.

Both chemicals began to burn their way through his flesh as Dorin writhed in agony and let out an inhuman shriek. Within seconds, the bones of his skull and his ribcage became visible, and his left eye began to seep down his cheek like sagging glue. Dorin suddenly flared with a red aura and his body rapidly revert back towards its normal state. His red, deformed eyes landed on Freddie, before a telekinetic blast threw him away with enough force to make a cracking sound when he hit the ground.

Edward let out an ear-piercing scream. His panic attack turned into sudden rage. He transformed at once into the huge, muscular beast he'd been when fighting the assassin, growing to twice his size and ripping through his clothes. Then, he brought his huge fists down on Dorin. The vampire stopped them all with an invisible barrier over his head. He took a moment to shoot more blue flame at Desdemona. Then he was focused back on Edward. His mind caused Edward's arm to spontaneously snap in half. Edward cried out in pain before another mental blow threw him away.

Jason was the only one left standing. He checked his Glock-17. There were still five rounds in the clip for all the good they would do.

Dorin's eyes locked on Jason. His face and chest had already finished healing the last of the acid burns. Now he looked as beautiful as ever, like a fallen angel. He turned slightly and started sending a constant jet of flames towards Desdemona. The last Vigile was still withstanding the attacks of all three Royalist champions, but she was clearly on the defensive and only focused on stopping attacks. Not delivering any of her own. She couldn't hold like this much longer.

"I'm truly sorry, Jason," Dorin said. "You seem a good man. But I need the High King as an ally if I'm ever to defeat Reynold. Velouette will hate me for this, but in time, she will understand. She's lost two husbands before you."

"I thought family came first with you, brother," Jason growled. "Or was that just another lie in your long list?"

"A cop shouldn't dare lecture me on lies!" Dorin snapped. He still had his left hand facing Desdemona, but his right hand reached out towards Jason and shimmered with heat without any visible flame. "Still, you have my sincerest thanks. You helped me find my sister. I'll take care of her from here, I promise."

"Go fuck yourself."

Dorin gestured with his hand, but the blast of heat shot upwards into the roof, as if redirected. Both Jason and Dorin glanced around the room and saw Leslie walking towards them again.

"Take a lesson from me, oh *king in waiting*," Leslie sneered, speaking like a teacher giving a lecture. "History repeats itself. Everyone knows that. But what we forget is that history never repeats itself in the exact same way. That means even if you repeat the mistakes of history," Leslie raised their voice to a bold shout, "you still cannot bring back the past!"

"Bloody historian," Dorin growled. "I will bring back the monarchy. You'll see. History will remember me for it."

Leslie shook their head. "History will only remember another fool on an already tragically long list. The monarchy is dead. The world has moved on. Why can't you?"

Dorin growled. "You love history so much? I think it's time you join it."

Jason hummed, "That's actually not ba—"

Pain suddenly exploded in the side of Jason's head. It took him a moment to regain awareness. Dorin had clearly backhanded him before launching himself at Leslie. Jason could barely lift his head to see what was happening.

The ancient witch and empowered vampire had thrown themselves into a duel, even as Dorin continued throwing his constant barrage of flame towards Desdemona. Dorin shot multiple blasts towards Leslie. The witch waved their hands and created multiple teleportation bubbles that swallowed up each attack. Leslie was straining, but clearly keeping up with the fight. Jason looked around for his weapons. His gun and sword lay nearby. He checked his allies. Khadija was out cold. Both Freddie and Edward were too injured to fight anymore. Portia had not returned, and he still had no idea where Silvana was. No, if anyone was going to help Leslie or Desdemona, it was up to Jason. He crawled to his gun and raised it in a shaking hand.

"We should be working together," Leslie cried. "We want the same thing."

"I doubt that!"

"What if I said there was a way to destroy the Imperium without killing millions?"

Dorin sneered. "I'd say you were naïve."

"That's a bold thing to say to someone in their eighth century, boy."

Jason took aim and prepared to fire just as Dorin gave a scornful laugh. "Boy?" he jeered.

Dorin moved with superhuman speed and was suddenly standing up against Leslie. It took Jason a moment to see what had happened. Dorin was touching Leslie's chest. In fact, the vampire's hand was *inside* Leslie's ribcage.

"*No!*"

Leslie collapsed to the ground, and Dorin gave a satisfied grunt as the witch fell. "Old fool," he growled. Then, he turned his full attention on Desdemona. The roar of the battle became deafening again as the final Vigile took on all three challengers at once. The sound of Alexei's laughter could still be heard loudest of all.

Jason scrambled across the floor towards Leslie. He gripped the witch's head in gentle hands, tilting their head up. "Leslie, just keep breathing. I'll try to stop the bleeding…" but one look at their chest and Jason knew there was no stopping this. In fact, Leslie should already be dead. They probably only had moments…

"Damn," Leslie spat, blood in their mouth. "Worst possible timing. I had so much more to teach you."

"Leslie, I'm sorry." Jason's eyes stung with tears. "All of this, everything I've done, it was to save you. But it was all for nothing. I've… I've failed you. I'm so sorry."

Leslie looked Jason in the eye, and Jason could see all that precious wisdom and knowledge in their ancient mind starting to slip away. Leslie murmured, "Talk to the cat."

Jason blinked. "What?"

Leslie gave a smile. "You'll make… a good… king."

"Leslie, you're not making sense. Stay with me! Keep breathing!"

But Leslie slumped down in Jason's arms. And Jason knew they were gone.

Chapter 31

Leslie Toussaint was dead.

The ancient and powerful witch, historian, and keeper of secret histories had been killed in an instant. It was a tragedy on a scale Jason could barely comprehend. This great Immortal had come to him for help, and he had failed to keep them alive. *This is all my fault.*

No. It was Dorin's fault. Dorin fucking Tepes!

Jason was absolutely blinded by rage. That vampire had lied and conned his way into their lives. He had said all the right things at the right time, but he had misrepresented himself until the final moment. Now Jason knew exactly what type of monster he was. He had killed a good person, simply because they were in his way.

"Well, great king?" Dorin roared, and the sound of his voice made Jason's blood boil. "Our enemies have fallen. Desdemona is the only one left, and she will soon fall. Are you satisfied now?"

"She still draws breath," Alexei answered, his tone flat and his voice amplified by magic.

"Thou fucking better believe it!" Desdemona shrieked. "I thought thy fools would at least pose a challenge!"

"Fucking die already, bitch!" Hana yelled back.

"Face it," Dorin cried. "She may hold out a while, but the match is over, and we have proven our strength to you. Now go. Fulfil our bargain as you promised."

Jason waited, his heart pounding in his throat. Surely Alexei would betray the Royalists now. There's no way he would go through with it. He would want to stay and watch Desdemona die. There was still a chance she could win all on her own.

"You are correct," Alexei said with resignation. "The match is won, though the bitch doesn't know it yet. I will perform the Act of God, as agreed."

No...

Alexei stood up from his throne. He stretched each side of his neck and rolled his shoulders. Then he cupped both hands together. The air around him began to bend and fold through space, and when it finished, the High King had disappeared entirely.

Jason gasped. Alexei had teleported. Meaning, he was probably in New York this second. How long would it take him to carry out his massive act of destruction? An hour? A few minutes? There was no way to tell. Was there even a chance to stop him now?

Desdemona is our best chance. Maybe she can tell Reynold, and he'll fight Alexei?

He had no idea. He just knew that if Desdemona failed now, eight million people would die. Then who knew how many more would die in the following war between Reynold's kingdom and the combined might of Alexei, Dorin, Glucksburg and Yamato.

Jason struggled to his feet. This was his last chance. No one else was left to help. Desperately, he scanned the broken throne room one last time, hoping for a glimpse of Silvana. He hadn't seen her since her leg was broken at the start of the battle. He still could not find her. Had she fled? Did a personality take over and make her flee? Or did Dorin teleport her away? That last one felt likely. Still, he wished he could see her again. Just once more before what was likely to be his end.

Desdemona was standing up ahead in the middle of a maelstrom. A massive tornado of swirling flame trapped Desdemona in the eye of a storm. The deafening roar of a fierce wind echoed through the throne room as the three Royalists pushed the firestorm on her, and she pushed it back from within the centre.

Jason staggered forward. Dorin was up ahead, his back to him. No one paid any mind to the lowly mortal amongst a battle of gods. He walked right up to Dorin without being seen, though he had made no effort to hide himself. Jason's shoulder and chest was aching now that the initial shock of his injuries had worn off. He had only moments left before his body collapsed entirely. He fought with every ounce of energy he had left.

He wrapped an arm around Dorin's neck to hold him in place and, with the other hand, put the gun to Dorin's head. He pulled the trigger without hesitation.

He emptied the rest of his clip into Dorin's skull.

Dorin flinched at each bullet's impact. The jet of flame coming out of his hands faltered slightly, and for the smallest second, Jason had hope.

Then Dorin jerked his head back and head-butted him in the face. Jason dropped to the ground. His weapon was empty and it hadn't made a difference. Desdemona was still trapped, and Dorin had shrugged off the attack like it was nothing more than a tiny inconvenience. He turned around, revealing a bloodied face and a gruesome dent at his temple. He snarled at Jason.

"Oh, I'm going to enjoy this more than I should," he growled. He held one hand towards Desdemona, pushing on the fire storm around her. He reached his other hand towards Jason.

"You're an asshole!" Jason growled. It wasn't his best insult. But by God, if he was going to die, he would do so cussing at his enemy.

Even Dorin gave him a look of respect.

"No!"

A bubble of space warped in front of Jason, and a heartbeat later Silvana stood before him, placing herself between Jason and her brother.

"Silvy!" he cried in relief.

It took him a moment to realise she was standing. Her legs no longer broken. But how had she healed them? She could never heal that quickly before. Unless… was she empowered too? She had just teleported herself back into the throne room. Surely, she must be empowered.

Jason gave a broad smile. Maybe she could stop Dorin.

"This has to end," Silvana cried. "I'm giving you one chance, brother."

Dorin tilted his head in bewilderment, and the flames cast dark shadows over his face. "Surely you're not threatening me, Velouette. I'm the only family you have left."

"My name is Silvana," she roared. "And Jason is my family!"

Dorin sighed at her before striking at her with the back of his hand.

Except, Silvana caught his wrist. Then bent her mouth towards his hand and *bit him.*

Dorin screamed and tried to yank his hand away, but her teeth had fully impaled his palm. She jumped up and wrapped her legs around his neck and arm in a wrestling lock, using her entire body to keep his hand in her mouth. He staggered while keeping her whole weight raised off the ground. He slapped and screamed at her. Shockwaves of telekinetic energy burst out of him, but Silvana shrugged off each blow and kept her jaws firmly clamped on his hand.

What is she doing? Is she bleeding him dry?

"Stop it!" Dorin howled. "You can't do this!"

The power he was sending at Desdemona was shaking, losing its strength. The firestorm trembled wildly. The other Royalists cried out in panic, but Dorin couldn't get Silvana off him.

In desperation, he ended his attack on Desdemona and bent his full power entirely on Silvana. He grabbed her physically with his hands and with his telekinetic grip as well, using every shred of power he had left to pull her away. Blood squirted from his hand as some of her teeth were torn from his flesh. Still, she held on.

"Impossible!" Dorin screamed. "You cannot steal souls! It cannot be done!"

Silvana gave a wild laugh that was muffled by Dorin's hand. Finally she let go, and it looked like it was her decision to do it. The siblings fell to the ground next to each other.

"We have the same venom, brother," Silvana cried, even as blood dripped down her lips. "We are a copy of each other, siblings as both mortal and Immortal. So I didn't steal your power. I simply transferred half of it to me."

Dorin's eyes widened in utter horror. "No!" he cried.

Just then the firestorm buckled. The whole formation shook, before bursting apart in an explosion of flame and stone. A thick wave of heat washed over the throne room and seared every inch of Jason's exposed skin. The torrent seemed to last an eternity and the heat in the air made Jason's lungs burn. He held his breath, covering his face and eyes until the last of the flames passed.

Desdemona gave a shrill cry which seemed to be equal parts elation and madness. Jason looked up just in time to see her sprinting up to Ingolf Glucksburg, who was still stumbling backwards.

"No!" Ingolf cried, just as Desdemona thrust her hand against his core. Instantly, he went rigid. Raw heat flowed out of her hand into his stomach and burned him from the inside. The old wizard let out a strained, gargled gasp as fire burst out of his mouth. Desdemona laughed maniacally as she kept pouring in heat until

Ingolf's hands, feet, and head burst into flames like an active furnace. Finally, his chest cavity caved in and he dropped to the ground, his body shattering on impact into fragments of red, hot coals and flakes of ash.

"Master!" the knight Wilhelm appeared nearby, his weapons dropped from his hands, staring in disbelief.

Desdemona raised her hands. The fire rose from Ingolf's body to form a red whip of flame, and with a flick from the Vigile's hand, it lashed at the knight and sliced his head clean off his shoulders.

"Damn it!" Dorin growled. "This isn't over between us, Velouette. You cannot outrun your blood." The world warped around him, and Dorin disappeared.

Nearby, Hana Yamato and her knight started to warp as well.

"Oh, I don't think so!"

Desdemona reached out a hand, and Hana was seized by magic and yanked from the middle of her teleporting sphere. She flew across the room and landed right in Desdemona's outstretched hand. The Vigiles fingers closed around her throat.

On instinct, Jason turned away. This time, he only heard Hana's screams as she died. He had no desire to know exactly what manner had caused it. The sounds continued for over a minute, and somewhere in there were the sounds of ripping flesh and snapping bones. Jason looked up only when the screaming finally stopped. Hana's body was in pieces at Desdemona's feet, and her knight lay dead a few steps away. Jason could see the cause. All of Hana's limbs had been removed. Bile rose in his throat. It was the same death suffered by Mikeru, and Desdemona had done it deliberately as psychological torture. At least Hana's knight had been decapitated quickly in the same manner as Wilhelm.

As quick as that, all the Royalists were dead. The chaos of battle became an empire of silence. Only Dorin had escaped.

Jason feared that Desdemona would turn on him now. She had a crazed look in her eyes. But the older Vigile turned aside from Jason and, instead, found Portia's prone form and started administering aid. So, Jason ignored her and turned to Silvana, who was still laying on the ground where she had collapsed earlier.

"Silvy," he called. He staggered towards her and reached out a hand. "Are you ok?"

She gave a shrill laugh that sent cold chills up Jason's spine. *No*, he told himself. *If that is another personality, you can't be afraid of it.* He kept reaching for her and took her hand in his.

"I'm here," he said. "You were brilliant, Silvy."

Silvana gave a satisfied smile. "I figured, we're full-blooded siblings, and we share the same venom. Surely we could transfer power. His life force filled me like it was balancing out the difference between us. I think we're perfectly fifty-fifty now." A tremor ran through her body. "And I only took half. How did he hold twice this much? Jason…" she cried out in distress. "It's… too much!"

"It's ok, Silvana. You can do this."

"You're right." She suddenly floated off the ground until she was in an upright position, only then, did her feet touch down on the floor again. She glimpsed her own hands and the blood covering her fingers, then clenched them into fists. After a few deep breaths, she seemed to settle. "Oh, Jason, you're injured."

"I've had worse." But even as he said it, he had to collapse onto his knees.

"The others?"

"They're injured too. And… Leslie was killed."

Silvana closed her eyes in pain. "By Dorin?" she didn't wait for his answer. "I think I can heal you. Can I try?"

He was going to answer her. Instead, he said what was really on his mind.

"Silvana, I'm so sorry I didn't tell you the truth," he cried. She went completely still and stared at him with her mouth agape. Jason struggled to sit up and face her while literally on his knees. "I was so scared that I would hurt you, or I'd lose you in some way. But that's no excuse. I should have done what was best for you. I was being selfish. I promise I will always tell you the truth from now on. Because I love you and you deserve that."

"Jason." She shook her head. Jason tensed, waiting for her to get mad. Instead, a laugh burst out of her, and he couldn't help smiling back. "My darling." She crouched and knelt before him, taking his hands in hers. Her skin was cold, and the blood made her hands sticky, but at her touch, he felt all the reassurance in the world. "I love you," she said. "We still need to talk about this more, but I accept your apology, and I forgive you."

"Really?" he blurted.

"Truth is, I was going to apologise for telling you to leave. And for vouching for Dorin so much. I'm the reason we trusted him, and he manipulated us both."

"That was not your fault at all. He knew exactly what he was doing. He told you the truth a little at a time, leading you along until you were under his control. I'm so proud of you for turning on him when you did. You saved us all."

She winced. "I'm not proud of myself. I turned on my only brother. I feel disgusting."

"Silvy, if you love someone, you'll call them out if they're making a mistake. Especially, if they're doing something evil. You did what any good family member should do."

She gave him a pained smile. "Oh, Jason… can I kiss you? I know things have been—"

Jason leaned forward and kissed her on the mouth. It was a short kiss, and he was wincing from the pain in his head and side, but it might have been the most sincere and heartfelt kiss they'd ever shared.

"If you two are done," Freddie called out, "I could probably use some medical attention. If it's not too inconvenient."

"Shit," Jason groaned. He struggled to his feet and stumbled over to Freddie, though Silvana got there first by a large margin. Freddie was slumped forward, clutching the side of his head and grimacing. Edward lay next to him in human form again, though his arm still hung at an odd angle. Nearby, Khadija was lying on her back and clutching her head in her hands.

"What are your injuries?" Silvana called to the group. "I need to triage. Anything life threatening?"

"Just a hell of a bruise," Freddie groaned.

"My arm," Edward groaned, but offered nothing else.

"I might be dying," Khadija croaked, "from humiliation!" She let out a long sigh. "Dorin tore through us all like we were nothing. We're only alive because he was busy fighting Desdemona. I was the strongest I've ever been, and I still didn't even make him pause."

"Where's the High King?" Freddie asked. "I thought he was watching this like a fucking sicko?"

"Fuck," Jason groaned. "He left for New York." He looked up at Silvana. "Alexei is still going to destroy it. He doesn't know the Royalists failed."

"I… I can't possibly stop him," Silvana cried. "I'm still nowhere near that strong."

"Thou art mistaken."

The group turned to see Desdemona standing before them. Her clothes and hair were partially torn and burnt through, and blood seeped down her cheek from a head wound, yet she was still standing, proud and defiant.

Jesus, what does it take to kill this woman?

"Vampire," she said, addressing Silvana. "Thou hast the power from thy brother?"

"Yeah. About half of it."

"It will suffice. Come. Thou will aid me."

"Aid you? With what?"

Desdemona's lip curled upwards. "Defeating a High King."

Chapter 32

Silvana didn't know how she was supposed to feel. Yes, she was brimming with more power than she'd ever imagined, like a goddess walking the earth. But, the thought of taking on a High King made her feel smaller than ever. It was insanity! What was Desdemona thinking?

"You want the two of us to fight Alexei?" she cried. "What about Portia?"

"She's too injured."

"But the other Vigiles? The other High Kings? Can't you call Reynold—"

"There is not the time. There is thou, and me. That's it."

"It's impossible."

Desdemona's lip curled up again. "No, it's necessary."

Portia limped up behind the other Vigile, clutching her chest and wincing with every movement. "I'll care for your loved ones," she told Silvana. "You best care for mine."

"I'll... try?"

Portia rolled her eyes and gave Desdemona a nod. But something happened that surprised everyone. Desdemona snatched Portia by the hand, yanked her close, and kissed her hard on the mouth. It was a long, deliberate kiss, and both women let their hands grip each other, clutching tightly in desperation.

That's... really hot. Silvana blinked at the thought. Where had that come from?

Desdemona pulled away with a gasp, grinning widely as she let Portia go. "Come on, vampire. We shouldn't delay any further." She held out a hand to Silvana.

She paused to look at Jason. She gave him one last kiss too, though nowhere near as decadent as the Vigiles' kiss had been. Then she looked to the others in the group. She wanted to run to Freddie and embrace him, but he simply gave her a nod and smile. "Give 'em hell, baby," Freddie cheered. "Go fuck up that High King."

"Kick his ass," Khadija growled.

"You can do this," Jason said.

Silvana gave them all a nod of thanks. Then she took Desdemona's hand, and they warped away.

Her feet touched solid ground. In front of her was a viewing deck with floor-to-ceiling glass panels, and beyond, the sparkling night time cityscape of New York City.

They were in an observation room, far above the other buildings. They had a three hundred and sixty-degree view of the entire city and the building lights glittered like a sea of man-made stars. Yet, the first glimmer of sunlight was just visible on the horizon. Silvana could see the World Trade Centre in the distance, and twin-rivers running along each side of the island. If she turned and faced the opposite window, she could see the vast green park far below. She considered the layout for a moment.

"We're in the Empire State Building," she said.

"One hundred and second floor," Desdemona said. "The middle of the city. I need to sense where the attack is coming from."

"What type of attack are we looking for? It's an Act of God. It could be anything, right? Hurricane, earthquake…"

Desdemona shook her head. "I know Alexei. He's been obsessed with nuclear weapons for decades now. He's been all too trigger-happy to test them further, but Reynold stops him because he doesn't want the mortals growing more powerful. So thou can bet Alexei will use this chance for revenge against Reynold. He's going to recreate a nuclear strike with magic."

Silvana paled. "Is that even possible?"

"Once a wizard has seen it done, they know it is possible."

"Jesus," she gasped. "But that won't look like an Act of God. It'll look like a man-made explosion. It will start a war."

"A nuclear war," Desdemona said in a flat tone. "And the Immortals will finally be tested by mortal power. Thy brother was too young and naïve to see the problem with working alongside Alexei."

"No argument here," Silvana said. "So how are we going to stop him? What's your strategy?"

"I will take the brunt of his efforts. Thou shalt be the feather that tilts the scales in our favour."

Silvana blinked as she processed Desdemona's plan. "Yeah, I can live with that."

Desdemona smirked and went back to staring into the distance. She held her arms at full length, palms outwards, and breathed deeply as if drawing power from the air around her. Silvana decided to do the same. She meditated on the massive wellspring of magic in her core. She had only to think it, and that power would rush to fulfil her command. The mental trigger was easy to find. What had Dorin said was possible? She thought back on his explanations.

Stronger physical powers. She was faster, stronger, and more agile now. She had incredible telekinesis, and that included moving other wizard's magic. There was some telepathy, such as Dorin sharing his memories through blood. And he talked about absorbing power. *Of course, we absorb power, because, at a fundamental level, that's what vampires do.* She wished she had time to practise. But for now, she'd have to use everything she had if she wanted to stop Alexei and save the city.

Not to mention stop a nuclear war.

A light flashed in the distance and Silvana looked up. It had come from a tiny island in the middle of the bay. Had she imagined it? The flash happened a second time. It looked like a little flicker at this distance, but it must have been huge up close.

"Did you see that?" she asked.

"I can sense it. It's the High King." Desdemona reached out her hand. Silvana took it and they teleported again.

She landed on a grassy knoll. Ocean breeze filled her nose, but even stronger was the scent of sewage waste and pollution. Waves were lapping against the retaining wall around the perimeter of the island. Silvana spun in place, searching for the High King. Instead, she saw a massive statue looming over her, and instantly recognised the form of Lady Liberty, lit up by floodlights facing upwards, standing nearly one hundred metres tall on top of her bronze platform.

Silvana searched through the empty island. There were only a few scattered street lamps still turned on. But she could *feel* the magic around her. It was vast and terrible beyond her comprehension. It was like she had taken her first piano lesson and was feeling proud of her talents, but now she was listening to a grand master play a piece too complex and nuanced for her to fully appreciate. It was magic on a scale that frightened her.

And it was being conducted just a few metres away. Her vampire eyes spotted her target in the darkness ahead.

"There he is," Silvana pointed him out, and Desdemona growled.

The two women walked calmly towards the shadowed figured.

The lone wizard king stood with his back to them at the end of a long wharf. He faced the city to the left side of the mighty statue that loomed above. He held his hands outwards. Nothing was happening at first, then a single brilliant flash of light shot up into the sky. A tingling sensation hung in the air, like static before a lightning strike. He had summoned an incredible amount of power.

"Can we strike him in the back?" Silvana asked.

"He is a High King. By Imperium law, a challenge must be issued."

"Fuck that. We should just kill him."

"I am the law, vampire. Thou shalt not challenge me."

Silvana shivered at her tone. She was awed by Desdemona's self-confidence. But then, the Vigile was about to challenge a High King, one of the seven greatest powers in the world. If anyone could do it, it would be her. Silvana wisely decided not to question her further.

Desdemona approached the High King, and when she was a mere twenty metres away, she called out in a loud voice.

"Hail, High King Alexei Russia."

Alexei had no reaction for a moment. Then he gave a loud, frustrated growl before slowly turning around. "You fucking whore. Why are you still alive?"

"Thy Royalists allies are all dead," Desdemona gloated. "I burnt the Glucksburg wizard into a pile of ash. I tore Yamato limb from limb. I cut the heads from their knights. Their lines are broken."

Alexei chuckled darkly. "But no mention of Dorin. I see he escaped you."

"Not for long. Face it, thy majesty. Thy allies have fallen. Thou hast made an agreement with those now dead. There is no point in continuing this alliance. Return to thy lands and abandon this futile effort."

His face softened for a moment and doubt flickered in his eyes. Then, a look of steel snapped into place. He sneered back at them, his tongue pushing at his bottom lip in disgust.

"You think I can't fight this war alone? I am a god in shackles, you filthy bitch. I have been chained by the Imperium and their pointless rules for far too long. The High Kings squander their power, wasting their magic by sitting behind desks. It is time we remembered our godhood."

A brilliant flash of light burst out of thin air. It looked like a rainbow prism, and the ground seemed to shake at its appearance.

"It's time the mortals fear us as they should. It's time Reynold stepped down and died, like the withered old crow he has become. And I will finally have the kingdom I was promised."

Silvana looked at Desdemona and simply raised an eyebrow. "Satisfied?" she asked.

"Indeed. Let's kick his ass."

Desdemona stepped forward. Alexei growled and copied her movement, his hands clenched at his side. Silvana followed a half pace behind the Vigile. They moved closer, one slow step at a time. The distance between them shrank until only a few steps parted them, and they came to a stop.

The High King and Vigile prodigy stared each other down. Nearby, the waves rolled in and clapped softly against the island walls, and the wharf creaked with the movement. A single gull squawked high above them. A constant wail of car horns and sirens sounded in the distance.

Alexei roared and threw his hands out. Desdemona silently pushed her hands at him, and a thunderclap rang out as their Wills collided.

And the island split in half.

The ground opened up underneath them and formed a massive crater. The water rushed in to fill the gap. There came a great groan and squeal of twisting metal as the great statue above them tilted on its pedestal, then came crashing down into the pit of earth and shattered like clay fragments. The carnage only spread out further with each passing second. Soon, the island had been completely demolished into a burning hellscape. Floodwaters rushed through the newly formed canyons and still, the two wizards simply *pushed* at each other.

Silvana finally came to her senses. She'd been shocked to see it all collapse so quickly, she hadn't consciously decided to start floating off the ground, but that's exactly what she was doing, holding herself suspended above the rushing ocean with the power of her thoughts.

"What art thou waiting for?" Desdemona roared. "Strike now, girl! Lest the city crumbles in our duel!"

Silvana gathered herself. Now was the time. She had to make this count. She reached deep into the wellspring of her power, and with a simple thought, sent it all forward towards the High King.

It hit a wall.

Silvana felt like she'd been smacked in the head with a sledgehammer. The experience was no less painful for being metaphysical. The power of the High King was an immense, immoveable object. It had not even budged a little when she added her Will to the fight.

No, don't think like that. You're an Immortal. An empowered vampire. Make him submit to you!

She felt her Will harden, crystallising into diamond. Now she understood she'd been capable of so much more than she first believed. Her Will had power to shape reality itself, raise up mountains and tear down empires. *I am Silvana Romanov, heir to a lost line of royalty. And I am Velouette Tepes, the heir of Dracula. I may be young, but my blood is ancient compared to this... usurper! This false king! I will tear him from his throne!*

Now, she could feel a slight trembling in the battle of Wills. A growing tension of uncertainty where the combined balance of power could tip either way. She was making a difference. She could stand among these giants and hold her own.

An alarm sounded in the distance. Silvana tried to ignore it and focus on her battle. Then car alarms began to howl in the distant city, and she looked up.

The battle was causing an earthquake. The ground was shaking for kilometres in all directions and the sea had become tumultuous with great swells. Silvana could see that cracks were forming in the distant city streets. Plumes of gas and water sprayed into the air from broken underground pipelines. Fires were catching, cars were disappearing into gaping holes, and a rising tsunami tide was starting to flood its way through the city.

Dear God... what have we done?

Silvana's Will started to falter. She couldn't keep doing this. She knew, objectively, that she had to beat Alexei to save the city. But the act of fighting was causing destruction, and probably the deaths of innocent civilians. Could she be responsible for that?

"Vampire!?" Desdemona roared. "Ignore the mortals! Keep fighting!"

"I… I'm trying!" she screamed back. But Alexei could see the doubt on her face, and he leered at her with a vicious grin.

A warehouse by the dock collapsed into the water. Ships were capsized and strewn along the city streets as a tidal wave of sludge and debris made its way deeper inland. She could hear the sounds of people's screams for help.

"No…" she whispered. Her power trembled, and the weight of the High King's Will seemed to magnify. Alexei saw his opening and focused more of his attack on her. All three of them knew the truth. If Silvana failed, so would Desdemona, and the city would burn.

"I must protect them," she cried and squeezed her eyes shut. "I… must…protect…"

* * *

Ana's eyes snapped open.

She took in the sights of destruction all around her. She could feel the immense power baring down on her, and the shockwaves rolling out from their conflict. And before her was the wizard responsible for all this.

"You bastard!" she screamed. The fat man with the stupid hat blinked at her, and she shrieked wordlessly in his face, before launching her full, savage Will against him. "I'll fucking kill you, dumb cunt! I swear I'll fucking kill you!"

"What in God's name?" the old king cried.

"Hello?" the black Vigile said with an amused tone. "Where hast thou been hiding?"

Ana sneered at her. "Under your mother's saggy tits! Now are we going to kill this bastard? Or let a few million mortals die while we make up our minds?"

The Vigile gave Ana a wide, full smile. "I couldn't have said it better myself."

They pushed again in unison, and the world seemed to groan with the strain. The old king winced in pain as he tried to hold them back. Ana didn't watch him. She watched the destruction being wrought on the city docksides and waterfront. Street poles collapsed and building fronts were ripped apart by the flow of water. If another few minutes were allowed to pass, then a skyscraper might topple down and kill thousands. Ana wouldn't allow it. She would save them all from this evil bastard. She was going to fuck him up. She screamed a terrible, high pitch battle cry, and the Vigile beside her matched her shriek in both volume and ferocity.

The power shifted and buckled. Alexei gasped as his magic was torn apart and shattered.

The great battle of Wills was won.

The king gave a great cry of agony. He clutched his head and hollered like a raving madman. The Vigile let him scream, so Ana waited as well. It looked like he was suffering, and she didn't want to interrupt that. Besides, the destructive power from their battle had ceased. The tsunami still maintained momentum, and a lot of damage had already been done, but it wouldn't get any worse. So she waited until the king seemed to come to his senses.

"What have you done?" he screamed, his voice feral and savage. "You fucking whores, what did you do to me?"

"We have shown thee thy limit, oh king," the Vigile sneered. "Thy Will hath been broken. Now thou knowst thy limits, and thou can never surpass the power thou hast shown tonight. Thou cannot grow in power, never rise to the level of the other High Kings. Thy magic is… crippled."

"Impossible! I have no limits!"

"Pitiful fool. Thou hast been shown thy limits. This is all thou shalt ever be, forevermore." The Vigile couldn't stop a chuckle from building in her throat. Finally, she smiled openly at the king, and Ana roared with laughter.

"You… you…" the king stammered.

"Aw, what's wrong, little king?" Ana giggled. "You gonna cry?"

"Fuck you!" he screamed. She only laughed all the more.

He struck out at her with a blast of lightning. Ana didn't have time to react. It was too powerful for her to stop…

…but the Vigile blocked him with ease. "There, dost thou see the truth now?" she said. "Thy power is *limited*. Go and live out the rest of thy days in shame, and beg Reynold not to announce thy weakness to the world."

"You fucking whore!" the king screamed. "I will find a way to kill you. Mark my words, you filthy black ape, I…"

Desdemona moved right up to the king's face and slapped him with the back of her hand.

It was a pitifully weak blow. The wizard had no physical prowess to speak off. Ana could have slapped his head clean off his shoulders. It made no sense. Until Ana saw the look of utter humiliation on the kings face, and understood. He had been degraded like a little school boy getting spanked by a parent. And, he knew it too.

His lip started to tremble. Ana leaned forward in excitement, ready to watch the great king burst into tears. But he waved his hands and the world bent around him to swallow him up and carry him away. He was gone, leaving Ana and the Vigile floating above the roiling waves below.

"The slap was a nice touch," Ana said. "Though if it were me, I would have kicked him in the balls. But then, if it really were me, I would have kicked his balls up into his throat." The Vigile gave her a sideways glance. "What? You got a problem with me now, honey?"

"No, no. I just… didn't know this about Silvana. The other side of thee. She's so timid all the time."

"And fucking boring."

The Vigile gave a broad smile at that. "I'm Desdemona. What's your name?"

"Ana."

"Well, Ana, I think thou and I can be friends."

Ana blew a raspberry. "In your dreams, girlfriend."

Silvana arrived back in Edward's mansion with a sigh. But relief was replaced almost immediately with a sense of panic.

"How the hell did I just get here?" she cried. She stood in Edward's library where a massive hole in the roof lead to the floor above. Yet the only person nearby was Desdemona, watching her with a curious expression. "Where's Alexei? Did we stop him? What happened?"

"Ah," Desdemona said with a nod. "Silvana, I presume?"

Silvana blinked. Then her mind caught up with Desdemona's body language and calm face. "Oh," she said. "You met… Ana?"

"I did. She was quite lovely."

"Not the word I'd choose." She shrugged. "Did she… help?"

Desdemona froze in place with her mouth half open. Then, she shook her head. "Ah, thou deserves the truth. Ana made all the difference in the end. It was a mere pinch of a difference but enough to break the stalemate."

Silvana couldn't help a smile. "I see. So you did ninety-nine percent of the work, and Ana did the one?"

"More like point zero one."

"Yeah, yeah," Silvana drawled. "I appreciate you telling me that Ana was helpful. I'm still…" she gestured at her head, "figuring it all out."

Desdemona tilted her chin up in a serious pose, like a judge deciding someone's life sentence. Silvana felt strangely naked in her view. "If thou wert to ask my advice," Desdemona said, "I would say to listen to thyself. These other parts of thee are powerful and useful. Thou would be a fool to hide them away. They exist for a reason."

"Oh… thank you, Desdemona."

"Besides, I would like to see Ana again. Preferably in front of thy family, or at another public event. It would be most amusing for me."

"Uh-huh." Silvana studied the Vigile, taking in those dark, ancient eyes. "You're incredible," she muttered. "You took on a High King. One of the seven most powerful wizards in existence. Hell, you held off all three Royalist champions at once. How did you… get so good?"

Desdemona chuckled. "First, in terms of magic, Alexei was the weakest of the High Kings. He was more *politically* influential. There are a few other wizards who I suspect could have beaten him if required to. Several from Jin's court alone. Remember, the position of High King is just the top of the pyramid, and Alexei was the top of a relatively small pyramid. Reynold and Jin hold the real talent."

"I see."

"As for how I got this good," she chuckled. "Perhaps I'll tell thee one day, since thou made a good ally. But thou hasn't earned it just yet."

"All right then, keep your secrets."

"I will."

Silvana gave her a satisfied smile, and Desdemona returned it.

They found the others upstairs in Edward's laboratory. The alchemist had administered healing elixirs to everyone, including himself, and all seemed to be in better health if only a little frazzled. Jason came running at the sight of her, with Freddie barely a step behind. The two of them squeezed her in a tight hug that might have crushed a mortal woman. They cried out at how worried they'd been and how they knew she could do it, cutting each other off yet somehow finishing each other's sentences too.

"What happened, Mistress?" Portia asked in a flat voice.

"It was a battle of Wills," Desdemona said. "And the king's Will was broken."

Portia and Khadija both gasped in amazement, though the others had to have it explained at length. Silvana didn't mind being patient. The feeling of accomplishment burned in her core, and she brimmed with fierce pride. Now she knew for a fact that she wasn't weak. She could finally trust herself to be brave. Her aunts and uncles would never believe this.

"Silvy, there is something you should know," Jason said. "About Leslie…"

"Yes, I know they died. I was here for that."

"Yeah…" Jason grimaced. "Leslie's body is downstairs, in the basement. Edward insisted on trying his resurrection elixir on them."

"Really? So there's a…"

"It's not working."

"…chance," she finished. "Oh."

Edward gave a frustrated grunt. "Nothing's working. I'm certain I've done every step the same way I did for Samantha Kennedy. Leslie's body just will not respond the same way. It's like I've flicked the light switch, and there's electricity, but the bulb is just gone."

"Wait a minute," Portia drawled in a bemused voice. "I thought your resurrection elixir was outlawed by the Imperium?"

The room went deadly quiet for several long seconds. Freddie cleared his throat. "We… uh… forgot." Portia glared at him, and he shrugged.

"It doesn't matter now anyway, since it didn't work," Jason said with a sigh.

Portia rolled her eyes. "I suppose."

"But all things considered," Silvana said, "We still won. We finally stopped the Royalists after three separate battles. And we broke the mind of a High King. Not bad for a bunch of misfits and mortals."

Jason groaned. "But the chimera assassin got away again. It is likely they will come for us once more, as witnesses."

"Then we'll kick its ass," Silvana said. "I'm empowered now, and we're basically the X-men!"

"Oh! I want to be Cable!" Freddie cried.

"Shotgun Wolverine," Jason answered.

Khadija rolled her eyes.

"I am more concerned that Dorin got away," Desdemona muttered. "Can thou at least tell me the source of his power?"

Silvana winced at the question, but didn't hesitate. "He runs a charity. He's beloved by his staff."

"Aha," Portia said. "An elegant solution." Jason gave a bewildered look, but Silvana waved him down.

"Please promise me you won't hurt those people. They're good people who had no idea they were serving a monster."

Desdemona held up a hand. "As a favour to thee, I will shut them down with bureaucracy, not force. No one will get hurt."

"Thank you."

"Maybe we'll be fortunate enough to find Dorin. But my guess is he'll go into hiding. He's good at covering his tracks. Our best hope is he'll settle into a quieter life somewhere else." Desdemona shrugged. "As unlikely as that seems."

Silvana gave a sad shrug. She knew she would have to face her brother someday. After all, she had taken some of his blood. Even now, she could sense his life force in the distance, and could probably teleport to him if she had to. Though, she kept that fact from the Vigiles. That connection would fade in time, but she was certain they would meet again. *'You cannot outrun your blood,'* he had said.

"Now there is one last matter to attend to," Desdemona said. "We must report this to Reynold. And all of you will come with me to testify."

"What?" Jason cried. "Why do *we* have to be there?"

"Because Silvana broke Imperium law and became an empowered vampire. Yes, she used it to save millions of lives, and Reynold will see this as a huge personal favour. Yet even now, thou art in an empowered state, art thou not?" Silvana gave a reluctant nod. "The punishment for merely reaching this state is death."

Silvana felt her skin go cold at her words. "You mean…"

"Don't abandon all hope just yet," Desdemona said. "I will vouch for thee. It is more than likely my opinion will carry much favour, having just defeated High King Alexei. Yet, Reynold is the greatest of the Kings. He will do what he wills."

"It will go better for us," Portia said, "if we are all present and own up to the parts we played."

There was a collective sigh of frustration from the group, but no one raised any objections. Jason moved to Silvana's side and held her hand, and Freddie stood on the other side with a hand on her shoulder.

"It'll be ok," Freddie whispered. "No matter what, we'll be right here with you the whole time."

Silvana nodded and gave them a grateful smile. She looked at the Vigiles with a hard stare.

"Let's get this over with," she said.

Chapter 33

Jason hated this place. It didn't matter how many times he'd seen Reynold's throne room with its vast stone columns and painted golden surfaces, it still chilled him to the bone. The painting of Jesus Christ loomed from its place high above the throne, sending down divine judgement and wrath from heaven. Jason wanted to wipe that cold stare from the Lord's face.

"You may approach the throne," cried the herald. It was a different man to last time. Jason hoped they just worked alternate shifts.

The hall was filled with other petitioners. People of all ethnicities were dressed in dozens of different versions of wizards robes, suits, and formal gowns. All two hundred odd guests parted like the red sea to make way for Desdemona and those following in tow. Many stared at them in fear and wonder, but a few sneered with malicious delight like spectators at an execution.

Desdemona came to the foot of the stairs and knelt before the High King. The others formed a single row a few steps behind her. Portia, Silvana, Jason, Freddie, Edward, and Khadija each bowed to one knee.

"Come, my good and faithful servant," Reynold rasped. His throat sounded dry and worn. "Enter now into the joy of the Lord."

"Thy Majesty," Desdemona purred. "I come with glad tidings.

Thy enemies, the Royalists, have been destroyed. Only Dorin the vampire escaped, though his power is severely weakened. They had allied themselves with High King Alexei. It was he who caused the destruction at New York an hour ago as part of their plan to challenge thee." Murmurs ran through the crowd, but Desdemona simply spoke all the louder. "I challenged him in a battle of Wills. I, Vigile Desdemona, was victorious, and the High King's Will was broken."

The crowd broke into a roar of shocked exclamations and cries. The name Alexei was said over and over but in open derision and scorn now, and with none of the deference a High King would normally receive. Jason couldn't hide the grin spreading across his face.

"You defeated a High King?" Reynold asked, disbelief clear in his voice.

"Yes, thy Majesty."

He stared at her, and the crowd went silent in anticipation. Yet all the king said was, "Interesting." Jason couldn't help feeling a bit annoyed on Desdemona's behalf. It was hardly the praise she deserved. "I am more concerned that Dorin escaped. How was his power weakened?"

"It was drained by his sister." More murmurs escaped the crowd as Desdemona gestured to Silvana and bid her step forward. Jason's heart nearly leapt into his mouth.

"Sister?" Reynold asked. "You are Silvana of the House Romanov. How are you related to Dorin?"

Silvana glanced at Desdemona, who nodded for her to speak. "Your Majesty, I was adopted by my aunts. I was found wandering the refugee fields during the Second World War as a newly turned vampire. They took me in. But when I met Dorin, I discovered he was my brother. My younger brother. When I disappeared, I was presumed dead, and he inherited the family power."

"Two vampires?" Reynold growled. "From the same family? This breaks our oldest laws, stating that only one Immortal may rise from every generation. The law is clear on this. One of you must die. immediately."

Jason nearly cried out, but clenched his fists and waited. This wasn't his fight. He had to start trusting Silvana.

She rose to the challenge. "I am the elder. The Immortal birth right is mine. If one must die it must be my brother. And as I understand, he is already on the run from the law. Nothing has changed."

Reynold squinted at her, though it wasn't clear if from displeasure or poor eyesight. "How did you drain him?"

"I bit him, your Majesty. Half of his empowered vampire state transferred to me."

"So you come before my throne, empowered?" Reynold growled.

"Great King," Desdemona cut in. "Silvana absorbed this power *only* to stop one of your enemies. She was brave and did a great service in your name. Then, she used that power only once more to aid me in my battle with Alexei."

"She aided you?" Reynold did not sound pleased.

"There is a slim possibility that her involvement changed the outcome of the battle. It is likely her actions saved New York City, thy greatest centre of power. She did this, knowing she risked death, in order to serve thy Will. Now she has wilfully submitted herself before thee. In the opinion of this humble servant—who has done great deeds in thy name—I believe she is undeserving of any form of punishment."

Jason's heartbeat raced as he watch Reynold for any signs of his reaction. The High King sat motionless as he studied Silvana. The hush of the audience was a tangible presence as everyone waited for his decision.

"Your House, child," Reynold said. "Which was it, originally?"

Silvana swallowed nervously. "Tepes, of Romania, sire."

The moment she said Tepes, the room erupted in cries of awe. Jason nearly screamed at them to shut up. The last thing they needed was Reynold fearing Silvana's power and influence over others. Yet, that's exactly what seemed to be happening. People were looking at Silvana with newfound awe and respect. No one whispered out loud the name they were all thinking. The name of the most famous vampire of all time.

"Order! Order!" the herald shouted, and the room obeyed him. Jason had to admit this herald was a lot less timid.

"Ah," Reynold said. "The heir of that line has finally revealed themselves again. Your family always hid in fear of me. Perhaps, you would have been wise to do so yourself, rather than coming before me."

"Begging your pardon, great king, but I believe that would be foolish."

"Indeed? Now word will spread through the Immortal world like the gospels of Christ. The last Romanov is also the heir of Vlad the Dragon. There will be those who seek to make you a puppet of their goals. And you are still empowered this very instant as you stand before my throne. Should I not end you right now, and spare any risk to my throne?"

"Sire, there is no risk."

Reynold scoffed. "Because you swear fealty?"

"Because it's your throne. There exists no power capable of causing it risk. None can challenge the heavens."

Jason pressed his lips together to stop them forming a smile. It was a clever bit of rhetoric from Silvana, forming a verbal trap. If Reynold killed her now, it would be like admitting he was vulnerable. In a way, she had forced his hand indirectly. Surely he would not punish her now.

"It is at the recommendation of my greatest servant," Reynold said, gesturing towards Desdemona, "that I will deign to spare your life. I decree you acted in my interests. However, your empowered state must end. You must spend that energy until it is used up and never again take hold of power beyond your allotted portion from your husband, as per vampire law. If I ever have cause to suspect you are not conforming to this decree to the exact spirit in which it was uttered, I will consider you in open rebellion, and I will destroy you utterly. Is that understood?"

Silvana bowed her head. "Absolutely, your Grace."

"Herald," Reynold ordered, and the man in red gowns knelt by the king's throne and let him whisper into his ear.

"Yes, sire." The Herald stood at the edge of his podium and made a declaration in a loud voice. "Hear ye, Hear ye, High King Reynold English has decreed that the Vigile Desdemona, in honour of services rendered to the crown, shall henceforth bear the new titles of Lady High Constable and Earl Marshall of his court. She has, from this day on, the power to command every last able bodied Immortal in Reynold's courts into active deployment. She is commander of his armies, master of the Vigiles and shall answer to no other voice in his court beside the great king himself."

The crowd erupted into cheers and applause. Desdemona merely bowed before the High King, once more. Jason found himself smiling and clapping as well. He didn't understand what half of that meant, but it sounded like she was basically a five-star general now. She deserved it.

And yet... he wondered if she really needed any more power.

"I still want Dorin found, you understand," Reynold said.

"It will be done, my lord," Desdemona said. "I have discovered his source of operations and power. I will begin dismantling it right away. I'm certain he will reveal himself soon."

Reynold called the herald and whispered in their ear again. Jason checked the others in his group and found them all smiling in relief. Only Khadija looked nervously at Desdemona's back. Jason couldn't blame her. Only six months ago they had fought each other. It must be hard to see herself as the Vigile's ally at this time.

Don't fool yourself, Jason thought. *She's only your ally today. You must always watch her carefully.*

"The King has decreed," the herald said, "that his court is now adjourned. All other matters will not be seen today. You are requested to leave this place immediately. Any delay will result in immediate punishment."

A cry rose up from the crowd as people eagerly started teleporting away or sprinting for the exits. "That's our cue," Portia said. "Everyone come together, I'll return us to the mansion."

Jason's group all reached for each other and formed a circle around Portia in as short a time as possible. But they couldn't hide their looks of joy any longer. They had finally won.

'Jason Turner'.

The voice echoed inside his head. He flinched and covered his ears, looking around to see who had spoken, though no one else reacted. Who the hell had said that?

'You will stay.'

It was the High King. Reynold was looking him dead in the eye. The words repeated inside Jason's mind, and he recognised the king's voice. *'You will stay.'*

"Jase? Come on man, we gotta go," Freddie said.

"The king," he murmured. "He's asked me to stay."

"What? No he didn't, I was right here, man. He asked us to leave."

"But I heard his voice—"

"Say no more!" Portia said. She stepped forward and shoved him out of the circle. "You obey the king. We'll see you at home."

"Wait, Jason!" Silvana cried but Portia was faster and warped them away half a second later.

The hall was already empty. Where a crowd of hundreds had stood seconds ago, now there was vast empty stillness. Even the herald was gone. Only Reynold remained, sitting on his golden throne, and Desdemona standing at his side.

The Vigile—or perhaps Jason should start thinking of her as Lady Earl Marshall–had already changed her suit and vest into an elaborate long gown of black and gold. The front of her robes were surprisingly low, showing much of her clavicle and bosom as if she were drawing attention to her femininity. But Jason could just make out two golden lions appeared in the centre of her robe. Despite her regalia, her hair was still in dreadlocks.

"Earl Marshall," Reynold said. "I need you to witness this. You will speak of this to no one."

"Yes, thy Grace."

"Jason Turner." Reynold's puffy eyes creased at the corners as the hint of a smile twitched at the corner of his mouth. "I told you I would be keeping an eye on you. And I must say, you did not disappoint."

Jason had to push aside a lot of questions and answered flatly. "Thank you, sire."

"I have to ask. Were you actively seeking my favour?"

Jason took a moment to consider that. He knew, for all intents and purposes he was speaking with a god. He would not be able to predict what this wizard king would want to hear. So he decided to tell only the truth. "No, sire. If you're asking about my fighting the Royalists, well, that was just me doing my duty. I couldn't let them commit mass murder."

"Interesting. So you have no idea at all? Truly? I thought your escapade into the Library would have revealed the truth?"

Library? Now he was even more baffled. He blurted out, "I guess not, since I have no idea what you mean."

"Ah."

Reynold took a moment to pause as if considering something. Then, his eyes lit up into a smile. *Why does he look so damn happy? What the hell is going on with him?*

"I guess I better explain. I told you six months ago I would keep an eye on you. But the truth is, I've been watching you for far longer than that."

Jason felt a chill crawl over his skin. "I was… not aware of this."

"A fact I am just realising. Jason Turner, I learnt your name the very day you were born."

Holy shit. The day I was fucking born? What the fuck is this?

"I heard you were living in Plymouth. I heard when your mother died. And I was intrigued to hear that you attacked your father, though, I would have been a little more impressed if you had succeeded in killing him."

"Believe me, you weren't the only one disappointed." Jason wondered how he managed a full sentence with all the shock he was experiencing. Reynold seemed to appreciate the input.

"Nothing else drew my attention through your years as a delinquent. I feared your potential had left you. I was intrigued when you became a police officer. A noble profession in keeping the peace."

Oh god… what does it say that Reynold considers police work a noble profession? I don't like that we have this in common. Maybe Dorin was right.

Reynold cleared his throat, and his deep voice came through all the clearer. "But then you truly gained my attention. Surely, you can guess how. It was when this woman," he pointed to Desdemona, "reported to me of a Royalist movement in Plymouth that attempted to destroy the old Romanov line. She told me that one mortal, Jason

Turner, had slain a wizard." Reynold let out a genuine chuckle that abruptly turned into a cough and wheeze, until he cleared his airway. "There have been precious few instances of a mortal slaying a wizard in battle. It's only occurred a small number of times in history. What are the odds that Jason Turner should be the one to do it? Surely that was not a coincidence."

Jason had to bite his tongue to keep from blurting out his questions. The king was happily monologuing now, growing more excited with each new line of thought.

"And that is why, six months ago, the Romanovs suddenly found themselves invited—for the first time in a century—to a gathering of Immortal elites. Because you distinguished yourself as a wizard killer."

Jason thought back to that time. Silvana's family had been so excited by the invitation. They had told him how rare something like this was. Yet, everyone was far too excited to question *why* it had happened. They had overlooked the coincidence because it was convenient.

"Oh my god," Jason said. "Everyone was shocked that you were there that night."

"Indeed," Reynold acknowledged. "I can't stand parties." He spat the last word. "Nothing but mewling sycophants begging for a blessing. As if I don't already get enough of that. No, Jason, I was there for one reason only. To see... *you.*"

Reynold chuckled before continuing. "I was hoping to see you distinguish yourself again in some way. Instead, you were blown off the side of the building and knocked out, barely surviving. I must say, a rather disappointing start. Yet, I was confident my little test would bring out the best in you."

"Little test?" Jason frowned. Then it clicked. "Mikeru Yamato. You hired him to kill Samantha Kennedy and Khadija, and I worked to solve that case." Jason's mouth fell open. "That was all for me? That was just… a *test?!*"

Reynold shrugged. "I am a capable tactician, boy. I can accomplish multiple goals with one stroke. But yes, one of those goals was to test you. And I must say, I was impressed. You discovered the culprit when no one else could. You also knew your limits as a mortal and therefore brought in allies to fight for you. You acted the general, giving orders to your troops."

"I had a lot of help. And there was some luck involved too."

"Ah, but what is help if not a sign of the worthiness of people's trust? What is luck if not the divine Will of God acting on our behalf? No, your victory was your own." Jason noticed Desdemona smirking ever so slightly at that, like she quietly disagreed. "Now, I knew you were capable. But the final test was the greatest one yet."

Jason started shaking his head frantically. "Oh, no. Don't tell me *you* hired the assassin?" he cried. "You were the one who started this as well?"

"No," Reynold said and held up a finger. "In fact, I had nothing to do with the assassin, though it is a fair guess." That surprised Jason, but it didn't bring any sense of relief. In fact, it made him feel even more frustrated and confused. "The final test meant I could not instigate anything myself. If the time was truly right, I had to trust the Hand of God to move you. You had to distinguish yourself on your own."

"If the time was right?" Jason blurted. "Sire, I don't understand."

"Yet it came to pass exactly as I hoped. Tonight, a High King fell from grace. No one in the Immortal community will ally with him now. His business ventures will drop considerably. His rising star has just began its long descent back down from heaven. And while it was the Lady Marshall's sword that dealt the blow," he nodded to Desdemona. "I see your hand clutching the blade."

"You give me too much credit."

"Was it not you who led the charge into Alexei's court? You who began the very venture that led to his demise? You found even greater allies than last time. By God, I was sceptical of your choice of wife. A vampire. And yet, she ended up being the heir to Dracula himself. She has the potential to be the greatest living vampire of our age. You chose wisely."

"I love Silvana."

"Then your heart chose well. Admit it, Jason. Everything you have done has shown me you are strong. You are capable, and you are a tactician with a keen intellect and sharp mind. It's exactly what I prayed for."

"Sire, please. I don't understand all this. Why me?"

Reynold sat back in his chair. His eyes were more alive with excitement than Jason had ever seen. "Jason, do you know why all the High Kings are men?"

He nearly said 'misogyny' before he clenched his jaw to stop the word slipping out. "No, sire."

"Because God has declared that men should rule. As I taught you all those months ago in Dubai. It is given to men to rule, and so men shall. It is not that women are weaker or inferior, of course. I place great trust in women, as you can plainly see." He gestured proudly to Desdemona. "But we must obey God in his decrees. That is how we prosper. That is how the world remains ordered and functional."

"Ok." Jason forced himself not to say anything more. Reynold was not the kind of person who welcomed debate.

"Do you know your history?" Reynold asked. "Do you know your royal lines?"

He nearly laughed. "Some of them."

"Mortals dare to debate the line of succession. They fight and war and die over it, sometimes for a hundred years at a time. But there is no debate. There is no moral grounds to challenge the line that God has declared as His choice. No, Jason, the line must be male. It must always be male."

Fucking chauvinist.

Jason cursed himself for thinking that in the King's presence. He had no idea what this wizard could do, and if that included reading minds.

If he did hear Jason's thoughts, he was not perturbed. "That is why I don't recognised the royal family of England today. They split from the male line nine centuries ago when it passed through William's daughter, Adela, to her son Stephen. The fact they have done so dozens of times since, only heightens their sins. But I remember the male line. I have never forgotten it. And the line of men has remained true. From the sire of my brother William the Conqueror across nine hundred and sixty years. Right up to today."

Jason felt an icicle of dread seep into his heart and plunge his entire body into a chill. He finally thought he understood what was happening. And the thought was too terrible to comprehend. His mind buckled at the very idea.

Please God, no, don't let this be true.

"There are millions of English mortals who still carry my brother's blood. The line is strong, though not hallowed. My line does not have powerful names like Windsor or Romanov. No, they have the names of commoners, the lowest of the low, and some of the oldest most common names in all of England. Like Smith, Baker, Clarke..."

Reynold leaned in and whispered, "...and Turner."

Turner. Jason remembered what Emberline had said the day they met. She had mocked him for having a common name. *Maybe... not so common.*

"In all my seven hundred years ruling as High King, I have never named an heir," Reynold said. "Because I have never in that time seen a man from my line prove himself worthy."

"No," Jason cried out loud. The word slipped out, but Reynold didn't care.

His excitement was starting to make sense.

"I waited centuries. Nearly my entire life. I tracked the male line and watched each one rise and fall. You come from a long, long line of failures and miscreants. Licentious scum and vermin who squander the blood in their veins. Until you came along. You, who had the bearing of a king. You even had the audacity to ask me here, in my very court, at the seat of my power, if I had an heir! I nearly proclaimed it then and there. Finally, I thought, someone worthy of my name."

"Please," Jason said, holding out his hands. "I didn't ask for this."

"Yet God has clearly chosen you for it. Your timing couldn't be any more perfect. I am nine hundred and eighty-two years old. No Immortal has ever lived passed one thousand years. So my death will come soon. Whether in six months, or in seventeen odd years, I will die. And you have until then to prepare."

"No," Jason cried. "Please have mercy. I am mortal."

"It matters not. The signs are clear. The time has come, and God's will has been manifest. So here today, before my witness, I make this declaration."

Jason felt tears brim in his eyes. His mouth hung open in horror, but he could think of no words to say. It made him sick to his stomach. He was powerless here. Nothing in the world had the power to stop Reynold the First.

"Jason Turner," the High King declared. "I hearby name you as my heir. From this moment onwards, until the time of my death, you shall be a king in waiting."

Chapter 34

J ason's hands were shaking.

One year ago, he hadn't even known Immortals existed. He thought Silvana had been lying about being a vampire. God, how deluded had he been? Now, he was kneeling before the leader of the Immortal world, a tyrant, a madman and a monster.

And accepting a formal adoption.

"From now on," Reynold said. "You shall be my son. In public you will address me as king. But between the three of us here, you will call me… *Abba, Father.*"

Jason could feel the tears spilling from his eyes, yet no sound came from his mouth. He was related to this man. He was a direct descendant from over a thousand years. *And I thought my birth dad was a piece of shit. Maybe it's because he came from this monster. Oh my God… this is everything I never wanted to become.*

"Take these two rings," Reynold said.

The High King reached out his hands, and two black coiled rings appeared in his palm. There were no jewels or signets in a crest, just a single loop that wove around in a circle like an ever-flowing serpent. They looked totally unremarkable. Jason realised the king was waiting, so he took them from his wrinkled, weathered hand.

"I have granted these talisman to men before," Reynold said smugly.

"As a sign of my blessing. Genghis Khan received them from me at the summit of Burkhan Khaldun and wore them till the day he died, and they returned to me. He used their power to create chaos in the Far East that distracted my enemies and allowed my rise to power."

Jason couldn't even process that. Reynold had created the Mongol Empire as a distraction? Who the fuck was this man?

"The rings won't grant you magic. But my magic is in them and they will offer you some protection. Think of them as lucky charms. Strange fortunes will follow you as you hold them. If you deliberately touch them together and say my name three times, I will be able to speak to you. Use this power wisely, as my time and counsel are limited. And when the day comes that I die, they will form a signet that will prove you as my heir.

"Now pay attention," Reynold instructed. "You cannot tell people what has happened here today. If word gets out, the other High Kings will be quick to destroy you or turn you into a thrall for their control. Keep this a secret. That's the reason I attacked you earlier when you asked why I hadn't named an heir. I could not indulge you in any way lest anyone suspect you. That's also why I sent everyone away just now in the manner I did, so no one would know that you and I spoke. Keep it secret.

"And use these next few years to prepare to assume this throne and hold it against the other powers. Learn the intricacies of the court and who your enemies will be. Consider eliminating them before you ascend to the throne. Make powerful allies."

Reynold held out his hand again, and this time, a brown leather book appeared in the middle of his palm. "This is yours now, by birth right. This is a book of magic, a grimoire. In fact, it is mine. This book taught me my magic. It is the birth right of your family line now. I regret that you are too old to learn this. Although," Reynold laughed, "if you were the first adult to ever learn magic, I would hardly be surprised at this point." He broke into a coughing fit again, and Jason had a panicked thought that the king was about to die here and now. But he recovered. "Give this to your child one day. Have an ally teach them from the book, and they will become Immortal."

"Thank you," Jason said in a lifeless tone. The movement of his lips allowed a single tear to fall down his cheek.

"Well, praise be to God Most High!" Reynold gave a happy, contented sigh. "I have waited a long time for this moment. I enjoyed it even more than I imagined. I am excited to see what the Lord has in store next. Now, I fear I must rest these tired old bones." He checked Jason and took note of his unshed tears and shocked expression. "Do you have any questions, my son?"

My son.

The words nearly made Jason scream in fury and despair. He clenched his jaw shut to keep from speaking. He had to focus on something. What had Reynold said? Did he have questions? Well, sure, he absolutely did.

"The Lisbon Earthquake," Jason whispered. "Was that you?"

Reynold raised an eyebrow in surprise. Desdemona gave an impressed twitch of the lips. Yet the king was not stalled for long. A broad grin stretched his weathered face, and he whispered back to Jason.

"It was an Act of God."

Something about the way he said it made the term feel different. Now Jason understood exactly what Reynold meant. When he said 'act of God', he was referring to himself. Whenever he talked about God's Will or the Lord's plans, he merely meant himself. Reynold had called himself God's representative on earth. Yet somehow, he had mentally removed any distinction. Hell, that was why he was such a powerful wizard. Unmatched in all the world.

Because deep down on a fundamental level, Reynold believed he *was* God.

And that made him even more dangerous.

"Thank you, sire," Jason said.

"Ah," Reynold corrected. "Among the three of us do not address me as king."

Jason felt bile rise in his throat, but he got the words out. "Abba. Father."

"Good. You may go now, my son."

Desdemona stepped forward and took Jason's hand in her own. She surrounded him in warping space and finally carried him away from Reynold's throne room. He watched the stars shimmer and spin around him in a sort of fever dream, barely able to comprehend what was real.

His feet abruptly touched grass. He stood in the countryside where the scent of grasslands and ocean salt told him he was back in his own country again. Edward's mansion loomed above him.

Desdemona stood beside him, nearly half a foot shorter, but looking all the more powerful for her new gown and title. She cleared her throat as she let go of his hand.

"Art thou well?" she asked. Jason could only give a helpless laugh and shrug. She nodded in a way that said she expected as much. "What will thou tell the others?"

"I have no idea."

"I would tell Silvana, if I were thee. But that would be all." He nodded in response. "And Jason?"

Hearing her say his name like that made him snap out of his stupor. She spoke to him with sincerity, using his name instead of some sassy insult or threat. She looked at him with respect, even sympathy. "I know thou didn't want this, but it cannot be changed. My advice, make the most of it. And if thou ever needs me, simply ask…" she took a long time to say the final words. "My *prince*." She lowered her head in a slight bow. He almost laughed at the sight. He knew what a big action this was for her.

"Thank you," he said. Then added, "Lady Marshall."

She gave him a rare smile. "I am not sure how I feel about the title. It is a bit long." She nodded. "I must return. Fare thee well, Jason."

"And you."

She disappeared.

Jason stood outside the mansion for a long time. He had a lot to process and was grateful the others hadn't spotted him. He held the grimoire in his left hand, and the two black rings in his right. How would he explain what these were?

'Oh hey guys, I'm now the heir to Imperialism and tyranny. Who wants to commit atrocities?'

Yeah, he knew how they would react. For a moment, he considered just dropping the king's boons in the nearest bin or throwing them into the ocean. But somehow, he doubted they would stay there if he did.

There was no denying it. The course of his life had changed. He wasn't going to have time to become a detective after all, even if he did get back to work and explain his week-long absence. Now he was going to have to… what exactly? Build a political empire? Google how to run a conglomerate? Ridiculous.

Yet the worst thought was that, somehow, he deserved this. Because despite trying his whole life to be a better man, he was still *tainted* by his father's evil. He had been let down by his father, then by Nicholas, and now by Reynold. Every single father figure in Jason's life had been a monster. So, of course, he was always going to be a monster too. Everything he'd ever done to change or improve himself was just a desperate act of denying his true nature. Reynold had seen the truth.

But none of that was reality. Jason knew in his heart he was just scared and overwhelmed by it all. He needed time to think. And he needed to see the people he loved. His closest friends. Everything would start to make sense after that.

He slipped the rings into his pocket. He tried shoving the book into another pocket but the edge was too wide. So he tucked it into the nook of his elbow and walked up to the front door.

A few minutes later he was hugging Silvana and Freddie. They asked about what happened, but he couldn't think of how to answer them. Though, he knew he was going to tell both of them the truth immediately and avoid a repeat of his earlier mistakes of keeping secrets. He just wasn't sure if he could convince them it was real. Hell, he was already trying to deny it himself.

Khadija and Edward were in the lounge room, sipping hot tea after a stressful morning. Both leapt to their feet when Jason walked in. They started asking him questions, but Jason was too dazed to even comprehend what they were saying. Jason wondered if he could tell them the truth. Could he trust these two as much as he trusted Silvana and Freddie?

"Where's Portia?" Jason asked.

"That's the first thing on your mind?" Freddie asked. "She left a few minutes ago. Though, she gave us her number in case the assassin comes back."

"I thanked her for figuring out the whole New York thing," Silvana said. "It saved me from siding with Dorin. I owe her for that."

Jason nodded and stared absentmindedly at the wizard and the alchemist. He was holding a powerful secret. Khadija was a formidable, influential member of the Khalifa family and part of the court of High King El Siddig. Could he trust her with this much information? And Edward was a strange man with a lot of idiosyncrasies.

No, he pushed that aside. Both of them were his friends. Khadija had put her life on the line to save him twice, at the Library and again during the fight with the Royalists. Without hesitation, she had positioned herself to shield him. Yes, she had attacked and tormented that girl Aakriti six months earlier. But she had sworn to do better, and she had proven the truth of her vow many times since.

And Edward had fought to save him too. He had been loyal and devoted to Freddie. He even leapt in front of Dorin to save his friend, even though he had been suffering from a panic attack at the time. He was a good man of the highest quality.

It was time for Jason to start trusting the people in his life.

"Everyone, sit down," Jason said. "I need to tell you something."

* * *

Twenty minutes later, the room was deathly silent. Everyone had taken the news with a hint of scepticism at first, but Jason had convinced them of the truth in his words when he showed them the two rings and the book of magic.

"That's the real thing," Khadija said with awe. "I can sense the power of those artefacts from here. And the grimoire is legit. I learnt my magic from a similar book. By the way, Jason, if you want, I can teach your firstborn magic. Though, Silvana can't have biological children," she shrugged. "So you would have to adopt. But I could teach them when you adopt, I mean, *if* you adopt. Although you'd have to adopt at least twice. One to be a wizard, one to be a vampire." She paused for a moment. "I'm sorry, I'm getting way ahead of myself. That's none of my business."

"Wow," Jason whispered. "That's a huge undertaking. Thank you."

Silvana was trying and failing to hide her smile.

"Can I see the rings?" Edward asked. "I could probably tell you something about how they were made." Jason handed them over, and the alchemist held them up close to his face. "There's definitely an enchantment woven into the rings at their creation."

"Please tell me it's like the One Ring," Freddie said.

"No, but a similar process. These rings have a Will of their own. Or should I say, they have Reynold's Will. They will influence the throw of a dice or the path of a bullet. It should mean they'll protect you to some extent. But it will also make it difficult to defy him."

"You know, he claimed he gave these to Genghis Khan," Jason scoffed. "How crazy is that?"

Freddie was furiously typing on his phone then he pulled up an image. "Buddy, I think that's true. See this pic?"

Jason recognised it. It was the classic picture of the great Khan that appeared in all his school history books. "Yeah, I know the one."

"Check out the earrings."

"Yeah? I don't see—" he cut off. Genghis Khan was wearing two black earrings of coiled steel. "Holy fuck," he cried. "They're the same rings."

"Exactly. You read much about that guy? He often fought in battles himself. Once, he got shot in the neck with an arrow, but survived. I think those rings protected him."

Jason looked down at the black circles sitting in the palm of his hand. He couldn't bring himself to wear them. He already had his wedding ring on one finger, and he was supposed to be wearing the golden signet of the Romanov house on his left index finger. To mark himself now as Reynold's heir felt like a betrayal to Silvana and his family. But if the rings would protect him... maybe he'd work up to it.

"Reynold is right about one thing," Khadija said. "His time is almost up. He will not live past one thousand years, and he's nine hundred and eighty-two. Which means we have less than eighteen years to get you ready." She scoffed. "Probably a lot less than that."

Jason gave a small chuckle. "You said 'we'."

"Of course." Khadija smiled. "I'm aware of how much trust you've shown me, and I do not take this lightly. Besides, this is an incredible opportunity."

"Don't you mean curse?" Freddie said. "He's got a target on his back for the whole world to see."

"That's true. But we need to consider the possibility of what happens if you succeed? Jason, you are a good man. I think you are more moral and ethical than I am." Khadija gave an embarrassed shrug. "Could you imagine what you could achieve if you ascended that throne and held it? You could instigate massive reforms! You could change financial systems, rewrite laws and greatly improve the lives and freedom of mortal society. Hell, you might even have the authority to share magic with the mortals. Isn't that what you want?"

Jason gave a reluctant shrug. "Partially. But I also think we'd be better off getting rid of the Imperium and High Kings altogether. Get some democracy in the Immortal sphere."

Khadija nodded excitedly. She leaned in and whispered slowly, as if begging him to understand her every word. "Jason, that's not a crazy idea. If you became High King, democracy would become a legitimate possibility."

"Oh."

"So why are you so afraid?"

It was the question that he had been dreading. It cut to the heart of his fear and anxiety. Yet he realised he already trusted these four people with his biggest secret, so he might as well open up and be vulnerable.

"What if I become evil?"

A laugh burst from Khadija before she put a hand over her mouth. "Sorry, that was inappropriate."

"I mean it. Khadija, you don't know this, but my father was abusive and violent. He tormented my mother so much that she committed suicide to escape him. I grew up as a foster child."

"By Allah. Jason, I'm so sorry."

"I've always been afraid that I would become like him. And now Reynold says he's my distant ancestor, and I'm to inherit the throne of imperialistic rule. Could you imagine a more evil thing than that?" He let out a long sigh. "It's like evil is in my blood. Like I can't escape it."

"Jason," Silvana said. She had been the quietest out of all of them. She took a moment to gather her thoughts. "When you met me, I was a quiet, submissive housewife and perfect daughter. You taught me to be more confident in myself. Then, just a few hours ago, I dared to fight a High King and win."

"That's true."

"When you found Freddie, he was in a cult. Now, he helped us to stop a world war and save all of New York."

Freddie droned and rolled his eyes. "Thanks, but you know we don't have to keep bringing up the cult thing every time, right?"

"Wait, you were in a cult?" Khadija cried.

Freddie groaned.

Silvana went on. "Khadija has had her darker moments. But she's sacrificed herself to save us in the Library and did so again while fighting Dorin. She's a true friend and a proper hero." Khadija held a hand to her chest and pressed her lips together in a sad smile. "And Edward, well, you taught me what an amazing person he is. You helped him make friends for the first time. Now look at him! He's so comfortable socialising with us."

"I'm not that comfortable," Edward said flatly, causing a few amused chuckles.

"Ok, fair, but it's still progress. My point is, Jason, that you've improved all of us by being in our lives. I know you will improve the whole world in the same way because you're a good man. You always will be."

Jason had to wipe a tear from his eye. "Thank you Silvana. I'll… I'll try to believe that."

"Take your time. But I believe it right now. You can make big changes to the Imperium if you successfully claim a throne."

"Yeah, like the king of Spain," Freddie cried. "You guys heard of Juan Carlos?"

Jason sighed. "Freddie, how the fuck do you know so much history?"

"I'm an Asian nerd, man. I know everything."

"I find that stereotype offensive."

"Yeah, well fuck you." The two men laughed uproariously, making a lot more noise than the joke deserved. Clearly, they needed to vent a little. "But putting aside being fucking hilarious," Freddie said. "You heard of Franco? The Spanish dictator?"

"Just explain it, Freddie. Assume I know nothing," Jason drawled.

"Fine. Spain has a bad civil war in the thirties then Franco takes over as a fascist dictator. Literally performs purges and turns the country into a police state. Spain did not side with the Axis during World War Two, but it gave them permission to use their land and docks. It's why Germany was able to attack the British and American ships."

"Ok, Franco's a dick, got it."

"Exactly. Now Franco brought back the monarchy and appointed Juan Carlos as the new king, but didn't let him have any power. Kept it all for himself. Carlos plays along and waits thirty years until Franco died, and finally took over in nineteen seventy-seven. Everyone expected him to continue the rise of fascism. Except, it turns out Juan Carlos was secretly cool the whole time. As soon as he came to power, he implemented mass reforms on the entire country and turned it into a democracy."

"Shit, that is cool."

"Yeah! The guy played the long game and won. He reigned for like forty years and spent the whole time giving away all his power."

Silvana gave an impressed chuckle. "What a legend."

"Well, he did have a bunch of affairs and illegitimate children. And he used to illegally hunt animals and once killed a bunch of Romania's bears." Everyone looked at him. "What? It's true! I'm just saying, people are complicated. Good people can still do shitty things."

"Very deep of you," Jason drawled.

"The point is, you could do the same thing, Jason. Play the long game, and when you take power, you can dismantle the whole fucking system."

"He's right," Khadija said. "You would make a fine king."

A fine king.

The phrase clicked in Jason's mind, and, just like that, several ideas started falling into place like dominos. He understood it all in a flash of understanding.

"Guys," he said. "Leslie knew."

Everyone stared back at him, uncomprehending. "What do you mean?" Silvana asked.

"The last thing they said to me as they died was 'You will make a fine king'. I thought it was delirium. But they knew." Jason suddenly launched to his feet with a great cry. "Oh my god! Oh my fucking god, I can't believe it!" He clutched at his head then slapped himself in the forehead. "I am so damn stupid."

"Jase! What's wrong man?" Freddie asked.

Jason turned to face the group and threw up his hands.

"Leslie hired the assassin!"

The room went completely silent. Everyone frowned as they exchanged confused glances. Freddie rubbed his chin in thought.

"Think about it," Jason cried. "Leslie arrived at our door, claiming they'd just fought and killed a chimera assassin and that more would be coming. Then one appears in the damn room to prove the point. Leslie hits it with a spell, but it backfires. Why? To sell the story! To show beyond a doubt that Leslie is a victim too, and that we're all in a fight for our lives."

"Son of bitch," Freddie muttered. "Wait, I can't call Leslie son of a bitch. Eh, child of a bitch doesn't have the same ring—"

"Shut up," Khadija snapped, but without any real venom.

"But why the act?" Silvana asked. "Why not just…" She trailed off. "Oh my god… the signet on their arm."

Jason pointed at her. "Yes, exactly. I bet that Leslie looked in the official records and found my name as Reynold's potential heir. But they couldn't just tell me because it would break their vow as a historian. So, everything they did was to guide me into discovering the truth on my own."

"But that's so risky," Freddie stated. "How would Leslie know what we would decide to do?"

"Because Leslie was right there, subtly guiding us the whole time. They were steering the conversation without being too direct until we reached a decision to break into the Library."

"Of course," Khadija said. "Witches are known for their clever manipulations. Leslie tricked us into that plan."

"Exactly," Jason answered. "Leslie went to great efforts to get us inside that Library. And you remember when we got there, the section on Reynold was literally the first category. It was Reynold's lineage. Leslie planted it there in the first place we'd look. But it would have been a complex mess to unravel, since I'm only the heir through an obscure male line. So we needed to collect all the information in order to discover the truth."

"Jesus," Freddie groaned. "That's why Leslie lost their shit at me when the cameras failed. Because you went all the way there, right up to the information they'd planted for you, and you missed it by that much because of me." Freddie laughed. "I'd be pissed too! Man, I actually feel much more forgiving of the old witch now."

"But the assassin attacked us in the Library," Silvana said. "Why would it do that if it was working for Leslie? We were doing what they wanted."

"No we weren't," Jason said. "Remember *when* it attacked? At the very instant we decided to leave the Library and go with Dorin."

"Of course! Because we were getting away from what Leslie wanted," Silvana cried.

"And I think that's why Leslie was so polite to Dorin. As cover, so we wouldn't suspect their disapproval. But once Dorin arrived, Leslie started losing control of the situation. They were scrambling, trying to find ways to get us back on track. That's probably why the assassin found us again, here in the mansion. Leslie called them."

"Oh, because we had run out of options at that stage," Freddie said. "We had no idea what to do next."

Jason nodded. "Yes. Then we beat the assassin and Leslie removed the shield, bringing the Vigiles here. Perhaps that was a long shot attempt to lead them to Dorin and remove him as a distraction. Then, Leslie took on a role of just trying to keep us safe through the danger."

Jason shook his head. "Now I understand. Leslie wasn't just fighting to protect me. They literally died to save me. Because they… believed in me." Jason's voice dropped to a whisper. "They thought I was their best chance at fixing the Imperium." His eyes began to fill with tears. "When they were dying, they said they had so much more to teach me. That was Leslie's plan. They wanted to teach me how to be king. They would have become my advisor. God, that's what Leslie was doing the whole time. *Teaching* me!"

Khadija nodded. "I remember they taught you about the words imbecile and cretin. I thought it was a random lecture, but they were actually mentoring you on morality."

Jason nodded. "Leslie talked constantly about leadership, history and the right of kings. Hell, I just thought they were a big nerd. But it was the start of my education."

The adrenaline that had built up in him finally began to drain, and Jason slumped down into his chair with a long sigh. "I knew Leslie's death was a tragedy, but I didn't realise just how much. They wanted to equip me for rule. When Leslie was dying, they literally said, 'I had so much more to teach you'. " Jason's voice dropped to a whisper. "But they never got the chance." His unshed tears finally began to trickle down his face.

Edward quietly got up and left the room. There was some rattling in the kitchen, then he returned a minute later with a bottle of whisky and six glasses on a tray. He poured one out for each of them. He gestured to the drinks, and everyone stood to take up their glass.

Then Edward poured a sixth glass and left it on the tray.

"To Leslie Toussaint," Edward said. "Who was smarter than us all, the kindest person I've ever met and a true friend. They will be missed." He raised his glass. "To Leslie."

"To Leslie," they echoed as they raised their glasses and drank.

Silvana wiped her eyes. "Thank you, Edward. That was perfect."

Everyone agreed and offered their thanks in turn.

"So," Freddie said, his voice unusually sombre. "Silvana is the heir of Dracula. And Jason is the heir of Reynold." He shook his head. "Yeah, this is great for my inferiority complex."

Everyone laughed.

"People know about me," Silvana said with a heavy sigh. "I had to tell Reynold in front of his court. We can assume the whole Immortal community will soon know the truth."

"Pandora's box is open," Khadija murmured. "Even with Reynold pardoning you, you must be careful. You will have enemies who will see you as a symbol of vampire liberation."

"Dorin said people would rally behind me." She took a long breath and let it out slowly, then looked at Jason. "At least you can operate in secret."

"For now," he groaned. "When Reynold dies... I don't know what I'll do."

"You'll change the world," Edward said. All heads turned to the alchemist who was looking at the floor. "If only one of you had a throne, you'd probably fail. But together, you're more likely to succeed. Together, you can change the world."

Jason felt a strange surge in his chest. Maybe there was cause to be hopeful. Silvana took his hand, and he squeezed it back. No matter what, at least the two of them were together again. As long as they stayed that way, they could handle anything.

"I love you," he said.

"I love you too," she replied, squeezing his hand tighter.

"There is one bit of good news, though," Khadija declared in a firm voice. "This means the assassin is not coming for us now."

It took them a moment to understand. "Oh. Are you sure?" Jason asked.

"Their contract is up. We were hunting for the person who hired the assassin because if we killed them, the contract would end. And Leslie died, so..." She gestured around the room. "The contract is complete. That means we're finally safe. We can all go home."

Jason could have cried out of relief. He wanted to go home so badly.

He desperately needed to get away from all this and feel like himself again. Besides, now that he was free, he wanted to call his boss.

"Can we do that now?" Freddie asked. "Go home, I mean?"

"Yes, please?" Silvana asked. "I'm so tired."

"I think that would be an excellent idea," Khadija said. "I have affairs to tend to as well. Edward," she turned to the alchemist. "I'm sorry to leave you with such a messy house. But I'd like to pay to have it cleaned." She seemed to reconsider. "And repaired."

"How would money help me?" Edward said. "That's a lot to organise."

Khadija blinked. "Or I could hire people to just do it for you."

"Yes, please."

They all laughed. One by one they said their goodbyes to Edward, though only Freddie hugged him. The alchemist was more comfortable with that anyway.

Khadija took the trio's hands, and magic began to carry them home.

Chapter 35

It felt so good to be home. That is, until Silvana saw the massive gaping hole in the dining room roof, the broken back door and the carnage that covered half the house.

"Son of a bitch," Freddie groaned. "I forgot about this part."

He stepped over the debris of broken plaster and the layer of white dust that covered everything as if hoping it would get cleaner further in. Yet the shards of the broken table and chairs had left wood splinters everywhere. Worse, the hole in the wall had clearly allowed rainwater to blow in sideways, and now the whole place smelt of mildew.

"My dad is gonna freak when I tell him about this," Freddie cried.

"No one's been here for days," Jason said. "I can't believe none of the neighbours said anything. Weren't there gunshots and animal noises coming from here?"

"They probably thought it was a weird sex thing," Freddie said. Jason glared at him. "What? I'm just saying, you guys could be a little quieter."

Khadija held a hand over her mouth to stifle her laugh, then pretended she was just scratching her chin. "If you need help with this, just let me know."

"Thank you," Silvana said. "We'll see if we can't figure it out. You'll be ok?"

"Yeah. I'm going to make a petition to get Samantha released. Hopefully, helping to stop a High King has earned me a favour or two with the Vigiles." She shrugged, the action making her curls bob. "It's worth a shot."

"Tell Sam we said hi."

Khadija gave her genuine smile.

"Come here," she said and gripped Silvana in a hug. It was sudden, yet completely welcome. Silvana hugged her back. The wizard felt warm. When Khadija pulled away, she waved to the boys and gave a nod. "Stay in touch. We've got a lot of work to do." Then she summoned her magic and teleported away.

Jason let out a sigh. "Suppose we should clean this up. I'll get a bin."

"I'll get a broom," Silvana said.

"I'll get the beer," Freddie replied with a grin.

Silvana walked to the hallway closet and pulled out a bucket of cleaning supplies, but she couldn't find the broom. She rolled her eyes, figuring the boys had probably left it somewhere dumb. She checked the garage and found the broom standing in the corner. *Why do we even have the broom closet if the damn broom is never…*

Something moved in her peripheral vision. Silvana tensed. The garage was dark, and it took a second for her vision to adapt. In the middle of the room were two yellow eyes, peering up out of the blackness. Her heartrate spiked, and she prepared her mental power to seize the creature with her Will. The creature didn't move, just continued to stare at her. Now, she understood what she was seeing.

It was a cat.

She gave a short laugh and turned on the light. Sure enough, a furry black house cat with yellow eyes was sitting on the bonnet of Jason's car. It blinked at her and licked its paws.

"Guys, get in here," she called. The boys arrived a second later. "I think someone came through the back door and made themselves at home."

"I've heard of this," Freddie laughed. "This is how you get a cat, right? It just adopts your house? Hey, puss puss." He clicked his fingers and held out his hand. The cat showed no interest. "We're certain it's not an assassin, right? Absolutely certain?"

"I think it's just a cat," Silvana said with a smile. Jason watched the cat with open suspicion. "Relax, Jason. I'm sure it's fine."

Jason marched up to the animal until he was an arms width away. The cat remained disinterested and focused on licking its paw, then wiping at its forehead.

"Hello," Jason said in a formal tone. "I am Jason Turner of House Romanov. Welcome to our home."

The cat shook its head, and its ears flicked upright.

"Hello, Jason," the cat replied.

Silvana let out a gasp. The tiny creature had a shockingly deep voice. It took a long moment for them all to accept what they'd just heard.

Then Freddie groaned. "I should have known."

"What is your name?" Jason asked, completely unfazed.

"I have many names, Mortal Knight," the cat said. "And I am all of them and none of them. What are names, if not ways to get one's attention? You can gain my attention by simply speaking to me."

"I have a question," Freddie said, raising his hand. The cat ignored him, so he just asked, "Why do you sound like Darth Vader?"

"Yes, that's it!" Silvana cried. "I thought I recognised the voice. I was thinking Mufasa."

"James Earl Jones, *RIP*," Freddie said. "Wait, is that who you really are?" The cat ignored him again. "Perhaps we should call you James—
"

"Absolutely not," the cat said in its deep voice. "If you must call me by a human name, you can call me Morgan."

Silvana cleared her throat. "Welcome, Morgan. Now, may we ask, why have you come here?"

"To fulfil a bargain," Morgan said simply and resumed grooming themselves.

"Well, perhaps the more pertinent question," Freddie said, "if maybe not the most polite, is *what* are you?"

The cat did not answer, but Jason did. "I know you now. You're Leslie's familiar," he said.

Morgan made a chittering noise of approval. "You're smarter than I thought, Mr Turner."

"But Leslie said they didn't have a familiar," Freddie said, a frown pinching his brow.

Jason nodded to himself. "I know. They said so twice. But among Leslie's last words were also 'talk to the cat'. It seems they had one last surprise up their sleeve. And speaking of surprises." Jason leaned down towards the cat and whispered, "Morgan, were you also the assassin?"

The cat stopped grooming and turned its wide, yellow eyes up to Jason. As quick as blinking, it started to transform, shapeshifting like the chimera assassin, until a humanoid figure appeared before them, lying along the bonnet. Silvana was surprised to see a beautiful young woman. She had bright blue eyes and alabaster skin with a sprinkling of freckles. Her long red hair formed flowing waves that reached her waist and brushed up against her white silk shift that clung to her ample bosom. Her form was lithe and feminine.

After the shock wore off, Silvana noticed the woman's face. She'd seen the woman only briefly across the throne room of the Russian High King, but she recognised her easily. It was the assassin. Last time, she had short black hair and was covered in dirt. Now, she glowed like she'd had a professional team of hair and makeup artists working on her from dusk till dawn. She looked queenly.

"Morgan?" Jason asked. "You're not… what I expected."

"A man?" Morgan said, and now her voice was a husky, sensual purr. Distinctly feminine. "I change everything about me when it suits. My form, my name, my gender. All is as clothing to me to suit my desires."

"Makes sense," Freddie said. "Leslie was gender neutral, you're gender fluid. It has a symmetry."

"Freddie," Jason shushed him, then asked the woman, "Why are you here? You said to fulfil a bargain. So what did Leslie ask you to do?"

Morgan gave a distinctly cat-like smile. "To give you this," she said, and held out an empty hand to Jason. He frowned back until light glimmered and a red rock appeared out of thin air and dropped into her palm. The rock was only four centimetres long and refracted the light and sparkled in a dozen places.

"It looks like a diamond," Freddie said.

"A blood diamond," Silvana cried. "I can sense its power. It's made of vampire magic. It must be Leslie's old key to get into the Library of Alexandria."

"And now it's yours," Morgan said. "If Leslie died before they could teach you how to be a king, I was to give you their pass into the Library so you could go and teach yourself."

Jason let out a wordless cry. "Oh, thank God! Oh, shit." He clutched his chest and cried out again. "You have no idea what a relief that is."

"Leslie, you genius," Freddie cried, facing up to the roof and nodded. "They really thought of everything."

Morgan's voice purred as she held out the stone. "That was my deal with the witch. Now take the stone, and our contract is fulfilled."

Contract? Something about that made Silvana suspicious. Morgan seemed eager for it. Why would that be the case if she was just a courier passing something along? She was acting like she had a personal stake in this matter. Jason reached out to take the stone, but Silvana gently pushed his hand down.

"Silvy?" Jason asked.

"You dodged the question before," Silvana said. "Freddie asked what you were, and you didn't answer. Jason said you're a familiar. But there are many types of creatures that can take on a familiar role. It can be animals under a spell, but you're not an animal. You shapeshift into many forms, including human. So are you a Metamorph?" Silvana looked sceptically at Morgan. "I can't say, but I've never seen a Metamorph with multiple names and genders."

"And have you met every Metamorph, or are you just stereotyping?" Morgan asked.

"Some witches make deals with spirits," Silvana went on. "They give something away in exchange for services, knowledge or power." She smiled, feeling sure of herself. "I know what you are now, Morgan. You're a faery." She pointed to the blood diamond. "And you're trying to trick us into ending a contract early, aren't you?"

Morgan's beautiful face hardened with cold fury. She shifted form again, making Silvana flinch. Morgan became nine feet tall and male, covered in muscles. His chest expanded and his hands became the size of a baseball mitt.

"I should crush you for your disrespect, vampire," Morgan growled, his voice deep like the cat again. "I have walked this earth for millennia. I witnessed the rise of wizards. I know of the Old World and the Ancient Ones who ruled there." The garage was plunged into a supernatural darkness, and Silvana shivered with the blistering cold that swept over her skin. "I saw the seraphim fall. I saw cities burn with dragon fire. And you dare to dictate to me what I should do? You dare question—"

"Yes, I dare!" Silvana roared, hands clenched into fists at her side. "You will *not* intimidate us, cur! Now, you will spell out our contract to the very letter before we go any further. Do you hear me, Morgan?"

The giant man growled deep in his chest, then shifted down in size to a young girl with blue eyes and red hair, appearing no older than five. It looked like she was the younger form of the woman she'd been before.

"Fine," the child said in sweet voice that gave Silvana chills. "Leslie Toussaint's contract was arranged to pass to Jason Turner at the time of their death. The contract can only end when I make a request to end it, and my master grants it. Until such a time as that happens, I am to advise you in all matters that you ask about, as long as doing so will not compromise the welfare of the Fae people. However, I am under no obligation to obey commands or participate in your endeavours. If you are attacked, I need not act in your defence. If you are killed, my contract is considered void, however, I may not take any action that may contribute to your untimely death." The child tilted their head up at Silvana. "Satisfied?"

"So that's why you left," Jason said. "You abandoned Leslie in their final fight because you were under no obligation to help them." He frowned. "Then why did you agree to be the assassin? You clearly followed Leslie's instructions in that regard."

"I made two contracts with Leslie. The assassin role was separate. Only the role of familiar transfers to you."

"What did Leslie pay you?" Silvana asked. "In exchange for all this? You're clearly a powerful being, and it sounds like we have you on retainer until we accidently release you. That must have cost a lot."

Morgan gave Silvana an innocent, child-like smile. "Their soul."

The cold air sent a shiver up Silvana's spine. "Their soul? But... how?"

Morgan blinked. "I thought you knew. You tried to take it back from me just an hour ago, though a feeble attempt it was."

"The resurrection elixir," Freddie cried. "Edward was trying to bring Leslie back, but it wouldn't work. We had no idea why." Freddie glared at the small child. "Because you were holding on to Leslie's soul. They couldn't come back to life without it."

"Unfortunate," Morgan said flatly. "Leslie's life force has now added to my power, and what a sizeable addition it is. Leslie was powerful after nearly eight hundred years of life. It was a worthy bargain."

"You have their soul?" Jason cried. "What are you doing to them? Are they suffering?"

"No, no. They are truly dead, no longer sentient. I simply hold the piece of the universe that combined with their body to create life. They are not in any pain, I assure you."

"And I should believe you?"

"I cannot lie. It is the nature of Fae."

"Of course," Jason sighed. "All right, so Leslie sold their soul to you in exchange for your services. And now you're here to advise me in Leslie's absence, except you will try at every turn to escape me through verbal trickery." He nodded. "All right then. I would like to receive the blood diamond now. However, I do not release your from your contract."

Morgan glared at him as she shifted back into the adult woman. She held out the stone once more. "Very well," she said and offered it to Jason. He took it. "If you should have need of me, say Morgan three times, and I shall appear."

She disappeared. There was no flash, no swirling vortex of space and stars, no visible warning signs of magic. Morgan was simply there one second, and gone the next. As soon as she left, the garage lights shone brightly once again.

"Jesus," Freddie said. "That was really fucking scary."

"Yeah," Jason said, clutching the diamond in his hand. "But this is a good thing. Leslie had a backup plan. It's a risky plan, but it gives us something to work with. Now, we can access the Library." He blinked. "Hopefully we can get through all the other barriers."

"I'm sure Leslie thought of that and made arrangements," Silvana said.

"You saved the day, Silvana," Jason said. "I never considered it was a trap. I nearly lost our new ally in our first exchange. But you were brilliant."

"I'll say," Freddie added, and Silvana blushed. "But what I'd like to know is what was all that about the Old World?" He shuddered. "Morgan said he saw dragon's fire? Seraphim falling? Holy fuck man, we're in some heavy shit."

Jason groaned. "Let's just clean up the fucking house."

Silvana nodded, grabbed the broom at last, and left the garage.

Chapter 36

Jason swallowed nervously as he pressed dial on his phone.

"Officer Turner!" Captain Kader snapped on the other line a second later. She sounded furious. "You better have a damn good excuse for disappearing for a week!"

"Hi captain. Yes, I have a good reason—"

"God damn it, I filed a missing person's report on you. Your face is about to start appearing on milk cartons."

"Oh, no."

"Then, I go to your house, and it's a scene of carnage. I got the forensic team in there, and they find lion hair? And snake skin?"

Jason frowned. "Wait a minute, you were here? Then why isn't there police tape all over…" he looked out the window, and found police tape covering the entire front of the house. There was even a cop car in the driveway. "Oh," he said. "We teleported past it."

"And then I hear the Statue of Liberty is blown the fuck up, and there's scenes of devastation all over New York. Why am I certain you were involved, rookie?"

"Captain, I wasn't even there."

"I didn't say you were there, I said you were involved. Am I wrong?"

"Well… no."

"Exactly. They report that over sixty people are confirmed dead, and a hundred more are missing. Apparently, the subways flooded."

"Oh, god."

"And what were you expecting? To call up and have a chat about catching up for tea?"

Jason could barely get a word out. When Captain Kader finally paused to inhale, Jason jumped in.

"Someone was trying to destroy *all* of New York. We had to save it. And we did! Save it, I mean. It was literally us that made that happen."

There was silence for a long moment on the other end before the captain asked, "Are you safe now?"

"Yes. We are one-hundred percent out of danger. I called you the minute I could."

"Ok. I will report that you've been found, and you will show up at work first thing in the morning. We are going to have a *long* debriefing session, you understand?"

Jason stammered. "Uh, captain? About that. I'm not certain if I… should return to work." Captain Kader was quiet on the end, so he took his time to get the words right. "I've been offered a job within the Immortal community. It's dangerous, and I'll need to train before I take it. But if this works, I could do a lot of good. I'm wondering if that should be my one and only focus right now."

"I thought you wanted to be a detective, rookie. More than anything in the world."

He gave a long sigh. He wanted to be a detective because he and his mother used to like watching crime shows. How childish that dream seemed now. "I wanted to help people. I think I can do more in this role than I ever could as a detective."

Kader seemed to think about it. "You said you need training. Will your police work help with that?"

"Well… maybe."

"Then consider staying on a little longer. I think there's a lot more we can teach you that will help you in your next job, whatever that may be."

"Ok. I'll think about it. Thank you, captain."

"Don't get too sappy. I'm still going to chew the fuck out of you tomorrow."

He chuckled. "Yes, ma'am."

* * *

By the evening, the dining room had finally been cleaned up. Every piece of debris had been collected, every surface had been wiped clear of dust and Jason had taped two blue tarps around the wall and the roof to keep out moisture and bugs. It wasn't pretty, but it was effective.

Jason sat down on the couch with Silvana and Freddie on each side. They each had a box of pizza and a beer, and they ate in silence. Everyone was too tired to even bother turning on the TV. They stared at their own reflections on the blank screen.

"Hey Jase," Freddie said at one point. "Do you want to talk about it? The whole... king in waiting thing?"

Jason snorted. "No."

"Ah, ok." Freddie relaxed back in his chair, before suddenly shooting forward and facing Jason. "You know what? Too bad! I want to talk about it, so spill."

Jason chuckled. "All right. Look, I honestly have no idea what to feel right now. All I know is I need to start studying at the Library and talk with Morgan as much as possible. Learn all I can about the Imperium, start networking and finding allies. It's a long shot, but

I've got to try."

Freddie nodded. "And what about you, Silvy? Heir of Dracula. That's kinda a big deal."

She laughed darkly. "To hear Dorin tell it, he'd insist half the Immortal community would rally behind me, if they only knew."

"Do you two want to… oh, I don't know… collaborate?" They all gave tired laughs. After a few moments of silence, the mood became more hopeful.

"It is a funny coincidence," Jason said. "You, Silvana, wanting to date me because I was a nobody from no Immortal House."

"Yeah, instead you're from the biggest House of them all. And now, I'm from Dracula's House. We should be mortal enemies."

Jason shuddered. "Oh, don't remind me. I can't believe we found ourselves on opposite sides of a battle. I never want to do that again."

"Then you better watch yourself," Silvana quipped. She gave him a cute smile, so Jason leaned over and kissed her before wrapping an arm around her shoulders.

"We'll figure this out," he whispered.

She grumbled. "I don't know. Dorin is still out there, and I have no idea what he'll try next. I can only hope he takes a long time to recover his power. But he'll come for me. One day."

"You're just as strong as him. And we have allies."

Silvana gave a grim chuckle. "The crazy thing is, Dorin is not what scares me the most. That honour goes to this thing in my head. The other personalities…" she went quiet for a long time. "It's scary. I'm scared. Even though I know Ana helped us. She's the reason we were able to beat Alexei. She fought harder than I could. So I know she's on our side. It's just…" she trailed off again.

"It's a lot to deal with," Freddie said.

"Yeah."

"But we *can* deal with it," Freddie went on. "You're not alone,

Silvana. Jason and I both love you and will always be here to help. We'll find you a good therapist. You'll get some professional help, and you'll figure this out. And one day, you'll look back on today and wonder why you were ever so scared."

"Aw, Freddie," she sniffed. She brushed her eyes and let out a laughing sob. "That was really sweet."

"Well, I meant it. You're going to be ok."

"And you know what?" Silvana said. "I love you, too. Both of you. I'm so lucky to have you both in my life."

Jason was surprised to find himself happy in that moment. He wasn't jealous to hear Freddie and Silvana say they loved each other. He knew they deserved it. If anything, he was feeling nervous. Should he say he loved Freddie too? Was that expected now? Somehow, it felt too personal a thing to say.

Or maybe… he wasn't thinking of love in terms of friends.

"One thing bothers me," Silvana said, and Jason was disappointed to feel the moment slip away. "My family knew about my personalities, and they never said anything. That hurts. I wish they'd told me the truth."

"Oh, dear," Jason said.

Both of them looked at him. "What?" Silvana said.

"Ok, don't be mad." Jason clenched his teeth together in discomfort. "Silvana, you know how I didn't tell you about the other personality because I was scared? Well, technically, there was one other thing I should have told you."

"Ok," she said soothingly. "I won't be mad. Just tell me."

"You know how Mikeru was the one who killed Samantha Kennedy? But before he died, he claimed she was already dead when he found her? Well I figured it out six months ago. Nicholas was the one who killed her." They were both silent, so Jason rushed through. "I confronted him about it, and he confessed. He said he knew Samantha was going to tempt us to rebel against the Imperium, and so he killed her to protect us. This is why I haven't spoken to him in six months. I've kept it a secret so no one in the Imperium punishes Nicholas. But also, I kept it secret because… I was still trying to protect you."

Silvana sat quietly in thought for several minutes. Freddie loudly sipped from his beer, then whispered, "Sorry!"

"Thank you for telling me," she said at last. "I am also mad at Nicholas. He's always been overprotective of me. Now I know he killed someone because of it. It doesn't matter if she's alive now, he still committed the act." She sighed. "We have to talk to my family again at some point. I want to hear the truth from them. But I don't think I want a relationship with any of them going forward."

"I understand," Jason said. "And yet… I'm undecided about it, myself."

"Oh?"

"I was furious with Nicholas, because I thought he was going to be the father I always wanted. Then it turns out he was a murderer, just like my real father. Well, now I've learnt my ancestor is Reynold, a genocidal maniac. I can't help but think Nicholas is the least bad of the three."

Freddie said, "That's a pretty low bar, mate."

"I know. But… there's something else. Nicholas killed her because she was opposing the Imperium. He said sometimes you had to obey the Imperium to survive. Well, that's kinda what we were just doing. We fought for Reynold! We beat his enemies for him. Plus, now I have to work with Reynold if I want to take his place. Suddenly it's like… it's so much harder to avoid working for the Imperium than I realised." He sighed. "I don't condone Nicholas's actions, but I'm beginning to understand."

"I know," Silvana said. "It's just like Dorin. He had so many clever things to say, and he made really good points about the world that I agree with. But I can't condone his actions." She took a long breath and let it out slowly. "I think that's human nature. We're not superheroes, fighting in a world between good and evil. We all have capacity for good and evil, and I'm not sure any one person is entirely one or the other. We just… do the best we can."

"Well said," Freddie cheered.

Jason looked down at his hands. They were covered in pizza grease. "I don't know about that. If I ever take Reynold's throne, then I fear my own hands will be stained with plenty of blood by that point. And even more after. I'm not sure if there is a way to do this morally."

Freddie put a hand on his shoulder. "We'll be with you, mate."

"I know."

They finally turned on the TV and sat in silence for a while, each alone with their thoughts and barely focusing on the screen. It took about five minutes before Jason even realised they were watching Fawlty Towers for the millionth time. It was one of Freddie's favourites.

"Jase," Silvana said. "I'm sorry to ask this, I know it's rude, but was that everything?"

He blinked. "Everything?"

"You know. You said you had to tell me the truth. You've told me about my personalities and now Nicholas. But there's no other secrets you're keeping from me, right? I just… need to hear you say it."

"Well…"

Silvana abruptly pulled out of the hug and sat up straight, her eyes fixed on him. "Are you serious? I thought I was just being paranoid. But there is something else!"

"I… oh, no."

"Should I go?" Freddie checked.

"No, it's ok," Jason said. "I just… crap, there's no way out of this now."

"No way out?" Silvana cried. She was trying to smile and stay calm, but she was clearly getting concerned. "Did you *want* to keep this hidden from me? Jason, what the hell? You said you were going to…"

Jason stood up from the couch, turned around, and faced both of them. "I have feelings for Freddie, ok?" he snapped. "There, that's what I was going to say."

The room went very, very quiet. Both Freddie and Silvana stared with their mouths hanging slightly open. Jason cleared his throat.

"Sorry, sorry, I didn't mean…" He gave a loud huff. "Look, I'm not saying I want to act on my feelings. I'm just admitting that I have them, ok? Cause I still love you, Silvana, and I don't want to leave you. And Freddie, you're my best friend. I'd hate to ruin things between us. But I'm just confused cause… you're awesome! I can't help that I've been feeling this way for a while now, and it's not going away. I don't know what to do about it, it's just how I feel, ok?" He threw up his hands. Neither of them said anything in response. "Well, ok, now I've ruined the whole night. I guess I'll just go sleep in the car."

"I do too."

Jason blinked. It took him a moment to realise what he'd heard. *I do too.* He'd heard the words… twice. Silvana and Freddie were looking at each other in surprise.

"Ha, jinx," Freddie said. Then he grumbled and cleared his throat. "Sorry. I just meant to say… I like you too, Jase." He laughed nervously. "But I wasn't going to say anything cause I don't want to come between you two. It's my problem to deal with. I never thought… you'd feel the same way."

"I like Freddie too," Silvana whispered. She glanced between them both. "I thought I was a terrible person for it, but I can't help it either. I like both of you."

Freddie's mouth hung open. "And I really like you too, Silvy."

The three of them glanced nervously back and forth between each other. Then one by one, the tension in their faces relaxed.

"Huh," Jason said. "That's not what I expected."

Chapter 37

Jason finished his first day back at the station.

His fellow officers had been mildly curious to hear about his sudden disappearance and the mysterious assassin chasing him. Meanwhile, the two detectives couldn't care less. His captain wanted to hear every last detail, and Jason told her everything, except about being a king in waiting.

He had spent the whole day with his mind elsewhere. All he could think about was Reynold. *Why is that guy in my head? I'd much rather think about Silvana, and Freddie.* His cheeks heated every time he remembered their conversation from the night before. Yet, he struggled to be happy.

I'm the son of a monster.

The thought had persisted so much that Jason finally gave in. He did something he promised himself he would never do. He logged into the police database and looked up a single person. He found their last known residence. They were still in Plymouth, England.

So when he finished his work day, he hopped straight into his car and drove to the address.

Jason parked just a little ways down the street from the townhouse he was looking for. It was exactly like he remembered, even though he hadn't been here in thirteen years. It was a dual occupancy townhouse made of red brick and split down the middle by two garage doors. Two cars were parked on the left side, but he was here for the half of the house on the right. Several green pot plants stood out the front. Some even had pink flowers in full bloom.

This was where his mother had died. Where his father had beaten Jason so severely that he'd been forced from the home.

And this was where his father still lived.

Jason had forgotten the exact address over the years, and he promised himself he would never look it up again. But now he understood something. His father came from a long line of violent men, tracing their cruelty and dominance back nearly a thousand years to Reynold, himself. Jason had been running from this place all his life. Yet, he found himself drawn back here. Perhaps, it was inevitable after all?

He watched the windows. There was no sign of anyone inside. Maybe his father wasn't home. What if he came home and found Jason waiting in his car? What if he had a new family with him? Would Jason introduce himself? Or should he warn the new family about what happened to the last one?

Or maybe he'd just beat his father to death. Finish the job he attempted all those years ago.

No.

Jason started up the car. He did a three-point turn and drove back down the street, leaving his father's house behind.

He drove north for over forty minutes. The sun was setting. Silvana and Freddie would be wondering where he was, but he had to keep going. He'd put this off for far too long. He had to face this now.

He parked the car again, this time among an empty grove of trees. He stepped out from the driver's side, his feet crunching against the forest mulch and twigs. Surrounding him were a horde of dead trees that swayed in the gentle sea breeze. Jason walked over a nearby crest, and saw a great stone mansion in a little valley below.

I'm back here, where it all began.

Jason raced down the hillside to the grand entryway of wooden doors, guarded by two stone lion statues. The strong scent of wood polish overpowered the fresh smells of nature. He considered knocking on the door, but there was only one person he wanted to see right now, and he didn't want to alert the whole family. Jason tried the door and found it unlocked. *It's not breaking and entering if it's unlocked, right?* He ignored the thought and snuck inside the mansion.

He recognised the two suits of armour by the door and grinned. No one was around, so he snuck down the hallway towards the library. He walked past Silvana's old bedroom on the way and found himself feeling nostalgic. The sad, quiet, confused woman who had lived there had just beaten a High King in battle. She had come so far.

Jason saw the door at the end of the hall was shut. That meant the room was occupied. Inside, he could hear soft jazz playing on an old speaker. He raised his hand and politely knocked on the door.

"Come in," the voice inside called.

Jason froze. He hadn't heard that voice in six months, but it still drew out deep feelings of trust and security. How that voice had let him down in the past. *No, I'm here to work past that.*

"Hello?" the voice called. Jason steeled himself, and entered.

Nicholas the Third was sitting in an armchair and reading a book by the fire while an old record player spun on its track beside him. He reminded Jason of Reynold in his old age. A maze of wrinkles covered Nicholas's face, and age had given him splotchy skin and red puffs beneath his eyes. He was still lean and appeared even wiser than Jason remembered. Strangely, he was still in the exact same place where Jason had last seen him six months ago, as if he'd never left.

Nicholas hadn't looked up from his book, so Jason spoke. "Hello, sir."

Nicholas raised his head, and his eyes settled on Jason. His mouth fell open, and the book dropped from his hand onto the floor.

"Jason?" he whispered.

"Yeah, sorry to barge in. Actually, I didn't barge in, I snuck in. The front door was unlocked. You know you really should lock that…" he trailed off when he realised he was rambling.

"It's good to see you," Nicholas said while trying to hide the smile on his face. "How have you been?"

Jason just waved away the question. "Nicholas, I…" he struggled to find the words. Yet, he wasn't feeling awkward. Something about Nicholas put him at ease, and he knew he could be himself. So he spoke bluntly.

"Look, I still think you were wrong to kill Samantha Kennedy. And you were definitely wrong to make that decision on my behalf." Jason let out a long sigh. "But I was wrong too. I was naïve to think we can survive in the Imperium without getting our hands dirty. Sometimes there is no perfect solution, and you have to cross moral lines if you want to survive long enough to make a difference. Oh, I don't know," he cried. "I'm still figuring this out. I just know that I judged you too harshly, all right?"

Nicholas gave a sombre nod. "Thank you for saying so, Jason. I think you are very wise."

Jason nodded back. "So, I guess I'm saying… I want to try again." Nicholas started to smile. "I'm not ready for the whole 'father and son' thing just yet. Let's just… start talking again. Ok?"

"Ok!" Nicholas held up his hands in a gesture of surrender, no longer hiding his broad grin. "I understand, I need to work to earn your trust again. I will do that work, I promise."

"Ok. Good."

"Good," Nicholas echoed. He cleared his throat, "That said, would it be too soon if I asked if I could hug you?"

Jason huffed in mock annoyance. "Yeah all right," he drawled. Then he knelt before the old man's chair and wrapped him in a firm hug. Nicholas hugged him so tight, he seemed to be attempting to crush Jason's ribcage. The scent of old soap and musk filled Jason's nose. And yet, he found himself relaxing into the embrace.

"I'm still really mad at you, you know," Jason whispered.

"I know," Nicholas said and hugged him tighter.

"And you know next time we're training together, I'm going to kick your ass."

Nicholas chuckled. "Go ahead, make my day."

"Oh, you're back on Dirty Harry again?"

"I never left!"

Epilogue

Portia stood at attention with her hands behind her back as her world changed around her.

Desdemona was packing up their home with the assistance of magic. Books flew off the shelves and straight into packing boxes. Wooden furniture was being stacked in the corner with chairs tucked under table legs and bookcases packing in the sides. Even the bedframe and mattress were already prepped for transport.

"I still don't see why you have to move at all," Portia said. "You can teleport back here in about five seconds. This won't exactly save on travel time."

"I must be near the High King at all times," Desdemona said. She was still wearing her new black and gold robes of the Earl Marshall. "And I will not be parted from thee, hence why thou art coming too. Fear not, thou wilt be in a separate wing of the palace altogether. Thou need not ever lay eyes on Reynold."

"It's not that," Portia replied. "I find it suspicious that Reynold would promote you after all this time. He's been deliberately ignoring your achievements for a century."

"Isn't it obvious?" Desdemona's tone was blunt. "He wanted to impress people by having me near. I won him a great victory, and my presence will remind others of that fact."

"But Reynold is a chauvinist. And a white supremacist."

"Indeed. I am but a token, I have no doubt. But I will use this opportunity all the same."

"To do what?"

Desdemona smiled. "Grow in power."

The last of the books reached their boxes and joined the pile of furniture. Now that they were tightly packed together, she would teleport her things to the new location. The real question was, would it take only one trip?

"Mistress," Portia said. "Before we go…" she trailed off, tugging at her curls to straighten them before letting them bounce back into place. Desdemona watched her for a moment as she kept stroking her locks. Then Portia scrunched up her hair around her fist and gave it a firm tug. She let out a soft breath and took a single step forward. A coy smile slid over Desdemona's face.

"Art thou certain?" she checked, her rich voice showing a rare tenderness.

"I want nothing more," Portia whispered, and knew she meant it.

Desdemona made a quick gesture with her hand, and Portia felt herself whisked off the ground by magic and straight into her lover's arms. Desdemona's lips press down on her own as a gentle hand clutched the back of her head. Portia could feel Desdemona's patience straining to its limit, her desire having built up over months of unsated longing. Even now, she was trying to be gentle.

Oh, how she loved this woman.

"Get out of those damn robes," Portia purred.

Within seconds the bedframe was set up once again, and their clothes were on the floor beside it.

Silvana held hands with Jason as they walked down the hillside. And on her other side, she held Freddie's hand too.

The trio stepped through a grove of dead trees whose skeletal branches stretched into the evening sky. The air smelt of mulch, damp ground and beech trees.

"This takes me back," Jason said, as piles of dead leaves crunched underfoot

Before them, a bleak stone mansion rose up from the forest ground. Bright blue tiles lined the roof, their pattern broken up by turrets every twenty paces. Twin statues of lions stood at the entrance, and a massive wooden double door loomed above them in silence.

"Huh. They redid the paint," Silvana noted.

The whole mansion seemed to shine brighter than it did in her memory. Even the door had a fresh coat of paint, plus a new glossy outdoor polish. Maybe they'd used some of her money after all.

"Still not very welcoming, is it?" Freddie said. "You guys ready for this?"

"I don't know," Jason replied.

"I am," Silvana answered. "I took down a High King. I can face these old crones." She chuckled. "Thanks for being here, you two."

"Of course," Jason said.

"Anything you need," Freddie added.

Silvana let out a long sigh. "Who wants to do the honours?"

Jason reached for the door knocker, but Freddie leapt forward and banged it down several times.

"Sorry. It just looked so cool."

The latch clicked, and the door silently swung open. A woman with short black hair and a stern face filled with hard lines stood inside the doorway. Another woman came rushing up the hallway with long blonde hair swaying as she moved. Her soft, graceful face lifted into a smile, only accentuating her beauty.

"Hello aunts," Silvana said. "We need to talk."

"Silvana," Lisbeth cried, hand to her breast. "My darling, it's so good to see you!"

"Jason," Emberline said coldly.

"And Freddie!" Freddie announced himself.

Emberline pointed to him. "Who's the boy?"

"He's my new boyfriend," Silvana said without flinching. Freddie beamed up at her.

"Oh, sweet hell, take me," Emberline huffed.

A black cat stalked slowly through the crystal palace.

Every surface of this court was made of white stone of the purest cut, placed with exact care to create a grand pattern of reflected light. It was a monumental undertaking of architecture. Yet, amidst the architectural precision were giant tree trunks with their roots growing through and around the structure as if they had always been there. A perfect blend of nature and design. The air smelled of old oak and stone.

The cat did not care for the beauty of the Fae court. He had seen it countless times over the millennia. He was a true Immortal, not like one of those pathetic interlopers who thought their extended life gave them power over creation. Morgan could not die. If power existed that could kill him, he hadn't found it yet.

After all, that power had been sealed away long ago.

Morgan shifted form until he became a young woman. Her graceful feminine form drove the mortal men out of their minds with desire. She still wasn't sure which of her forms would please the master the most, but this was her most appealing.

Other creatures chittered nervously as Morgan stalked the courtroom. Goblins, dwarves, and lost souls lined the room and drew silent at her approach. She ignored them, and instead, focused her eyes on the mighty figure that sat on the oaken throne. The ancient pedestal had been carved out of the oldest tree in existence, and had aged even more during the millennia since then. Morgan reached the foot of the dais and bowed before the King of Faerie.

"Great King Oberon," she announced. "I come at your summons."

Oberon was bare-chested. He wore plates of steel around his muscled arms, shoulders, and armoured greaves from the hips down. His form was inhuman. No human's eyes were ever that big, or face that disproportionately long. He had six great wings that stretched out behind him, covering half the throne room in their shadow. He wore a crown made of olive leaves that wrapped around the two great antlers that grew from his head.

"Have you made contact with the heir?" Oberon asked.

"I have, my lord. He is committed to his claim on the throne and will seek my counsel in pursuit of that end."

"You seem to have done well, Morgan," Oberon sneered. "Though, you neglected to speak of the problems you encountered."

Morgan winced, but there was no avoiding it. Oberon knew every verbal trick in existence. "He knows I am Fae," Morgan said. "He will now watch my words for traps. And I am still in his service."

Oberon gave a deep laugh. "He is no fool. This one has promise."

Morgan wanted to skim past her mistake. "What is your will, my lord? How shall I guide him?"

The Fae King leaned forward on his throne, and his six wings sent a gentle breeze flowing through the hall. "Convince him to clear the path *before* taking the throne. You must turn him against the other High Kings."

Morgan couldn't help smiling as she bowed again. "It will be done, my lord." She stood to leave, but a voice cried out from the hall.

"I would speak to the king!"

Oberon growled, and the denizens of Faery trembled at his displeasure. "Who dares interrupt the great king?" Oberon whispered with the promise of death in his voice.

"I do."

A man stepped forward. A vampire with piercing blue eyes and a handsome face. He wore a white vest and trousers with golden embroidery, though his clothes showed the scorch marks of having tasted flame. He stood before Oberon and only glanced at Morgan before turning his full attention back to the king.

Oberon tilted his head, his antlers swaying. "Who are you, interloper? And how did you come to this realm?"

"My name is Dorin Tepes," the stranger cried out in a loud voice. "I wish to make a bargain with the King of Faerie."

The End of Book 3 of the Immortal Investigations

Acknowledgments

This book is an enigma.

It's the eleventh novel I've written, but unique for several reasons. This is the first book that was planned in its entirety before I'd written a word. It was the fastest I've ever written a book. The book that required the least revisions. And the first book written on a brutal deadline.

And it's the novel I'm proudest of. So far.

Once more, thanks to my wife, Kit, who waited patiently until I asked for her help in designing book covers. Only then did she reveal she'd already planned covers for all twelve books in the series. I think she believes in me.

To Emmie Hamilton, for developmental edits and catching a huge plothole that would have ruined my life. And to Kirsty Inic, for line editing this one on a punishingly tight deadline.

To Wouter K, for doing such a great job proofreading books one and two that we increased the pressure and gave you even less time to proofread this one. It was poor repayment for your generous lending of talents.

This book exists indirectly because of YouTuber, Elliot Brooks. I planned to take two or three years to grow a YouTube audience big enough for me to self-publish, with no guarantee of success. But Elliot shared a video of mine, helped me gain followers early, and drastically shortened that timeline. If not for her, this book would still be another year away at least, if it even got written at all.

To every single person who has followed The Book Guy and participated in the channel's growth, thank you. To those who backed the Kickstarter and got these books out there, thank you. This is still just the beginning. There are more stories to tell.

Finally, to Kit (again), for not laughing at a dorky twenty-two year old who tried to impress you by explaining the book he was writing. And for giving him your number. And for being willing to look past that god-awful drum kit pun I made exactly three seconds after meeting you. How you ever married me after that is beyond my comprehension.

***

A sneaky note from Kit, since I'm the one finalising these internal page layouts.
Bad puns about my name aside, you had me at "I'm writing a fantasy novel". Some 12 years later... we're finally here. You did it. I always knew you would - and this is just the beginning.

I'm so proud of you. Now and always.

About the Author

Michael Cronk is an independent author from Brisbane, Australia.

He has a special love for fantasy stories and can often be found trying to convince random strangers to read The Wheel of Time. Or Discworld. Or anything by Robin Hobb. Or... well, you get the idea.

Michael is passionate about encouraging others to read on his popular YouTube Channel, The Book Guy. He firmly believes that reading has the power to change our lives - and the world - for the better. With that in mind, this debut series is written to be easy and enjoyable for both voracious readers and those who haven't read in a while.

When he's not reading or writing (or having nightmares about endless editing), Michael enjoys playing all sorts of music from heavy metal to classical on his many instruments. Much to the delight of his cats and neighbours.

You can connect with me on:
- https://michaelcronk.com
- https://www.youtube.com/@cronkthebookguy

www.ingramcontent.com/pod-product-compliance
Lightning Source LLC
Chambersburg PA
CBHW050844210726
48290CB00004B/1080